GRAY WAR

A PALLAS GROUP SOLUTIONS THRILLER

Peter Nealen

CHAPTER 1

They say that the loudest sound in a firefight is a *click*.

When a door that's supposed to be locked opens with that same sound, it's pretty damn loud then, too. Especially when you're supposed to be guarding a covert meeting that nobody outside that room is supposed to know about.

Drew had been playing solitaire, and I'd been reading a book while we waited. Neither one of us were so wrapped up in our diversions—keeping the crushing boredom of a close-protection gig at bay—that we didn't notice the sound. Both of us snapped our eyes to the door. I let the book drop to the floor as I moved my hand to the Glock 19 in my waistband.

I was on my feet as Drew got up, facing the door as he took a step back toward the inner room of the hotel suite, his own Glock already in his fist. Ordinarily, even on the overseas contract the two of us had last worked, we wouldn't have drawn that quick, but *nobody* was supposed to be coming here. Nobody was supposed to have access to the suite, and we'd made sure to hang the "Do Not Disturb" sign outside, too, so housekeeping should have fucked off.

Granted, we *were* in Atlanta.

About two seconds later, the door was kicked open with a *bang*, and two men in jeans, black t-shirts, and balaclavas burst in, weapons in their hands.

I never did suffer from the sort of tunnel vision many other people have described experiencing in life-or-death combat situations. I just sort of get calm and clear. I noticed the M&P Shield in the first man's hands even as he swung it toward my face, and I punched my Glock out, already letting him go blurry as all my focus turned to my front sight.

The 9mm barked deafeningly in the entryway, my first round going low into his guts, the next three walking up his chest and blowing bloody bits of his shirt off his chest as the Critical Defense hollow points punched through his ribs and lungs. He staggered, his eyes widening in shock behind his balaclava, and the Shield slipped from his fingers to land on the carpeted floor with a *thump* that I barely heard as I put one last round through the bridge of his nose. We were close enough that I'd barely aimed until the last one or two shots.

The second man triggered a blast from the sawed-off shotgun in his hands into the floor as Drew dumped him with a failure drill, hammering two 9mms into his chest and a third into his head.

A barely coherent curse in Spanish sounded outside the door, and I caught a glimpse of movement through the opening as someone scrambled out of sight very quickly. There were more than two.

A part of me wanted to push the fight, make entry on that hallway and kill everyone out there. That wasn't the job, though, and in a place like Atlanta, it could very well mean mission failure in the long term. We weren't in a foreign country with the full weight of the US government to get us out of jail and send us home, this time. The client had good lawyers, but that wasn't going to get us off the hook in any sort of quick timeframe.

So, I fell back, keeping the Glock trained on the now empty doorway. The hydraulic door closer should have swung the door shut, but it was caught on the corpses, one face down on the carpet and the other slumped back against the doorjamb, drops of red running down the wall behind it. "You good?"

"I'm good. You?" Drew kept holding on the door, too, at least until I answered.

"I'm up. Check on Strand."

With my gun trained on the door, Drew turned back and opened the door leading into the suite's bedroom. The Hyatt House Atlanta Downtown had some pretty nice rooms, and the one bedroom king suite had been perfect for Merritt Strand's purposes. He'd been ensconced in the bedroom with the nerdy little dude he'd come there to meet for the last two hours. Not for the sort of thing you might be thinking, either. They'd been confined to the bedroom because it meant that Drew and I could stay out in the entryway and kitchenette, where we could keep eyes on the front door without sitting in the middle of the meeting. Both of us knew some of the depravity that we might have been asked to watch over as private security contractors, but Strand wasn't that kind of guy, billionaire though he was. We hadn't heard much of the meeting, but they were talking some heavy financial stuff in there.

Which probably explained why these two weirdos had kicked in the door. Possibly why someone had provided them with a keycard, too.

Drew threw the door to the bedroom open. "Meet's over. We need to get ready to move."

"What's going on?" The little nerdy guy sounded scared shitless. Even if you're not familiar with gunfire, there's really no mistaking the sound of gunshots in a hotel room.

I had just kicked over the table. It wasn't the chintzy sort of plastic I'd expected but appeared to have an actual marble top. That would make some decent cover if I needed it. Right at the moment, though, I wanted more room. I eased toward the wall, my Glock still trained on the doorway, looking for targets. If the dead guys' buddies had turned tail and run—which seemed most likely—then we could roll out and get off the X. The cops might object to our leaving a crime scene, but I'd leave that to Strand's lawyers. Our responsibility was the client's safety.

They hadn't run, though. One stuck his pistol, a cheap Ruger P90, around the doorjamb and opened fire.

I dropped behind the overturned table then, as bullets smacked into the partition behind me, shattering the TV. Drew had ducked into the bedroom, getting out of the line of fire and keeping himself between the bullets and the client. Just getting on the floor was enough to avoid the .45 caliber rounds, as the guy was shooting one-handed and not well, so he was drilling holes in the ceiling tiles within half a mag. Bad news for anyone on the floor above us, but better for me.

Unfortunately, I now had that table between me and the door, so I couldn't exactly rush him, even if that had been a good idea. He wasn't exposing himself aside from his gun hand, either, so I could either shoot him through the wall or wait until he gave me something more to shoot at.

Neither felt like an ideal solution but sitting there and waiting for them to try something else felt like the worse option. They should have run for it as soon as we'd smoked the first two. Something was off.

Right then wasn't the time to analyze the situation, though. I judged roughly where he was on the other side of the wall, shifted aim, and dumped five rounds through the drywall.

The scream of pain that followed was almost drowned out by the bark of my Glock, and the gunman dropped his Ruger. For a moment, everything went quiet, except for what might have been frantic screaming somewhere else in the hotel, even though it was mid-afternoon, so there shouldn't have been that many people checked in.

"Drew! Call 911!" It wouldn't have been my first choice, in all honesty, especially not in a big city like Atlanta. Even in the middle of a firefight, I was still more than a little worried that Atlanta PD was just going to slap us in handcuffs for shooting back. It seemed like the sort of thing they'd do in a big city in Current Year. But I knew that if we were going to make sure we were legally covered, we needed to call the cops. Let us book our way out of there *without* calling for help, leaving bodies, bloodstains, and empty brass behind, and it would damn near *guarantee* that we'd have the cops looking for us.

I waited, still on my side behind the table, my weapon trained on the doorway, while Drew called for help. He would have already alerted Phil and Marcos, who were supposed to be outside, waiting in the backup vehicle, and they'd have the rest of the team alerted and moving, just in case.

We weren't *supposed* to be running quite like we had overseas, in war zones, but Pallas Group Solutions had noticeably recruited guys who'd done time in Special Operations before working various high-risk overseas gigs with various three-letter agencies. Some things were hard-wired into us, and right then, that was a good thing.

"There are two squad cars on the way," Drew reported from the bedroom. "Sounds like they're spinning up a SWAT team, too."

That could be good or bad. I'd been around enough cops—even trained some of them—that I didn't trust their marksmanship or target discrimination very much. *Especially* when they were all amped up because shots had already been fired.

I held my peace, though, just maintaining my coverage on the door. For now, all we could do was strongpoint the room and wait.

My ears were ringing from the gunshots. Not the first time, but it's not always feasible to have ear protection on when you're working a gig like this. Nor are most people *expecting* to actually get hit when working close protection.

It's a weakness, even among professional paranoiacs like me. It usually only gets remedied when something bad happens, or *almost* happens.

Over that ringing, though, I could hear voices out in the hallway. The hitters weren't being particularly quiet and having just seen three of their shooters killed or wounded had them rattled. From the sounds of things, that just made them angrier.

They were speaking Spanish, too. I filed that detail away for later. It wasn't what I would have expected in Atlanta.

Time seemed to slow down as I waited. I hastily reloaded, stuffing the partially empty magazine into my back pocket. I had a moment, so I used it to get my weapon back into the best condition possible.

My phone buzzed. I had it connected to a Bluetooth earpiece, which looked retarded but could be useful for times like this when I needed both hands. I tapped the button on the earpiece. "Talk to me." Hopefully it wasn't some dumbass telemarketer.

"Backwoods, it's Ziggy." We tended to use callsigns over comms, even supposedly secure ones like the phones. "We're listening to the police scanner, and something's definitely up."

"Need a little more than that, Ziggy." Phil and I were old friends, but right then I was in the middle of a fight, and I was a little terse.

"It sounds like one of the squad cars that's heading our way just got in a wreck. They're not coming, and their backup just got called to help them out." There was something more to it, though. I could *hear* the frown in Phil's voice. "The weird part is that I haven't heard any other units get reassigned, *and* the SWAT team just got told to stand by."

6

That *was* weird. It might just be incompetence.

Or it might be something else. Under the circumstances, we had to assume both.

Actually, under the circumstances, we had to adjust our plan. Legal worries aside, our primary concern was Strand's safety, and from the sounds of things outside the door, that was going to get a lot more tenuous the longer this went on.

Then Phil made it worse. "Uh, brother? Looks like you've got some more company coming. Two vehicles just pulled up and a good half a dozen more *cholo*-looking dudes got out and hustled inside."

He'd barely finished speaking when one of the Spanish-speakers out there yelled something, and while I couldn't understand all the words, something about that sound told me that I needed to do something, or we were about to get overrun.

And I needed to do it fast.

CHAPTER
2

While I take some pride in having been a professional gunfighter for the better part of two decades, it still took some doing to pick myself up off the floor and move to the door. All it would take would be another one of those gangbangers sticking his weapon blindly through the doorway again, and I'd be dead. We had body armor with us, in the car, but I didn't have it on. One more oversight, one more bit of complacency born of working Stateside.

So, I felt pretty damned naked as I got up, moving to my left to cut off more of the fatal funnel, though I was also cutting off Drew's field of fire to do it. If the bad guys followed my example and just opened fire through the wall, I was in trouble, but so far, they hadn't reciprocated. I needed to move quick to get this done before they did.

I had to quickly haul the bodies out of the way before I could get the door shut, and that took some doing. The first one was easy, but the one I'd shot was well out in the fatal funnel, and I couldn't grab him solidly without exposing myself to the hallway. So, I grabbed his ankle, braced myself against the door, and hauled.

Someone out there saw the movement, and I heard a yell. I moved quickly, and barely got the body out of the way of the door before I drove it closed, pushing faster than the door closer. I slammed it shut, snapping the deadbolt and the swing lock closed.

You know, like I should have done the first time.

Right at that moment, one of the gangbangers outside decided to get desperate, and more bullets smashed through the wall and the door, tracking up toward the ceiling again, which was the only thing that kept me from getting my head blown off. I still dropped to the floor and crawled out of the fatal funnel as fast as I could, rolling to my back and aiming my Glock between my knees.

I *almost* shot back through the wall, but years of training to never shoot at what I couldn't see held me back. I might have made an exception when I could see the bad guy's pistol, but blind firing through the wall was a bridge too far.

So, I scrambled backward and through the door to the bedroom. Drew had Strand and the nerd down on the floor, while he stayed on a low knee, with his own weapon pointed at the door, lifting the muzzle toward the ceiling as I came through.

"Cops or no cops, we can't stay here." I stayed low and looked at the door connecting the suite to the next one over. There was no doorknob or door handle, just a lock. It was for maintenance and housekeeping, not guests.

We weren't ordinary guests, though. I glanced at Strand for a second. He might not like what was about to happen, but it was his life and ours on the line. We had to get out of that room. "You still got that bump key?"

Drew glared at me for a second for dropping that dime in front of the client, but this wasn't a situation where we could afford to be delicate and subtle.

"Yeah, I got it." He'd brought his pared-down go bag in with us, mainly because he could fit a blowout kit into it. There were a couple more weapons we could have fit in there, too, but of course it was Stateside, so we'd brought two pistols and left our carbines in the vehicle.

I was rapidly reassessing our mission loadouts, even though this was probably the first actual firefight I'd been in in *years*.

Fortunately, Drew didn't argue or waste time and energy getting pissed that I hadn't been able to ask him about it out of the client's earshot. He saw what I was getting at and started digging in the sling bag, coming out with a key ring carrying about half a dozen keys. They looked normal at first glance, except that all their teeth were the same size. The only differences were the grooves, as there were enough different locks we might need to get through that a single bump key wouldn't necessarily do the trick.

He had that door into the next suite open in two seconds flat and then he rolled out of the doorway, snatching up his own Glock again as I grabbed Strand, keeping his head down with one hand while my other kept my own handgun up and ready, and pushed through the open door into the adjoining rooms.

I'd been a little worried that either the next suite would be occupied, or that the bad guys out there in the hall might have thought ahead and were flanking us, but the room was empty.

We cleared it quickly anyway, Drew hustling through the door behind me with the nerd that Strand had been meeting, pushing the door shut and hastily re-locking it with the bump key. Drew was a lot better with locks than I was.

Keeping Strand and his buddy down as much as possible, even as we heard more banging and swearing from out in the hall—the gunfire had stopped for the moment—we repeated the procedure on the next door. There was no way in hell I was going to pop out into that hallway with an unknown number of bad guys still out there.

Unfortunately, that room was occupied.

The couple in the bed were holding the sheets up over them as we burst through the door, and the girl started screaming, while the guy's voice started to rise in volume and pitch as he screamed into the phone he was holding to his ear. Sounded like he was talking to 911, understandably so.

Drew put a finger to his lips, though it proved to be completely fruitless. The screaming only increased in pitch, so much so that I couldn't hear enough to tell if our little buddies out in the hallway had heard it and were adjusting their plan of attack.

We still had to move faster.

I switched places with Drew, pushing past him with Strand and the other guy, taking the bump key from his outstretched off hand as I passed. He covered the couple in the bed, his Glock held at his sternum, not *quite* pointed at them but ready to engage if he needed to.

I went to work on the next door.

We got through three more rooms without further incident, then we popped out into the hallway right next to the stairs. I went through the door fast, punching my handgun out to cover down the hall.

We'd actually come out just around the corner from the hall where our room had been set, so we had a little bit of cover. The door swung shut behind us with a *boom*, however, and any evasiveness we'd bought by cutting through the other rooms was immediately lost.

Another command was shouted in slurred Spanish, and two more shooters, in t-shirts, baggy jeans, and black jackets came around the corner, barely ten feet from me.

The first guy, with a teardrop tattoo at the corner of his eye, looked more than a little shocked to see me. His own Glock was pointed at the floor, in a pretty decent two-handed grip, which told that icy calm, analytical part of my brain that he'd had some training.

His training didn't matter a damn a moment later, since his handgun was pointed at the floor and mine was pointed at his chest.

12

I blew three holes through his heart and lungs and his knees buckled, the Glock falling from limp fingers as he stared at me, his tough guy look dissolving in a look of confused fear as his soul left his body. He fell on his face a moment later, but I'd already shifted my aim to the guy in the untucked black button up behind him. That one was already bringing his own weapon up, but I shot him through the eye a second later and he crashed onto his back on the floor.

He fell partway out into the hallway behind him, and a yell went up. They knew where we were.

Drew was already clattering down the steps with Strand and his interlocutor, and I turned and ran to join them. Speed was our only security, now. I was down to two mags, and there were still a lot of bad guys in the hotel.

The fact that we could *not* in any way rely on Atlanta PD to help us out just meant we had to move faster.

Not that I'd been eager to lean on the cops in the first place. There's a certain liberating feeling to the knowledge that no one is coming to save you.

It's also damned terrifying if you spend more than a few seconds thinking about it.

We tore our way down the stairs as fast as Strand and the little guy could move, which wasn't nearly as fast as Drew and I could have. I kept stopping at each landing, pivoting to point my Glock back up the way we'd come.

The door slammed open above us, as the hitmen—or *sicarios*; I wasn't sure which we were dealing with, and that was a question that could be addressed when we were out of the fight—came after us. They didn't immediately run down the steps, which told me that they were being a bit more cautious after we'd smoked at least four, maybe five of their buddies.

It took them a second to realize just how big of a head start we had. Another yell echoed down the stairwell, and then they sped up, rushing down the flights of steps as fast as they could move without tripping and biting it.

I leaned out into the gap between flights of stairs, aiming up through the narrow opening and shot past the railing. I didn't have much in the way of targets, but I needed to discourage them from coming on too fast. A bullet caromed off the railing and I heard a howl of pain, then I turned and threw myself down at the second to last landing before we had a way out.

It took seconds to get to the bottom of the stairs and the glass door leading onto the parking lot on the side of the building. Unfortunately, the Hyatt House Atlanta, Downtown was an L-shaped building with only one parking lot, so we were going to be exposed as soon as we pushed out onto the asphalt.

I halted on the landing and took up security on the stairs above again as Drew paused by the door, keeping Strand and the other guy—who now looked pale and nauseous—pressed back against the wall. I could just hear him on the phone, coordinating with Phil and Marcos outside, and then he called out to me, "Moving!"

I almost held my position anyway. I was getting brief glimpses of movement above us as the bad guys pursued, but not enough to get a shot, and I'd already stretched my luck far enough the last time I'd shot blind up the stairs. I collapsed my handgun back to my chest and practically jumped down the steps to the semi-enclosed entryway, with another fire door leading toward the hall of the first floor.

Drew threw the glass exit open and then he was moving. I herded Strand and the finance guy he was meeting out after him, taking up the rear with my Glock pointed at the sky for the moment.

Unfortunately, the bad guys hadn't just left their vehicles unattended.

A gunshot *crack*ed across the parking lot, but fortunately the shooter wasn't really aiming. I pivoted toward the noise, my own pistol coming back down as I pushed myself between the shooter and Strand. I didn't care as much about the other guy—we hadn't even been told his name—but we'd brought him along because we couldn't just leave him to get shot or kidnapped.

The guy shooting at us didn't even have a clear shot. He was reaching over the hood of a sedan with one hand, blasting away and not even trying to control the recoil. Unfortunately, that meant I didn't have much of a shot at him, either, so I grabbed Strand's shoulder and forced him down almost double as we ran for the cars.

Phil and Marcos had been waiting for us, though. Even as we ran for our vehicle, parked about halfway across the lot, they surged into the gap between us and the bad guys' cars, pivoting to face the shooter. We didn't have armored SUVs— Strand was rich as Midas, but he hadn't sprung for that kind of hardware, and PGS didn't have that kind of money, either—but Marcos was down behind the dash, and Phil popped the passenger side door open, staying almost as low as Marcos as he opened fire through the "V" of the door. He fired twice, and the bad guy's pistol clattered to the ground.

Something made me turn, just as we reached the little strip of landscaping that ran between the rows of parking spaces. Just in time, too. The door we'd exited slammed open and two men with guns burst out into the parking lot.

My sights had already come level as the first one came through the door, and I dumped him with a single round to the face. His head jerked and his knees collapsed under him, though the bullet's impact wasn't enough to stop him in his tracks. He just sort of dropped on his face, still moving forward with all the momentum he'd had as he came out the door.

The second man was a step behind the first, and he flinched as I shot the guy in front of him. He was already

15

committed, though, and he got one shot off into the asphalt about ten feet in front of me before I slammed the rest of my mag into him. The slide locked back as he toppled, and then I turned and sprinted for the car.

Drew already had Strand and the other guy crammed into the back and was starting the engine with one hand, the other holding his Glock out the driver's side window. "Get in, Chris!"

I rounded the back so as to avoid crossing his line of fire, yanked the passenger side door open, and threw myself inside. No sooner had I slammed the door shut than Drew was stomping on the accelerator, leaving black tire marks on the pavement as we screamed out of the parking lot.

CHAPTER
3

We hadn't cleared the fence yet when I shoved my Glock into the center console, flipping the cover off the Recce 16 carbine wedged between the console and the seat and hauling the rifle out onto my lap. I couldn't see any more threats out on the street, not yet, but it didn't pay to be complacent.

I'd already made enough mistakes on that count for one day.

Drew turned right coming out of the parking lot, heading south on Luckie Street, but then immediately took a fast right turn onto Ivan Allen Jr. Boulevard. A horn brayed indignantly behind us as an oncoming car just missed rear-ending our Acadia. Drew didn't even react, but just put the pedal on the floor.

I snatched up the radio handset and turned the comms on. "Ziggy, Backwoods. We're clear."

"Roger. We're breaking contact and heading north. See you back at the house." We'd driven to the hotel as a two-vehicle element, but splitting up might give the bad guys more than one route to take and thus spread out the threat, provided they pursued.

They'd have to be nuts to try to push things after we'd smoked at least seven of them, but the fact that they'd pushed the fight after we'd dumped the first two who had busted into the room told me that they were really hot on killing or capturing Strand.

There wasn't time to think through all the implications just then. I still had work to do.

Security was my primary responsibility as the right-seater. I had my head on a swivel, checking every vehicle I could see around us, looking for threats. The guy Drew had cut off was a threat, if one presumably unconnected with the gangbangers who had kicked in the hotel room door, but road rage was still nothing to discount, especially in a city like Atlanta.

So far, though, I didn't see anyone else on the road who might be obviously gunning for us. Drew was driving fast, weaving through the midday traffic, though he was still keeping his speed just low enough that we *probably* wouldn't get pulled over.

What role the cops were going to play over the next few minutes to hours was going to get interesting.

"Ziggy, Backwoods. Any updates on police response?" We had a scanner in our vehicle, but I didn't have it up yet, and Phil had been listening in since we'd gotten into position at the hotel.

"It's a mess." Phil sounded simultaneously disgusted and somewhat disturbed. "Sounds like things are getting ugly at the wreck, and they're calling for backup. SWAT is still in stand-down mode, though I've got to give the team leader some credit. He's pissed."

That might have been a bit of extra detail over the radio, since we only had regular commercial encryption on the black gear Motorolas. We were still being *mostly* aboveboard, though, especially considering most of the guys recruited by Pallas Group Solutions as close protection operators had some experience with clandestine operations in foreign and mostly hostile countries. We were wired to be sneaky, and nothing that had happened over the last few years had made any of us the particularly trusting types.

We did have completely encrypted comms, but they were a little bit less reliable, and we needed clear communications right at the moment.

Still, it wasn't good news. Something was up, in a big way. And the more I thought about it, now that I had some breathing room while Drew drove, the worse it got. "Good copy. We're en route to the house. See you there."

Drew took the next right immediately, heading north on Northside Drive. He pulled a right turn on red, once again just barely avoiding a collision as another sedan came tearing up the street behind us. It was risky, and I could feel as well as hear Strand and the other guy freaking out a little at the double close calls, but Drew was doing it deliberately, and I knew why. The more traffic he could put between us and any tail that might be following us, the better. It wouldn't only make it more difficult for them to catch us, but it would force them to drive more recklessly just to *try*, which would make it easier for us to pick them out of the other traffic.

I was watching the mirrors as well as the windows. I didn't have as good a view of the rear as Drew did, but I could see most of our surroundings. Right at the moment, aside from some irate Georgians behind the wheel, we didn't have any bad guys to worry about.

Which meant I had to take care of the next thing.

Twisting around in my seat, I faced Strand and his companion. Merritt Strand was a relatively young man, maybe in his early thirties, which made his considerable fortune and financial savvy that much more impressive. Clean shaven, his sandy blond hair was slightly long, more from neglect than style. He was thin and with a slightly receding chin. Physically, he wasn't much to look at.

The other man was considerably heavier, if slightly shorter. His black hair was cropped short, and he was trying to grow a beard, though his genes didn't seem to be up to the task. He wasn't quite flabby enough for a second chin, but he was getting close to it.

"Did either of you get hit?" I didn't see any blood at first glance, but that didn't mean it wasn't there. I was already reaching across the cab to start doing blood sweeps on Strand, running my hand over his arms, legs, and torso, checking my palm for red with every move. Strand submitted to the indignity, though he looked uncomfortable. He'd been briefed on our procedures, even though at the time it had felt like a formality that we more than likely wouldn't ever need to follow through on.

Strand shook his head as I kept checking him over. "I don't think so." He'd gathered himself a little, though he was still looking a little pale and shaky. The other guy was too dark to look pale, but his eyes were wide as I finished with Strand and turned to him.

"Well?" I held up my hand, having to twist around even farther in the seat, shoving my carbine back between the seat and the center console. "Did you get hit or injured in any way? I need to know."

When he shook his head, his eyes still so wide that I could see the whites around his black irises, I held up my hand again. "I need to check, just to be sure, okay? Sometimes you don't feel it, because of the adrenaline." If we'd been in a warzone, I probably wouldn't have bothered to ask, but this guy was already completely freaked out, and the last thing I needed was a fistfight in a car just because I was trying to keep him from bleeding out.

For a moment, he just stared at me. I could almost see the static behind his eyes as his brain failed to process what I'd just said. I was about to repeat myself, as much as I hate doing that, when he nodded, a sudden, spasmodic movement. "Oh. Yes. Of course. Thank you."

He started babbling as I started running blood sweeps over his body. I didn't really listen, since it was mostly just adrenaline dump chatter about how scared he'd been.

I didn't need him to tell me that. I could smell it on him. Fear sweat has a particular odor that's unmistakable once you've smelled it.

It took seconds to confirm that he wasn't leaking, at least nothing life threatening. He might have pissed himself a little.

I turned back forward, re-settling myself in my seat and getting my rifle back to where I could use it quickly. "We clear?"

Drew glanced at the rear view mirror again. He was in his late thirties, maybe a year younger or older than me, with his blond hair now worn somewhat long. Long and lanky, he hadn't changed that much since I'd first known him almost sixteen years before, in the Marine Corps. He had grown a luxurious mustache since he'd moved over to the contracting world, almost in defiance of both the military grooming standards and all the guys in our line of work who felt obligated to grow lumberjack beards as soon as they left the service.

I *had* grown a beard, though it seemed like there was more gray in it than black, these days.

"Looks like it." He kept scanning as he drove, having slowed to the pace of traffic. "Unless they're sophisticated enough to follow the traffic cameras, but that seems unlikely."

Something about the tone of his voice and the way he glanced in the rear-view mirror again told me he wasn't entirely convinced. He hadn't been looking out the back. He'd been looking at Strand.

Drew knew what was up. He was as suspicious about what had just gone down back there as I was.

"Let's hope they're not." I took a long moment to check that I couldn't see anything that Drew might be missing, then turned back toward the rear of the vehicle. "We're going to need to drop him off." I nodded at the pudgy guy.

"Aarav's car was at the hotel, though." Strand didn't quite get it. He was a smart dude, and one of the better clients I'd ferried around over the last decade or so, but there were still some elements of our world that he wasn't quite attuned to.

"He can get a cab to pick it up after things cool down." I wasn't going to have Drew turn around, though Strand wouldn't have asked us to do that, not from what I'd seen of him. But there was a reason why we'd gone to the Hyatt House for the meeting and having this Aarav guy hang out with Strand even longer seemed to defeat that purpose.

Besides, though I wasn't going to say it in the car, I was pretty sure that the leak that had led the bad guys to our location hadn't come from our side of the house.

Strand looked over at his companion, then reluctantly nodded.

I turned back forward with a faint nod. I'd wondered if Strand's assurance that he'd listen to us on all security matters was genuine, or if he was just trying to placate the high-dollar security he'd hired. Apparently, he was serious.

Maybe he'd been placating us until the bullets started flying and he realized that maybe he really did need to take this seriously.

I woke up the tablet affixed to the dash and pulled up our CivTAK app, a civilian version of the military ATAK mapping and tracking software that most of us had gotten to know overseas under various circumstances. It was a good way to keep track of our location and plan routes without worrying about some potentially compromised Big Tech software leaking a back door to someone we didn't want looking over our shoulders.

We were near Berkeley Park. I pointed to the screen as Drew took his eyes off the road momentarily. "Let's head for

Atlantic Station. Nice public place where he's not likely to get moved on right away. Lots of entrances and exits."

Drew nodded, taking the next right to get us moving that way.

I could hear Aarav fidgeting in the back. Drew glanced in the rear view again. "You good back there?"

"Yes. I just have never experienced anything like this." The fear in his voice was palpable. "Will the station be safe, do you think?"

"As safe as any other public place." I wasn't going to sugar coat it. As far as I was concerned, we were back on a warzone footing. In a way, it felt good. "Just keep your head down, go use the bathroom or something, then come back out by a different exit and get a cab. Oh, I wouldn't go straight back to the hotel to get your rental until tomorrow or the next day."

I had turned back over my shoulder as I spoke, and so I caught his faint, shaky nod.

It took minutes to get to Atlantic Station. It was essentially a planned residential and commercial complex on the site of the old Atlantic Steel mill. The whole place was very modern and nicely laid out, with brick sidewalks and landscaped and manicured medians down the middle of the narrow streets. The older, turn-of-the-century brick buildings were offset by much more modern steel-and-glass skyscrapers and stores, and entire streets were blocked off for use by pedestrians.

It wasn't the most covert place, but it was relatively low crime, and that was what mattered at the moment. Besides, there were thousands of people who came and went through Atlantic Station every day, which meant Aarav had plenty of crowd to get lost in.

Drew pulled over in front of an Atlanta Falcons Team Store. The brick sidewalk was lined with park benches and clay pot planters, with several picnic tables on the corner. "This is your stop."

For a moment, Aarav didn't move, and I was afraid we were going to have an issue. After a few seconds of hesitation, though, he cracked the door.

"I think we should proceed with what we talked about, Merritt." He'd steadied a little bit, just over the last few minutes. "Not right away, but after this afternoon..."

Then he was out and heading for the Falcons store, letting the door slam behind him.

Drew didn't wait. We were moving as soon as the door latched.

CHAPTER
4

It still took another hour to get to our safehouse. I didn't think that was the way Strand was thinking of it, but then again, he had wanted to set this meeting up in Atlanta, some distance away from his Dallas-Fort Worth headquarters. He might have been far more security conscious than we had given him credit for.

The safehouse itself was a massive, sprawling Frank Lloyd-Wright sort of nightmare, a blocky, one-story L-shape set back in the trees in South Tuxedo Park. It wasn't the sort of thing you'd expect to be a safehouse, but an AirBnB rented by a billionaire with room for his security detail was another matter.

Drew drove past the fountain set in the octagonal concrete courtyard out front and pulled the SUV around the back. Phil's and Marcos's vehicle, a white Nissan Pathfinder, was parked back there already. I didn't see the big Excursion that was our QRF vehicle, so Tom, Brian, Ken, and Custus must still have been out there.

Jake and Rob were waiting at the door, and I thought I saw KG lurking somewhere behind them. They ushered Strand inside quickly, while Drew and I got our own gear and weapons sorted out and the vehicle secured.

The trees surrounding the estate were thick enough that we weren't especially worried about any of the neighbors looking in. We still took care to cover up the weapons and go bags before we headed inside. This was Georgia, not California or someplace like that, but this was still a rich neighborhood, and the locals might get the wrong idea if they saw a bunch of rifles and chest rigs openly displayed.

The Quick Reaction Force rolled up in their big, black Excursion just as Drew locked the doors. The passenger side door opened almost before it had come to a full stop, and Brian got out.

"You guys couldn't even have left any for us?" Short, bowlegged, and with a chest that was almost perpetually puffed out, Brian had earned the callsign "Scrappy" long before he'd even come to PGS. He'd tried to evade it, but Rob had known him before, so it had followed him along.

"Do *you* want to be the ones talking to the cops about getting into a firefight in a Hyatt?" Drew retorted, barely even looking at Brian as he headed for the house.

"Of course not." Tom had just gotten out of the driver's seat and leaned around to speak over the hood before Brian could say a word. "He just hadn't thought that far. You know, as usual."

"Says the senior citizen who's probably getting too old and tired for this line of work." Brian turned back to his partner as he started pulling his own gear out of the Excursion. "If you were this scared of getting in a fight, why would you take a high-risk security contract?"

"Maybe because kids like you need some wisdom so you don't go off half cocked and get all of us thrown in the slammer." Tom wasn't looking at Brian as he spoke, but he still raised his voice enough that everyone could hear him.

Ken and Custus were already halfway to the door, duffel bags full of weapons, ammo, and first aid gear over their shoulders. Ken came to his big partner's shoulder, but he wasn't a small man. Salt-and-pepper hair and beard were offset by a deeply tanned and weathered face that looked about ten

26

years older than he really was. Custus was massive, pushing three hundred pounds of muscle, his skin just light enough to account for the Creole part of his background, his own hair still jet black, drawn back in dreads and with a small patch of beard on his chin.

"You clowns are the same age." Ken shook his head. "Grow up."

"A wedding made in hell, right there." Custus still grinned a little as he said it. There was a reason that Tom and Brian were partners.

KG was waiting inside as Drew and I entered. "Need to see you guys once you get your gear secured." Since he was thick around the body and going bald, a man might look at KG and think he was just a middle-aged nobody going to fat. The truth was I didn't know a single man stronger than that balding, sad-eyed, barrel-chested man. He powerlifted for fun.

"We'll be there in a second." I'd known this was coming, and I had plenty to go over in the hot wash myself. It was going to be brutal, and the mistakes we'd made needed to be laid out, but then the rest of it needed to be dealt with, too. And Strand probably needed to be in on that conversation.

The house was massive, with ten bedrooms, most of them with their own bathrooms. The wood floors and the furniture provided about the only color, as everything else in the house was stark white. It was blinding turning the lights on in the bathroom first thing in the morning.

With twelve of us in the house, it still got a little cramped, as big as it was. We'd staged our weapons and gear in the bedrooms next to our beds, out of sight if Strand had any visitors. There hadn't been any so far, but he had family in the area, and it would have seemed strange if none of them visited.

Of course, after today, things were probably going to get interesting regardless.

Leaving my rifle and gear under my bed, reloading my Glock mags, and making sure everything was ready to go again, I headed back out into the living room.

Phil was leaning against the hearth, under the massive wall-mounted TV. He and I had been taken for brothers more than once, though we were no relation at all, aside from our mutual history as Recon Marines and contractors. Dark haired, hatchet-faced, and lean as a whip, Phil had more than once suggested on contract that we have some fun by impersonating each other.

Marcos was even thinner than Phil, but it was a lean, dangerous thin. He'd never confirmed his history in my hearing, but I knew enough dudes to know that he'd been with Task Force Orange before he'd gotten out and gone private sector.

KG and Strand were sitting on the sectional in front of the hearth, while Marcos and Phil stayed on their feet. I decided to follow suit, though Drew pulled one of the chairs away from the little breakfast nook next to the big picture window off to the side of the hearth and sat down.

KG started things off. "Okay, first things first. We've been talking to the cops. They'll have detectives over here shortly to take statements. I know nobody's eager, especially after what happened, but this is important to cover our asses so that we don't all end up in jail and fighting charges for the next two years. Georgia law is on our side, as long as there wasn't any excessive force used." He looked around at the four of us. "I hope I don't have to explain any insurance rounds to the head on a man who was already on the ground?"

It wasn't that KG was squeamish. He was probably less sensitive than I was about such things. No, he was hoping that the company wasn't going to have to pay lawyers to defend against a murder charge. Insurance rounds might be one thing in a combat zone. Stateside, they tended to turn a good shoot into a homicide.

Strand was frowning. He might not have quite understood what KG meant by "insurance rounds." I hoped that he'd back me up.

"There are some guys on the floor with holes in their heads, but no one was shot after they were no longer a threat, no." I could say that with some confidence since I'd done *most* of the shooting, after all. Strand's expression cleared and he nodded as I said it. *Whew. He is going to back me up.* I should hope so; it was the truth. I'd worked for clients who'd throw you under the bus in a heartbeat, though, whether the accusation was remotely true or not.

With a glance at Drew, which drew a nod, KG accepted it. "Good. I didn't think I had to worry about it, but I had to ask. If it had been Scooby and Scrappy..." He suppressed a shudder.

"That's not really being fair, bro." Drew folded his arms. "Scrappy talks a lot of shit, but he's a pro. He wouldn't be here, otherwise."

KG inclined his head to acknowledge the point. "Fair enough. Okay. Let's have it. From the beginning."

I launched into the hot wash, starting with our departure from the safehouse. I went over the route, then our arrival at the hotel, checking in, meeting up with Aarav, and then the assault itself.

I hoped that I was being sufficiently honest with myself and the rest as to the mistakes I'd made. I'd been the right-seater, which meant I was the team lead for the mission, so I took responsibility for trusting the electronic lock on the door and leaving the carbines and spare mags in the vehicle. Drew interjected a couple of times with clarifying details, but nothing that outright contradicted my own memory of the incident.

Strand, for his part, held his peace. I didn't know if he just had little to add, since he was pretty much down on the floor or being steered around the hallways and the parking lot for most of the fight, or if he just didn't think he was in a place to add to our debrief. I was sure that he'd probably noticed a lot, but whether or not he understood what some of it signified I didn't know.

KG was taking notes while I talked. Some debriefers might have asked questions or made comments, but that wasn't KG's way. I hadn't known him before I'd gone to work for PGS, but from what I'd seen since he'd taken charge of this detail, I thought he was a solid dude, and he wasn't going to snipe me while I was relaying what had happened.

What he said after I was done could be another matter.

I finally finished up with the drop off at Atlantic Station. Strand was looking at the floor with a faint furrow between his brows. KG stared at his notes, while Drew, Phil, Marcos, and I watched him.

"Well, that was a hell of a day, and no mistake." KG finally dropped the notebook on the coffee table and leaned back on the couch. He turned to Strand. "Have you got anything to add, sir? Anything you noticed that my guys didn't?"

Strand seemed to come out of a deep reverie. "No." He shook himself a little. "No, I think Chris got everything straight. He certainly saw a lot more than I did. I was a little focused on the meeting."

Any further debrief was interrupted by a knock at the door. "Cops are here," Jake called out from the entryway.

"We'll table the rest of the discussion until we're done with these guys." KG stood up. "Mr. Strand, I took the liberty of calling our company lawyers as well, and we've got someone on the way."

Strand nodded, pulling out his phone. "Sorry, I've been a little distracted. I'll get my Atlanta office moving."

"Hopefully we won't need them immediately, but it pays to be prepared." KG started toward the door. "Let's go talk to the nice policemen."

***

30

The conversation with the detectives from Atlanta PD actually went far more amicably than I had any business expecting. Apparently, the receptionist at the hotel had been threatened before she'd given up the keycard, lending further credence to our assertion that all of the shooting on our end had been in self-defense. There were some extremely shaken guests, but we hadn't threatened them. So far, no one was talking about charges being brought against any of us. The surviving attackers, however, were in the wind, with no leads that they could or would tell us about.

The cops were still reserved enough that I was a little leery. Their expressions were shuttered as they took down our statements, and any questions about what had happened to the SWAT team that was supposed to have intervened were ignored. They took down our information, thanked us for our cooperation, and left.

"I don't like this." Tom had been listening on the periphery, without anything to add since he and the rest of our QRF had been blocks away as the shooting had gone down. "They were way too aloof. They're gonna try to hit us with something."

"Maybe." KG rubbed his chin as he stared at the door where the detectives had left. "It's possible that they screwed the pooch by telling the SWAT guys to stand down, and now they're worried because there are bodies on the ground."

"That might be it." Strand hadn't said much during the interviews, except to give his own statement, which had been brief and leaning heavily into the fact that we'd saved his life. But he'd been thinking. Been thinking hard. And Merritt Strand was a thinker. "There are a few things about this that don't add up."

"Indeed they don't." KG turned and headed back into the living room. "Which is what we need to talk about next."

He sat back down on the sectional. "Everybody grab a chair. This could take a minute."

31

Strand sat next to him, that furrow between his eyebrows getting deeper. "This wasn't just a random violent crime, was it?"

A chorus of derisive snorts and curses went around the room, and even KG joined in. "That's putting it mildly. A random violent crime is a mugging on the street. Even a vehicular ambush might have been a random violent crime. This was a targeted attack on a meeting that no one outside that room was supposed to know about. Furthermore, while it *was* over fairly quickly, *somebody* told that SWAT team to stand by instead of intervening." KG leaned back on the couch again. "Neither of those two things are necessarily connected, *but* they're awfully coincidental, and I don't usually believe in coincidences, especially when they result in deaths."

There was a pause as Strand thought that over. Under different circumstances, with a different team lead and a different client, I might have kept my mouth shut, but I'd had to kill people that afternoon. This was dead serious and status games no longer had any place in my mind.

"I know that corporate espionage was one of the big things you said you were worried about." I watched Strand's face carefully as he turned his eyes on me. "There were threats, too, but if I read the dossier right, those seemed to be the usual aimed at a man with a lot of money." I lifted my gaze to encompass the rest of the team. "Ten guys is a big detail for one man. We're fine with the work, but I think we've all been asking a couple of questions. Under the circumstances, we might need a little more information, if you've got it."

Strand thought that one over for a moment, every eye on him. Finally, he took a deep breath and leaned forward, his hands clasped in front of him.

"Okay. That's fair. I'm afraid I don't *have* much more information than I provided. I don't know who the opposition is, but they appear to be a lot higher placed and more powerful than I would have thought."

He paused for a moment, as if gathering his thoughts. "So, the meeting with Aarav was about bringing him and his fund in on a bit of an intervention that I've become involved with. I wouldn't even have found out about the situation if it weren't for a social media post that a friend brought to my attention.

"I found out that there's a concerted effort underway by a group of private equity firms to force a leveraged buyout of a family ranch down in southern New Mexico. Now, that might seem to be no big deal. Leveraged buyouts happen all the time. *Especially* in the land and development business. There are a lot of developers salivating over every bit of agricultural land they can find lately, for whatever reason. There are some theories about that, for better or worse, but I'm somewhat agnostic about them.

"As soon as I started digging, though, it became obvious that there's something more going on here. The leverage doesn't seem to be limited to financials." His eyes hardened slightly, an expression I admit I'd never expected to see on his somewhat soft features. "There's been sabotage, livestock killed, and several assaults on members of the family. And all of it started *after* the first rather aggressive offers to buy the property were extended."

I frowned. "Where is this ranch?"

He laughed softly. "In the middle of nowhere, east of a little town called Columbus. It's all high Sonoran desert and far enough outside of El Paso that nobody would want to make the commute. There's seriously nothing of interest there for anyone but a cattle rancher. Except that *someone* wants it badly enough to resort to criminal activity to force the owners to sell out. Which is why I took an interest.

"I don't like leveraged buyouts in general. I know, that sounds weird coming from a big finance guy like me, but I like to think that I've earned my wealth honestly. I sure as hell didn't hire thugs to try to force the issue when I wanted to buy something that the owner didn't want to sell."

"Who's trying to buy the place?" KG asked.

"That's the question." Strand lifted his eyebrows. "The opening offer was from a shell company. Lots of money, but almost no other footprint anywhere. I traced it back to another shell company, which got traced to yet another. My analysts are still working on exactly who's behind it, but they've got a *lot* of resources, whoever they are, and they're being very careful about covering their tracks."

Drew and I shared a look at that one. Some of the pieces were coming together. The hit hadn't been at all random.

Which opened up a whole new can of worms, but one which I doubted PGS was going to back down from.

When Strand didn't appear to have much else to add, KG leaned forward again, tapping his pencil against the notebook sitting on the coffee table. "So. We've got some unscrupulous actor working against the client on a financial level, who is apparently willing and able to leverage violent crime to get what he wants. We have Hispanic hitters who knew exactly where to go, in an apparent targeted kill or capture mission against the client. *And* we have a SWAT team get called off an active shooter situation." He tapped the pencil again, his eyes narrowing. He suddenly looked up at Strand. "Did you have your phone with you on the meet?"

Our client looked a little surprised. "I mean... Yeah. I did. I needed it for a couple of things."

KG nodded. "That might explain it."

"Does it?" Phil sounded a little skeptical. "I haven't heard anything about MS-13 or whoever having phone tracking capability."

"Neither have I," KG said grimly. "Which raises a few other questions, that I suspect are linked to the fact that our police help got called off."

34

"So, what are we going to do about it?" Drew asked. From the way he asked, I suspected he knew just how thorny a question it was. If we already had enemies in the local police department...

Hell, we hadn't even known we were in the middle of a war when we'd gotten here.

"For now? Nothing much." KG had to know that such a course of action wasn't going to sit well with anyone in the room. He'd been in our shoes before, even if he was supposed to just sit back and direct these days. "Taking any sort of overt interest or what might be construed as offensive action could easily backfire on us. If there *is* somebody in the Atlanta PD, or higher, who is actively working against us, things could get really ugly, really fast." He scratched the back of his neck for a moment. "Do you mind cancelling your meetings for the next couple of days, Mr. Strand? Begging off because of how shaken you are over the violence, something like that?"

Strand hesitated, but then he nodded. "We can do that. I try not to let personal issues get in the way of business, and most of the people I've worked with understand that, but ordinary personal issues are not the same thing as having someone try to kill you." He laughed nervously. "I think I can sell that. May I ask why the postponement? Because that's what it's going to have to be. Several of these meetings are vital to this project."

"It'll give us some breathing room and let us narrow a few things down in the meantime. The lawyers can get here and start doing their lawyer-fu. Like I said, I don't want to give any bad guys with access to local government or law enforcement any openings." KG looked around at the rest of us. "While they do their thing, we can run a few 'errands' out in town and see if we can pick up any surveillance. I know." He held up his hands before anyone could protest. "I know. Everyone did surveillance detection routes to and from the meet. I don't care. Get out there and make damn good and sure that we're not being watched *here*, because if we are, then someone could have gotten a tail on us on the way to the hotel. If not, well, then we'll have to look more seriously at the phone tracking possibility."

"Or that Aarav wasn't as aboveboard as you thought." Drew wasn't accusing, just stating facts, but Strand looked at him as if he had made such an accusation.

"Aarav's a good guy. He wouldn't do something like that."

Drew shrugged. "If you say so."

"We'll keep looking into things while the lawyers do their thing and make sure that we're not going to have to go to court to stay out of the slammer." KG glared around the room, his gaze finally halting on Brian. "So, nobody stick their neck out or do anything stupid for the next few days, at least."

Brian held up his hands innocently. "Why are you looking at me, KG?" When he got nothing but a heavy-lidded stare, he subsided. "Okay, okay. I'll be good."

With a heavy sigh, KG got to his feet. "Let's lay low for tonight. Y'all can start going out and beating the bushes tomorrow."

CHAPTER
5

Surveillance detection is an important part of the job. A large portion of close protection work is looking for trouble with the intention of seeing it coming so that it can be avoided. If you're getting in fights on the regular, it might be thrilling, but you're not doing what you're supposed to be doing. You're getting paid to keep the client safe, not to kick doors and shoot bad guys in the face.

That can be a hard pill to swallow for a lot of guys who enter the business from the Marine Corps, SEAL Teams, or the Ranger Regiment. I'd known a few who had come from Special Mission Units for whom it was excruciating.

And, truth be told, most of us still long, on some level, for something to happen like what had gone down in the Hyatt House, so that we got a chance to once again be the high-speed death machines that we'd been years before, in Iraq, Afghanistan, or, for some of the younger guys, Syria. Even those of us who had long since made our peace with a new role in the contracting world still wished for the rush of combat one more time.

We'd gotten it. And while I went for a walk through the *extremely* posh neighborhood that I could never afford to live in, even if I'd wanted to, I had some time to think it over.

It had been a lot of years since I'd actually been in a firefight. Oh, I'd trained for it. Trained hard. Constantly. Spent a decent amount of my own money on it, since contracting companies and clients, even governmental ones, don't like to pony up for training when you're Stateside. All those years I'd spent overseas, I'd been in some very dangerous places and situations, but when your job is to keep the client out of trouble, it's got to be a well and truly desperate situation to fire a shot in anger.

Now I'd done it. I'd killed at least six men the day before. And after all that time, I had to reflect on it.

I hadn't lost my edge. There was that. And while the weight of the potential repercussions of that fight was starting to bear down on all of us, I wouldn't have missed that fight for the world.

Killing a man isn't something to take lightly. I'd done it enough to know that. Yet there's a satisfaction about coming that close to death and being the one who came out alive. An exhilaration that is unmatched anywhere else in life. And I'd successfully kept a man alive whose safety had been my responsibility. I wasn't going to apologize for that.

I was keeping my eyes open as I walked along the road under the shade of the trees on either side, thinking things over. I wasn't just out for a stroll to clear my head. I wasn't the main effort for our little surveillance detection dragnet, either. I was the rabbit, the bait sticking my neck out to see if I could flush somebody who might or might not be watching the house and therefore taking stock of our comings and goings. I could still watch for any indicators that I might be able to see.

After all, if we were up against gangbangers, they were not usually the most professional recondos.

Still, as I walked around the sweeping curve at the base of the low hill where our AirBnB sat, I didn't see anything. No cars on the side of the road that might be out of place, no little sneaky wannabe ninjas in the trees and the bushes. I tried not to look too much like I was looking, but from all I could see, I may as well have stared intently and scanned the woods with binoculars. There wasn't anyone around to think it was strange.

My phone buzzed, and I stopped by the fire hydrant out front of a house that looked like a miniature Monticello as I pulled it out of my pocket. I swore silently as I answered it, trying not to wince as I brought it to my ear. "Hi, honey."

"Is everything okay?" Julie didn't sound mad, which was good. She sounded scared and worried, which was kinda worse. "You didn't call last night."

I had often had to be intentionally vague over the years, but I never could lie to my wife. "Sorry, hon. We had a bit of an incident yesterday, and things got a little hectic."

She was quiet. That wasn't a good sign. It meant she'd already suspected.

Julie and I had been married for a long time. Divorce wasn't on the table, and never had been. We'd agreed on that before we'd tied the knot. That didn't mean that things couldn't get extremely uncomfortable, though.

She'd been happy as could be when I'd quit going overseas. The government agency that was the client and I had finally had certain irreconcilable differences, so I'd left. I'd been home for a whole year before the Pallas Group Solutions job had come up. She wasn't going to be so happy that I was in danger again.

"Was it bad?" She wasn't freaking out, which was good. It wasn't that my wife was a hysteric. She wasn't. But she'd gotten used to the idea that I was done, and when it turned out that I wasn't, it hadn't sat well with her.

Once again, though, I couldn't lie to her. "It was bad enough. I might have to stay here for a little extra to get it sorted out. There are cops and lawyers involved, now."

"Are you in trouble?" At the tone of the question, I actually started to relax a little. She'd slipped back into her deployment mindset. She'd never wanted to upset me while I was deployed—which had gotten a *little* out of hand a couple times, when things had happened at home that I'd needed to know about—and while she'd been upset herself that I was going back into the business, now that it was what it was, she had simply flipped that switch back.

"Not that I know of." I was being vague again, but even though this was an encrypted call—we'd been using one encrypted messaging and calling app or another for years to talk long distance—she didn't need to know all the gory details. Especially when I considered how much speculation was mixed in with those gory details. "The client's lawyers are getting involved now."

"Good. He can certainly afford it." She knew who the client was, though not why he had essentially a special operations team for a protective detail. "Is there anything I need to get ready for? Is there media attention?"

"Not so far." That was a *little* strange. A shootout in a downtown hotel seemed like something that should have been on the news that evening, but there was a strange silence about it. "I'm sure there will be, but I don't think any of us were identified. We kind of had to get the client off the X while things were still hot, so I'm pretty sure none of us were identified on the scene, anyway."

She got quiet again, putting the pieces together. "Chris?"

"Yeah, Julie." I knew that tone, and it was worse than her getting angry. She was scared.

"Please be careful. We can't lose you."

I sighed faintly. "I'll be careful, hon. Trust me. I've been in a lot worse places than Atlanta."

"I know. That's why I'm worried." She didn't need to elaborate. She'd known some of the friends I'd had to bury over the years. She'd been at more of their funerals than I had. She knew the phrase "Complacency Kills" as well as any of us. And she knew that we were all mortal, and that clock was running out for all of us, sooner or later. "I love you."

"I love you, too. Are Sammy and Rick there?" Our two boys were eleven and thirteen, and they both tended to be little wild men most of the week. If they weren't in homeschool with their mom, they were out in the woods being frontiersmen. Or would-be Recondos, like their dad.

"They're out fishing with Tyler." Tyler Rutledge was our neighbor and an old friend. We'd worked together in more than one Third World shithole. Her voice got a little lower. Not ashamed, not really. "I didn't want them to hear if things were bad. Not yet."

"They're not that bad, Julie. Not yet." I grimaced as I said it. There it was again. I couldn't just reassure her. I had to be honest.

"Well, I know I already said it, but please be careful. And even if it's just a text, make sure to let us know that you're all right, okay?"

"I will." I had to. Hell, I'd had enough rough times downrange when I hadn't heard from her in a couple of days, usually because of something unforeseen. I couldn't expect her not to worry. Especially not after what had just happened. "I love you."

We hung up and I took one more scan of the area. Still nothing. I turned and headed back toward the house. Maybe KG had something new.

CHAPTER
6

I got back to the house to find a new car parked out front. Frowning and immediately taking in not only the expensive Mercedes but also the rest of our surroundings, I was on alert at once. Not that I'd been especially in "The White," as it were, but after what had happened at the hotel, I was more paranoid than usual.

When I walked in the back door by the garage, however, no one seemed to be any more keyed up than normal. An attractive blond woman in business attire was sitting in the living room across from KG. She looked up as I walked in, and KG held out a hand to beckon me into the room. "This is Chris, he was one of the primary security detail on Mr. Strand during the incident."

She looked me over, standing as I walked over to the couch, and held out her hand. I shook it, trying to gauge just what was going on here.

"Chris, I'm Amanda Tavington. I work for Mr. Strand's legal team. Please, have a seat. I have a few questions."

I suppressed a grimace, but I had already known that repeating the same debrief over and over was probably going to be a part of this process. I sat down on the sectional at an angle to her, since KG was holding down the other leg of the "L." "What do you want to know?"

"First of all, gentlemen, let me state from the beginning that I consider everything said in the course of this conversation to fall under attorney-client privilege. Technically, Mr. Strand is my client, but he's asked me to extend the same courtesies to you, as you are contracted to him and his enterprise for the moment." She took a notebook and pencil out of her briefcase and set them very precisely on the coffee table. "I can record this, but if you'd prefer, I can also stick with written notes."

I glanced at KG, and he nodded slightly. "Let's just stick with the notes, shall we?"

She didn't seem surprised at my decision. "Very well then." She took a deep breath and her demeanor seemed to change slightly. As if the formalities were out of the way and she could be more straightforward. "First thing. Is there *anything* you left out of your official statements? I'm not saying you were deliberately concealing anything, but might there have been some detail you overlooked? Something you forgot in the adrenaline dump?"

I felt my suspicions starting to mount. "No. The statement was as complete as I could make it. I haven't had any sudden revelations in the hours since, either. Why?"

She pursed her lips as she leaned back slightly. "Hmm." She sighed. "There's something extremely strange going on. When I first talked to the DA, she was hostile and combative. The sort of thing I'd expect from a DA who's about to file charges dealing with a defense attorney. It was not a happy meeting. Especially not when I started asking questions about whether or not she intended to press charges. I couldn't confirm it, since nothing had been filed, but I was pretty sure from her answers that she wasn't interested in the attackers, but was looking at charging you, Mr. Radford, Mr. Tull, and Mr. Gonzalez with murder. When I made some calls afterward, I did get confirmation that she was working on such charges."

44

"That was a clear-cut case of self-defense, with multiple witnesses, including the hotel security cameras." I'd like to say I was shocked to hear that the local district attorney wanted to burn us for killing some thugs who'd broken into our hotel room with guns, but after the last few years, I really wasn't. I still had to say it, though.

"It was." She nodded in agreement. "There's no two ways about it, and while I didn't *exactly* say it during our conversation, I did make it clear that that's precisely what it had been, and that if she pressed charges, I would personally end her entire career." A tight smile. "I've done it before." She frowned slightly, the faintest cleft forming between her eyebrows. "Then, less than an hour later, the same DA calls me up, very conciliatory, and wants to get everything tied up and all the statements clear. No charges. No trial. No fuss. She admitted when I pressed her that one of the dead perps had been identified as a known felon with multiple priors and at least five outstanding warrants. She didn't have information on the others, but she said it was likely the same situation. That it looked like a cut-and-dried armed robbery gone bad. As if that was it."

There was silence for a moment. "As if that was it." KG's eyes had narrowed. "We all know that's not *it*."

"Yes, we do." Tavington eyed me narrowly. "I don't know for sure what you gentlemen stumbled upon, but it's clearly something big enough that someone very connected wants it buried." She got even more sober. "I can't prove it right off, but I suspect that if you try to push on this, then charges *will* be preferred, even if they have to wait until I can't easily get here to defend you. If nothing else, they'll drag things out so that the process itself shuts you down."

KG nodded, his expression otherwise blank. Probably a well-practiced expression, given how much he'd more than likely dealt with lawyers and governmental functionaries over the years. "As is generally to be expected. Even without the unlikely series of coincidences we're looking at here, I would have expected the government and law enforcement to bend over backwards to cover their own asses, *especially* if they could publicly crush a private security company in the process."

For a moment, Tavington looked downright frustrated, as if she had hoped that we had some perfectly revealing bit of information that we'd somehow held back that would blow the whole case wide open. There was definitely an edge to her, and I believed her when she'd said that she'd ended district attorneys' careers before. She seemed like the type. There was blood in the water, metaphorically speaking, and she smelled it.

Well, so did we, but we had different ways of dealing with it.

"Unfortunately, unless you gentlemen have anything more to tell me that I can use, there's not much more to say. The police won't be pursuing the investigation further, and won't refer it to the DOJ, even though the would-be victim was from out of state. According to the official story, it was a random, local violent crime that was stopped by concealed carriers, and that's that." She stood. "Like I said, whoever is behind this is connected. We *could* try to go public, try to push. I'm amenable if that's the way that you and Mr. Strand want to go. He expressed to me that your assessment of the security situation and your opinion on our course of action going forward mattered as much as his. *However.*" She tilted her head slightly as if to emphasize her point further. "Understand that the current situation is probably the best case. Without saying as much, they're offering you an out. If we all accept that it was a random violent crime, none of our people were killed or seriously hurt, and the bad guys are all dead and gone, they'll let us off unmolested.

"If, however, we push, they're going to push back. There will at the very least be smear campaigns in the media. Something about trigger-happy, armed-to-the-teeth security contractors getting into a firefight in downtown Atlanta. Deep dives into all your backgrounds to find a reason to accuse you of looking for a fight. Then there will almost certainly be charges, if only to continue the Kabuki theater."

I hoped that my expression was as much of a mask as KG's. "So, you're saying we should just accept it and move on."

Her eyes flashed. "That's not what I'm saying at all. I'm just saying that if you decide not to, you need to be ready for a fight. You need to have a plan. You need opposition research at the very least."

"We appreciate the input, and we very much appreciate you bringing us the word." The tone of KG's voice made it abundantly clear that the current conversation was over. I wondered just what he had in mind. While I'd come to respect him as a team lead, at least in this close protection context, I still didn't know him well enough to be able to read his mind yet. The things he'd already said had made me suspect that he wasn't going to take this lying down, but then, he had to take Strand's wishes into account, not to mention the Pallas Group Solutions directors. I'd never met anyone above KG's position, though references had been made to a Mr. Walker, the founder and CEO. The name sounded familiar, though without a first name—which was never forthcoming—I couldn't be sure. "We'll definitely be in touch, but you understand that I can't make any long-term decisions on policy for the company without consulting higher."

Tavington wasn't happy with the answer. She'd clearly been on the warpath when she'd come here and having the guys who'd shot their way out of Hyatt House without taking a single casualty suddenly become cautious and not jump at the chance for a fight hadn't been on her list of expected courses of action. She was enough of a professional not to make an issue out of it, though.

47

"I understand." The coldness in her voice and her eyes said that while she might understand, she didn't approve. As far as she was concerned, she was our only hope of finding justice and not getting nailed to the wall, or at least dragged through legal purgatory until we wished we *had* been nailed to the proverbial wall. "I'll be in town for the next week, and Mr. Strand can always contact me, should he need me." There was the faintest emphasis on Strand's name, as if to remind us that we didn't necessarily get the final say here.

"Thank you, Ms. Tavington. We'll be in touch."

KG escorted her to the door, though she shot a look over her shoulder at me just before she left. She wasn't happy, but she was starting to sense that there was more going on here than just a bunch of aging security contractors who were worried about their future employment.

He waited at the door until she had pulled out of the driveway, then turned back to me. There was a hard look in his eye. "What do you say, Backwoods? You and Smokestack ready to do some of that PI work that PGS paid to get you certified in?"

"You want to know who's pulling the strings." It wasn't a question.

"You're damned right I do," he bit out. "And I want every bit of information I can get to hang 'em with. I'll talk to Strand about starting to backtrack some of those shell companies and see if we can't find a link from that direction. I want you guys out there, tracking down leads. Start with the receptionist at the Hyatt House, if you can find her. Find me targets."

His expression got even harder, and if I'd had any doubt that KG had been a gunfighter in his day, that look dispelled it. "If we can do this legally, fine. If not..."

He let the words hang in the air.

He didn't need to finish them.

CHAPTER
7

We got a lead a lot sooner than I'd expected. In fact, it came even before any of us hit the streets to try to follow up.

While the idea most people might have of Private Investigator work—and PGS had required that we all get certified as PIs before we went on an active detail—might involve a lot of stakeouts and spying, the truth of intelligence work in this day and age is that open source intelligence—also known as OSINT—is invaluable. And the internet is *teeming* with OSINT if you know where to look.

As it turned out, an independent Atlanta news site was the source of the first lead. "Hey, Chris, come take a look at this." We were sitting at the kitchen table in the safehouse, laptops open and connected to the house's wifi through VPNs from hell, using a few specially programmed news aggregators and social media search engines.

I got up and moved around the corner of the table to look over his shoulder. He had a news site up, the banner displaying the words *Atlanta Daily Independent*. It looked professional enough, though I hadn't heard of the site before. Not that I was any expert in Atlanta newspapers, but this looked somewhat small.

Which was probably why they had published the story that was splashed across Drew's screen.

DID ATLANTA PD DELIBERATELY ALLOW A DEADLY KIDNAPPING ATTEMPT TO GO FORWARD?

The Atlanta Police Department has finally released a statement concerning the shootout that happened at the Hyatt House Atlanta, Downtown two days ago. While the statement was delivered with suitable gravitas, and the Chief of Police assured everyone that the attempted armed robbery in a hotel room was a one-off violent crime, one of hundreds that happen in the city every day, there are any number of immediate and obvious holes in the story.

According to eyewitnesses, the perps initially intimidated the receptionist into giving them a keycard, indicating that they knew exactly who they were targeting. This was not a random act of violence and greed. Furthermore, there are eyewitness reports that several of the initial attackers—to be distinguished from Merritt Strand's personal security guards—were seen fleeing the scene, putting the lie to the police chief's claim that all of the perpetrators were killed by Mr. Strand's security personnel. (Which would mean, by extension, if not said, that there is nothing more to worry about.)

This might only be a matter of public relations for a police department that has struggled to deal with an exploding violent crime rate, while politicians blame their political opponents for either allowing lax laws or inflating the crime statistics for partisan selling points, and police continue to leave the department in droves. However, recent information points to something even more sinister.

This reporter had the opportunity to speak to an Atlanta Police Department patrol officer who was in the vicinity during the shootout. He received the initial dispatch call and was prepared to respond when, he says, he received a call ordering him to divert to a minor altercation several blocks away, which had resolved by the time he arrived. He told us that he heard several other such diversions take place over the police radio, and he believes that more might have been issued via phone. He did state that he had heard the Atlanta PD SWAT team told to stand by rather than intervene.

When asked why he thought that the police were diverted from the hotel, his answer was simultaneously vague and damning.

"Somebody in our office wanted Strand dead or taken. Somebody with a lot of money, who wanted more."

I turned from the screen to Drew, straightening up from where I'd been leaning on the table. "Who's the reporter?"

"Ella Brolin." He scrolled back to the top of the article to read the name off. "You thinking what I'm thinking?"

"If you're thinking that we need to make contact with Miss Brolin, then yes. I'd like to have a chat with that cop." I turned toward the bedrooms where my gear was. "Let's see if we can't hunt up some contact information for her."

***

We were about to make the call when KG came in. I'd briefed him as soon as I'd finished reading that news piece, while Drew had set out tracking down Ella Brolin.

"Hold up. We've got a call with corporate, first." He set his own laptop down on the coffee table. "Get over here."

I frowned. Drew mirrored my expression. We had work to do, and so far, KG had been our insulation from corporate. He was the team leader on the ground. I'd hoped, based on what I'd seen, that PGS wasn't one of those companies that had idiots in corporate offices somewhere in Northern Virginia making calls on operations that they weren't qualified to make. Even some of the worst contracting companies I'd worked with during my time overseas hadn't done that, though they'd certainly screwed with personnel to the detriment of operations from time to time.

KG waved at us impatiently. "Come on. The boss wants to talk to you. Both of you."

51

"Hey, Kevin." The voice on the other end of the videoconference sounded vaguely familiar. I frowned as I stepped around the couch and came in behind KG.

The face was a little older than I remembered, and the beard and the long hair were gone, but I'd recognize those craggy features and bright green eyes surrounded by crow's feet anywhere. "Goblin?"

He grinned. "Hey, Backwoods. Long time no see, buddy."

"Wait." I ran a hand over my face. "Of course. Thad Walker. Why the hell didn't I think of that?"

The grin got wider. "Because you had no reason to. Most of us who went to work on staff with the client either stayed there or quit the business altogether. Or went contract again." He pointed to his close-cropped hair, which had a lot more gray in it than I remembered from those long ago days, when Goblin and I had been driving an up-armored Land Cruiser through the streets of Baghdad. "I have to say that I earned every single one of these gray hairs, getting to where I am. Which is a position where I can see that you guys get employed the best way you can."

He sobered. "I'll get into that later, when we've got more time to talk. Right now, I need to bring you up to speed on what we're seeing out here.

"I spoke at some length with Strand about this job when he first put out feelers for security. There's a reason that we got hired on, and that he agreed to a ten-man detail. He didn't have all the information that we do at the moment, but he had a feeling, and it's starting to look like that feeling was entirely justified.

"We've been doing what we can to trace a bunch of the shell companies that are behind this buyout he's trying to head off. Most of them are based in Panama. One in particular that we're taking special interest in is actually a foundation based in the Bahamas. Lots of money going in and out, and since it's a foundation, there's next to no accounting required. It's no smoking gun, but when an offshore foundation is involved in a land deal, it's usually organized crime at work. We'll keep digging, but I needed you to know so that you're going into this op with the reporter that KG told me about with as much intel as we can get you. There are some bad actors involved in this buyout attempt, and they may well be connected to the attack the other day. If you can trace the links from your end, we'll do what we can from the more IT-centric end and see if we can come up with some answers. Maybe even leading to some criminal charges."

I didn't react. I wasn't sure how much Goblin was playing for an audience, in case someone was monitoring the call. The man I remembered had been a hell of a lot more cynical. On the other hand, he had gone to work full-time for a three-letter agency, then gone corporate. It had been a long time since we'd worked together.

He had to take this tack, I realized. There was a lot at stake for the company, and therefore all the guys he had working for him. Things get different when you're not just a trigger-puller anymore.

At the same time, I remembered that I had more at stake, too. If we went rogue and ended up on the wrong side of the law, then Julie and the boys would suffer for it, too. We *had* to work within the system, no matter how much the better part of two decades working for that system had soured me on it.

"Roger that. We're about to contact the reporter now, see if we can set up a meet."

Goblin nodded. "KG will keep me posted. I've got a lot to do here, but I might come out to join you at some point if this gets weird." He grinned again, though the expression was only a ghost of what it had been before. "Good to see you again, Chris." He blinked out.

Drew was standing at the end of the couch with his arms folded. "Well, I'll be damned. Never would have expected Goblin to be running a show like this. Figured he'd be up on the seventh floor somewhere by now."

"In a way, I guess he is." I straightened from where I'd been leaning against the back of the couch. "Let's see if we can talk with our reporter friend."

CHAPTER
8

I'd kind of expected an indie journalist to want to meet in a coffee shop, for some reason, but since it was the middle of the afternoon, Brolin had asked to meet at the Hudson Grille, a small sports bar on Peachtree Street in Midtown. The area was narrow enough that it took some time to reconnoiter it, pick out countersurveillance positions, and plan how we were going to cover this.

Ordinarily, Drew and I might just go in and meet with her. After all, we were Stateside. This was Atlanta, not Baghdad, or any number of other nasty Third World warzones where the two of us had worked. We could watch our own backs.

But there was more to this than just watching our own backs. More information that we hoped to glean from this meeting than just what she knew and how to contact her source. She might not realize it, but publishing that piece in the *Atlanta Daily Independent*, as small as it might be, may well have put a bullseye on her back.

Ideally, we might have someone sitting in a car, ready to react quickly to whatever developed. However, after a few moments in that part of Midtown, it didn't look like a good idea. The only places where someone might park reasonably long-term were the parking lots in front of or behind several of the businesses, and they didn't have good lines of sight.

We still needed a quick reaction force nearby, but that would be Ken and Custus, doing lazy loops around Midtown, trying not to look like they were just wandering around aimlessly, waiting for a call.

Phil and Marcos would be our countersurveillance, and after a frustrating couple of hours, they decided that they were going to have to bite the bullet and use the Sweet Hut bakery and café as their position. There was outdoor seating on the sidewalk, so they could get a good view up and down the long axis of the street.

If anyone was following us or the reporter, they should be able to spot them from there. And so, they were in position thirty minutes before Drew and I pulled into the parking lot behind the sports bar and made our way around to the front to go inside.

At a glance, the street was relatively empty and quiet. It wasn't a busy part of the day, though there was a box truck about a block down making a delivery. For the most part, it didn't look like a lot of people came down here in the middle of the afternoon. Peachtree Street wasn't quite deserted, but there were only a handful of pedestrians on the sidewalks.

That could be good or bad. On the one hand, it would make it a little easier to pick out anyone on surveillance. On the other hand, it made it more difficult for us to disappear into the crowd when there was no crowd.

There was nothing for it, though. We weren't in a position to dictate times or places for these sorts of meetings. If we'd pushed, we might have spooked the reporter, or simply pissed her off and made her cancel the whole thing.

So, with one more scan of the street, which didn't show me anything suspicious, we turned into the restaurant.

The place wasn't that large. It was dark, with the venetian blinds drawn so as to keep the sunlight outside from washing out the TVs. And there were a lot of TVs. Two rows of booths faced the bar, which had a double row of screens above the taps, all showing the same game. The whole place was warmly lit aside from the bluish glow of the TV screens, and the yellow walls and cream colored tiles on the floor added to it.

Since it *was* mid-afternoon, there weren't many people inside. Hell, there wasn't even anyone behind the bar at the moment. That made it a little easier to spot our contact.

Of course, "danger hair," as Drew had called it, is pretty easy to spot anyway. Our reporter contact was in her mid-twenties, with thin, sharp features, wearing a sleeveless shirt and with her hair dyed bright green. Fortunately, while her profile picture on the *Atlanta Daily Independent* had shown her with purple hair, the color change wasn't nearly enough to suggest this was a different person.

Neither Drew nor I were dressed like gunfighters, though that's a rather subjective criteria at the best of times. Drew was wearing khakis and a button-up shirt, while I had on a polo shirt and jeans. Phil had grinned as he'd told me that to *really* blend in, I should be wearing skinny jeans and Chuck Taylors, but there was only so far I could really bring myself to go when it came to the gray man stuff. Besides, not *everybody* in Midtown Atlanta was wearing skinny jeans.

The clothing made it a little difficult to conceal all of our usual toys. I've never been a huge fan of appendix carry, but with the Glock 43 that I was currently packing, it kind of made sense. The other reason I refused to wear skinny jeans was the first aid "blowout kit" on my ankle. The rest of my gear was momentarily limited to a knife and a cell phone, with the remainder left in the vehicle.

There were those who would say that I shouldn't even have that much on me. I've known instructors who've taught surveillance and counter-surveillance who insist that guys running that sort of mission should be unarmed, since clothing that's truly low-profile in a majority of places within a city makes it difficult to carry concealed. After what had gone down in the hotel, however, there was no way in hell I was going anywhere without a weapon. *Especially* not when we were meeting someone who just might be on more target lists than just ours.

She looked up from her beer as Drew slid into the booth across from her, and I grabbed a chair to bring it around to the end of the table. Brolin had picked a seat facing the door, which would have left both of us with our backs to the one main route in and out. There was a back door, and Drew could see that well enough, but I wasn't leaving front and rear security to a contact who we'd never met.

Brolin looked simultaneously nervous and combative as she looked us over. She recognized that my placement had put her in an L-shape, even if she didn't understand enough tactics to realize what that was.

Of course, I didn't really think she was enough of a physical threat to take such a posture and intimidating her wasn't in the playbook. I just wanted to be able to see anyone coming in the front door.

"Ms. Brolin?" We'd decided that Drew would do most of the talking. He's got a slightly softer voice than mine, and even with that lip caterpillar of his, he can look a lot more non-threatening, especially when he's wearing business casual. "My name's Andrew." We'd also decided to use real names, although first names only. They wouldn't communicate too much, and pseudonyms can be too hard to remember if you haven't practiced with them for a while.

While she might have been nervous, she wasn't a shrinking violet. She stuck out her hand—somewhat to my surprise; the brilliantly dyed hair would have led me to believe that she was the sort who didn't want to be touched—and Drew shook it. "You said you were at the hotel?" She didn't seem to have noticed that I hadn't introduced myself, which was just as well. "You saw what happened?"

"We did. Most of it, anyway." He launched into the wavetops version of the story that we'd worked out ahead of time, since no one on the team, least of all KG, thought it was a good idea to let her know that we'd been the hired gunslingers who had killed over half a dozen gangbangers there.

I sort of tuned out, since she was only asking questions and taking notes while Drew talked. This wasn't quite what we were there for, but it was still a necessary step. We had to build a rapport with her. If we'd just sat down and demanded contact information for the cop who'd talked to her for her story, she'd have told us to piss off and left. There'd be nothing we could do to stop her, either. Not if we wanted to avoid attention and still be the good guys here.

So, Drew talked, she took notes, and I only half listened while I watched the rest of the bar. I couldn't keep my eye on the bartender all the time, but he looked like he was in his late twenties and if he was in league with a bunch of Hispanic gangbangers, he was awfully devoted to his cover as a hipster bartender. The other three people in the Hudson Grille were a pair of older people at another booth, closer to the door, and one more twenty-something sitting at the bar itself, his eyes riveted on the soccer game playing on all six screens. Like the bartender, he was lily white. Unlike the bartender, he was fairly chubby. Unlikely to be part of the gang we'd crossed swords with in the Hyatt.

Of course, that still left whoever had pinpointed Strand in the Hyatt. An organization with that capability might very well not look like a bunch of *sicario*s or *marero*s. They could easily have surveillance personnel who looked like that little marshmallow sitting at the bar.

If I hadn't had years of experience in all sorts of irregular warfare environments, ranging from Iraqi and Afghan farmland to Iraqi, Yemeni, and Qatari cities, my finely tuned paranoia might easily have started to run away with me. As it was, however, I noted his presence, keeping an eye on him through my peripheral vision as best I could. He wasn't paying us any attention and didn't even have his eyes on his phone most of the time. He was paying rapt attention to the game.

The two older people were similarly intent on their conversation, neither one even so much as looking up at us.

It really wasn't a good place or time for surveillance. I had to admire Brolin's choice. Whether she'd been aware of its tactical suitability or not, she'd picked a meeting place that was both public and difficult to eavesdrop on.

Drew was nearing the end of his story as I looked down at my phone. It buzzed quietly with a message from Phil, coming up as just, "Ziggy."

Got two dudes sitting at the table next to us that look about as out of place in this joint as we do. He attached a surreptitiously taken photo of a pair of slightly younger men at the next table over. Both of them were dressed a little too "covertly," meaning they stood out. Cargo pants and fishing shirts were black and khaki. One of them was looking at his phone, while the other was watching the Hudson Grille. *They got here shortly after we did, at almost the same time your girl went inside. Been watching the front of the Grille ever since. They haven't even ordered anything.*

That sounded like surveillance, alright. Extremely amateurish surveillance, but surveillance, nevertheless.

Thank goodness for small favors. Professionals would have been more difficult to spot.

It didn't mean I could relax, though. There still might be someone out there who was a pro. It was even conceivably possible that these guys were the bait, the diversion that we were supposed to be watching, while the real surveillance went unnoticed. It was what I'd do.

Of course, I'd spent a good part of my career thinking about stuff that I'd do that the people in charge were either too lazy or too complacent to actually put into action. I kept looking, anyway.

The conversation at our table drew my attention again. Drew had started to shift the topic slightly. "Do you really think that somebody in the police department deliberately kept the cops from responding? Is that why nobody came after we called 911?"

Brolin was a bit sharper than I'd thought. At least, she was more suspicious than I'd expected. Her eyes narrowed as she looked back and forth between us, her lips pressed together. When I glanced up from my phone, I saw the wheels turning behind those blue eyes, and it was abundantly clear that she didn't like the conclusions those wheels were leading her to.

She studied us with increasing suspicion for a few seconds. "I never said *I* thought that." She took another sip of her beer, but she was buying time. I could see a faint shake in her hand as she brought the glass to her lips. Her eyes kept moving back and forth between the two of us. She was adding up what she saw. Two men in their late thirties to early forties, though both of us were in good enough shape that we could probably easily pass for younger than that, if not for the gray in my hair and beard. What had we been doing in the Hyatt when a firefight had broken out?

"Maybe not, but would you have published a source saying as much if you didn't at least suspect it?" Drew was trying to steer things toward the anonymous cop. He was our target. She wouldn't necessarily know as much as he might. Unfortunately, she picked up on that almost immediately.

She set her beer glass down with exaggerated care. She was even more nervous now, her eyes moving even more rapidly between us. "Is that what this is about? My source in the PD? Who are you guys, really? Internal Affairs? Are you trying to get me to reveal my source so that you can burn him? Were you even there at the Hyatt?"

Drew stayed calm. He was better at that than me. "Yes, we were there. And we called 911, *and* we saw no response while bullets were flying. Of course we're interested. If there *was* malfeasance involved…"

His calm demeanor wasn't wearing off on her, though. She sat farther back in her seat abruptly, her eyes a little wide with both fear and anger. "Who the hell *are* you guys?"

This interview was going to hell in a handbasket, fast. I'd been afraid of this since I'd looked at her profile picture. Brolin came from a different world from the two of us, and there wasn't going to be any immediate rapport there. Especially if she sniffed out that we were private security contractors with long histories in the military and overseas operations both overt and clandestine. I decided to step in. Drew was doing an okay job, but sometimes it just takes a different voice to change course in a conversation.

"We're private investigators, working for someone who was very nearly killed in that incident. You can understand why they're concerned about the fact that the police didn't respond after being called." I kept my expression composed and my voice friendly and reasonable. "We're just trying to get some answers for our client, possibly as groundwork for some legal action later on."

"If you're just looking into this for someone who was there, then you were lying when you told me you were there," she bit out accusingly.

"No, we weren't. We *were* there, on a separate assignment." That was *technically* true, since that had been close protection, and this was intelligence gathering. "This business doesn't always allow us to follow up the way we'd like."

We were losing her, though. She abruptly grabbed her bag and slid out of the booth. "I'm sorry, but I think we're done here. I didn't come to get used in some kind of entrapment scheme for one of my sources." Without waiting for an answer, she turned her back and stormed to the bar to pay her tab, her back stiff and straight.

I watched her over my shoulder, though I was also watching the other clientele at the same time. The bartender was taking her card, but the chubby guy at the bar may as well have been alone, for all the attention he paid her. The older couple at a booth had looked up at her raised voice, but quickly returned their attention to their food and their beer.

Brolin kept her back pointedly turned to us as she paid and left. I turned back to Drew, who had leaned back in the seat with his arms folded. "Well, that didn't work quite so well."

"Not yet." Drew was a bit more of an optimist than I was. "What was the message from Ziggy?"

I finished tapping out a text to Phil, warning him that she was on her way out, before I swiveled the phone around so he could see the message and the attached photo. "Seems like we're on the right track, anyway."

"Yeah." He spun the phone back around to show me Phil's follow-up message.

Roger. Got eyes on her, heading south. Our buddies have just gotten up to follow, too.

I nodded. Drew slid out of the booth to go pay our own tab while I tapped on the screen.

Good copy. You trail them. We'll leapfrog ahead and see if we can get eyes on.

The chase was afoot. I only hoped there were answers at the end of it.

CHAPTER
9

We didn't go out the front, the way we'd gone in. With active surveillance on the front of the sports bar, we didn't want to make things that easy for our mysterious opponents. Instead, we headed for the back. We were parked in the lot behind the Hudson Grille, anyway.

As we left, I spared one last glance at chubby at the bar. He was still paying rapt attention to the soccer game, barely blinking. Maybe he was what he appeared to be. Just an ordinary, slightly overweight sports fan, sipping beer in the early afternoon.

I kind of hoped so. It would make all of this much easier if all we had to worry about were gangbangers and those amateurs currently trailing Brolin.

Drew led the way out the back door into the parking lot. I almost unconsciously checked the vehicles in the lot, just in case.

It would have made sense, if the opposition—whoever they were—wanted to keep a close eye on the place, to put another element in the back. However, the hiccup there was the fact that there really was only one way in or out. The parking lot was set above the entrance to the parking garage for the apartment building behind the Hudson Grille, so there was no exit onto Peachtree Place.

That would have been a game-ender for us, except for the need to park off the street. We *could* have just parked out front, but we'd decided that a spot a little more out of sight was preferable.

There are a distressing number of compromises that you sometimes have to make in this business.

I was half expecting another pair of Covert Charlies to be sitting in a car back there, waiting for us, but all the other vehicles in the lot were unoccupied.

It was nice to work for a client who wasn't shy about spending money to make our job a little easier. Strand had quickly signed off on the expense of renting several more vehicles in addition to the SUVs that we'd already been driving. The explanation KG had given him had been about reducing our footprint so that anyone who might want to come after him again would be kept guessing, and that was certainly part of it. It also helped to keep us underneath the opposition's radar, lest they'd made a connection between the us and the vehicles we'd fled the Hyatt in.

So, Drew and I got into a completely ordinary looking blue Chevy Malibu, our go-bags and carbines on the floor in the back seat. I hated sedans on principle, in no small part because they never seem to be built with a man my size in mind, and Drew was half an inch taller than me. I also prefer trucks because I'm a redneck and I like something a little bit higher off the ground, better off road, and able to haul stuff. I didn't get the callsign "Backwoods" for nothing.

But a modest sedan was perfect for disappearing into big city traffic. We wouldn't stand out at all, and the fact that it was a rental made it even better. Anyone trying to connect us to the license plate would have to do some digging, which would buy us time.

By the time we got out onto Peachtree Street, Phil and Marcos were gone, already following the two clowns who were trailing Ella Brolin. That shouldn't be too difficult; those idiots

66

were so easy to pick out that both of our guys could hang well back, and even leapfrog up parallel streets to switch off.

We had a longer drive ahead of us. Research into Brolin hadn't just revealed her contact information. She might have been smart about her journalism, but her privacy awareness sucked. It hadn't been difficult to get her address. That might seem creepy at first glance, but to be fair, we hadn't even really been looking for it to begin with. It had come out in the dossier that Brian had been putting together—he might talk like an over-aggressive child, but Scrappy was actually a pretty smart dude—and we'd filed it away for contingency planning. Then, while working on those contingencies, it had come up that if things got weird, she might become a target, and we might need to protect her. So, we'd included the information in the brief.

Now it looked like that was going to be useful, because somebody *was* following her, and she was, presumably, heading for her apartment.

And we'd be there ahead of her, just in case the opposition did anything shady.

***

We could have been there in less than five minutes, but that might have entailed crossing either Brolin's path, or her shadowers'. So, we took a slightly more roundabout route, circling around to the east before pulling into the parking lot of J.R. Crickets, where we could see the front entrance to the 131 Ponce Apartments.

There was no guarantee that she'd come to the front, but Phil and Marcos should be able to walk us on if something went sideways.

The truth was, we were less interested in her at this point than we were in the guys who were following her. We'd stumbled into the middle of something nasty, that much was clear.

While we waited, watching the street, I got back on the phone. There's a certain advantage to texting, but there's also something to be said for voice comms, especially when you're in a rental car and there's nobody around to overhear. I called KG.

"How'd it go?" He didn't beat around the bush, KG.

"Not great. She kinda freaked out when we started asking *her* questions." I kept my eyes on the lot, the phone on speaker and sitting on the center console. "She thinks we're trying to get at her cop source, so she bailed. *However*, we've got two amateurs in 5.11 tuxedos following her. Ziggy and Drizzle are following them."

"Interesting. The 5.11 tuxedo doesn't really go with the MS-13 vibe you guys reported from the hit on the hotel." Being KG, he was analyzing as fast as he could get the information in.

"No, it doesn't. It *might* go with somebody who can track phones and leak that tracking info to MS-13 types, though." I didn't *know* that the hitters who'd tried to kill us in the Hyatt House were *Mara Salvatrucha*, but it fit for the current conversation. "On the other hand, these guys might not know anything about that, and might just be Atlanta PD trying to intimidate her into either shutting up or revealing who's talking out of school." I'd just thought of that part, though from the sound of KG's monosyllabic acknowledgement, he'd already added it to the list of possibilities.

It can be good, sometimes, having a smart boss. It can also be a pain in the ass.

"Keep an eye on the situation." KG sounded slightly distracted. "Try not to get in another shootout, but your task right now is protective intelligence. We need to know who set our client up, and who's trying to sweep it all under the rug."

"Roger that." I almost cringed as the old saying slipped out, but some things get hard wired whether you want them to or not.

The phone buzzed as I reached for the "End Call" button. It was a message from Phil.

She just went inside on the west side. The two clowns walked past and are heading toward the south side. What's your loc?

I typed my reply quickly after showing Drew the message. *We're on the south side, across the street.*

Roger. You should have eyes on shortly. They stutter-stepped a little as they passed the door, and one of them was on the phone immediately after she went inside. We're going to pull off, get back to the vic, and then we can switch out when you need us.

I acknowledged and started watching the pedestrian traffic on Juniper Street as best I could. It wasn't that we were in a bad position. Even the trees planted every few yards on the sidewalk didn't obscure the view that much. The trouble came from sitting in a damn sedan, in a parking lot. That was what limited my field of view.

Fortunately, our two little would-be spies were pretty easy to spot. One, in a black fishing shirt and green cargo pants, was still on the phone, while the other one was looking around, trying to act like a tourist.

What kind of tourist travels to Midtown Atlanta?

Granted, I'm biased. I'd never willingly go to a city for vacation. Once again, see my callsign.

They kept walking across the street toward us. I started to feel the tension rise. Were we made? Were these maybe undercover cops?

If they are, they need to go back to school for the "undercover" part.

Neither one of them gave our car a second glance, however. They just went into J.R. Crickets and disappeared inside.

That made some sense. They'd stand out a lot more hanging out on the streetcorner, and inside the bar and grill, they could sit down, order something, and keep an eye on the entire southern side of the apartment building while someone else moved in to watch the other three sides.

I had to assume at this point that there was someone else involved. I couldn't imagine that these two would pick such a limited position to surveil their target if it was just them. Granted, from where I sat, I couldn't see much in the way of better surveillance positions. There was a radiation therapy center just to the west, and while I couldn't see what was off to the east, it wouldn't be particularly easy to hang out in a cancer center without a reason for being there, especially when the place had no windows facing the apartment building.

There weren't many other buildings nearby where someone could just hang out for a while and stare out the window at the blindingly interesting sight of a modern brick, steel, and glass apartment building. J.R. Crickets was about it. Which meant that, if there was another surveillance team, they were probably going to have to use a different method.

Almost like clockwork, as soon as I'd thought it, a white van pulled up to the curb on the side of Juniper Street and parked. No one got out.

I pointed it out to Drew. "It's like something out of a damn movie."

He snorted. "Probably where they got their tradecraft from." Then he tilted his head slightly as he studied the vehicle. "Though, to be honest, look around you. How many people are really going to notice?"

He had a point. There weren't that many people on the streets at that hour of the day, and most of them were absorbed in their personal affairs, their phones, or both. You can actually get away with a lot in a city, especially one like Atlanta, where the cops were spread thin, where they still even gave half a damn.

That didn't mean it was a good idea to get sloppy. Quite the opposite, in fact, because that meant there were more bad guys out there who would have their eyes open. Fortunately for us, though, these guys were sloppy.

We sent photos to the rest of the team and settled in to wait.

***

Surveillance isn't thrilling. Most of the time it's boring as hell. I'd learned that in the Marine Corps, spending hours, sometimes days, just sitting in a hole in a berm, staring at some Iraqi intersection just in case some AQI terrorists or somebody else of interest showed up. Usually, nothing happened, except the usual traffic going by until we got pulled off to go stare at a different empty objective.

That street in Atlanta was the same for hours, as the sun went down, and the streetlights came on. We saw nothing out of the ordinary, except for the fact that those two dudes in tactical clothes never left the J.R. Crickets, and no one ever got out of that van. There wasn't anyone in the driver's seat anymore, but no one had gotten out the back, either, I didn't think.

That was ominous. The van didn't have any windows in the back. I might have been paranoid, but it looked like a good platform for a snatch team.

I wasn't the only one who thought so, either. We switched out with Phil and Marcos twice, even going back to the safehouse to change vehicles. There was no disguising ourselves, but we could disguise the car. By the time we'd returned the first time, Phil had confirmed via text that he and Marcos had the same feeling about that van. We could still be wrong—I'd certainly seen it before, where the heebie-jeebies turned out to be nothing but a bad feeling—but it really looked like someone was *very* interested in Ms. Brolin.

The streets got empty quickly once full dark fell. Midtown was one of the most affluent parts of Atlanta, surpassed only by Buckhead, where the safehouse was. Yet that didn't spare the area from the change in security status

71

over the last few years. I could see it as people returned to the apartment building we were watching. There was a furtiveness, a haste to get indoors, that I'd only seen in warzones, and then only when the violence was entirely too close by.

Almost at the same moment I thought it, a series of *pop*s sounded somewhere to the south of us. Sirens wailed in the distance. Night had fallen in Atlanta.

As if on cue, the back doors of the van swung open and four men got out, moving quickly toward the east side of the 131 Ponce apartments.

I knew a hit team when I saw one, even though they weren't showing weapons. So did Drew. We were both out of the car and moving a moment later, even as I sent an already preset text to Phil to get him on the way.

CHAPTER
10

The hit team moved fast, getting across the street in seconds. We'd observed over the afternoon that the side doors needed a key; only the front door on the south side appeared to be open all the time, and then the elevators and stairs probably needed a key, as well. I found it slightly interesting, given Midtown's general affluence, but times were changing. At any rate, we could generally expect that the door might slow a hit team down.

It didn't. They had a key, and they were inside before we could even reach the edge of the parking lot.

The sound of music and talk coming through an open door, followed by a footstep, drew my attention. The two guys in the tacticool "covert" clothes had come out of the bar and grill, and they seemed entirely too sober for the amount of time they'd spent in there.

They hadn't seen us yet. I reached out and caught Drew, drawing him back to where we might just have been getting out of the car to go inside the J.R. Crickets. If they were connected to those guys from the van—and it sure looked to me like they were—then things could get almighty interesting there in the parking lot if it looked like we were about to interfere.

We hung back, trying to act as if we had just parked. The two of them paid us no attention but moved quickly toward the street and the apartment building. They weren't even trying to be sneaky anymore.

I was about to follow them, already reaching for the Glock 19 I'd returned to after the meeting, but the snatch team had moved fast. They were already coming out, and even at that distance, I could tell that the figure in the middle wasn't moving well and had a bag over her head.

It had briefly crossed my mind that maybe this was an undercover police hit, but that clinched it. Even undercover cops didn't drag prisoners out limp and bagged. Not in any jurisdiction I'd ever heard of. Certainly not in Atlanta, where they'd be crucified in the media as well as publicly from City Hall as soon as it got out.

No, this was a kidnapping, and I was reasonably sure that Ella Brolin was the figure in the bag.

We should have held back and called the cops. Any reasonable citizen would have. We were past that, though. Drew and I didn't even look at each other as they hustled Brolin into the van and shut the doors while the two surveillance goons jogged across the street to join them. There was no trusting the cops after what had happened at the Hyatt, and even if we *could* trust any of them, there was no way they'd get to Brolin in time. These guys were about to disappear.

It took seconds to get back to the car. There wasn't time to alert Phil and Marcos to what we were doing before we did it, so we were about to stick our necks out, though hopefully we could bring them up to speed and have backup before things went loud.

The van was already pulling away from the curb, having waited just long enough for the two surveillance guys to get in. We were already in the car and Drew started after them.

"Give us a bit of space. We don't want to spook 'em."

"I've done the course, Chris." Drew didn't sound pissed, just focused. "I know how to do this. You just worry

74

about comms and what the hell we're going to do whenever we catch up with these clowns."

I accepted the rebuke in silence, partially because I deserved it, and partially because I was busy hammering out a fast SITREP to Phil. *Bad guys grabbed our girl. They are on the move, heading south on Courtland Street. We are taking up a close follow until you can move to support.*

It took a second, as Drew turned out onto North Avenue, even using his turn signals so that it should look to any casual observer—or the driver of the van—like we hadn't noticed a thing and just happened to be going the same way, before Phil responded. I expect that he was cussing me roundly inside their car.

If he was, he didn't show it over comms, though. That might have simply been because we didn't want to risk Strand or even KG seeing our message history and getting upset over a lack of professionalism. We tried to keep the shit-talking to voice or in person. Even when it was richly deserved.

Need a bit more of a plan than that.

I had to think as Drew followed the van. The target vehicle wasn't moving all that fast, which meant we had some time, but how much time was necessarily limited. They had a hostage, and her life could now be measured in minutes if we didn't do this right.

Phil was actually ahead of me, presumably once he got done spitting nails about the mission suddenly changing from surveillance to interdiction and hostage rescue. *What if we engineered a wreck? Nothing catastrophic, but enough to stop the van.*

It was an idea. Risky, but it might be our best bet. *Might kill or injure the package.* We were in professional mode now. Brolin had just become "the package."

They're probably going to kill or injure her if we don't stop them. I could almost hear Phil's snort through the text message. *She's got a better chance in a car wreck.*

He didn't go into detail, but he didn't need to. We all understood that there was probably no returning from this ride if we didn't stop it. It was possible, but something about the whole setup suggested to me that someone wanted Brolin disappeared. Probably after she was interrogated to find out the identity of her source within Atlanta PD.

We'd stumbled on a snake-pit of corruption, alright. Someone had tried to get our principal murdered or kidnapped and was willing to resort to more kidnapping and murder to cover it up.

That was a declaration of war as far as we were concerned.

We might be able to PIT them. The Precision Immobilization Technique was a time-honored method for vehicle interdiction. We'd pull up next to the van, just behind the rear wheels, and steer into the back, spinning the vehicle sideways, possibly putting it into a lightpole or other obstacle.

That might be too obvious. Phil was thinking ahead. He was good at that. *If this goes sideways, it's got to look like an accident. We're moving to get ahead of them. Keep me posted on their route. We'll find an intersection and run a red light.*

I glanced up at our quarry. *Still going south on Courtland, just passing over the 85.*

Roger. Nothing came for a few seconds, as we followed the van over the overpass and kept going toward downtown. *Coming in from the east, next intersection.*

Making the hit downtown was risky as hell, but we had eyes on, and it wasn't likely that they'd killed Brolin yet. If they'd just wanted her dead, they'd have done it in her apartment. The longer this went on, though, the shorter her lifespan was going to get.

"How are we doing this?" Drew had his eyes fixed on the van, two cars ahead of us. There wasn't a *lot* of traffic out at the moment, but there was enough that we could get somewhat lost in the noise. It also might give them a chance to slip away if our timing was off. "Pistols or carbines?"

I watched the van slow and stop at a red light. They were being careful, too, observing traffic laws and keeping a low profile. Maybe they didn't have the entirety of the police department suborned. Or maybe they did, but only so far. Kidnapping, torture, and murder might be a step too far for some of the cops who would otherwise turn a blind eye.

"I'd prefer carbines, but if we're still trying to keep this quiet and relatively deniable, we should probably stick with pistols." A plan was starting to coalesce around Phil's interdiction idea. "We can pretend to just be concerned bystanders rushing to make sure no one was hurt in the wreck. If they get froggy, we draw and smoke 'em. If they're too rocked, we grab Brolin and get the hell out." I didn't mention calling 911 for the wreck. That would probably be counterproductive and might cut off our escape.

Besides, fuck these guys. Play stupid games, win stupid prizes. I had zero sympathy for them.

The light turned and the van started moving. At first glance, I thought that Phil and Marcos had been blocked from the intersection by another car. I didn't recognize the midsize SUV sitting at the light on John Wesley Dobbs Avenue.

Marcos was inventive, though. He came in fast, zipping around the SUV on the right-turn lane, and darted into the intersection to slam into the van's front quarter panel.

The *bang* of the impact echoed off the skyscrapers to north and south of the intersection, and the brick First Congregational Church just to the east. Glass shattered and brakes squealed as the other vehicles on Courtland skidded to a halt to avoid joining the pileup.

Drew had thrown the car into park, and we were both out and moving, still keeping our weapons holstered and out of view. A couple of the other motorists were getting out and moving toward the crash, while at least one was on the phone.

Pity. One of the cars ahead of us accelerated, swerving around the wreck to disappear to the south on Courtland. Apparently not everyone in Atlanta was a Good Samaritan. Shocker.

We hustled to get ahead of the other people who were already moving to help. I did *not* want them getting between us and our targets, and Drew was of the same mind.

Phil was already out of the car, letting out a loud, "Holy shit!" Marcos was moving a little more slowly, but he might have taken the brunt of the impact. The sedan's hood was crushed, and the windshield was cracked. Shattered headlights were scattered across the pavement. That car wasn't going anywhere anytime soon. Fortunately, it was a rental, and insured.

The van had been shoved halfway across the intersection, and its half-crumpled front bumper was now only a few feet from the light post on the corner. The driver's side door was stove in, and unless I missed my guess, the driver was in none too good shape. Phil had talked about making sure the wreck wasn't catastrophic, but the risk of missing the target had added a bit of lead to Marcos's foot.

Drew and I got to the rear doors a second later, and we both reached up to pull them open. We didn't stack up, didn't give each other the nod. We were still just supposed to be helpful, slightly shocked bystanders.

Fortunately, the doors weren't locked. I'd half expected them to be, which would have made this a lot trickier. There were windows in the double doors, blacked out, which would have given us a way to reach in and unlock them, but that would have given the bad guys in there a bit more time than I wanted.

We snatched the doors open and took in the scene.

The back of the van had been stripped, to my lack of surprise. Four men, two of them dressed all in black and the other two being our friends in the cargo pants and fishing shirts from the surveillance team, were still picking themselves up and shaking off the impact. Two had been thrown against the side of the vehicle, and two others were on the floor, one of them on top of Brolin.

It was definitely Brolin, even with the bag on her head. She hadn't changed clothes since our meeting.

"Is everybody okay in here?" Drew took the lead, since he was generally better at playing a normal, inoffensive human being than I was. I tended to come off as threatening to a lot of people, even when I wasn't trying to.

Drew's non-threatening act didn't work, though. Not when these guys had just been caught with a kidnap victim. The man in black closest to us grabbed for a Scorpion EVO that had fallen on the floor next to Brolin.

I was a split second behind Drew on the draw. Before that first guy even got a hand on that shorty, the four of them were staring down our muzzles. "Ah, ah, ah. That's no way to treat somebody who's just trying to help out."

They all froze. I heard the passenger side door open a moment later, and Phil's voice telling the driver and passenger to keep their hands where he could see them.

In retrospect, it was a little surprising that we didn't just smoke all of them as soon as that guy grabbed for a gun. It might have saved us a little trouble down the line. On the other hand, it might have bought us far more.

We were all used to different rules, and I think we were still in the middle of figuring out just how different the rules had become.

"Ella, can you hear me?" I kept my eyes and my gun on the two guys up against the sliding door. Neither one of them seemed to want to try their luck.

She might have mumbled something. She still had one of the bad guys on top of her, plus the bag over her head. I suspected she might have been tased or drugged, too.

"Get off her." Drew's voice had gone cold as the Arctic, his Glock's muzzle not moving a millimeter.

Marcos appeared at my elbow. "I've got 'em."

Holstering my Glock 19, I clambered into the back. None of the goons moved at first, until Drew, without moving a muscle, and in that same icy tone spoke up. "Either you two get over against the wall, or I start shooting. Now."

They moved slowly, but that was more out of carefulness than anything else. Both of them still had their eyes glued to that gun. I don't think they'd expected anything like this to happen. In fact, I was starting to suspect that they'd been confident that no one was going to mess with them. That would explain why they had just been driving straight to wherever they were going. No attempt at surveillance detection or anything like it. This ambush shouldn't have been so easy.

With the way clear, so that I wasn't going to cut off either Marcos's or Drew's lines of fire, I crouched over Brolin. She hadn't just been bagged; her hands were tied with flex cuffs, drawn tight enough that her hands were swelling and starting to get discolored.

I pulled the bag off her head and hauled her up to a sitting position. She blinked, even though the interior of the van wasn't all that bright. She looked dazed, only about half conscious.

There wasn't time to do a full evaluation on her. We needed to get out of there. We had the bad guys buffaloed at the moment, but they were six to our four, and they probably had backup somewhere nearby. I stepped back to the bumper, pulling her along with me. She struggled at first, clearly unclear as to what was going on, but I held on and dragged her out of the van, pausing just long enough to make sure she was on her feet before I started to hustle her back toward the car.

The rest fell back, keeping their weapons ready but having retracted them so that we weren't running past other vehicles on the street with guns up. I made a beeline for the car, towing a dazed, faintly protesting Brolin with me. The whole way, I expected gunfire to suddenly erupt, but the street stayed relatively quiet, except for the distant wail of police sirens. They didn't sound like they were coming this way, but sound got tricky in the concrete jungle of a big city. It was harder to gauge direction and distance, especially when your hearing is as battered and messed up as mine was.

I got to the car first, pushed Brolin into the back seat, and then slid behind the wheel. My gear and carbine were on the passenger side, but we needed to move fast.

Drew was right behind me, and then Phil and Marcos piled in, Phil dragging both of their go bags and carbines with him, the weapons clattering against the door as he squeezed in, crushing Brolin against Marcos.

Then the doors slammed shut and I had us moving, going over the curb to get past the cars between us and the intersection, around the corner and down John Wesley Dobbs Avenue as fast as I could without losing control.

CHAPTER 11

The bad guys might not have run a surveillance detection route on the way off their target, but I wasn't going to repeat that mistake. I'd already made about five turns before we even got out of downtown, heading east into Edgewood.

Drew was on the phone as soon as we got off Interstate 20 and into the residential areas. "This is Smokestack. Package is secured and we appear to be clear, but we're going to need somewhere to take her."

He hadn't put the phone on speaker, so I couldn't hear KG all that clearly, but what I could hear didn't sound happy. Or particularly calm.

Drew, for his part, stayed as deadpan as usual. "Sir, we had to move fast. If we hadn't done something, they'd have been gone, and Brolin with them."

I could hear KG barking something else over the phone. "That's true, but we didn't *have* any other vehicles. What were we supposed to do? Let them take her and sew everything up nice and neat just so that we didn't get identified?"

We both knew guys who'd do just that. Knew even more erstwhile clients from our days in the overseas contracting world who would have insisted on it. Most of them had been in various government agencies, too.

I also knew for a fact that KG knew just as many such people, if not more. He had to know that we couldn't just let it go.

From the pause in the conversation, I figured that he was mulling over that in his head and weighing it against what that night's escapades had probably already cost us.

"Tell him that if it's any consolation, it doesn't *matter* if we're connected to the crashed rental car." I kept my eyes on the road as I continued to drive, watching the rear-view mirrors for any sign that we were being followed. Of course, ground traffic wasn't the only way they could follow us. Drones were getting more and more ubiquitous, commercial as well as governmental. There was only so much we could do about that, though. "If these are the same people who tried to grab our principal, then they *already* know who we are. And there's a damned *mountain* of circumstantial evidence pointing to them being the exact same people."

In the quiet that followed, I heard KG tell Drew to put him on speakerphone. When he complied, setting the phone on the dash, KG sounded a lot calmer.

"I hear what you're saying, Backwoods, but this was a hell of a thing to pull on zero notice, and *downtown, for fuck's sake!*" Okay, maybe not *that* calm. "You should have maintained contact and followed to wherever they were going to go to ground. *Then* we could have planned this properly and done a good hit, quietly, without fucking eyewitnesses in the middle of the fucking evening!"

I wasn't backing down, though. "We thought about that, boss, but we had a limited time window. We had no guarantee that they weren't going to interrogate her in the vehicle and then kill her. No way to know that they even *had* a place to go to ground. How hard would it be for one of us to put the screws to somebody in the back of a van, garotte 'em, and dispose of the body in a ditch outside of town?"

84

It was a rhetorical question, but I had to make the point. And from KG's silence, I'd made it. I still needed to reinforce it. "Ground truth, boss."

Unfortunately, while it needed to be said, I'd said it within earshot of a dazed, scared, and not-entirely-all-there Ella Brolin. Who promptly started hyperventilating. "What do you want from me?"

"Take it easy, Ms. Brolin." Phil didn't look much less threatening than I did, but he had a softer voice and a talent for offsetting his resemblance to me by widening his eyes a little. It was weird, but it had usually resulted in me letting him do most of the talking when we'd worked together. "We're not the bad guys here. We saw them take you and knew that we had to act before they could hurt you."

With a glance in the rear-view mirror, I saw that she was staring at Drew and me, trying to see our faces. She recognized us, that was sure. "Were you watching me?" There was just enough anger in her voice, filtered through the fear, terror, and the aftereffects of whatever they'd used to subdue her, that I was pretty sure she'd be okay. Provided she didn't become a handful and get us into a wreck in the next thirty seconds.

"Strictly speaking, no," I replied flatly. "We were watching the goons who were following you."

That didn't seem to reassure her much. KG didn't care, though.

"Ms. Brolin, you are not safe in this city anymore. Some very dangerous people want your source, and they want you silenced in the process. Now, those men in the car with you right now also qualify as very dangerous people, but they're not going to hurt you."

There was still a quaver in her voice, but she sounded a little steadier, and less like she was about to freak out and try to fight us in the car. Marcos had already cut her flex-cuffs. "Where are we going?"

"That's a good question, boss." I took another turn, working our way deeper into Edgewood. "Do we take the chance that they know where the house is? I still maintain that the connection with the rental cars isn't something we need to worry about, but if they caught the license plate, they might track this puppy back to the house. I don't know that they've got a drone on us—I doubt it—but if they could track cell phones…"

"I hear you." KG still sounded pissed. "I'll get a van out and then send you the coordinates to switch out." He sighed, and the sound rasped in the speakers. "You guys are going to give me a damn heart attack, you know that?"

"All part of the job, boss." I couldn't resist the dig. "We'll keep moving until we hear from you."

KG might have grumbled some more before he hung up.

Silence descended inside the car as I kept driving. Brolin was clearly shaken, and none of the rest of us had much to say in front of her. The hot wash could come later. She didn't need to hear it.

I kept us wandering mostly aimlessly for the next half hour, easing our way toward Decatur, keeping an eye on our back trail, watching for the same vehicle showing up multiple times. Correlation over time is the best indicator that you've picked up surveillance. Unfortunately, as it got darker it got harder to tell whether we were seeing the same vehicle over and over. The glare of headlights made it difficult to see much of the car behind them, never mind the people in the car.

Finally, Drew's phone rang again. I fully recognized the issue with continuing to use the phones after we were pretty sure that the bad guys had tracked Strand using his, but we had few options. We'd simply bulletproofed the phones as much as we could and used encryption every chance we got.

"Send it." He listened for a moment. "Roger. On our way." He ended the call and returned to his vigil, scanning the darkness outside the window. There were plenty of streetlights and porch lights in the slightly run-down neighborhood we were driving through just outside Decatur itself, but there were so many trees that the light never went far. "The van's parked at the Walmart. KG wants one of us to return the rental tonight, before they put a BOLO out for it. He's got Hybrid on the way to meet up with us there, so the van can go back to the house."

I waited for a second, as I took another turn. "Which Walmart?"

Drew squeezed his eyes shut for a second. "Shit. Sorry. The Decatur Walmart. I'll walk us in."

"You do that." It had been a long couple of days, so I let it slide otherwise, though I was pretty sure Phil was already tallying up the snarky remarks that would be forthcoming once we had Brolin somewhere out of earshot.

* * *

I would have expected a Walmart to have a pretty big parking lot, but this one didn't. Instead, it appeared that our ride was in the parking garage. That went partway toward explaining why this had been picked for the changeover. It's harder to surveil parking garages, either from the air or the ground.

Of course, if you've got access to CCTV cameras, it gets a lot easier, but even those can't be everywhere. And we couldn't get so deeply paranoid that we started seeing threats where there weren't any. That could be just as damaging as complacency.

The van might have been the twin to the hit squad's vehicle that we'd left smashed up in the intersection of Courtland and John Wesley Dodd. White, boxy, and without windows in the rear, it was sitting in the shadows as far from the entrance to the garage, as well as the escalators up into the store, as possible.

Brolin started to hyperventilate a little again when it became apparent that we were making for the van. She might not have seen the bad guys' vehicle when they'd thrown her into it, but she'd seen it on the way out. Apparently, the trauma of her ordeal had made that mental connection with a white panel van.

"It's okay." Phil was still playing conciliator and trying to keep her calm. "It's just a van. There are seats in this one."

I sure as hell hope there are, Phil. Maybe don't say something like that before we get a look at the inside, next time? I couldn't exactly say it, and Phil ignored my glare in the rear-view mirror.

I pulled the car in next to the van and Drew and Marcos piled out, their pistols once again concealed, turning to scan the parking garage around us carefully before moving to the van itself.

Phil and I were already grabbing the carbines and go bags. The carbines were a little tricky, since we didn't want to just flash them in the parking garage, shadows or no. They had to go under jackets or other covers, which made carrying them a little bit trickier.

Drew found the keys in the back wheel well, unlocked the van, and slid the door open. Sure enough, there were seats inside, even though there weren't any windows. I was too busy getting the gear transferred to notice Brolin's reaction, but she didn't start screaming and trying to run away, anyway, so that was progress.

"I'll take the car back." Marcos held out his hand and I dropped the keys in his palm without comment. I'd have done it, but I wasn't going to turn him down if he'd rather take it.

Minutes after we'd pulled up, we were leaving in the van, Drew once again behind the wheel. Marcos would wait for a few minutes before he followed, if only to make sure that the van and the car weren't too closely associated.

***

It was getting close to midnight by the time we got back to the safehouse. Drew hadn't gone straight there, but done another long, meandering surveillance detection route on the way. We were all exhausted by the time he pulled the van into the driveway at the back. None of us were young bucks anymore.

KG was waiting in the living room, along with Strand. The financier looked almost as haggard as I felt. KG, for his part, looked a lot more chipper than any of the rest of us, though I knew the man well enough to know that he was just hiding his weariness.

Strand was sitting on the couch, staring at a laptop as we came in. Drew and I were escorting Brolin, since we were the ones who'd met with her in the sports bar, though we both had our go bags and carbines over our shoulders. She still wasn't *comfortable*, exactly, and she'd withdrawn into herself even more on the van ride. The fact that we'd saved her life, most likely, wasn't a comfort to her just then. She had a certain mindset about men like us—even though she hadn't said it, there were signs—and the cognitive dissonance involved in owing us was messing with her in addition to the shock.

So, she wasn't in the greatest frame of mind when KG stood up to greet her. She just stared at his outstretched hand.

"Ms. Brolin. I'm sorry we had to meet under these circumstances." KG looked down at Strand and tapped the financier on the shoulder, with a look on his face that suggested he wanted to do a lot more than tap. "Unfortunately, we find ourselves in something of the same boat at the moment."

Strand looked up with a start, but Brolin overcame some of her withdrawal before he could speak.

"I'm sorry, I don't see how. You're apparently armed for a war in Atlanta, Georgia." She folded her arms. The defiance she was going for was somewhat offset by her disheveled hair and smeared makeup. "I'm a journalist who's apparently become a hockey puck for gangs of armed thugs."

Frankly, I'm surprised KG didn't snap at that. Between the stress of the last few days and my decision to rescue Brolin

89

at the last minute, he had to be getting thin on patience. He was a professional, though.

"We didn't ask to be in this position, Ms. Brolin. Yes, we brought weapons, because security is our trade, what we were hired for. I don't know what kind of college education taught you that you can defend against violent crime without weapons, but it clearly came from someone with no experience in the matter. We're all here because someone decided to take a shot at our client, someone else with at least access to the Atlanta PD's chain of command took action to prevent interference in that attack, and then that same someone, apparently, tried to take you off the board for threatening to expose it." He folded his arms, fixing her with an unblinking stare. "Now, my associates could very easily have left you to your kidnappers and tried a different tack." He smiled then, though the expression never reached his eyes. "I'd say a little gratitude might be in order, but I'm old fashioned."

I was honestly a little surprised. It was far more diplomatic than I might have been, but KG had been working the corporate side of things for a while. Still, I was used to him being a bit softer on the touch. I realized then that the man was rattled.

No small wonder, really. We were playing with fire, and he knew it. It was one thing to fight off a random kidnapping attempt at a known site or on the road. We'd been ready for that. This was deep, dark, shadow war stuff. The sort of stuff that a lot of PGS's contractors had gone overseas with certain government agencies expecting to do and had never really done.

Nobody had been ready for this. Even as hard as some of us were, as many hours and days we'd spent thinking about how *we'd* do it, no one in this company had expected this turn of events. We were *Stateside*, for fuck's sake.

Nobody, except for maybe Goblin. I was starting to get a nagging suspicion about some of our preparations.

90

Brolin tried to stare KG down, but he was in full hardass mode, harkening back to the old days. There was no way this green-haired waif was going to stare him down.

Strand stood up, finally. "We got off on the wrong foot, I think." He stepped forward and offered his hand. "My name is Merritt Strand. You probably never heard of me…"

Brolin blinked, forced to break eye contact with KG. "Of course I've heard of you, Mr. Strand." She hesitated, then shook his outstretched hand. "You were involved in rescuing KTL Industries from getting sold off."

I glanced at Drew and cocked an eyebrow. I'd never heard of that one.

Strand tilted his head, looking down slightly self-deprecatingly. "It is kind of what I do. I made a lot of my money on speculation and saw a lot of distasteful stuff going on in the market. Now I try to help out struggling businesses where I can." He sobered and looked her in the eye. "I was meeting with someone who might help me do something like that again when we were attacked." He motioned to indicate KG, Drew, and me. "I owe these men my life, as much as you do. I don't always agree with them, but they got into this because of me."

He stepped closer to her, lowering his voice as if speaking in confidence. I could only watch. No wonder this guy was a good businessman. He knew what he was doing, and not just with money and figures. "I know that you're scared, Ms. Brolin. So am I. I'm still trying to figure out just what I've stumbled into, but it's become very apparent to me that some very wealthy, very powerful people want to stop this deal. I don't know why, yet, but they've shown themselves willing to use criminals and a corrupt police department to try to get to me." He gently took her by the shoulders. "You have the key that these men might be able to use to find out what's going on, what corrupt bastards are doing this. You've been a champion of accountability before, Ms. Brolin." He let go over her and stepped back. "Does it only count toward people *you*, personally, dislike? Or maybe those your political masters prefer you hold accountable?"

That went right in between the ribs. Damn.

She recoiled slightly as if she'd been slapped, but recovered quickly enough, given what she'd already been through that night. "How dare you? How *dare* you accuse me of having 'political masters?'"

Strand smiled sadly. "Oh, but you do. They might not tell you what to write, and you might not be able to identify them by name, but they've shaped your perceptions, formed your opinions by sheer volume of noise. They've shifted your Overton Window to see things through the lens they hold up for you." He laughed softly. "Believe me, I was the same way, not all that long ago."

Her answering smile held no humor. It was the sarcastic expression of someone convinced that she knew far better than what she'd just heard. "Oh, really? And what makes you so different? What gives you this blinding insight into the real world?"

"Experience." Strand tilted his head to one side as he studied her. "Something that my associates here have in spades, and you've started to gather, yourself. Just tonight's events should have you thinking differently, though perhaps it will require a bit more time for it to really sink in."

While I wasn't expecting much to come of his little speech, Brolin actually paused, a thoughtful expression crossing her face. Strand straightened and stepped back.

"You're safe here, at least for tonight. You can stay as long as you need to. I don't think that these men need to tell you that it won't be a good idea to go back to your apartment anytime soon. They'll be watching it…whoever 'they' are."

For the first time, she seemed to relax. No, not relax. She started to slump as the adrenaline drained away and the shock and exhaustion of what had just happened came down on her. Most of us contractors had some experience with that, even if our combat time had been a lot of years in the past. She didn't. Her knees started to shake, and she nodded, tears welling in her eyes as the full import of what had just happened finally came crashing down on her. "I'm…" Her voice broke.

Strand moved to stand next to her, putting his arm around her shoulders, and started to steer her toward the back and the bedrooms. "You need some rest. Come on."

If I hadn't known Strand for a little while by then, that could have come across as creepy. I was pretty sure he was entirely sincere, though. He was good with money, and he could turn on the charisma for his purposes when he needed to, but there was something about him that was almost guileless in certain areas. Like he had blind spots in all but a few specific realms of human activity. He probably wasn't even thinking about how his gesture might be misinterpreted.

Fortunately, while I could certainly see Brolin jumping to that misinterpretation in a heartbeat, right at that moment, she was so strung out that she just kind of leaned into the contact and let him guide her to one of the rooms in the back.

It meant that one or more of us were going to be sleeping on the couch or the floor in the living room for whatever was left of the night, but if we finally had a source, so be it.

"We've got a lot to do in the morning, but it's been a long day." KG took a deep breath. "Jake and Rob are on shift for the moment, so you guys rack out."

Neither of us argued. It had been that kind of day.

CHAPTER
12

We hit the ground running all too early the next morning.

"We got probed last night."

I squinted at Rob as I poured my coffee. "The sun isn't even up, Bone, and you're already getting weird. I don't want to hear about whatever escapades you got up to last night when you were supposed to be on security."

Rob, for his part, just grinned. He'd never been shy about the incident that had earned him his callsign, as disgusting as it was. That *was*, in part, a defense mechanism. You let a callsign get under your skin at your peril.

"Oh, I wasn't going to get into that." He sobered a little. "No, there was somebody rolling through the neighborhood last night, acting suspicious as fuck. Pulling into driveways and going around and around for a couple of hours. Either they were casing places for burglaries…"

"Which isn't outside the realm of possibility," I put in.

He shrugged. "Sure, but after what's already happened, do we *really* want to just wave it off?"

I grimaced as I took my first sip. The coffee was scalding hot, but at least Strand had sprung for the good stuff. I'd had employers who could afford even better than Strand who'd still given us the rotgut instant crap. "No, I guess we don't. You got photos?"

That lopsided grin again. "Of course I got photos. In HDR, no less. We've already got a couple of IDs." He pointed toward the living room. "In fact, that's only scratching the surface. I don't think the company's cyber team has slept for the last two days. KG's got a ton for us." He yawned. "Well, for you, anyway. Imma gonna crash out."

I waved a hand at him, grabbed a plate of bacon and eggs, and headed into the living room.

I'd gotten dressed, in part because Brolin was up and around, but also because I was already back in a combat mindset, where I might need to move and fight at any moment. That meant that while my gear and carbine were back in the room, I still had my Glock 19 on my hip, along with reloads and the ankle blowout kit just above my boot. At a glance, as I joined Drew, Phil, Marcos, Ken, and Custus in the living room, I wasn't the only one.

KG wasn't paying us any mind as we found a spot to sit down, eat, and drink our coffee. Or, in some cases, energy drinks. Custus was drinking a Wild Tiger. I had no idea where he'd scored that, but at least it wasn't a Rip It. The ground team lead was absorbed in his laptop, though he was putting down some pretty serious coffee, too.

Finally, he sat back on the couch, swiveling the laptop around so that we could see the screen. "Okay. The guys who have been up all night are already caught up, so this is the tail-end brief. It's still gonna take a minute."

He took a deep breath. "Okay, first thing is to cover the entirely reasonable question that Chihuahua asked this morning. 'Why the hell are we still in Atlanta?'" He rubbed his hands together. "It's an even more legit question since the DA has decided to wash her hands of the entire incident and declare it case closed, so we don't have any legal entanglements to keep us here. Well, the answer is simple: the client isn't willing to leave yet. He didn't finish his meeting with this Aarav guy, and he wants to get that nailed down. So, that's going today at 1300. Different venue. We've got another AirBnB outside of Athens. A cabin on some pretty good acreage. Backwoods, you'd be right at home."

"Which is why I'm not going there, right?" I sipped my coffee with a raised eyebrow.

"Not *why*, no, but you're right that you're not on the detail this time. We've got some more street work for you and Smokestack." He tapped the laptop, which was open to a photomap with a mark somewhere out in the weeds, off to the east of Atlanta. "Scooby and Scrappy will have the detail, with Rip and Hybrid on backup. We can't necessarily afford a dedicated QRF at the moment, so stay on your toes. The client's phone isn't going, and you'll use the van from last night, so there shouldn't be nearly the footprint that we had the last time, *however*, we don't know that this Aarav guy wasn't identified, and he might drag somebody to the meeting site. So, heads on a swivel.

"I know Bone's already been talking about it, but I'll go ahead and put it out from the top, anyway. A hostile reconnaissance element rolled through this neighborhood last night. We've already gotten an ID on the driver. Raoul Garcia, it turns out, really *is* MS-13. Two priors, outstanding warrants in Georgia and Tennessee. It's still possible that they were casing for burglaries, but it seems awfully coincidental. We don't have a line on where they went, but for the moment we need to treat it as hostile recon.

"That's not all our cyber guys have pulled off, though. See, when our bad guys hired thugs to be their shooters, they made a bit of a mistake. Even with MS-13, it can be hard for these guys to keep their mouths shut, *especially* when things have gone wrong. Most of these assholes are on social media, though they tend to filter and code what they say most of the time. Garcia had a buddy on that hit, though, and he's been losing his shit for the last couple of days. He's been hinting at getting new friends who are going to point him at the people

97

who killed his buddy." KG looked around the room, the faint shadow of a wolfish grin on his face, seeing a similar expression mirrored on every one of us. "I think you know where this is going. We're working on pinning down his location. We'll still have to step carefully, and there's a lot of prep that will need to be done, but you guys don't need to worry about that. That's my job.

"Finally, the other thread that we want to pull on. Seems that our guest couldn't sleep a couple hours after her initial crash, and we had a nice, wee hours of the morning chat. Got a lot of the air cleared." He turned the laptop to face him again, switched windows, then turned it back. Now it displayed the grinning face of a police officer, about in his mid-thirties, square-jawed and dark haired, clean-shaven and sporting a flattop. The guy could be on a recruiting poster for the Atlanta PD. Hell, he might have been. "This is Officer Aaron Lang. Been on the force about ten years. Details are a little hard to come by, but it looks somewhat like he's been in trouble with his superiors over integrity issues before. Not his integrity issues, but theirs. He seems to be a bit outspoken and uncompromising, and he is *not* the Chief of Police's favorite person. Which is largely why she kept him anonymous."

"What are the odds he's already on somebody's target list just *because* of that past trouble?" Phil asked around a mouthful of scrambled eggs.

"Give the man a gold star." KG pointed at Phil with a wink. "The easiest way to handle this would be to leverage Brolin. She's already talked to him. They've got *some* sort of rapport, if he opened up to her, even knowing she's a journalist. Most cops have about as much time for journalists as we do."

"Will she cooperate?" Marcos sounded doubtful. "She didn't seem all that thrilled to be here or to have anything to do with us last night."

"I think she will. The prospect of getting the scoop on major police corruption might well be enough all by itself. I wouldn't necessarily expect her to treat us all that nicely in the final story, but that's somewhat to be expected." He grinned a little, without much humor. "She's an asset, not a friend. We need to remember that."

There were a few grunts of assent. Most of us had seen that mistake made more than once, usually to the detriment of operations.

"So, which do we get?" I asked. "Bird-dogging the reporter, or hunting for the MS-13 dude? 'Cause I know which one I'd pick."

"Sorry, Chris." KG didn't *sound* sorry. "We're not ready to go after Garcia yet. Still some legwork to get done there. You're bird-dogging Brolin when she meets with Lang. She's contacted him already, and while he doesn't sound happy, he's agreed to meet with her." He checked his watch. "You've got about an hour before wheels up." When he looked up and met my eyes, his own were grim. "After everything that's happened, I wouldn't put it past these people to try to take him off the board. It might seem like babysitting, but keep your wits about you. I don't need to tell you that things could go pear-shaped *real* quick."

No, he didn't. From the look on Drew's face, he didn't need the reminder, either.

We'd be there, and we'd be loaded for bear.

CHAPTER
13

We drove Brolin this time. There was a risk, taking one of our vehicles instead of public transportation, since it was entirely possible that Garcia and his homies had fingered our rentals the night before. Carrying go bags and carbines into a cab, however, could be a non-starter, and we didn't have the time to spare to go swap out the rentals again, anyway.

It was another restaurant meet, this time in the Hattie Marie's BBQ in College Park. It was a pretty long drive to get there, which was why we didn't have time. It would still have been a relatively long haul, even if we hadn't taken the long way, using the surveillance detection route from hell to make damn good and sure we were clean before we even got to College Park. We must have hit every single suburb of Atlanta on the way down. Bit of an exaggeration, sure, but close.

The place looked like it belonged on a postcard. Brick front, big glass picture windows, with a couple of old-style lampposts and a big ceramic planter on the brick and concrete sidewalk outside. We pulled into a parking spot across the street after circling the place, looking for anything suspicious, and I put the car in park. Drew twisted around to address Brolin before she got out of the back seat. "We'll be right here. You've got both of our numbers on your phone. If *anything* feels weird or threatening, get out. You don't even need to call us first. Just get out and get back here."

Brolin nodded. She'd been almost silent the entire drive. She was clearly nervous, and if anything, Drew's solicitude made her even more nervous. She just as clearly wasn't used to thinking of guys like us as human beings, let alone protectors who would actually stick their necks out to keep her safe. "Do you really think that those guys who tried to kidnap me might come here?"

"We don't know, but it pays to be careful." I met her eyes in the rear-view mirror. "Again, that's why we're here."

She nodded, then slid out of the back seat and headed across the street toward the BBQ place. We settled in to wait.

Ideally, she'd record the meeting, but we hadn't asked about it. She was a reporter, which meant she was essentially a spy. From looking at her work, while I might seriously disagree with more than a few of her opinions, she was still good at ferreting out information. Some of her pieces had seriously embarrassed a few very wealthy, influential people.

I'd been on a lot of these sorts of movements and spent a *long* time waiting in the car. On many of those meetings, I'd passed the time reading a book. I could read and maintain situational awareness at the same time pretty well.

I didn't this time. I just stayed where I was, leaning my elbow against the door, and watched the street. There was too much going on. I couldn't have focused on reading if I'd tried.

The silence went on for a few minutes. Drew and I could sit in companionable quiet for a while, though this time it was a bit different. Each of us were watching our sectors, mulling over what was going on.

Drew broke the silence first. "So, if somebody in the police department is running interference for a gang hit on our principal, presumably at the behest of someone with a *lot* of money and political pull, then who was it that hit Brolin's place last night? They weren't pros. Not like us. They weren't gangbangers, either."

"Off-duty cops?" I was being flippant, but the thought suddenly brought a frown to my face as soon as I'd said it. "Boy, there's a can of worms if it's true."

"No kidding." Drew didn't stop watching our surroundings. "I could see them being contractors. Nobody tried to pull the 'I'm an undercover cop' card when we had the drop on them. They just froze."

"Pretty shit contractors." Granted, I might be biased.

Drew snorted derisively. "You and I have both met plenty of shit contractors over the years."

"True enough." I shook my head. "What was that one dude's name? The guy who insisted he was going to teach a class on the MAG-58 and then *broke* the damned thing?"

Drew chuckled. "Was that Crow? I don't think I was around for the broken machinegun bit, though I sure heard about it."

"I don't think it was Crow. Crow was weird, but he wasn't dumb *and* weird."

Drew snapped his fingers. "Peewee."

I thumped the wheel with my fist. "Peewee! That's it. The only guy I know with a worse origin story for his callsign than Bone."

"Dude, I was on that flight." Drew sounded disgusted. "If I'd been the task order manager, he'd have gotten right back on the first thing smoking home. That was gross."

"You weren't next to him, were you?"

He shook his head. "No, thankfully. But I didn't have to be. Half the plane heard it, since he didn't turn the volume down and didn't use headphones."

"That definitely sounds like Peewee. Boy, he sure stayed around longer than anyone expected."

"Just goes to show, man. Vetting only goes so far."

"More like sunk costs." I'd seen guys who'd gotten a job only to get lazy as hell as soon as they started, and never get fired.

I didn't think PGS was going to work like that. Not with Goblin in charge. It had been a lot of years since we'd been partners, but I didn't get the impression from the way things had been run so far that he was going to make many of the same mistakes we'd bitched about in the car, all that time ago.

I sure *hoped* PGS wasn't going to start acting like some of the other companies I'd subcontracted for over the years. Companies that had started strong, then sold out to some hedge fund and started to worry more about stock returns than the guys they were sending into harm's way.

I was still musing about it when a black Suburban rolled past, moving slightly more slowly than seemed normal.

That caught my attention. Sure, the black Sub was such a cliché at that point that I could hardly expect anyone who was serious to use it as an operational vehicle. It drew eyes like white on rice. Still, given the professionalism we'd seen displayed by the snatch team the night before, it bore watching.

The Sub didn't stop, didn't suddenly swerve into the curb in front of the BBQ place and spill a SWAT team. It just kept rolling, still maintaining that slow pace as it passed the columned, red brick College Park City Hall. After a moment, it was beyond the curve, hidden by the trees that lined the road.

"It'd take some balls to pull a hit right in front of City Hall." Drew had noticed the Suburban, too.

"If they've got the connections they seem to, they probably wouldn't care." I glanced in the rear view again, just to make sure somebody hadn't snuck up on us while I was watching the black Sub.

"Good point." Drew shifted to rest his hand on his carbine where he had it hidden underneath a sweatshirt, while he leaned forward to peer out his side mirror. It was angled for me to be able to see, not him, but he could still use it.

The street remained calm and quiet, and the Suburban didn't reappear. Probably just some soccer mom in her expensive SUV.

Or maybe not. It was hard to tell. Even way outside the city, there was so much noise that it was hard to pick out the signal that was actual bad guys.

This was why recon and surveillance usually are best carried out over a long period of time. Without building a pattern of life, it's hard to tell what's a threat and what's not. It gets too easy to either overreact or get complacent, because you simply don't have the reference points necessary to make a solid assessment.

Granted, when somebody kicks in the door and tries to shoot you, or breaks into an apartment and drags a girl off with a bag over her head, that makes things a little easier.

Movement caught my eye. "Here she comes." Brolin was easy enough to pick out, even though she'd put on a ball cap and pulled a hood up over her head to cover her green hair. I would have suggested that she dye it something at least a little less eye-searing, but there hadn't been time.

She hustled across the street, looking around her with the quick, nervous movements of someone who was well and truly rattled. Whatever she'd heard in there, it wasn't good. By the time she reached the car, she was almost running.

I let her in, then locked the doors before pulling out of the parking space and heading out the same direction the Suburban had gone. "That was pretty quick."

"He didn't want to stick around for very long." Brolin sounded a little out of breath. "After what he told me, I'm not surprised. He said he's taking an extended leave of absence and getting out of town for a while. This was probably the last chance I'd have to talk to him."

Drew didn't turn around to look at her. He was still watching for any tail or ambush. "So, what did he say?"

Instead of answering, Brolin pulled out her phone and brought up the voice memo app, opening a file and setting the device on the center console.

"I can't stay long. This got worse in the last twenty-four hours." That had to be Lang. He talked with only the slightest drawl, and he sounded dead tired.

"I know. Somebody tried to kidnap me." The fact that Brolin didn't go into the whole story was a good thing. I didn't know exactly how Lang would have reacted if she'd told him that she'd been rescued by gunmen who'd deliberately crashed a rental car into her kidnappers' van. *"But it sounds like you're thinking of something else."*

"Someone tried to kidnap you?" Lang hadn't missed that detail, as tired as he sounded.

"I'm here and I'm fine." Brolin seemed to have realized that she might have just derailed the conversation. *"What did you want to talk about?"*

For a moment, Lang didn't say anything, probably trying to decide whether or not to push. *"An old friend came to see me last night. Told me that the Chief knows I was the one who talked to you, and that he's pissed."*

"Isn't that kind of to be expected, though?" Brolin sounded slightly confused.

"Sure, except for the next part. Seems that the orders that nothing be done during that 911 call the other day came down from the Chief himself. I wasn't the only one wondering what the hell was going on, but nobody else wants to risk their job. Things have gotten real nasty around here with the drop in manpower. The Chief's been threatening all sorts of punitive measures for anyone who gets out of line, and everyone who's left is worried that they won't be able to pick up and start over somewhere else. Especially not in this economy."

"Does the DA know about that?"

There was another long pause. *"Ella, the DA is worse than the Chief. That woman would let someone murder her own grandmother if it bought her some kind of advantage."*

"But why *would they just let this happen?"*

The silence stretched for almost a full minute. "I could tell he was really worried about telling me this next part." Brolin was leaning forward in her seat, her elbows on her knees, staring at the phone even though she'd recorded what we were listening to.

"My friend told me that the Chief and the DA have both been going out of the office for 'meetings' that they don't want anyone coming along for over the last two weeks. That's odd. Usually, meetings happen at City Hall or one of the precincts. But they've been disappearing and not even taking their phones. Nobody seems to know why."

Brolin turned off the memo and took the phone back. "That was about all he had to say, but it seems ominous enough." She looked from one to the other of us. "That's suspicious, isn't it? The Chief of Police and the District Attorney sneaking off to secret meetings?"

Drew smoothed his mustache. "In the big picture, I'd say it's probably pretty standard, these days. Under the circumstances, though, I'd say it's damned suspicious."

I held my peace for about a mile, thinking it through as I drove. "I'd tend to agree with Drew. These days, politicians acting shady seems to be the norm, rather than an anomaly. But if he's telling the truth that the Chief of Police ordered his people not to answer our 911 call..."

"Add it to the DA wanting to charge us with murder and then suddenly pulling a one-eighty as soon as Strand's lawyers got involved, declaring it a nothingburger?" Drew nodded. "It makes sense. So, who are they meeting with?"

"I think we might have a couple more surveillance targets soon."

Brolin didn't have anything to say to that, which spoke volumes about how far she'd shifted her own perspective since we'd first met her the day before.

Either that, or she was staying quiet so that we didn't lock her up before she could turn us in. Either to the Feds or the Atlanta PD for a deal or something.

She's an asset, not a friend.

It wasn't the most reassuring thought as I started onto the return route to the safehouse, carefully checking our back trail all the way.

CHAPTER
14

Tom, Brian, Ken, and Custus were still out with Strand by the time we got back. Jake and Rob were still on site security. Rob didn't seem to mind; after all, it meant he was getting paid to pretty much sit on his ass and watch YouTube videos. Jake, on the other hand, was *not* a happy camper.

"If I'd known I was going to be stuck housesitting for the whole fucking contract, I wouldn't have taken it." Short, baby-faced, and blond, Jake often looked like a kid playing at being a gunfighter, even though he was every bit as good at the job as any of the rest of us. His height and his features had left him with a hell of a complex, though, which had given him his callsign of "Chihuahua."

"You got two days of the short straw." I admit that Jake's combination of impatience and eagerness kind of grated on me. "It'll change. Especially if this thing is as weird as it looks." I looked over his shoulder. "Where's KG?"

He jerked a thumb deeper in. "Been on his computer all day. I think he's trying to do more of that cyber shit, or whatever." The tone of Jake's voice said what he thought of that.

I just shrugged and headed for the living room, which had essentially become the team office, tactical operations center, and where KG spent most of his time.

He'd expanded things. He wasn't on just one laptop but had a tablet and a second laptop on the coffee table, as well as a radio repeater on an end table that he'd hauled over from somewhere else in the house.

Putting this place back together before we vacated was going to be interesting. We *could* be assholes and leave it to the owner, but that might also mean leaving target indicators that would tell anyone trying to trace our actions and movements in Atlanta more than we wanted them to know.

"Just in time." He looked up from the screen just for a moment before turning his eyes back down to whatever he was working on. "I didn't hear anything on the scanner, so I'm guessing no one crashed the party." It wasn't exactly a question. "You good to start prep for a hit in the next thirty-six to seventy-two hours?"

That was a question I hadn't expected to hear on this job. Not that I was complaining. I wasn't alone among many, many contractors who would have *killed* for a chance to get back into the door-kicking business overseas.

"We got a location on Garcia?" I was a little tired from all the driving, but not *that* tired.

"We do. At least, we've got a starting point." He shook his head. "Those cyber guys are freaky. Pinpointed the locations of at least three of his social media photos and videos, and that was with the location data turned off. We've got some more recon and surveillance to do, but I'm sending Chihuahua and Bone out for that, if only to shut Chihuahua up." He leaned back on the couch, watching me as if he was waiting.

He was waiting for me to get something. I studied him for a moment, then shifted my attention to the laptop, notes, and tablets on the coffee table, forcing my tired brain to think it through. It's astounding, sometimes, how draining hours in a car can be, even when nothing really happens.

Then I got it. "We're not just going off half-cocked on this, are we? I mean, it's one thing when the local cops have already sat on their hands once, but unless we're going to go all the way rogue, we can't just roll up and start shooting. Self-defense is one thing. This is declaring war on US soil." I knew I wasn't alone in the fact that I was actually fairly comfortable with the idea, after everything I'd seen over the years, coming from both the bad guys and the supposed "good guys" in our own government, some of whom I had, at times regrettably, worked for. But there was more than just my own skin and my hankering for action to think about. My family would face some serious consequences if I went off the reservation and it went bad. It might be the *right* thing, taken on its face, to put down some *Mara Salvatrucha* thugs, but there were second- and third-order effects to think about.

KG cracked a faint smile. "That took less time than I expected." He sat up again, leaning toward the computers and the coffee table. "You're absolutely right. There's only so far we can push this, right off. We're on Atlanta PD's turf, and unless they are absolutely off the board, we can't just roll as if we were in J-bad or somewhere like that." He shook his head. "No, we're going to feel things out a little bit, which is why I gave you a thirty-six to seventy-two hour window."

He handed me one of the tablets. "We called in an anonymous tip to Atlanta PD about an hour ago, pointing them at Garcia. He's got outstanding warrants in Georgia, so there *should* be a reaction." He pointed to the scanner. "We're monitoring every bit of police comms we can. The nature of that reaction will determine what we do over the next two to three days."

I was studying the brief dossier we had on Garcia. It wasn't much, but it was still more than I'd seen on actual target packages in Iraq, over a decade before. "So, we know that this guy's pissed that we smoked a few of his buddies in the hotel, but do we know that he's connected with whoever pointed them at us? Or is this just the same sort of spreading chaos that we saw overseas, back in the day, where some jihadi's cousin got pissed because we dumped him while he was setting in an IED? In other words, are we really tracking up the kill chain, or are we just getting dragged off on violent tangents?"

"It's a good question. That's part of why we're not just kicking in his door tonight." He grinned again. "The other part is putting together the misdirection that we're going to need to make sure that any hit doesn't get traced back to us, but that's not something you need to worry about yet." He sobered. "You know intel collection, Chris. This isn't going to happen overnight, and it's not going to be clear enough when it does."

I nodded, turning my eyes back to the tablet. There were a lot of questions, though I wondered just how open an answer I'd get. "I'm not backing out, just so you know." Hell, I couldn't *afford* to back out right now. "But it seems to me that we're getting into some serious mission creep, that might put us in a very bad position with law enforcement. I'm not one to equate all cops with the good guys, any more than I am to equate all of *us* with the good guys, by necessity, but there are going to be costs." I was trying to choose my words very carefully and felt like I wasn't doing a great job of it. There was a lot at stake, both for the company and for each of us personally. "Is our mission to hunt down some shadowy organization that might be working against the client, or to keep the client safe?" I was pretty sure that the *legal* answer was the latter, but that didn't necessarily make it the *right* answer, especially when we'd been confronted with the evidence of corruption that we'd already found.

For his part, KG listened to my concerns with a calm, impassive expression. "Those are good questions, and I'd be concerned if no one voiced them. You're right, this is a dicey position we're in. It would be entirely too easy for the bad guys to use Atlanta PD—or even the Feds—against us if we make the wrong move.

"But consider this." He leaned his elbows on his knees and folded his hands under his chin. "You're right that our primary remit, as per the contract, is to keep Strand safe. No question there. However, we're not dealing with a more-or-less random terrorism or target-of-opportunity armed robbery/kidnap for ransom threat here. This was an organized, targeted attempt to kill or capture our client, that had top cover from what appears to be the highest levels of local law enforcement, which also appears to be actively trying to cover it up. That changes things a bit.

"There are those who would say that to be good citizens, we just have to accept it and do what we can to mitigate the threat, probably leave town and adjust our signature to stay out of trouble, since the law won't help us. There's something to be said for that. There are places where we can be more or less confident that the law *will* be on our side.

"*However*, I'd advance a different idea. Goblin's on board with this, by the way." Since our first "meeting" with our company boss, everyone who'd known him before had stopped calling him "Mr. Walker" and just gone back to his callsign. "Since there obviously is an organized and powerful interest—though we don't know for sure who that interest is, yet—that has targeted our client's life, and has suborned local law enforcement to cooperate with that threat, then the best way to protect the client will be to expose that interest and neutralize it."

I nodded. I wasn't opposed. I was a little nervous about it. But all the same, I'd seen enough over the last few years to have fully embraced the understanding that in many places, we were on our own. No one was coming to save us.

When the bad guys had apparently bought off the Chief of Police and the DA, then we really and truly were on our own.

"So, what's the plan, then?"

"We've got the B Team flying in tonight. You guys are pretty good, but you're getting stretched thin already, and some

113

of you might have been identified. They won't come here, but we've got another safehouse for them to set up. They'll take over surveillance on the Chief and the DA. I have my suspicions about who might be pulling the strings on all of this, but that's going to be the B Team's job.

"We're going to continue to work close protection for Mr. Strand, while we deal with this immediate threat from the MS-13 douchebags. We'll have comms with the other team, but that should be the only contact for now, so we'll share any intel we get."

"And if Strand decides to pull off and go back to Dallas?" If he'd gotten what he needed from Aarav, then this all might turn out to be a moot point. There was a weakness to using this sort of job as a cover for other operations. That cover only lasted as long as the job did.

But KG just grinned. "Not going to happen for a while yet. We talked before he left with Scooby and Scrappy. He's got some other business in Atlanta to see to; after all, he *does* have financial interests all over the country as well as in several countries overseas."

I couldn't help myself. I found myself mirroring KG's wolfish grin. "So, we'll stay as long as necessary to accomplish *our* mission?"

With a shrug, KG put on an innocent expression. "We're here to protect the client, and he has reason to stay on for a while. Since protecting the client might mean taking some slightly more active measures..."

I nodded. "I guess we've got some mission prep to do."

CHAPTER
15

Nick "Croak" King looked around the small rental that was going to be their home for the next few weeks. "I've definitely been in worse places."

"I've been in better, too." Casey Moore looked around the house. "I've been in places with furniture."

Nick shrugged. It was true that the one-story, three-bedroom house in College Park was completely unfurnished, but there was room, there was power, and there was a kitchen. "It's not some Afghan farmer's barnyard. I'll take it."

"I don't know." George stood in the doorway, his luggage in hand. "I wasn't looking for another 'sleep on the floor' job when I switched to working for a fucking billionaire, Stateside."

Saul shouldered past George, knocking him a step into the entryway. George's eyes flashed for a moment, but Saul was half a head taller and outweighed him by a good thirty pounds. Long, black hair fell to the big man's shoulders, over the strap of his duffel. "Feel free to head back to the airport and get on a plane, George. I'm sure there are plenty of dudes who'd like a crack at this paycheck. Especially since there ain't no jobs in Afghanistan, anymore." He didn't even look at George as he spoke. The contempt was blatantly obvious.

George bristled, but he looked away as Saul finally turned toward him. He stalked off toward one of the bedrooms, muttering under his breath.

Well, that's a great way to start this off. Nick hadn't worked with Pallas Group Solutions before, and while there had been some training up front, not to mention all the certifications that the company had paid for its contractors to get, this team hadn't had a lot of time to mesh. And it didn't look like they were going to mesh all that well.

"Hey, one or all of you guys want to give me a hand?" The guy who'd just come to the door wasn't one of the usual team, but he wasn't just some rando, either. Nick thought he looked familiar, but he was clearly one of them. Something about the way he carried himself. "I've got the rest of the gear and some furniture to unload."

Nick craned his neck to look outside, to see a rental box truck waiting on the curb. He looked back at where George had disappeared, but the other man was still bitching, now somewhat louder since he was out of Saul's reach and baleful glare, and hadn't heard.

"Sure." Nick was always ready to lend a hand. He'd gotten into the habit in the Army, even when it had worked against him. Always give the unit a reason to keep you around. It was a habit that had been reinforced once he'd become a contractor, particularly during the times when jobs had started to get cut, and companies were looking for any excuse to send a guy home and not call him back. "Let's get this place set up."

***

It was past dark by the time they had the house essentially livable. The box truck had been almost full of equipment cases, folding cots, folding chairs, and plastic tables. Saul had just stared at George as the other man had taken his cot back to the rear bedroom, and George hadn't dared meet his eyes.

"I'm guessing we don't put Salt and Digger together on a team." The new guy with the box truck was at Nick's elbow, watching the two men avoid each other. Nick suppressed a start. The guy was quiet. "I wouldn't." He turned to him. "Sorry, are you the local contact?"

The slightly shorter man with the pockmarked face and prominent Adam's apple grinned lopsidedly. "Damn, Croak, that's cold. I know it's been a long time, but damn."

Nick did a double take. "Holy shit. Casper?"

Frank Moretti grinned. The two men shared a fierce one-armed bear hug. "I didn't recognize you with the short hair and no beard! When the hell did this happen?"

"When Goblin brought me aboard at PGS and I had to look respectable." He waved toward the kitchen. "Anyway, I've got a brief to give. Can we get everybody in?"

Saul looked up from his cot where he'd set up in the living room. "Team meeting! Time now!"

There were a few more grumbles. The team had met at the airport. They hadn't even had time to settle in as a team yet, and most of them were stiff and tired from their flights. He didn't think there was a man in the house who was younger than thirty-six. Which wasn't *old*, exactly, but when most of them had infantry backgrounds, age crept up fast.

Frank ignored the complaints. "We're on the clock, boys. It's been just over forty-eight hours since there was a hit on the company's biggest client, here in Atlanta. That would be significant enough, and a feather in our cap that the hit was stopped cold, with no friendly casualties and several dead MS-13 shitheads, but there's more."

He had set up a laptop on the table in the dining room, and he swiveled it around so that the whole team could see the screen. "Our guys called 911, but nobody came. And now we've got intel that the Atlanta PD and DA might well be working *with* the bad guys…"

***

Drone's up.

Nick sent a thumbs up emoji over the phone to acknowledge. A part of him would have preferred to use radios, but the phones were actually more secure at the moment and wouldn't attract attention. Everybody was on their phones. Not so many people were talking on radios.

He was sitting in their rental Audi, geared up much the same as he had been overseas, with a Glock 19 on his hip and a Recce 16 carbine in the back seat, watching the phone and a tablet with the drone feed on it while Matt drove them in seemingly random racetracks around the outskirts of the Atlanta city government buildings and the Georgia state capitol.

That was why they were using a commercial F11GIM2 drone for this particular surveillance duty instead of their Mark 1 Eyeballs. Setting up surveillance on the Atlanta Police Department wasn't impossible, especially given the evident declining quality of that department, but it was risky, and with only a few vehicles and personnel, they'd decided that the drone was going to be the best way to make their initial contact with the target.

Drones had to be registered in the State of Georgia, but after that, there weren't many restrictions. That was why Casper wasn't too worried about overflying the city government. They *might* get made, but the drone was registered with a local friend of the company, who would apologize, pay the fine, and then get reimbursed on the back end.

Coming up on the target building.

Nick sighed. *I don't need the running commentary, Money, I can see it. I have the feed.* He didn't send that, just because there was no need, and he didn't know Money that well aside from the initial conversation where he'd compared the man's callsign to "Moneypenny." Which was, apparently, where it had started, since Josh Costello had apparently gotten

118

a little too passionate about a James Bond theory while drunk when he'd been a SEAL.

He watched as the drone buzzed over roofs and parking lots. They didn't know exactly where Chief of Police Darren Wallace was at any particular time, but they knew what car he drove. That was going to be the choke point for him.

Nick checked his watch. It was still only about four in the afternoon. They could be sitting and watching for a long time. Most people didn't leave the office until around five, and if the Chief of Police was really busy…

"You know that we might not see *anything* for a while, right?" Matt took another turn, heading north on Grant Terrace. "I doubt he's meeting with his puppet masters every afternoon."

"I know, but I didn't want to think about it. Thank you for that." Nick kept watching the feed. "Wait a second."

It was way too early, but then, they *were* talking about a politician in uniform and wearing a badge. It was entirely possible that he was the type who would duck out early to go to the bar or whatever, while his cops were still sweating out their long shifts because there weren't enough of them to cover the streets.

Sure enough, the figure in blue, with gold epaulets and a badge shining in the sun, walked straight to the correct vehicle and paused at the side to get in. Josh had already seen the move and had sent the drone into a short arc to get a better angle on the face.

While it wasn't on Nick's tablet, Josh had the OpenFace software on his, feeding the video through it. An open-source facial recognition software, it would spot Wallace as soon as the software could get a full shot of his face.

That's our boy. Nick sent the "thumbs-up" again.

The drone gained altitude and backed off as Wallace pulled out of the parking lot. The plan was to shadow the police chief's car until he was out of the somewhat more secure part of the city, where a ground tail could pick him up.

He was heading east, getting on I-20 and heading for Glenwood Park. Matt started for the freeway while the drone continued to pace the car.

"Don't get on the interstate." Nick was occasionally lifting his head to check their surroundings, since security was his responsibility as the right-seater, but he was still watching the tablet carefully. "He's getting off. Looks like Glenwood Park is his destination."

"Weird choice. Unless our intel's completely off, he lives up in Buckhead, and this isn't what I'd call a normal time for a lunch break." Matt chewed the inside of his cheek as he took another turn, moving to intercept the target vehicle.

"Maybe our luck's better than we thought." Nick kept watching the overhead video. "Maybe things are getting hotter than he'd like, so he really is checking in with his handlers more often. If Strand's detail really did intercept an attempt at covering things up by kidnapping that journalist, then maybe they're more freaked out than we thought."

"I can hope. If we get our target tonight, maybe we won't be running around the city, dodging carjackers for weeks while we watch these political assholes." Matt Patric wasn't that thrilled with the assignment, but at least they were getting paid.

Nick didn't have much of an answer for that. He didn't know Matt well, though they'd been in 10th Group at about the same time. This was their first contract together, and their first time in the car.

Fortunately, his time contracting overseas had gotten him well-practiced at showing up, getting in the car with a stranger, and getting the job done. Most of them were used to that sort of thing. Thankfully, the really harsh personal differences, like the clashes between Saul and George, tended to be fairly rare.

"There he is." Matt had ducked them into the Waffle House parking lot for a moment, and spotted Wallace's car in the rear-view mirror. Nick didn't look up, but he saw the drone feed pick up the restaurant as Wallace passed by it.

Nick sent Josh a message that they had the target, and the drone pulled off. They were on their own now.

Matt was already pulling out of the parking lot, but he paused as Wallace turned right into the little business park just across the street. Apparently, he was coming right to them.

I sure hope he's not just getting a haircut. Nick hadn't really done this kind of long-term surveillance before, though he'd certainly trained up on it prior to earlier contracts, if only to know how it worked so that he could detect and avoid it. Coming from 2nd Ranger Bn, he hadn't *needed* to know this stuff in the military. His missions had been largely quick and kinetic. Now, though, he knew all too well that Matt was right, and that this could take a very, *very* long time.

Surveillance can be mind-crushingly *boring*.

Wallace pulled into a parking spot and got out. He'd shed his uniform jacket and shrugged into a black leather biker jacket. It wouldn't hide who he was, but it would hide his status as a cop, at least at first glance.

Nick frowned as he watched their target go into The Beverly. It didn't quite seem like Wallace's sort of place. Maybe he was just typecasting, but a sports bar in Glenwood Park seemed a little off from what they knew of the police chief's profile.

"I'll go in." They probably *could* just stay out in the parking lot and watch, but if Wallace was meeting someone in there, then they'd miss it. Worse, he might use the place as an escape route, and slip out a different door to a different car while they were watching only one side.

"Watch your back." Matt smirked a little. "You know, Glenwood Park is a dangerous place."

121

"From what I've heard, there ain't no safe zones in Atlanta anymore, no matter how much the yuppies wish there were," Nick retorted. He pushed open the door. "Don't get carjacked. I don't wanna walk back to the safehouse."

He shut the door before Matt could respond and made his way toward the bar. It took some concentration to look casual, like he was just going to get something to eat, maybe a beer. Not like he was stalking a man through an affluent neighborhood of Atlanta.

It was something that he'd trained to do, something he'd thought about a lot while he'd been working contracts after the Army. None of those jobs had ever equaled the rush he'd gotten in the Rangers. This might just be different.

He wasn't ignorant of the possible repercussions, but he was single, and he really didn't care. He was getting close to the action again.

He envied those guys who'd shot their way out of the Hyatt House. Maybe he'd get a chance at something like that on this job.

The bar wasn't all that full, which meant he was going to have to be especially careful. He wasn't really the kind of guy who stood out much, at least not until the second look. Brown haired, not especially tall, his beard neatly trimmed, he just looked like another guy. He usually wore long sleeves to cover his tats, as well as arms that made it clear he worked out regularly, more than the average civilian.

Wallace was already sitting in a booth at the end of the room, backlit by the blue and purple lights set into the wall and the ceiling, next to a wooden outset with "The Beverly" in gold lettering on a backlit black metal sign mounted on it. He was looking at his phone, not even bothering to check the rest of the room.

Nick found a seat closer to the door, at a tall bar table, and ordered wings. It was too early for a beer, in his estimation, and he didn't like combining alcohol with the job.

His wings hadn't come yet when a man in business casual, black slacks and a light pink shirt, came in the door, looked around, and made a beeline for Wallace's booth.

The man slid into a chair across from Wallace, and Nick started to video the meeting, covering the action by pretending to be absorbed in his phone. In some ways, the devices had turned out to be immensely helpful on jobs like this, since they had all sorts of useful surveillance tools that could be installed, and *everyone* had one. It never looked odd if you were staring at a smartphone.

The meeting wasn't long, but it sure was animated. Whatever they were talking about, the new guy was not happy about it. Nick could only see his back, but he could see that Wallace was not comfortable. The man in the pink shirt was stabbing a finger on the table, stopping only when the waitress came with Wallace's order. Once she was gone, the tirade resumed.

There was way too much noise to pick up voices, but when the man finally finished, he reached into the small attaché case he'd brought in and put something on the table. Nick couldn't see what it was, but Wallace quickly pocketed it. Then, without ordering anything, the man in the pink shirt got up and stormed out.

Nick got a good shot of his face as he left, but he didn't recognize the man. Clean shaven, his dark hair slicked back, he could be any number of businessmen around Atlanta. Still, whoever he was, he was comfortable dressing down the Atlanta Chief of Police. He was somebody. Nick would pass the video on. Maybe Pallas Group's little corral of analysts could make something of it.

I wonder what the hell that was all about?

CHAPTER
16

"Jock up." KG's voice wasn't loud, but it carried through the safehouse, anyway, carrying a jolt of adrenaline along with it.

"The hit's on?" Phil got to the question before Brian or Jake could, probably to both of their great irritation.

With a grave nod, KG turned back toward the living room. "Things have unfolded a lot over the last twelve hours."

Drew, Phil, Marcos, and I had been playing Spades. I hadn't played in years, not since my second combat deployment to Iraq, and I was rusty. Drew was getting irritated, so it was just as well that we could drop the game and get to work.

We gathered around the coffee table. It was somewhat notable that Strand was there, too. He wasn't supposed to be in on this part, but he was clearly interested.

That was a problem, though. "Sir, you might want to go in the other room. What you don't know can't hurt you."

Strand was sharp. He picked up the subtext. *You need plausible deniability about tonight.* He just nodded and left the room.

"Okay, so, the experiment has gone down. We dropped a dime on Garcia about a day and a half ago, then closely monitored the police response.

"In short, there was none. There was some activity. A squad car was dispatched, but it was quickly called back. After that, there was no more interest from Atlanta PD. On Garcia's part, however..."

He pulled up several screenshots of social media posts. In one video, Garcia ranted in Spanish at the camera, waving a machete. "I'll spare y'all the gory details, but suffice it to say that someone told him he'd been ratted out to the cops, and he's threatening to find them and chop them up for dog treats, *after* he kills Strand and everyone around him who killed his buddies."

There was a moment's silence. "So, that kinda tears it, doesn't it?" Rob sounded strangely subdued. "Somebody on the police force not only has the pull to cover for them, but actually leaked the fact that they'd been targeted."

"It does indeed." KG took a deep breath. "So, tonight's op is a go. We're not the law, so we can't exactly arrest them, but I want them neutralized. I also want intel. Phones, computers, tablets, fucking *sticky notes*. I don't care. I want all of it."

There were nods. I didn't think anyone in that room had a problem with *neutralizing* MS-13 killers. These were the guys who lived by the mantra, "Kill, Rape, Control." They weren't likely to surrender, anyway, not the way we were going in there.

"So, gear up and get ready to move. Wheels up to the staging point in thirty minutes."

***

The staging area was on the other side of Atlanta. It was necessary to keep the company—and Strand—disconnected from what was about to go down that night. The hit team—Drew, Phil, Marcos, Ken, Custus, Jake, Rob, and I—rode the van that we'd switched to in the parking garage, while Tom and Brian drove. They dropped us off with our duffels full of gear and weapons on the road, scattered across a couple of miles, and we made our way toward the fence on foot.

The old Atlanta Prison Farm was four hundred acres of city-owned, abandoned property, with the fire-gutted, graffiti-covered remains of a penitentiary sitting nestled back in the trees and the kudzu. It was technically a no-trespassing area, but that was generally ignored, so climbing in there wasn't going to be that difficult or even that big a deal. If we got caught, though, the trespassing would be the least of the things we might have to try to explain.

I came opposite a pair of gutted, roofless buildings and paused, checking up and down the road. No lights. No vehicles coming or going. As far as we'd been able to ascertain, the city didn't have CCTV cameras on the property, and they didn't exactly patrol it, either. There were certainly enough YouTube videos of people exploring it. For the moment, it looked like I was clear.

With a heave, I tossed my duffel over the bent, sagging cyclone fence, then followed it. I'd been careful to pad my rifle as best I could, so I wasn't worried about knocking the optic off zero. The fence swayed and creaked as I hauled myself over it and dropped to the ground, hardly pausing to haul the duffel back up to my shoulder as I hustled behind the slightly lower ruin and into the trees.

It took only a few minutes to get through the woods, under the high-tension power lines that buzzed nastily as I passed by them, and over to what was left of the main building. Apparently, there were all sorts of ghost stories about this place, and in the deepening dark, I could see why. The roof was gone, and the long, vaguely castle-like structure was visibly decaying, the plaster dingy, soot-streaked, and cracked, covered in vines and graffiti.

Ken and Custus had beaten me there, but then, they'd been the team that had been tapped to drop our ride for the night, so they knew the way a little better than those of us who'd never been on site. They were already getting geared up.

The massive, black silhouette of an armored Ford F550 was set under the trees at the end of what was left of the prison's driveway. It wasn't a SWAT vehicle, any more than our plain, sterile green fatigues, helmets, and plate carriers were actual Atlanta SWAT uniforms. We wouldn't wear badges or nametapes, and we wouldn't call ourselves police. We weren't. We wouldn't be adding "impersonating a police officer" to any eventual rap sheet, not really.

It was still weird. We were acting like we were overseas, in a war zone, doing things because they needed to be done, strict hierarchies of authority be damned. This wasn't supposed to be the way things worked Stateside, but there was a part of every one of us, I thought, who reveled in it, anyway. We were action guys. Trained, paid killers. Combat soldiers. Tonight, we were going to get our kill on, and we could be assured it was righteous, even if the legal authorities might not agree.

We told ourselves that we really didn't have any other choice. We might be out to kill people extralegally that night, but they'd struck first, and the cops refused to get involved. They'd certainly been given the chance.

I dragged my duffel over to the truck and started getting jocked up, as Drew, Phil, Rob, Jake, and Marcos joined us and followed suit. Nobody talked. We got our gear on in the dark, no one showing a light. We wouldn't do anything to attract attention. Even when we rolled out, it would be with lights off, Rob driving on NVGs.

Yeah, we had those, too. We had every bit of gear and weapons that Goblin could get us. He clearly had ideas for this company that went well beyond your ordinary, run of the mill security guards.

In minutes, we were mounted up, crammed into the armored vehicle with weapons buttstock down, in Condition

3—magazine inserted, chamber empty—and Rob had started the truck with a rumble, slowly rolling in the dark toward the gate.

That gate could have been a problem, but Ken and Custus had taken care of that the day before. They'd done a good job. I was pretty sure that the city had somebody check the lock on that gate regularly, because it probably got cut off just as regularly.

I couldn't see much from inside. There were windows, but they were as small and about as easy to look out as an MRAP's, and that was even without trying to look out an inch and a half of armored glass with NVGs on. I just rode the faint lurch of the big, heavy vehicle as Rob halted at the gate.

The door creaked open, Jake jumped out and ran to the gate, pulling it open after unlatching *our* padlock, and then we rumbled through. A moment later, Jake had secured the gate again and climbed back aboard, and then we were rolling.

We went a mile along a mostly deserted Georgia road in the dark before Rob flipped on the headlights. Then we were on our way, heading for Forest Park.

***

The target was a small, one-story brick house, with a chimney in the front, next to a door that had once been white, sheltered by a massive sycamore in the front yard. The sidewalk out front was cracked, and the street wasn't in much better shape. In fact, the street was so narrow that the F550 probably wouldn't have fit if there had been any oncoming traffic.

At that hour of the morning, fortunately, there wasn't any.

That didn't mean everyone was asleep, though. There were still lights on in a couple of the houses we passed, and even through the thick, armored sides of the vehicle, I could hear loud *corrido* music. Maybe *narcocorridos*, maybe not. I couldn't hear well enough to tell, even if my Spanish had been good enough.

The target house was lit up, too, and the music was painfully loud even on the street. I saw that as Rob lurched to a stop out front, Ken and Custus threw the rear doors open, and we went out.

The music was so loud that I couldn't hear any reaction to our arrival. At least, not for the first five seconds.

Glass shattered and muzzle flashes erupted from the front windows. Bullets smacked off the side of the armored vehicle with loud *bang*s, chipping the paint and leaving bright scars on the steel.

Men scattered across the yard, the plan suddenly gone completely to hell. Rob had just gotten out and he dropped flat on the grass and weeds. I couldn't tell if he was hit or not. I sprinted toward the corner of the building, just barely halting before I ran across Custus's muzzle. He snapped it up and we moved as a pair, even as Drew hunkered down behind that big sycamore and Ken ducked behind the F550 itself.

We were split up and half the team was pinned down, all in the first few seconds on target.

CHAPTER 17

There was no side door. I sprinted around behind Custus, heading for the back of the house. Keeping my head down as I passed the windows that covered the front corner, I kept to the outside of the couple of cars parked in the driveway. They weren't *cover*, strictly speaking, but they put *something* between me and the bullets.

"On me!" In some ways, after years of working more or less covertly, it went against the grain to yell, even in a firefight. But the plan had just gone completely to hell, and we had to shoot, move, and *communicate*. I sprinted for the back of the house as Custus and Phil fell in behind me, muzzles tracking toward the windows as we moved. So far, those windows were dark, and all the fire was coming from the front of the house, but it never paid to take chances, especially since I'd just called attention to myself by bellowing over the gunfire.

I slowed as I got to the back corner, though I didn't stop altogether. There was no time to stack up on the corner, as advisable as it *might* have been, so I pied off the angle as I kept moving, looking for a back door.

I found myself on a concrete back patio, with two more cars parked outside, along with a lot of junk. Clearing the corner, I didn't see any targets, but I spotted the back door, a light shining through the window and the screen. Keeping my muzzle trained on it, I closed in, only breaking that coverage to pie off the window between me and the door as I passed it. It was as dark as the windows out front had been; apparently the bad guys were all in one room, still dumping rounds at the not-SWAT vehicle out front.

Of course, even *mareros*, as aggressive and bloodthirsty as they were, weren't just going to stand and fight. The storm of gunfire out front was to cover the back. I'd barely gotten halfway to the door when it was wrenched open and two men in wife-beaters and baggy jeans raced out.

All I needed to see was the guns. The first man had a MAC-10 in his hands, but the second was carrying a folding-stock Mini-14. Shots had been fired, and guns meant threats, especially in the hands of guys with shaved heads coming out of that house.

I dumped the first one almost at the exact same time he noticed I was there. My first two shots ripped through that white shirt and into the man behind him, even as he triggered a burst from the MAC-10 into the concrete at his feet. I shifted to the guy with the Mini-14 and gave him another pair, those tracking a little higher and blowing out his throat, sending him over backward and back inside the house.

By the time I shifted back to the first man, he'd fallen on his face on the patio, twitching. I went straight in the door, stepping over the bodies, my weapon up and searching for more targets.

I was in a small mud room, opening on an equally small kitchen and laundry room. I could see through the kitchen to the living room, where at least a couple more gangbangers were crouched at the window, pouring automatic fire across the front yard.

While I might have tried to clear the house a bit more systematically, I had a shot through those adjacent rooms, so I took it. I didn't stop in the doorway, but kept moving out of the fatal funnel, which was going to close off my line of fire, but that couldn't be helped. I shot the first man twice in the back, then shifted to the second, who looked like he was leaning into an AK with a drum magazine as he sprayed rounds out through the window. My red dot was slightly higher on him, but I had the shot, so I splashed his brains across the windowsill with a single shot just before I fetched up against the wall, which opened more of the kitchen to my eyes, but that was about it.

Phil and Custus had crowded into the little mud room with me, and while Custus turned to cover the way we'd come, Phil joined me at the doorway and gave my arm a squeeze. He'd reached under and grabbed my tricep, making it difficult to mistake the signal for a simple bump.

It was enough. I went through the door and into the kitchen.

The kitchen was as trashed as the rest of the house that I'd seen so far, but I took that in at a glance as I hooked through the door and pivoted to clear my corner. I could hear someone screaming somewhere, either a woman or a dude with a hell of a high-pitched voice. They weren't in the kitchen, though.

It took a split second to clear my corner and then I was pivoting back toward the front. There was a dining room in the corner, on the other side of the fireplace from the living room, but I didn't see anyone there. There was dead space, however, that I'd have to clear.

Turning back toward the living room, I saw that both the men I'd shot were down. The fight wasn't over yet, though.

Phil pushed toward the living room and the two bedrooms behind it, and I fell in behind him. Once again, I had to rotate away from him to check the dining room.

Good thing I did, too, as a bullet whipped past my ear to punch a hole in the plaster ceiling. A third man—barely more than a kid, I saw a split second later—had thrown himself under the dining table as I'd shot the two at the living room window. He was still scrambling away from the bullets, which was the only reason he missed me, pointing his pistol with one hand while he tried to crawl away. I didn't have *much* of a shot, but I still stitched him up with at least five or six shots, two punching through the flimsy plastic tabletop.

Then I found myself at the back of the stack again, as Phil and Custus flowed into the short hallway leading to the two bedrooms and the bathroom.

Ideally, we might have left a man on the door, but with only three of us in the house, it was better to stick together.

We flowed into the hallway, and I followed just long enough to make sure I had no work in the hall before I pivoted back to check the six. We still hadn't cleared that laundry room, and I didn't know if the bad guys had friends elsewhere in the neighborhood who might try to follow us in that back door. With the pressure off the front, I hoped that Drew, Ken, Jake, Rob, and Marcos might have shifted to cover all the approaches, cordoning off the house.

I paused just long enough to make sure we weren't about to get shot in the back, then turned back forward while Phil and Custus made entry on the first bedroom. Then I shifted my position, pushing past that door to cover down on the last one.

No gunfire sounded from that bedroom. The screaming was still coming from the last one, and I pushed up as Custus came out and gave me a squeeze.

We burst through the last door and the screaming redoubled. I swept my muzzle across the shrieking, under-dressed woman crouched on a mattress on the floor, just long enough to make sure she didn't have a weapon in her hands, dug my corner for a split second, then pivoted back toward the middle of the room.

I'd seen it happen before that a seemingly panicked civilian suddenly produced a weapon and either got one of us or had to be killed first. So, I wasn't taking chances. It was a good thing, too.

In the moment that I'd been occupied checking my corner, she'd grabbed a knife from under the mattress and as I turned back, she lunged at me, screaming profanities in Spanish.

Custus double tapped her just before she got to me, since my rifle was off-line. Her screams were cut short in the sudden double thunderclap, and her head snapped to one side, blood and hair pattering against the bedroom wall. She fell at my feet, the knife hitting the stained carpet silently.

"Clear."

I nodded, keying my radio. "House is clear. Site exploitation, five minutes." We had to get clear *fast*. That fight had definitely attracted attention, as short as it had been, and while we weren't in a part of Atlanta where the cops usually responded with any kind of quickness, we had to expect some response, sooner or later. We had to be long gone before that happened.

Site exploitation, the way I'd been trained, meant we swept the entire house, turned everything over, and grabbed absolutely everything that might be of intelligence value, right down to the studs—or the cinder blocks, if you were in Iraq. We simply didn't have time for that thorough a search. We'd have to grab whatever we could find that might be of value and get out.

Fortunately, that was the pile of phones sitting on the table in the dining room and a couple more on the coffee table in the living room, surrounded by drugs, cigarettes, booze, and porn. Along with some more disturbing stuff that I didn't want to touch.

I'd heard that MS-13 had gotten started as a Satanic stoner club, but the evidence that they'd only doubled down on at least the first part was right there on the coffee table.

I moved to the two dead bodies on the floor beneath the living room window and turned them over. The guy I'd shot in the head wasn't that recognizable anymore, since the bullet had

135

punched out through the orbital bone and the bridge of his nose, but the one I'd shot in the back was still entirely identifiable. We'd gotten Garcia.

Custus was carefully looking at the handful of backpacks and duffel bags scattered around the living room, but finally, with a grimace, started shoving the phones in his dump pouch and cargo pockets. A glance inside one of those small duffels showed me a plastic bag full of small, multicolored pills. No wonder Custus didn't want to handle them.

Then we were moving out. Back in the day, I might have thrown a chemlight out to mark our exit for the cordon, but that would have left something behind that we didn't want any follow-up forces, whether they were cops or gangsters, to find. So, I just keyed my radio. "Coming out, front door."

"Bring it out." Things had gone quiet in the neighborhood. Everyone with two brain cells to rub together was down on their floor, hoping that bullets didn't come zipping through their walls to kill grandma or the family dog. I didn't hear any sirens yet. Either the Atlanta PD wasn't in any hurry to intervene in a gang dispute in Forest Park, or nobody in Forest Park was in a hurry to call the cops. Maybe both. Either way, it gave us a few more precious minutes.

"Get in, get in, get in!" Jake and Rob had already fallen back to the F550, and we scrambled to follow, getting aboard in seconds. Rob put the armored vehicle into motion with another lurch before we even had the doors shut.

I got myself into a seat and pulled out my phone, opening up a text message to KG. *Mission accomplished. No casualties. No survivors on site.* That last was necessary, if morbid. We hadn't necessarily *set out* to kill everyone in the house, but it did make things easier. There wouldn't be anyone left to identify any of us.

Good copy, and good work. Tell Rob and Jake to drop you at a good rendezvous outside the city. They're breaking off. That truck needs to be out of the state by sunrise.

Rgr. There wasn't much more to be said. I passed the word to Rob as we roared out of Forest Park and headed for the boondocks.

CHAPTER 18

It was almost dawn before we got back to the safehouse. Two guys from the B Team, who introduced themselves as Tonka and Whack, picked us up about half an hour after Rob and Jake dropped us off. We'd mostly changed in the armored vehicle, transferring gear and weapons to our duffels, so we didn't show any of the hardware we'd used to snuff out six people in a small drug house in Forest Park to anyone when we walked back out to a fifteen-pack van when it pulled up to the side of the road in Panola Mountain State Park. Not that there was anyone around to see us at that time of night, but it paid to be cautious, especially given some of the forces arrayed against us.

If I'd only known.

***

We crashed out hard once we got back. The van hadn't gone all the way to the safehouse, just to hopefully avoid any connection between the safehouse and the B Team. It might or might not work, if someone was monitoring traffic cameras or something, but so far, we didn't have any sign that anyone was aware of them. At least, none that I heard from KG before I went to my bed and passed out.

When I got up, things had definitely changed.

"Once everybody's gotten some coffee, dip, energy drinks, or all three, bring it in. We've got some interesting shit to go over." KG was standing in the hallway with a cup of coffee in his hand. Just judging by the light coming in the windows, it wasn't that long after we'd gone down to sleep. From the ache in my eyeballs, I decided that it *really* hadn't been long.

Strand was waiting in the living room as we straggled in, most of us looking pretty rough. It had been quite a few years since any of us could have pulled an all-nighter and bounced back immediately. Age takes its toll, especially on old infantrymen.

I studied our client as I sipped my coffee. He was staring at the laptop in front of him, his expression set and cold. Apparently, KG wasn't the only one who'd learned more about our situation overnight.

It came as a little bit of a surprise that it was Strand who kicked things off, not KG. "So, a report from y'all's B Team put a pretty important piece into place. I think I'm starting to understand what's going on."

He spun the laptop around so that we could sort of see the screen. It was small enough that not all of us could get a good look at it, so I watched Strand instead. "So, one of your guys got video of a meeting between the chief of police and this individual." He tapped a key and brought up a tab with a Linked In profile, showing a young man, clean cut but with slightly long hair, smiling toothily at the camera. "Now, we might not have identified him so quickly if not for one of the phones that you guys picked up from that gang house last night." He glanced at KG. "I'm not going to ask too many questions about where you guys got the hardware to rip a phone without the security code, but one of the contacts stood out, especially since some very interesting messages were coming from it. Someone was offering a considerable bounty—in cryptocurrency—for my head. Complete with photos of me, a couple of you, and several of the vehicles we've used here in Atlanta. Fortunately, one of those vehicles hasn't left this place recently, and the other was the rental that you guys took back to the airport, but the information is disturbingly current.

"Now, here's where it gets *really* interesting. Because we were able to trace that phone to this guy, Simon Cooper, we have some idea of just who's been the driving force behind the violence here. And it's not the gangbangers. They're just the instrument."

He pulled the laptop back around, brought up another tab, and then rotated it to where we could see it again. "Cooper works for a small financial firm called KNS Industries. They don't have much of a public presence. Their website is about as bare bones as it can get, and they have a tiny rental office in an industrial park in Alexandria, Virginia. They're about as opaque as possible.

"That would be that, if not for the fact that KNS Industries is technically a publicly traded company. While it's on the market, however, there are no publicly available shares. Those shares are all owned by Archer-Lin Investments, and were snapped up immediately, as soon as the company went on the market. Almost as if it was all planned that way."

"It's a front." Phil was frowning over his coffee.

"Got it in one." Strand smiled, though it was a strained expression. "Archer's been careful, but his cutouts haven't been careful enough. Bear in mind that KNS Industries is one of the companies that's been trying to pressure the Bowmans into selling their land."

"Who's Archer?" Brian spat a stream of dip spit into a paper cup. "I only know one Archer, but I doubt you're talking about the cartoon spy."

Strand raised an eyebrow at him. "Oh, I think you know this one. Devon Archer is the son of Senator Orrin Archer, a ranking member of the Senate Judiciary Committee. Devon's got a history of sketchy business dealings and foreign entanglements, mostly with the Russians and Chinese, though

141

he keeps getting it swept under the rug because of who his daddy is."

"That's interesting, but it still doesn't explain why he wants this ranch so badly, or why he'd hire *mareros* to try to kidnap or kill you." Marcos put a voice to what I think we were all wondering.

"I've been wondering that this entire time, myself, but I just got some news last night that might explain it." He leaned back on the couch and steepled his fingers in front of him, tapping them against his lips. "Apparently, there was an independent survey done of the Bowmans' land a few years ago. Mineralogical, among other things. Guess what they found?"

He waited, looking around the group, but no one was going to take the bait. We were probably all still too smoked from the night before.

Strand looked a little crestfallen when no one ventured a guess. "They found lithium. Quite a large amount of it. The Bowmans weren't initially interested in trading cattle ranching for rare-earth-mineral mining, but they did file the claim." He tilted his head slightly. "Now does the interest make sense?"

There was silence for a moment as we thought it over. On the surface, it made sense, but was also depressingly normal. Big government and big business corruption was nothing new. I think we'd all seen plenty of it on contract, even aside from some of the *really* shady stuff that we knew about but usually only talked about during those long conversations in the team room or the car, when we hadn't had much of anything else to do.

"There's more." KG hadn't inserted much into the conversation yet. "This Cooper guy wasn't the only one talking to Garcia about us. We haven't identified the other contact yet, but from what we can tell, it wasn't MS-13. It was cartel. Don't know which, but the language suggested that some very dangerous people south of the border were taking an interest in this target—meaning us—and that good things would be coming Garcia's way if he finished what his cousin started."

That was sobering. None of us, to my knowledge, had worked in Mexico, but we were all aware of it. Guys in our profession liked to keep our finger on the pulse of conflict, and Mexico was the place where the nastiest multi-axis irregular war on the face of the planet was currently raging. It was a place where we all sort of hankered to go try our hand, while at the same time recognizing the enormous risk involved.

The cartels weren't like jihadis. They were worse. Furthermore, they took things personally, and they had people north of the border who could find you and your family.

That gave me a chill. If some cartel *sicario* identified me, that could make Julie and the boys targets.

I'll kill all of them first. It might be hollow bravado, but I'd rather hunt than be hunted.

Strand was frowning. "That's interesting. That could mean something."

KG snorted. "I'll say it does. The cartels don't tend to limit themselves to just drugs and human trafficking. They've been making money on natural resources for over a decade now."

"You said that Archer's got friends in China, too?" Tom asked.

Strand nodded.

Tom took another sip of his Monster. "Well, then. Isn't China always looking to snap up lithium sources wherever they can?"

"Would they be dealing with the cartels?" Marcos asked.

"Sure they would. They'll do business with anybody. The shadier, the better." Phil took another sip of his own coffee.

"We don't *know* that this has anything to do with Archer's Chinese connections." Strand was getting uncomfortable. He must know a thing or two about the cartels, too. Though he should know enough that he wouldn't think that MS-13 was a cakewalk. Those guys were every bit as hardcore as the "*El Narco Diablo*" types.

"No, but it's worth investigating." KG was leaning on his elbows, sitting across from Strand. "Let's clear the air, here. This *could* be something that we very carefully investigate and turn over to federal law enforcement. This might just be a matter of ordinary criminal activity.

"On the other hand, it might be something more. The cartel involvement already has my Spidey Sense tingling. There are too many coincidences here, and Archer's status is going to make things even more complicated. People at that level tend to be pretty untouchable. If he was just an industrialist, that would be one thing, but he's a Senator's kid. That carries a *lot* of weight, foreign compromise be damned. And I don't believe for a minute that the Chinese have nothing to do with this. *However*, we're going to have to get some evidence before we can move." He looked around at the lot of us with a glint in his eye. "I'm not just talking about legalistic shit, here, either. If we miss a detail, it can get us all dead, or buried in a deep, dark hole for the rest of our natural lives."

That drew another grim silence for a minute. I decided to break it, since just brooding wasn't going to do much. "So, what's our next move?"

"My business is done here." It was Strand, not KG, who answered my question. "So, we'll be heading back to Dallas. Unless there's some other reason that I need to find to stick around Atlanta?" He turned to KG as if looking for his approval.

KG shook his head. "Unless we can start to get a profile on this KNS Industries, I don't think so. There's a thread to pull with the connection between them and the cops, but I think that's up to the B Team. We've done enough here, and our profile's already too high. I think we'd better pop smoke."

With that, the meeting kind of broke up, as we headed back to our rooms to pack our gear.

***

As I started to carry my duffel out to the vehicle, I paused at the sound of slightly raised voices in the dining room.

"I'm not going to become your corporate info-drone!" Brolin was clearly *not* happy.

"I'm not asking you to." Strand's own tone was markedly lower and more reasonable than Brolin's. "All I'm asking you to do is be an honest broker and be an investigative reporter. All I'm offering is the support to expand your reach *far* beyond the *Atlanta Daily Independent*. I just want you to dig."

There was a pause. I couldn't see her expression, since I was back in the doorway, listening in without exposing myself, but I'd been around her enough to imagine the angry look on her face. "And if I dig up something that doesn't reflect all that well on you?"

"Then I leave that up to your conscience."

That must not have been the answer she'd been expecting or necessarily wanting. The silence dragged on for a long minute before she spoke again, her voice even tighter and slightly angrier. "And if I find out that your hired guns might be crossing lines?" The tone of her voice spoke volumes. She at least suspected what we'd done the night before, and clearly didn't approve.

"Once again, I leave that to your conscience." Strand's own voice then got harder and colder. "If you really think that trying to burn the men who rescued you for the sake of murderers and drug traffickers is the right way to go, then maybe I misjudged you."

The conversation ended then, as Strand walked away. I stepped out of the bedroom and headed for the back door, my gear over my shoulder, trying to act as if I hadn't heard anything, and met his eyes as he stalked back toward his laptop. He wasn't terribly happy with the way the conversation had gone.

From the look on Brolin's face, neither was she, but there was something in her gaze as she looked at me while I walked past. Strand had hit a nerve with that last statement.

I just hoped that he was right about her.

CHAPTER
19

Nick sighed. They'd spent a whole seventy-two hours in Atlanta before word had come from the office to shift to Alexandria, Virginia. *Couldn't we actually get the time to settle in and familiarize ourselves with an area before we get yanked out to somewhere else?* He was having flashbacks to the Army. In, out, done, on to the next target. All without knowing all that much about the target, the area, or what their hit had actually accomplished. It hadn't been what Special Forces was supposed to be doing, but there was too much work, sometimes.

He hadn't minded while he'd been in. Door kicking was fun. As he'd gotten older, and moved into jobs where he got to see a bit more of how the sausage was made, though, he'd started to wonder. Wonder if it wasn't better to take it slow and careful, learning everything possible and therefore quietly getting into position to score a devastating blow before the enemy even knew what was going on.

While he'd never worked with the guy called Goblin, he'd heard some good things. Now, though, he was starting to wonder.

The office building that housed KNS Industries' headquarters looked like just about every other brick business park in Northern Virginia. The glass was smoked, there might have been lettering on the door, but there was otherwise no signage, and only two vehicles in the parking lot. That made surveillance a little more complicated, but only a little. There were enough corporate vans and cars parked semi-permanently in the parking lot set within the extended, slightly lopsided U-shape of the business park that one more wouldn't attract a lot of attention. Especially since they'd parked well away from both the entrance and the streetlights.

"Somebody's working late." Matt checked his watch as another car rolled past them and onto Braddock Road. The lights in the KNS office were still on, even as the parking lot steadily emptied.

"So much the better." Nick took another sip of his Red Bull. It wasn't his favorite energy drink, but it beat Monster in his opinion, and he wasn't willing to go back to dipping. "He won't get lost in the crowd."

"Maybe. Make it harder for us to get lost in the crowd, though." Matt tapped his fingers against the door. Unlike Nick, he hadn't given up tobacco, but he'd never been a dipper, either. He tended more toward chain-smoking, but wasn't going to do that in the car, not when they couldn't roll the windows down. Since they were trying to keep a low profile, a glowing cigarette ember and open windows venting smoke wouldn't look like an innocent parked car.

"Compromises." Nick shrugged.

The truth was, as mildly irritated at all the running around as he was, this was still better than his last couple of jobs. He'd quit working for the secret squirrels overseas only to take a training gig with the State Department, which had been considerably less than ideal. At least now he was back on the street, doing stuff that he'd never been *allowed* to do before, capabilities be damned.

The evening seemed to drag on, though when he checked his watch again, as yet another sedan rolled out, heading home for a Friday night, it had only been about twenty more minutes.

"Here he comes." Matt shifted in his seat, sitting up a little more. Sure enough, the lights in the KNS Industries office had gone out, and a man in business casual was coming down the steps, heading for a white Audi parked just outside.

Nick couldn't see the man's face all that well in the evening dimness, but the clothes, height, and build were right, as was the vehicle. Cooper was heading home for the night.

The next few minutes were probably going to be the most difficult. They had been sitting there, parked, for about five hours, and neither of them could exactly get out and stroll out of a nearby office as if they belonged there, and were just going home. So, they'd have to time their departure after Cooper right, so that he didn't notice that he was being followed.

Of course, they were in Alexandria, and Cooper had shown no particular concern about security so far. He hadn't even looked around as he walked to his car. If he was aware of his surroundings, it seemed to only be in the vaguest way. Far from the crime of Atlanta, he probably thought he was as secure as he could get. Especially with KNS Industries being as low-profile as it was.

Nick hoped he was that complacent. It would make the evening's activities that much easier.

Cooper didn't hang out in the car for very long. It seemed that he was in a hurry, now that his business in the office was done, so he quickly put the car in gear, backed out of his parking spot, and sped out of the lot, turning left on Braddock and accelerating toward the Little River Turnpike.

Nick quickly started the car and went after him. Cooper was moving fast, and they didn't want to lose him. There was a lot they could find out online, and a lot that they *had* found out about him. His social media was remarkably open for someone potentially involved in such shady dealings. He clearly wanted to be a mover and a shaker, constantly posting pictures of himself in high-end "insider" bars and eateries across Washington DC, Georgetown, and Alexandria.

The trouble was, they didn't know which snooty watering hole was going to be his stop for the night. Several other pairs of the B Team were scattered at some of the bars he'd posted pictures of—usually from a Friday night—but if they'd miscalculated, they could spend weeks trying to intercept him. That was why Nick and Matt were on him, provided Nick could maintain contact without getting burned.

He took the turn onto Braddock just in time to see Cooper turn east on Little River. He decided to take the risk, flooring the accelerator to make sure he got through the light before it turned red.

The next twenty minutes, however, went fairly smoothly. It quickly became evident that Cooper wasn't even remotely worried about being followed. He didn't do anything that might constitute surveillance detection or counter surveillance. In fact, after a few minutes, Matt checked his map and made a prediction. "He's going to Georgetown."

"Sure looks that way." Nick checked his blind spot and then merged to the right, heading for the exit ramp off the 395 toward VA-27/Washington Boulevard. He was two cars back from Cooper's, giving them some concealment, but he could still see the white sedan well enough not to lose it. If Cooper went into the tighter streets of Georgetown, he might still give them the slip, but there were a limited number of places he might go there. They could *probably* pick him up again.

Matt was already sending out messages to the rest of the team, tightening the net around Georgetown. It would take some of them a while to get there; Washington DC traffic is a nightmare at the best of times, and Friday evening was not what any of them would consider the "best of times." But even if Nick lost contact, they'd find him.

Yet while it came close a couple of times, traffic was such that Nick was able to keep close behind Cooper all the way to the parking lot beneath the monolithic brick edifice of The Graham, a seven-story hotel in Georgetown. Nick drove past as Cooper turned into the garage. There was no parking currently open on the one-way street, but parking right on site was probably a bad idea, anyway. They knew where Cooper was stopping.

"Looks like it's The Rooftop." Matt was already disseminating the information to the others. "Unless he somehow magically decided to flip the script and get wise right here, after driving in the white for the last half hour." Matt was referring to the Cooper Color Code, where "white" stood for completely oblivious to one's surroundings.

"Let's hope not." Nick took the next turn, grateful to see that the concrete jersey barriers that blocked off any parking on the sides of M Street stopped at the intersection, and there was an open space on the right just about twenty yards from the corner. "That would mean I had to drive in Georgetown for nothing."

He parked while Matt grudgingly shed and stowed his handgun, knives, blowout kit, and radio. With the gear carefully concealed, he looked over at Nick. "You sure you don't want to do this? You're the social butterfly here."

Nick grinned. "Driver drives, brother." When Matt grimaced and turned toward the door, he clapped his partner on the shoulder. "Look at it as an opportunity for personal growth."

Matt shook his head with the expression of a man condemned. "Don't worry, I'll get even. Eventually." Without another word, he was out of the vehicle, shutting the door firmly, but with the attitude that he would much rather have just slammed it.

Nick grinned. Matt didn't seem to be the most social of men, which was kind of funny when he considered that the other contractor had also been a Green Beret. Special Forces was supposed to engage with the locals, requiring a certain degree of people skills. Of course, Nick himself had seen—and had fallen prey to—the tendency over the last twenty years for everyone in SOF to want to be a door-kicker, at the expense of the rest of their primary skillsets. He wasn't putting that on Matt—he didn't know the man well enough—but it was a common enough problem.

He locked the doors out of habit as Matt headed toward the corner and the bar and settled in for a long wait.

***

It ended up only taking about two hours. The Rooftop at the Graham advertised itself as a place to "See and Be Seen," a networking bar for the connected and would-be connected in Georgetown and the Beltway. It had a dress code, but was first come, first served, so there were no reservations necessary, which was a good thing for the night's op.

What it wasn't was a dive where people went to get drunk, which made it that much more surprising when Matt came around the corner just after nine, supporting a clearly inebriated Cooper. The man looked like he could barely stand up.

Nick checked the mirrors and carefully scanned their surroundings, but no one seemed to be taking any undue interest in them. Just somebody who hadn't been able to hold their liquor. A little early for a Friday night, and pretty uncouth for this part of Georgetown, but nothing especially sinister. Just distasteful.

He unlocked the doors as Matt reached the car and opened the back. "Come on, man. We'll get you home. Cheaper than a cab." He levered Cooper into the back seat and got him buckled in. The financier mumbled something incoherent, but he didn't seem to be fighting, or even all that conscious that he was in a car with two strangers.

Matt got in the front, flashing what looked like a keycard and a keychain as he sat down. Nick nodded fractionally. Success.

So far, anyway.

"Who's this guy?" He had to play the part, just in case Cooper remembered much of this ride the next morning.

"This is Simon," Matt explained. "Met him in the bar. He's had a rough day, got a little carried away with the booze. I had to give him a hand just to get out. The staff wasn't that happy." From the way Matt said it, it sounded like he hadn't even needed the little extra that had been planned. It had been pretty simple. Get him drinking, then add extra alcohol to the drink, getting him hammered before he realized it. There were quicker ways, but those would involve carrying drugs that could cause issues if they were found. "He can't drive, so I offered to get him home." That *had* been part of the plan.

"Where are we taking him?" Nick managed to sound as long-suffering as he could. His was the tone of a man who was used to toting his drunk friend around, though he was getting tired of it.

Truth be told, it was probably more of an act than was necessary, given how obviously far gone Cooper was.

Matt relayed the address as Cooper mumbled it, and Nick found himself hoping that it didn't get so garbled that they were stuck with the guy for the whole night. They had a lot of work to do before sunrise, and they needed to drop Cooper off and get to it.

Fortunately, it wasn't *that* complicated. Cooper lived in a townhouse in Arlington, not that far across the river. They got him to the place easily enough, fortunately without him puking in the car. He did pass out at least once on the way, though, and was still unconscious when Nick pulled up outside the two-story brick building.

Matt sort of woke him up and helped him out of the back seat. From there it was a trek to the door, only for Cooper to discover he couldn't find his keys.

Nick watched the little drama play out in pantomime from the car. Their target still had his phone, so, with Matt's urging, he got it out and tried to call someone who might be able to let him in. He was going to have a hell of a time sorting his life out in the morning.

Of course, he was too drunk to figure out the phone, so Matt helpfully gave him a hand. Hopefully, he had the opportunity to install the keylogger onto the phone. One of PGS's cyber people already had the link all set up, so it shouldn't have been difficult. Still, one never knew when dealing with a drunk, and it's always harder to execute on the ground than it sounds like it will be in planning.

Finally, someone came down to let Cooper in, and Matt waved goodbye as he headed back to the car.

"You owe me, dude." He started rummaging under the seat to pull out his weapons and gear as Nick pulled away from the curb.

"It can't have been that bad. Hell, ten years ago you would have been drinking chai with some Afghan elder while his dancing boy cowered in the corner." Nick turned toward N Glebe Road, intending to get back to the 395 and from there to Alexandria.

Matt was silent for a long moment. "You know, when you put it that way, I don't have an answer to that. And I kind of hate you for it."

"Seriously, how did it go?" They may as well do some kind of debrief while they were still in the car.

"Well, I never want to be that surrounded by shallow narcissists ever again." Matt finally finished securing his reloads and settled back in the seat. "That place is a nest of the most disgustingly arrogant, worthless pieces of shit I've ever seen. And that *includes* on contract."

"Damn. Glad I didn't go in." Nick kept his eyes on the road and ignored Matt's glare. "He got pretty hammered. How many shots did you slip him?"

"Believe it or not, none. He was already going strong by the time I found him. I didn't even really have to chat him up much." Matt was visibly grateful for that fact. "He got really talkative as he got drunker, too, which got me some interesting info. Seems like his bosses aren't happy that Strand got out of Atlanta. He wasn't *quite* drunk enough to admit to hiring MS-13 thugs, at least not before he got incoherent, but he came awfully close. He's worried about something, and I think that cartel connection that the briefing mentioned probably has something to do with it."

"Probably has everything to do with it." Nick merged onto the 395 and sped up, heading west. "I know *I* sure wouldn't want those psychos after me if I was in his shoes." He thought it over as he drove. "Once he wakes up—and gets over the hangover—he's gonna be pretty panicked about losing his keys and his keycard."

"Not just the keycard." Matt held up their target's keychain. There was something that looked like a thumb drive dangling from the ring. "Looks like KNS is using YubiKeys for smart card access. This should get us into the computer without any hassle. We can get in, install the keylogger, and get out in a few minutes."

"Let's hope." Nick wasn't nearly that optimistic, but that came from a *long* career, and the accompanying observation that nothing ever went entirely according to plan. This op had already gone far more smoothly than he'd had any business expecting it to.

***

The parking lot was mostly empty when they pulled back in, once again parking some distance away from the target building. This time they both got out, though they walked nonchalantly toward the building, with just enough haste to suggest that they'd forgotten something at the office and needed to get it before they could go home.

At least, that was the impression Nick *hoped* they'd leave, if anyone was watching, either physically or over security camera feeds. Once again, it felt like maybe they were

155

overselling the act. They didn't have any indicators that their presence in Alexandria was even suspected.

No one had reacted by the time they reached the steps leading up to the KNS offices. Trotting up, Nick had to resist the urge to draw his Glock and hold security. They were conducting a break in, but the only way they were going to get away with it was by acting like they weren't.

Matt swiped Cooper's keycard against the pad next to the door, and it opened with a *click*. Matt pulled it the rest of the way open, and they went in fast, keeping their hands close to their pistols, just in case.

The office was dark and quiet. A couple of computers still hummed, but there was no one there, at least at first glance and listen.

Both men paused just inside as the door shut behind them. It was a version of the old patrolling SLLS that they'd both practiced in the Army: Stop, Look, Listen, and Smell. If there *was* one more KNS employee working even later, somewhere in the back, this could get ugly, fast.

Nothing. Silence, darkness, and the faint smell of industrial cleaning products. Just a typical finance office on a Friday night.

Except that they were pretty sure that this "typical finance office" was helping cartels, at the very least.

They threaded their way carefully between the cubicles in the back, looking for a particular desk. Nick had been afraid that maybe KNS wouldn't use nameplates, but the shady part of the business was all in the numbers and files. To all outward appearances, they were still ordinary office workers.

He found the plate "Simon Cooper" on one of three actual offices at the back. With Matt in the lead, they both slipped inside, Nick turning to hold security on the rest of the building while Matt got to work.

"Easy day." Matt might have been a Green Beanie by profession, but he and Nick had gotten the main effort assignment for tonight because he'd always had a bit of a side interest in computers. Given their profession, that interest had led him down some avenues that under different circumstances might have had the FBI knocking on his door. As it was, it still might, if they weren't careful.

Matt slid Cooper's YubiKey into a USB port in the computer, waiting until it unlocked before he inserted the next little surprise, a tiny thumb drive that looked entirely innocuous.

Nick didn't watch. There was nothing to see, anyway. He just kept his eyes and his ears open while Matt did his cyber ninja bit. It took about two minutes. Finally, Matt pulled both the drive and the YubiKey and moved to join him at the door. "Done. Let's get out of here. We can still get back to Georgetown and toss his keys and keycard in the gutter." That had been brought up in planning as a way to make sure it looked to Cooper as if he'd simply lost his stuff while drunk.

They headed out, carefully exiting and walking quickly but casually back to the car. Mission accomplished.

Nick just hoped that it turned out to be worth the risk.

CHAPTER
20

The first week back in Dallas was quiet. By that, I mean we didn't take contact. They weren't exactly uneventful.

Strand was on the warpath, in the way that only he could be, and that meant three or four meetings a day, most of them somewhere out in town. That meant we were hopping to keep him covered, complete with a backup vehicle and a Quick Reaction Force. *Especially* since Rob and Jake weren't back from disposing of the F550 we'd used on the MS-13 hit yet. They were driving back from Missouri, and they seemed to be taking their time.

What really had us running our asses off, though, was the extra intel requirements we now had to fill.

We knew that Strand was a target. We had a pretty good idea of who the players were. Unfortunately, with only so many of us on the ground—PGS wasn't a huge company yet—we had a limited number of areas we could cover.

That was what had Drew and I out on the street, looking for one of those potential players. Of course, since it was Dallas, a city of over one point three *million* people, looking for this one guy was like searching for a needle in a haystack.

Fortunately, we had a phone number. We didn't know for *sure* that this guy was connected with the bad guys, but who else would call an MS-13 *marero*—a dead one, but he hadn't known that—and leave a short, angry message in Spanish demanding a callback?

If we'd had a Stingray, or any one of several cell phone spoofers, we might have tracked the phone physically. Those were tools for law enforcement and spooks, though, and the companies that made them weren't going to sell them to a private security company, no matter what kind of connections Goblin had. I mean, I'm sure if he'd dug deep enough and pushed enough, he might have pulled it off, but those things had drawbacks, too. They tended to disrupt cell phone service, which could very well alert someone that there was somebody trying to run cell phone surveillance. Even if he didn't know that he was the target, that might spook him.

Fortunately, there are all kinds of spooky OSINT tools out there to enable people like us to find someone. Most of them open and commercially available.

A couple of searches of that phone number turned up a name, several social media accounts, several more photos, and even a current residential address. From there, the intel guys started in with their extrapolations, pinpointing locations of photos, working up patterns of movement, all sorts of things that had me wondering just how Goblin was paying them. There was a *lot* of work involved in the target package that KG had handed us. Maybe he had them chained up in a basement somewhere.

At any rate, that digital dragnet had narrowed our search zone down to South Dallas. Miguel Ochoa might eschew a lot of the *cholo* lifestyle, but there was just enough in his social media history to make him a target, in addition to the phone call to Garcia. He tended toward cowboy hats, flashy collared shirts, and cowboy boots, which wasn't out of place in Texas—unless you were in Dallas. Or worse, Austin. It was also, notably, a common style among northern Mexican cartels. Particularly Sinaloa.

Again, it wasn't a smoking gun, but it was an indicator. Put together with everything else we'd found out about him, and it amounted to enough circumstantial evidence to go looking for him.

What we hadn't quite counted on, though, was that he might be looking for us.

Not necessarily for Drew and me, specifically. But whoever Ochoa was working for or with, they understood that something had gone badly wrong in Atlanta, and they knew that Strand was back in Dallas. So, they were on alert.

Drew spotted them first. I was driving, trying to stay in the general neighborhood where our OSINT guys had figured Ochoa tended to hang out while trying not to make it look like we were casing the place. The odds that people in this part of South Dallas were going to call the cops were pretty slim, though not nonexistent. Dallas still had many of the problems that a lot of major cities did, though there hadn't been the concentrated push against the cops that had hamstrung Atlanta PD. It might be a big city, but it *was* still Texas.

"Black sedan, one o'clock." Drew nodded toward the indicated car, which had just pulled over to the curb ahead of us. I'd seen it in the rear-view mirror as it had closed in from behind, but I hadn't gotten a great look at it as I'd pulled up in front of the next house for rent. There weren't a lot of them in that area, and while they were dirt cheap, relatively speaking, they were still horrifically expensive compared to a few years ago. They'd presented us an opportunity to scope the place out and look for Ochoa, though, pretending to be a couple of bachelors looking for a place to crash. Still slightly sketchy, since neither of us were going to pass for college kids, but it was about the best we could think of.

I followed his gaze. The Ford Taurus wasn't that new, but it wasn't that old, either. There were no readily identifying marks on it, no bumper stickers or any of the flashy rims or decoration that some gangbangers and drug dealers liked to add, but the windows were deeply tinted. "What have you got? I saw the car, but not who was in it."

"Two military-age males." Even after all this time, we still defaulted to that designation, often shortened to "MAMs." The military had tried to stop using it well over a decade before, but everyone who'd served in Iraq and Afghanistan still went with it anyway. "They both mean-mugged the hell out of us as they went past. They're watching us."

"That's no bueno." I was trying to watch them without staring straight at the car. Our windows *weren't* tinted, so that made it a little harder to hide. Plus, we'd just pulled up in front of the house we were supposed to be looking at, and the landlord was going to be there any minute. Just sitting there was going to look off. "Wonder what got them looking at us?"

"Maybe they're just watching for anybody who doesn't quite belong. Maybe Ochoa upped security after Garcia went dark." He shrugged. "Maybe they think we look like undercover cops."

I snorted. "We've got way more firepower in this car than any cops would." That might be debatable, actually, since we were rolling with our usual pistols on body and carbines in the back, covered over, but I'd almost be willing to bet that we had more ammo than your average cop.

I glanced in the rear-view mirror. Our six o'clock appeared to be clear for the moment, but if these guys wanted trouble, there was no telling how long that was going to last. If there were enough bad guys in this neighborhood, this could turn into a massive dogpile in minutes if it went sideways. "Landlord's supposed to be here in five minutes. What do you want to do?"

Drew thought about it while he watched the black sedan. The car hadn't moved, but I could see the dim shape of a face in the side mirror. The driver was watching us.

"I'd almost say that we need to either just pull off or get out and see if there's a reaction now, before the landlord gets here and gets caught in the crossfire." He was already getting ready to get out, making sure he could get to his Glock quickly.

I wasn't sure if that was wise, though. "I think we call the landlord and reschedule while we drive away." It wasn't that I was opposed to popping a couple more gangbangers, but that wasn't the mission. The mission was surveillance, and if we'd been made, we needed to get the hell out of Dodge.

For a second, Drew looked like he was going to argue the point. I could kind of see his thought process. Probing these guys might tell us something. On the other hand, it might not. Getting into a fight with unknowns would only draw more attention, and there was no certainty that these guys were Ochoa's.

Finally, though, he settled back in his seat and reached for his phone with a sigh. "I'll call him. Guess we need to get somebody else in here to find our boy."

That could present some difficulties. We were perhaps better at playing the gray man than we had been on previous jobs, but it's still awfully hard to infiltrate a place like this if you don't belong. We might be able to play out the renter angle, but something about that car had my hackles up.

I pulled us away from the curb and took the next right turn, intending to head back toward I-45. Yet as I did so, the black sedan pulled a U-turn and followed us.

"Shit." So much for getting out of the neighborhood and disappearing. This just got far more complicated.

It was still possible that they were just going a similar direction. I was already adjusting my route in my head, glancing at the phone's map on the dashboard in front of me as I did so. A much more roundabout way back to the hotel where Strand's company had put us up was now called for. If they followed us more than a few turns, however…

Then things would really get interesting.

I turned aside from the entrance onto I-45 somewhat abruptly and headed back into the residential areas of South

Dallas. The black sedan stuck with us, and by the time I turned onto Highway 175, I had no doubts left. They were definitely following us. And neither one of us had any illusions that they were doing so with any sort of benign intent.

Drew could call the cops. We *might* get some uncomfortable questions about the weapons and gear in the car, but then again, it *was* still Texas. Getting the cops involved might scare these guys off and allow us to break contact cleanly.

On the other hand, it might not. They might back off, only to find a way to catch up with us later. I'd seen that happen. Hell, I'd done it while red teaming on a small training contract a while back.

So, that left a couple of different options. If we didn't want to go right to the cops—who might be able to protect us in the short term, but not in the long term—then we'd either have to get really inventive to lose these clowns, or we'd have to force a confrontation, and break contact the hard way.

If we'd been driving a purpose-built vehicle with a racing engine, we might have done the former easily. The Santa Fe I was driving, however, wasn't going to outrun a VW Beetle, never mind the Taurus that was following us. It was a decent all-around vehicle, but it wasn't a getaway car. It didn't have the power, speed, or agility.

That left forcing a confrontation. I wasn't looking forward to that. It was going to be dicey, and we were going to end up with bullet holes in the car—and quite possibly one of us—if we didn't handle this very carefully.

Drew was already on the phone. "Hey, Ziggy, it's Smokestack. We've got a tail, and they're getting more aggressive." He wasn't kidding, either. The Taurus had closed in on us to the point they were tailgating us now, and the driver had a pistol in the hand he had draped over the steering wheel. The threat was pretty damned clear. "We're going to need a hand."

He listened for a moment. I had actually sunk down a little in my seat, not that any part of the SUV behind me was going to make for good cover. It was more instinctual than thought through, but for the moment, the bad guys were holding their fire. The guy in the passenger seat was messing with something below the dash. I couldn't see what it was, but I expected it was a long gun of some sort.

Drew was now fiddling with my mapping software. "We need to head for Great Trinity Forest. It's on our way, and there are a bunch of places back in there where we can disappear, at least for a few minutes. That's where Phil and Marcos are heading."

A glance at the map told me that I didn't have long to turn off if we were going to do that. I wrenched the wheel over and took the ramp a few seconds later, braking just enough to keep from rolling the Santa Fe as I went around the curve, keeping left to head down Tune Avenue—which was a cracked, potholed one-lane road, not what I'd call an "avenue" and into the trees.

Bad call. We'd barely gotten a couple of car lengths in when I saw the closed and padlocked gate right in front of us. We weren't getting into the woods that way.

Unfortunately, that Taurus was right on our rear bumper. Things were about to get ugly.

Without slowing down much, I threw the SUV around the corner, heading for the wrecking yard just off the highway, then braked, hard.

There wasn't the room—and the Santa Fe didn't have the agility—to pull a full one-eighty, which would have put the engine block between us and the bad guys. That would have been about all the cover that vehicle was worth. Without it, though, I just braked, threw open the door and dove out into the junk, weeds, and trees on the side of the road, drawing my Glock 19 as I went.

I hit hard and out of position. Action movies to the contrary, trying to leap and manipulate a weapon generally don't go together, and if you're in active combat, it's that much worse. I rolled to my back, pivoting with my feet as I desperately tried to get my muzzle on the bad guys before I got shot to pieces.

The driver was already getting out, swinging around the door with that big, chrome Smith in his hand. I got a good look at him as I brought my sights to my eye. The baggy black jeans and equally baggy white t-shirt were topped by a scrawny neck and a very young face beneath close-cropped black hair. He had a little bit of a chin scruff, but that was it.

I shot him a split second before he could bring that 5906 to bear on me. His eyes widened for a second as my first hollow-point smashed through his guts just beneath his sternum, immediately staining the white shirt red. I walked the next three shots up into his throat and face, just as fast as the trigger would reset. The last shot took him just above the mouth as his knees started to buckle, snapping his head back and spattering the side of the car with droplets of red as he collapsed.

My ears were ringing—there hadn't been time for earpro—but I heard another shot from the other side of the Santa Fe. "Smokestack! You good?" I was already levering myself to my feet, my pistol still pointed at the dead *marero*.

"I'm good." Drew hadn't even gotten out of the vehicle. He'd already turned around as I'd started to brake, and he'd just cracked his door and stuck his Glock out through the opening. "Let's get the hell out of here before somebody shows up and starts asking questions."

CHAPTER
21

We got back more than half expecting an APB to be out for whoever smoked two *Mara Salvatrucha* goons just outside a wrecking yard, but when we walked into KG's suite in the Renaissance Dallas Hotel, the scanner hadn't even picked up any calls about the gunshots. The cops in Texas were getting harder and harder on the cartels and their proxies, but it was a big area to cover, and we hadn't exactly been downtown or in the middle of a residential area. It would take time for the car and the bodies to be found. Presuming the cartel didn't have a follow-up that would remove them first.

"Bad luck." KG wasn't shook up about it, even though we'd left two bodies on the ground. I was probably more bothered by what had happened. Killing generally didn't fall into the reconnaissance and surveillance realm. It can come *after* but, if it happens when you're supposed to be snooping, it tends to be counterproductive. "I think we can lay off Ochoa, though. We're working on some other avenues to maybe put the Dallas PD on him, but he's off *our* target list for the moment."

I frowned, folding my arms. "When did this happen? I only ask because it would have been nice to know this before we killed a couple dudes and potentially put more of a bullseye on our backs."

For a moment, KG just looked at me, and I wondered if I'd overstepped. He'd been a pretty good boss so far, but I still hadn't known him more than a little over a month.

He nodded, though. "That's fair. You can rest assured, though, that we just got this info in the latest dump from Goblin's cyber ninjas about forty-five minutes ago. I would have called you back as soon as we knew, provided you could have gotten clear." He tilted his head and studied me for a second. He could tell something was eating at me. "Look, brother, I've been there. Got blown out of an urban hide in Fallujah back in the day, then damn near got arrested in Baghdad, ten years later. It happens. Sometimes Murphy just brings the hammer down and you get spotted, no matter how good you are." He shrugged. "We didn't know that Ochoa was so nervous he'd have *halcones* out watching the streets. It gets hard to sneak up on a jumpy bad guy." He beckoned us toward his desk and the bank of laptops and radios strewn across it. "Come on. I'll show you *why* he's so jumpy."

We moved to join him at the desk, each of us leaning over one shoulder. He brought up a folder and started opening text documents that were clearly emails. "So, that keylogger that Croak and Toe-Tag put on Cooper's computer has been worth its weight in gold. I won't go through all of them, but I've got 'em if you want to read 'em.

"Short version is that KNS has been taking orders directly from Devon Archer himself. He's been a little careful, never saying anything outright, but he was clearly pissed that the hit on Strand failed. He spent an entire email just to cuss Cooper out for letting Strand out of Atlanta. Now, it doesn't look like Cooper or anyone else at KNS had anything to do with actually putting those *Mara Salvatrucha* goons on us, not directly. *However*, they *were* tasked with essentially buying as much information from the Atlanta PD and passing it along to Archer as possible. And it seems that they failed, or else they just didn't move fast enough. Again, there's a lot that's either vague or in code, but it sounds like Archer was passing that information on to someone else, who was passing it on to the *mareros*."

"So, the cops knew where we were, because of the shooting at the Hyatt." I was putting some of the pieces together in my head. "KNS had already established a 'special relationship' with the Chief and the DA and wheedled that information out of them. That got passed to Archer—the son of a long-sitting *US Senator*—who then passed it on to Garcia and his local MS-13 franchise?"

"That appears to be the short version." KG brought up another email. "There's quite a bit more to the long version, however." He pointed at the screen.

This whole situation is fucked. If we don't fix this, then we're not only going to be out a LOT of money, but the whole operation's going to come down like a house of fucking cards. There are some VERY dangerous people who are getting pissed that this is taking so long, and they want to just step in and finish it. I'm telling them—and so is Deng—that it's going to work out better in the long-term if we can do this with money more than violence. But they're getting impatient, and I don't think I need to tell you what happens when Lopez gets impatient.

"There are several like that. Archer, it seems, tends to repeat himself a lot. From what little has made it into the media about his drug use, that probably shouldn't be that surprising." KG switched to yet another.

Strand is back in Dallas. You fucked this up. Shut everything down, erase everything, and get back here. Unfortunately, but fortunately for you, Lin has some use for you. This is going to have to move fast, so make sure all the ducks are in a row. We need a full liquidation of half the shell companies by tomorrow night. Lopez thinks that Strand is going to get the money to shore up the Bowmans enough that they'll be able to hold on and replace the losses they've already taken. His people are going to dial up the pressure now. This buyout HAS to happen.

I straightened up. "Well, that might be determined to be somewhat circumstantial in court, but damn. That sure looks like a smoking gun to me."

"You're right, though it won't necessarily look that way to a judge or jury, especially once Archer's lawyers get involved." KG tossed a pen onto the desk as he leaned back in his chair with a creak. "And of course, *Archer*'s lawyers really means 'his daddy's lawyers.'" He looked like he wanted to spit. "Who's going to stand up to the army of litigators that *Senator* Archer can bring to bear? Hell, forget the lawyers. Just the name and position alone might be enough to torpedo any criminal case."

"That's awfully cynical." Drew turned and leaned against the desk with his arms folded.

KG rolled his eyes at him. "You've been in this business how long, and you're not a jaded cynic yet?" He glanced at me. "I didn't know your partner was such an innocent, Backwoods."

"He's not." I shook my head. "He's just looking for any reason not to completely lose faith here."

KG turned to Drew. "Oh, my sweet summer child. If it was local, it might be one thing. If it was *any* other private equity firm, even. But a senior Senator's boy?" He laughed without humor. "Not a chance. The record's there for anybody to look at."

"So, what, then?" Drew wasn't happy. "That leaves us with only two options. We shrug, say, 'Well, I guess that's the way it goes,' and let this happen—whatever 'this' is, which seems to involve paid hits by gangsters at least—or else we go all the way rogue and start assassinating people." He shook his head. "There's got to be a middle ground somewhere."

With a faint, almost sad smile, KG reached over and gripped his shoulder. "And if it's there, we're gonna find it.

Trust me. Goblin didn't build this company just to throw it right into the meat grinder against the Federal government. Not to mention whoever else is behind this. Did you catch that reference to 'Deng?' That looks an awful lot like a Chinese name, and it's not one currently associated with Archer-Lin Investments."

"So, what are we going to do, then?"

With a deep breath, KG folded his arms across his broad chest. "Well, much like Atlanta, we're going to quietly push the envelope while testing the waters. Goblin's got people putting these emails together into a series of leaks that will end up on an FBI desk within the next few days. Whether they go anywhere or not remains to be seen, but we'll adjust our course of action depending on what the Feds do about this. Again, it might not be a smoking gun, but it should be sufficient evidence to start an investigation. It definitely looks like Archer-Lin is partnering with criminal elements to force a buyout. Leveraged buyouts might be usually unethical, but this is downright illegal, if we can connect Archer-Lin to actual violent crime…"

I breathed a sigh. "And if the FBI comes after us, instead?"

He cocked an eyebrow. "Well, then we'll have to react accordingly."

With that thoroughly unsatisfying answer, he shifted gears. "Okay, so. Strand has one more meeting here, and then we're leaving Dallas for a while. Unfortunately, it's a pretty big meeting, and fairly public, so security's going to be rough. We're going to need the whole team."

"What about the B Team?" Drew asked.

"They're moving on ahead." KG grinned tightly. "Strand's already set up a trust to pay for site security for the Bowman ranch. One team might not be enough, but it should be enough to keep an eye on the place and hopefully deter any further violent attacks, at least for a while." He pointed at the computer in front of him. "I had a talk with Strand and Goblin, and we agreed that the talk about 'pressure' probably meant that things were going to get nasty down in New Mexico pretty soon."

"So, we get to keep doing the whole close protection thing in the meantime."

KG's grin was not promising. "Oh, yes. And you're gonna *love* it."

CHAPTER
22

Nick squinted into the sun as he got out of the truck. It was almost sunset, which meant they'd been driving into that sun for the last two hours, coming from Las Cruces.

"Great. The desert again." He spat in the dirt under a creosote bush. He'd spent a grand total of probably six years or more in Iraq or various hellholes in North Africa. He was sick of the desert. That was a large part of why he'd signed on with PGS. It was *Stateside* work.

"Shoulda thought of that before you went looking for a job that might get you into the action again." Matt was pulling the bags out of the back of the F150. The canopy had kept most of the dust off on the way in, but "most" still didn't mean "all." "The action Stateside ain't up north. Ain't in the nice places. It's in the shithole cities or down here on the border."

Nick shook his head and joined his partner, pulling his own bag out alongside him. The rifles were still up in the cab, though they'd had to stop on the side of the road after they'd picked up the vehicles to go hot. Not that Texas—they'd flown into El Paso, then driven across into New Mexico—was all that squeamish about guns, but loading up rifles in the middle of the city was generally frowned upon, even so close to Cuidad Juarez.

Some people just don't recognize the reality of their situation. And refuse to as long as it's happening somewhere else, to someone else.

"Should have taken that Ukraine gig." He heaved the bag over his shoulder and started toward the ranch house.

Matt laughed as he joined him. "No, you shouldn't have, and you know it. That was sketchy as fuck. If you hadn't gotten rolled up—especially since I'm pretty sure you speak as much Ukrainian and Russian as I do—then you'd have eventually gotten sent to the front and turned into a pile of mush under Russian artillery."

"I speak some Russian. Tenth Group *was* supposed to be the European Group, you know."

Matt snorted. "And we were deploying to the Middle East and Horn of Africa for forty years. Your Russian was hobby learning, not pipeline."

Nick had to concede the point. "Still. Why'd it have to be the desert again?"

Saul and Mike were waiting for them at the house. "I'll take the desert over that East Coast humidity any day of the week," Mike said, squatting on his haunches by the porch. He squinted up at the sky. It was still too early for any stars, though the sun would be setting shortly. The distant hills were purple against the sky. "Besides, this kinda reminds me of the old days."

Saul looked down at him with a heavy-lidded, long suffering look. "That's because you just got vacation deployments to Mexico, youngster."

Mike winced a little at that. He was probably the youngest guy on the team, if not in the entire company, at least the youngest operator. It was something he was still trying to live down. Not that he ever would. His callsign was Hoop, but Manny was pushing hard to get it changed to Baby Driver. Most of the rest of the team was starting to come around. Except, of course, for Mike.

"Hey, it was still dangerous." He got a little defensive about those "vacation deployments," too. "The cartels would have *loved* to get their hands on an NSW guy."

"Probably just to hire him." Casey had never disguised his general dislike of SEALs, and he tended to let it spill over whenever the subject came up, even when it wasn't really called for. "Come on. We're not just here to hang out. Work starts now. Casper's got the rotation up on the board in the living room." He grinned like a skull. "George is already bitching about the fact that we're gonna have to live in tents or the barn."

"I know." Saul heaved himself away from the post he'd been leaning against. "That's why I'm out here."

"Well, the sooner y'all get in here, the sooner the brief can start, and he'll have to shut up." Casey turned and led the way into the house.

The ranch house wasn't large. In fact, as Nick looked around, he couldn't see much of anything to suggest why Strand and PGS had taken such an interest in the place. It looked like just about any other small ranch or farm he'd ever been around. Nick himself was a bit of a city boy, though he generally tried to keep that to himself and did his best to be as much an outdoorsman as he could. He just didn't know shit about agriculture, so all these places looked the same to him.

Of course, the positioning was something. They were out in the middle of nowhere, but the Mexican border was only about three and a half miles away. He could see the cartels causing some trouble. That still didn't explain the company's interest. Maybe Strand's detail had gotten that brief, but this team hadn't yet.

The inside of the ranch house wasn't much more impressive. It was a wonder that the Bowmans hadn't gone ahead and sold out already, he thought as he looked around. With the amount of money they were apparently being offered, they could upgrade in a big way. Bigger house, probably more land, bigger and newer vehicles.

Maybe it wasn't about the money, though.

Frank was waiting inside next to a whiteboard propped up against the Bowmans' slightly threadbare couch. His chicken-scratch writing in fading dry erase marker was pretty small, but that was because there was apparently a lot of information to pass.

"We got everybody?" Frank looked around the room. It was getting crowded, with ten shooters and at least some of their gear. The family and the handful of remaining ranch hands had, for the most part, retreated to the kitchen and the dining room.

"Looks like it." They weren't in the military anymore, so there wasn't really a hierarchy as such, every man being a contractor, but Saul often sort of took lead. He was quiet, but he was that kind of guy.

"Okay." Frank rubbed his hands together. "Got a lot to go over, and we need to get the first patrol out quick, so listen up and hold all questions till the end."

Nick listened with growing interest as Frank laid out the situation as Pallas Group Solutions understood it so far. The targeted attacks on the Bowmans, many coming after the initial offer to buy the ranch out, and then the thinly veiled suggestion in a follow-on offer that the attacks would only get worse if they didn't sell. That alone had been enough to get Strand interested, and the assault on his meeting in Atlanta had kicked things into higher gear.

"Now, because of that implied elevated threat, we're going to be hanging out here for the next few weeks or so, to help secure the Bowmans and their property. I don't need to tell you that we're looking at a hell of a dangerous environment around here. The border's right over there, and this isn't Arizona or Texas, where we can expect the authorities to lend a certain degree of backup, if they won't just look the other way while we take care of it. New Mexico is a shithole of a state, and we can expect Santa Fe to screw us at the drop of a hat." He looked around the room, making eye contact with each man in turn. "Just so that's clear, we could find ourselves in a combat situation at any time, but we're still going to have to make damned good and sure that every shoot is justified, and we know exactly where every bullet goes."

"So, just like Iraq and Afghanistan." Manny was playing with one of his ever-present knives, twirling it between his fingers as he leaned against the doorjamb in the entryway.

A different corporate rep might have gotten ass-mad at that. Frank Moretti, however, was a veteran of both wars, both on active duty and later on contract. He was one of them. "Pretty much. I'd almost say worse, because you at least had a chance with your unit JAG if some haji came to the FOB and accused you of shooting at their house. These people won't even ask questions. They'll see dead Mexicans and contractors and immediately decide who's in the wrong, and it won't be the *sicarios*."

He turned back to the whiteboard. "Getting back to the brief. Recent incidents. Someone tried to drive off a couple dozen head of cattle two days ago, fleeing when confronted. Two of the hands took fire from an elevated position about a mile due west of here yesterday. Lights have been seen down by the border, and there have been tracks and trash dumps across the property for the last several months. One such procession got stopped by Trevor Bowman and one of the hands, Miguel Zapata, and they were fired upon. Trevor's described the group as consisting of about a dozen military age males, eight carrying large packs or duffels, and four carrying rifles.

"Furthermore, there have been at least three assaults on Bowman family members or ranch hands out in town, and Emilia Bowman was followed for two miles by a pair of military age males in a car about a week ago." He pointed to a printed-out timeline that was dense enough that it had been printed too small for Nick to read it from across the room. "As you'll see if you take a look at this report, there has been a decided uptick in these incidents since our client, Merritt Strand, got involved.

"So, with the situation laid out, let's get down to the mission. I'd like to get the first four guys out before it gets fully dark."

He pointed to the map of the ranch. "The mission is to secure the ranch against cartel incursions and protect the Bowman family and their employees. We've got just over nine thousand acres to cover, though before anyone panics, there are some choke points where we should concentrate our efforts. We won't be able to stem the entire tide of illegals and drug traffickers. There appear to have been at least six routes across the ranch over the last couple of years, mostly moving up the seasonal creek bed that runs through the center of the property here, cutting across the southeast corner toward the mountains to the east, or heading along the west side and the high ground over there."

He flipped the map over, showing a more annotated version. "We've only got eleven of us. I'll be taking shifts as well. I'll be damned if I'll be *that* corporate guy. But we've got some severe limits on how much we can do. So, we'll have two partner teams on duty at any one time. If things clack off, then it'll be all hands on deck. We might end up short on sleep for a while, but we're all getting well paid."

Nick thought about it for a moment while he watched his compatriots. He didn't think that the pay was the only thing that had brought these guys there. Pallas Group Solutions had been specifically headhunting shooters, spreading by word of mouth through the informal network of guys who'd worked certain contracts, all requiring certain military backgrounds. There had been no online advertising that he'd seen, not for contractors. For clients, certainly, but the company had been *exceedingly* careful in its recruiting.

Vetting had been every bit as brutal as any Nick had ever seen. The shooting quals had been unforgiving, the scenario and decision making exercises even worse. It had quickly become clear that the company was looking to weed out any contractors who'd gotten lazy or simply gotten too old to do the job effectively. That happened. Age catches up with a man, especially when he's done a hard job for a lot of years.

In the end, though, he was pretty sure that most of the men in that room weren't just there for the pay. It was a powerful incentive, especially during a recession, but it wasn't everything. These were the kind of guys who were addicted to the action and were willing to put themselves through the training and the pain to stay ready for it.

And while George, predictably, grumbled, the rest just accepted their assignments and got ready to go to work.

CHAPTER
23

Strand's next meeting wasn't a covert rendezvous like he'd done in Atlanta, unfortunately. It wasn't even a business meeting with a broker or anything like that.

It was a gala dinner for at least a dozen of Strand's business partners, in the Sheraton Fort Worth Downtown. Which meant that while it wasn't strictly speaking public, it was public enough, especially coming and going.

Worse, it meant we had to dress up for it.

It wasn't as bad as it could have been. Button up shirts and jackets were about as far as the dress code went. Most of us were still wearing jeans, and since it was Texas, boots were still fine, even though most of us were wearing low-heeled work boots that laced up and were easy to move in rather than cowboy boots.

The layout of the hotel made it almost impossible to get long guns in, even though most of us would have preferred for at least one two-man team to have the carbines close at hand. Not only was Strand a target, but all of these other millionaires would be, as well. The fact that they were even associated with Strand would put a bullseye on their backs.

Glocks it was, though. We still had to maintain something of a low profile. A few of Strand's guests might not like what Archer-Lin Investments and their proxies were doing, but that didn't mean they liked guys like us or our hardware, either.

Drew and I had managed to draw the advance team slot, so we showed up early, meeting with the hotel receptionists and the security coordinator. He was a younger guy, seemed to generally know what he was doing, but his primary go-to strategy was to try to talk the disruption down while his people called the cops. Which was fine for protestors, or drunk and disorderly idiots, which was probably most of what he had to deal with. It doesn't work so well with *Mara Salvatrucha* goons or cartel *sicarios*.

Still, neither of us disabused him of the idea that his plan was going to work. We weren't sure how he'd react even to the knowledge that we were armed, let alone that we were prepared for a balls-out firefight in the middle of the hotel. Well, somewhat prepared. There's no universe where that doesn't turn into an absolute nightmare in seconds.

The gala was set to go in the Cypress Ballroom, at the northern end of the hotel. It could be split into two separate rooms with a sliding divider in the center, but that wouldn't happen for tonight. While the guest list *looked* relatively small, each of those millionaires would have some kind of entourage, and none of them wanted to be crowded into half a ballroom. They were paying enough to get the full experience.

The hotel staff was already setting up as Drew and I walked around, checking things out. The carpet was covered in this weird, asymmetric orange, blue, and tan pattern, the ceiling was acoustic tile set above large, thick divider beams, and the chandeliers looked like a spray of glass coming out of a cone set in the ceiling. The whole place was modern enough to put my teeth on edge.

Once again, I didn't get the callsign "Backwoods" for nothing.

There were four doors around the outside of the ballroom, all of them opening onto the hallways, with stairs at three corners. In many ways, I would have preferred to be on the ground floor, since it provided more escape routes, but the hotel layout was what it was.

We found we didn't have that much to do for the last hour or so before the guests started arriving. There was no way to keep overwatch on the ballroom itself; there were no windows. Outside wasn't much better. There were a couple large paid parking lots to the east, while to the west was the Fort Worth Water Gardens. North was the Texas A&M School of Law, with the Fort Worth Convention Center beyond that. There weren't exactly any good places to set up a sniper hide. There weren't even many good places for any of us to park the vehicles and keep eyes on the hotel.

Finally, the first of the guests started to show up, as the staff was laying out the start of the spread. Drew and I kept our distance, letting the hotel staff handle the greeting and ushering. We were there to kill people and get Strand out if it came to that, not to coordinate the event.

Time seemed to slow down as the guests arrived, filtering into the ballroom, chatting, having drinks and hors d'oeuvres. It wasn't my first time having to do close protection on a venue like this, but it's never fun. It's boring as hell, worse if you get trapped into listening to any of it.

Ken and Custus showed up about ten minutes after the guests started to arrive, and then Tom and Brian came in with Strand and a couple other people from our client's office. I didn't recognize any of them, but right at the moment, I didn't care. They were with Strand, they weren't threats—one of the two women couldn't have concealed a weapon on her body to save her life—and that was all I gave a damn about.

The next four hours weren't the longest of my life, but they felt like it at the time. Strand moved through the crowd, gladhanding and wheeling and dealing, while the rest of us circulated around the ballroom and through the hallways, looking for the hitters who were going to try to get at Strand or any of his big finance buddies.

By the time things finally started to break up, I was tired as hell. My eyes ached and I just wanted to sit down. I grabbed a Red Bull off one of the drink carts near the exit and chugged it, instead. This was when things were probably going to get interesting.

Strand didn't wait until last to leave, fortunately. He appeared at the door, whispered to Tom, and then Tom moved to join me where I was leaning against the wall in the hallway. It was my turn to watch the approaches.

"Ten minutes." I just nodded. Nothing more needed to be said. We all knew the plan, and a moment later, Brian walked out past me, heading for the stairs. He'd need to bring the vehicle around. Hopefully Phil and Marcos still had eyes on it. Otherwise, Brian was going to have to check it over very carefully to make sure no one had planted anything on it or otherwise tampered with it.

Apparently, we were good, because Tom was escorting Strand and his entourage out a few minutes later, while the rest of us closed in and joined them, forming a loose ring around the principal. We headed down toward the ground floor and the vehicles in a big sort of knot of people. Several of Strand's associates had clearly had a good time, and the woman in the skintight outfit could barely walk a straight line. That was going to make this fun, even if the bad guys didn't show themselves.

Strand himself was sober as a bird, his eyes open and moving all over, watching us for our reactions as much as he was watching his surroundings. He knew he was under threat, and he didn't want to get ambushed.

We got to the ground floor in only a few minutes, despite Strand's lady friend's inebriation. She almost fell down the stairs twice, and Strand had to help her. They headed for the Suburban that Brian had pulled over out front with her draped against Strand, her head on his shoulder. It wasn't the best position if we needed to move fast.

I pushed ahead with Drew and Ken, stepping out of the front doors from the foyer and onto the brick-paved, partially enclosed parking lot out front. We spread out, alert and ready, though none of us were being so overt as to keep hands obviously close to weapons.

It took longer than it should have to get everyone loaded up. I was watching every angle possible without craning my neck, feeling my heart rate go up as I waited for the hit. This was the most vulnerable point. We were stationary, exposed, and there was no way anyone with an interest in Strand wouldn't have known that he was there that night.

Still, we got everyone loaded up. Drew and I had parked right across the street, in the dentist's office parking lot, and jogged over to get in while Brian pulled the Suburban out onto Commerce Street.

It was a good thing I hadn't relaxed. Someone *had* been watching.

Brian had to stop the vehicle as the light on East Lancaster turned red, just as Drew pulled our SUV onto Commerce Street behind them. Ken and Custus were still moving to their vehicle, and Phil and Marcos were either coming around from the paid parking lot where they'd been hanging out for the last few hours or else heading out for Dallas and the Renaissance by a different route.

For a moment, we were all stationary, without much of anywhere to go. A truck had come down Commerce Street behind us as soon as we stopped behind the Sub.

Then a box truck came around the corner and stopped right in front of the Sub's front bumper.

My alarm bells had started ringing as soon as that thing started to come through the intersection and instead of turning or going straight, had faded toward the Suburban. I was already moving as the back rolled up and men with guns started to pile out.

None of our vehicles were armored. We were going to have to solve this with speed, aggression, and firepower.

The truck behind us had closed in while we'd been watching the box truck. Fortunately, I was clearing our six as I came out of the door, so I saw the man with a pistol heaving himself out of the passenger side window. All I needed was to identify the weapon; I already had my Recce 16 in my hands. We'd kept them up front this time, just because of a feeling that we were probably going to need them.

I dropped the muzzle through the still narrow opening of the door, put the red dot on the guy's face, and shot him from about twenty feet away. It was an easy shot, made easier by the fact that they thought that they'd gotten the drop on us.

The man's head jerked as the bullet punched through the bridge of his nose, and his pistol fell from limp fingers to clatter on the street. I pushed out, slamming the door the rest of the way open and pivoting toward the driver's side of the truck, even as a burst of gunfire echoed off the surrounding buildings from behind me.

The truck's driver was trying to get out, so I didn't have a shot right away. It was a big F350 dually, lifted and covered in painted flames, so there was a lot of truck between me and my target. There also wasn't nearly enough space between our rear bumper and the grille for me to slip through.

So, instead, I dropped to my knees in the street and leaned down to almost put my forehead on the pavement, wrapped around my rifle so that I could pick up the red dot while I nearly laid the weapon on its side. The second man was behind the front wheel, but he thought he had more cover than he did.

I shot him through the knee. He collapsed with a scream, rolling away from the wheel and writhing in agony on the street. I would have left him there, but he still had his own weapon, what looked like a Tec-9, in his hand, and as he slithered away, dragging the bloody ruin of his knee with him, he leveled that junky 9mm at me, apparently still conscious enough past the pain to try to get in another shot.

My rifle thundered underneath the truck as I shot him three more times. He jerked under the impacts, and his finger tightened spasmodically on the trigger, sending a pair of 9mm rounds entirely too close to my head. One of them punched into the undercarriage, the other punctured the tire right next to me. Yet he slumped limply to the pavement, his head lolling as a pool of blood slowly leaked out from beneath him.

Drew was shooting through the V of the partially open door, engaging the men who'd piled out of the back of the box truck, as I moved quickly to clear the back of the pickup.

I swept around the tailgate, checking beyond it toward the hotel just to make sure there wasn't another element coming up on us. For the moment, I had six o'clock security.

In the infantry, or Recon, where I came from, that was often an ironclad position. You left your sector at the risk to everyone else in the unit. On this side of the house, when you only had a handful of dudes, sometimes you had to be more flexible. It didn't make things easier. In fact, it was considerably harder when you had to worry about just about *every* angle.

I kept moving, sweeping my muzzle around toward the front, looking for any more threats. At least three bodies lay on the pavement behind the box truck. Brian was partway out of the driver's side door of the Suburban, his own pistol leveled. The gunfire had stopped for the moment.

Joining Drew at the front of the vehicle, I took stock. It looked like all the bad guys were down, at least. "You good?" I'd bailed with just the rifle and my pistol on my hip, so my go bag with my reloads was still in the vehicle.

"I'm fine. I don't think these clowns got more than a handful of shots off." Drew had reholstered as soon as I'd come alongside, and now he was ready to drive again.

"I'm gonna move up to the principal vehicle and check on them." It might be self-evident, but communication is vital in a time like that. When guns have been drawn and shots fired, it can be a matter of life and death to make sure that the other guys with guns know where you're going to be. Just in case.

Drew nodded, pulling his own carbine onto his lap, twisting around in his seat and opening the door again so that he could cover the rear. There was still a chance that someone else would follow up, though the fact that no one had hit us again yet suggested that if the bad guys had backup, that backup had just watched us gun them down and decided that discretion was the better part of valor.

With Drew covering my back, I hustled up to the Suburban. I could hear the screaming before I even got there, though they were screams of terror, not pain.

"Shut the hell up!" Brian was at his Scrappiest of Scrappy. Unfortunately, his roar had absolutely no effect on the inebriated and shrieking women in the back.

"Everybody good?" I wasn't technically the team leader, but since I'd been the first one on the ground, I'd sort of stepped into the role. "Anybody hit?"

Strand finally got his lady friend to calm down enough that he could make himself heard. Either that or she lost her voice from all the screaming right then. "We're all fine. Nobody got hit, I don't think." Neither Tom nor Brian were checking at the moment, since both of them were still covering the front.

It was going to take a second to get out of there. The bad guys had pulled the box truck right up to within inches of the Sub's front bumper, and the truck behind us was almost as far away from our vehicle. There was just enough of a gap

188

between us and the Sub that we could get out, but it was going to take an Austin Powers turn to do it.

"Shouldn't we get the hell out of here?" Brian was clearly thinking the same thing. "It'll be faster if you guys move first, so I don't back into you."

"I'd say yes, except for that." I pointed to where I could already see red and blue lights flashing as a Fort Worth police car came screaming down Lancaster toward us. Sirens wailed in the night, and more were starting to close in from the north. "At this point, leaving a crime scene is probably a bad idea. Especially with this many bodies on the ground." The intersection was a bloodbath. I raised my voice. "As soon as the cops get here, everybody carefully put your weapons on the ground and keep your hands in view. We defended ourselves and our client, and this is Texas. We *should* be all right." I wasn't *entirely* sure of that, given everything that had happened in Atlanta, but we were out of time and options.

I suited actions to words, lowering my Recce 16 to the street with my off hand held high as the police screeched to a stop surrounding us.

CHAPTER 24

"Got a group about two thousand yards out. Coming right up that arroyo. Appears to be twelve military age males in dark clothing." Saul's voice was as deadpan as ever over the radio. Almost bored. That was just Saul's way, though.

Nick started the truck. "Time to go to work."

He and Matt had been stationed in an old Ford pickup near a watering tank about a mile from the ranch house. They didn't have a lot of elevation to observe the ranch land, but that was why Saul was running the drone from the house. Except for the rocky hills to the west, north, and east, almost all of which were off the property and none of which were close enough to interdict the arroyo that cut through the center of the ranch, the land was flat as a pancake, dotted with sagebrush and creosote bushes.

Those bushes made for some treacherous driving, but he was getting the hang of it. It was more fun than executive protection driving in a big city, anyway.

With Matt hanging onto the "Oh Shit" handle above the door, Nick started south, bouncing over the rocky ground, the tires crunching on the coarse desert floor. They had the windows open, even though it was hot. Both had been in worse, recently, and it allowed for some better situational awareness.

It took only a few minutes to cover the slightly over a mile distance to their interdiction point. "Got 'em." Matt pointed toward the thicker brush down in the arroyo. It was so shallow that it almost didn't deserve the description, but Nick had seen wadis in the Middle East that looked almost like just a regular part of the otherwise rolling desert landscape, too.

Nick peered over the steering wheel. There was a thin sheen of dust on the windshield, making it somewhat difficult to see, but after a moment he nodded. "I see them." He'd only spotted a couple, both wearing dark clothing. One was definitely carrying a large pack, but it looked like the other one just had himself.

That was probably the coyote or the armed security. They'd have to watch out for that one.

The brush down in the arroyo was thick enough that the illegals had plenty of concealment to work with. He thought for a moment as he continued to slow roll south, then braked to a stop. "Don't want to roll right into the middle of them."

"No, we don't." Matt was already getting out, dragging his rifle with him. While Nick grabbed his Recce 16, the company's standard carbine, Matt had drawn one of the two Aero Precision M5E1 designated marksman rifles, a 7.62x51mm AR-10 that had been modified from its original Aero configuration with a Geissele trigger and a JP Enterprises barrel. "Especially not if it's an ambush."

Nick pushed out to the flank, while Matt paused, looked over the terrain, then changed his mind and clambered up into the truck bed, laying the rifle's bipods on the roof of the cab.

As he jogged through the creosote bushes, Nick was acutely aware of just how little cover there was out there. And while he'd only seen two guys, he was pretty sure there were quite a few more than that. Which put the two of them currently alone against at least six.

That wasn't going to last; the rest of the team was mobilizing quickly. But it was a sobering realization that they were currently alone and unafraid in the middle of the desert.

With Matt holding overwatch, he started to creep forward, staying bent almost double, his rifle held at the high ready as he closed in on the arroyo. As tempting as it was to get down on his belly and crawl, he wanted to be high enough that he could get a better look at what was in front of him through the brush. The last thing he wanted was to crawl right up until he was eyeball-to-eyeball with some *sicario*.

Because he had no doubt that that was who these guys were. Those big packs tended to belong to drug mules. That, and the dark clothing. A lot of illegals tended to cross the border in regular street clothes, but the cartel people usually wore darker clothing that would blend into the landscape a little better.

Getting farther away from the truck, he could hear more clearly. The men down in the arroyo weren't being especially quiet. He could hear breaking brush, grunts, and curses in Spanish. The fact that he could hear them that well told him he was way too close.

He was sorely tempted to just stand up and open fire. Outnumbered, possibly outgunned, the only advantage he and Matt had at the moment was surprise and violence.

But this wasn't an overseas war zone. This was the US. Contract or not, illegal drug runners or not, there was no way that opening fire from ambush was going to be treated as anything but murder. Nick might not especially care about the legalities, but he knew the legalities cared about him, and while he might still be single in his mid-thirties, he still didn't want to go to a federal prison, especially not for doing what he knew was right.

A glint of light caught his eye, drawing his gaze momentarily toward a rapidly growing dust cloud. Another truck was roaring down from the ranch house. So, at least they had backup, but that didn't solve Nick's immediate tactical problem.

The voices down in the arroyo were getting a little more agitated. They knew they'd been spotted, and they knew that someone was coming. It had to be hard to miss that cloud of dust the rest of the boys had kicked up on the way.

He eased himself a little bit straighter, trying to get a look at the adversary over the brush without exposing himself all the way.

At first, he could see about three of them. Two of the drug mules were crouched under a single creosote bush, while one of the men with no pack was doing much the same as Nick himself was, craning his neck to try to see over the brush. All three had their backs to Nick, facing the oncoming truck.

It would be so damned easy. Except that he didn't have eyes on the others. He was sure there were more than just those three.

Carefully turning his head, rising just a little bit higher above the brush, he spotted one more, though he couldn't see much more than the ballcap the man was wearing. He couldn't tell if the man was another drug mule or if he was armed. He also couldn't see any of the rest of the dozen or so Saul had described.

Finally, as the truck came to a halt, Nick decided to go for broke. He stood up. "*Hola, amigos!* You guys lost?"

The man standing in front of the two drug mules reacted almost instantly, pivoting toward Nick and lifting an AK, letting off a burst that went high, the bullets crackling off into the distance over Nick's head.

For his part, Nick had already been at the high ready, and only needed to drop his muzzle a few inches to put the red dot right on the *sicario*'s chest. His finger tightened on the trigger and the Recce 16 bucked with a harsh *crack*, and the man staggered but didn't go down. Nick kept pressing the trigger, slamming round after round into the AK gunner's dark brown shirt as he moved up the arroyo. Staying in place was only going to get him shot, especially out there in the open desert.

Matt's M5 thundered then, and while Nick couldn't see the hit, he knew Matt well enough to expect that he'd dropped whoever he'd been shooting at. Two more shots *crack*ed over the desert, as Nick's target finally slumped to the ground, getting caught up on a particularly stiff patch of sagebrush.

The yelling down there had gotten even louder, though it was next to impossible to hear over the thunder of unsuppressed gunfire. So far, PGS hadn't sprung for suppressors, probably because NFA items required ATF paperwork to cross state lines. A hell of a tactical disadvantage, but one they had to work around.

Nick shifted his aim toward one of the drug mules. From the intel reports that Frank had supplied, the mules making their way across the Bowman ranch had been mostly unarmed, but it didn't pay to take chances.

It was a good thing he was being cautious. The first man with the backpack lifted a Desert Eagle and cranked off a round at him, the ridiculously massive pistol spouting an equally massive fireball.

Fortunately, the man hadn't really bothered to aim, while Nick had had the fundamentals hard-wired into his very being for a decade and a half. The man with the backpack didn't get a second shot off, as Nick drilled four rounds of 5.56 into his chest from fifty yards away, holding the muzzle steady enough that all four ripped through a spot about as big as his spread hand. Bloody froth erupted from the dying man's mouth as his lungs were shredded, and he collapsed, the big magnum semi-automatic falling to the desert floor.

More gunfire thundered from the other side of the arroyo, as Casey, Manny, George, and Josh cut down the rest before they could get a shot off. The crackling roar of rifle fire lasted about ten more seconds before it was all over and there were no more targets.

Nick straightened to his full height, rising above the top of the brush to where he could see the others, as well as be seen, himself. He raised his off hand just to make sure none of the other contractors mistook him for a bad guy. "Moving down to check. Watch your fire!"

Casey lifted his muzzle toward the sky and waved to indicate that he'd heard and understood. Nick started to push his way through the brush toward the bottom of the shallow gully and the bodies.

They hadn't formed much of a defensive position when they'd stopped, so they were scattered in a rough column along about ten yards. No trained infantrymen would have been that bunched up, not without having guns pointed in every direction, but it was doubtful that these guys had ever gotten much training.

The man he'd initially shot was dead as a doornail, as was the guy with the Desert Eagle. A couple of the others were still showing signs of life, and he moved carefully, never turning his back on any of them and keeping his weapon ready for action.

He had to circle around a little bit to come at the first two he'd shot without walking among the moaning and still-stirring dying men. He supposed that he really *should* try to treat them, but they were narcos, they'd tried to kill him and his buddies, and they sure as hell wouldn't extend the same courtesy if roles had been switched.

The first man was armed with an AKM, wearing a Chinese chest rig under a collared shirt. Nick had seen enough of the simple canvas load bearing rigs in the Middle East to recognize it immediately. Those things were everywhere there were AKs. He knew that Frank had said something about the client suspecting Chinese involvement in the play for the

Bowman ranch, but even if that was the case, this was no smoking gun.

A quick search of the body, after kicking the AKM away from the dead man's hands, revealed nothing else of use. He moved to the drug mule.

That one was younger than the first, with the gawky look of a teenager, but something about the body bothered him. Not the apparent age; he'd shot a fourteen-year-old Taliban fighter in Kunar ten years before, and that had gotten him over that hurdle. No, there was something else.

He lifted his head to check the others. At least two more of the narcos had succumbed to their wounds, going still and falling silent. Even as he tracked his red dot across the cooling corpses, he saw one more stiffen, then go limp.

Turning back to the dead man with the pack on his back, he looked him over more carefully. That was when he spotted it.

The kid hadn't just carried the Desert Eagle in his waistband or his hand. He was actually wearing a professional belt rig, complete with reloads, knife, light, first aid kit, and tourniquet. This was borderline military gear. Nick had seen paid gunfighters who were less well equipped.

Usually, drug mules were unarmed. Hell, they were usually indentured servants to the cartels, carrying the drugs across the border lest their families be tortured and murdered. To have a drug mule geared out like a gunslinger was weird.

He moved to the pack itself, though he was extremely careful as he crouched by the body, his muzzle pointed at the sky as he investigated the flap and the straps. If it was booby-trapped, he didn't want to be the clumsy ass who set it off.

Worse, he didn't want to die of a fentanyl overdose just because he was careless in handling narco gear.

Finally, as the rest of the support team came down into the low ground, except for Josh and Matt, who stayed on overwatch, he flipped open his knife and cut the straps holding the flap closed. Gingerly slipping the blade under the flap itself, he lifted it.

The pack had been cinched shut under the flap, so he had to cut the drawstring, as well, still unwilling to touch the thing with his bare hands. He wondered a little at the cartels using an old Alice pack to transport drugs, but they probably used whatever they could get their hands on.

Easing the pack throat open, he peered inside.

There were two large plastic bags of white powder, wrapped in packing tape, set to either side of the interior of the pack. Those were definitely drugs, though whether heroin, cocaine, or something else Nick was in no position to tell, nor did he want to find out. In between those two was where things got interesting.

Not only were there bags of food and a water bladder, but more ammunition, a spotting scope, and what looked very much like several incendiaries. This guy hadn't just been moving drugs. This was a patrol pack for an offensive military operation.

The last of the dying men had expired, and the only sound in the arroyo was the whisper of the wind through the brush and the crunch of boots on the desert floor as the contractors moved down to check the rest of the bodies.

Nick joined Casey at the next corpse carrying a pack, keeping his mouth shut for the moment. Casey wasn't the easiest to get along with, and Nick wanted to see if this one was the same as the first before he ventured an opinion. He had no desire to get into an argument with the surly, flat-faced man right then and there, and any comment that Casey considered out of line was going to result in an argument.

Especially since they'd just killed thirteen men on American soil.

He stood by while Casey cut open the second pack, displaying the same caution that Nick had on the first. He wasn't going to ask if Casey had observed his own search and modeled his caution after it. That would not be a good idea if he was going to avoid trouble with the other contractor.

Sure enough, as he peered over Casey's shoulder, he saw much the same load in that pack. Drugs, gear, sustainment, and incendiaries.

"Well, this is a little weird." If anyone else had said it, Casey probably would have bitten their head off, or at least responded with so much acid in his voice that he'd make the interlocutor wish he'd never opened his mouth. When Casey stated the obvious, however, it was okay.

"Maybe it was a twofer." Manny seemed to be the only one besides Saul whom Casey wouldn't mess with. He wasn't much to look at, but Manny was a hard little bastard for all his easygoing attitude, and it hadn't taken long to figure that out. Nobody knew exactly what all his background was, though Brett had mentioned knowing him in the Army, a *long* time ago. "Their primary mission was the ranch, but they brought the drugs to make some extra money after they'd done what damage they could."

"Sounds plausible." That was about as close as Casey was ever going to get to admitting that anyone who wasn't from the front office was right. He straightened up. "Let's get photos of everything. Then we'll burn the bodies. I don't want the Border Patrol to come along and start asking questions."

Nick suppressed a sigh. It was a pretty typical idea coming from those who had never tried to burn a body. *Guess I'm gonna have to poke the bear.* "That's…not a good idea."

Casey turned to look at him with eyes that looked like he wished he could shoot lasers from them and burn Nick to ashes on the spot. "Why not? We don't need the bad guys using this against us. We've seen what they've done to turn law enforcement in Atlanta."

Nick shrugged, trying to take a little bit of the edge off. "You ever tried to burn a body, Casey? Let alone thirteen?"

199

Casey frowned, momentarily holding off on the torrent of abuse that usually followed someone questioning his judgement or experience. "No, but it makes sense. Turn the bodies to ash, and there's nothing to identify."

"Yeah, well, I know a guy who tried it, and it didn't work very well." Nick grimaced a little, more at the memory of that story than at Casey's increasingly aggravated glare. "Turns out, without an actual incinerator, or some way of starting one *hell* of a fire, that seventy-percent water that makes up the human body doesn't burn too good."

For a moment, he thought Casey was going to argue the point anyway, but then common sense seemed to get through, and he grimaced. "Okay, wise guy, what should we do with them, then? I still don't think leaving them for the vultures half a mile from the road is a good idea."

"We've either got to bury them or drag them up to the north side where the folks on the highway won't see the buzzards." Nick shrugged. "Either way, we'd probably better get to work."

CHAPTER 25

We didn't need to be quite so worried about the cops. They still gathered all the weapons and impounded them as evidence, and we all had to go to the police station to get fingerprinted and statements taken. That took hours, well into the following day, but while we all were extremely careful about what we said and took great pains to make sure we asked clearly if we were under arrest or were being charged with anything, we all were finally assured in no uncertain terms that no charges were being filed against us, that it appeared to be a clear-cut case of self-defense.

I didn't think that any of us were entirely comfortable with these assurances. We'd all seen guys get burned before, often after believing they were in the clear. Some of the time that had been justified, as new information had come to light. Other times it had been entirely political. And like it or not, the connection of these events in any way to Archer-Lin Investments made this entire situation *very* political.

Finally, as I waited for the umpteenth interview in a small conference room—we were still on the outside of the jail, which was a good sign—a younger man in a dark, cheap suit walked in and closed the door.

"Mr. Grant? I'm Detective Salazar." He stuck out a hand, and I rose from my seat to shake it. His grip was firm, and he looked me in the eye before we both sat back down.

Another good sign. "I wanted you to take a look at a few of these photos, from the crime scene and elsewhere, and tell me if you recognize any of these men."

I refrained from repeating what I'd already said about five times, that I'd been worried about identifying weapons and hostile act, hostile intent. I hadn't studied faces. I just nodded and let him open the folder he'd brought in, spreading out several printed photos.

I'd seen several of the crime scene photos before. Some of the bodies were indelibly etched in my memory from the previous night, anyway. The headshots set next to those photos were new, but I still didn't recognize any of the faces. They were all cut from similar cloth, though. Sullen, mostly with shaved heads, maybe a few chin-scruff goatees, some sporting obvious MS-13 tattoos.

"Can't say as I do." I leaned back in my chair again and folded my arms, trying to stifle a yawn. I was exhausted. I didn't know for sure how long I'd been up, but it was definitely well past twenty-four hours at that point. "I recognize the crime scene photos, obviously, because I was there. None of the mugshots ring a bell, though."

He grimaced. "Damn. I was hoping you might have some more insight, since they were apparently after you and your client." He tapped one of the photos, of a particularly sullen young man glaring daggers at the camera. He had longer hair than most of the rest, though it was still relatively short. "This punk right here is Joaquin Michael Salazar. No relation. He's a known *Mara Salvatrucha* hitter. I've been looking for him for six months. So, I owe you some thanks. I might not get the credit, but I'm a happy camper, knowing that asshole is taking a permanent dirt nap." He waved at the other photos. "The rest of these have been picked up once or twice over the last month, always with different aliases, and they've all disappeared when let out on bail." He sighed. "I doubt I need to tell you just how fucked the situation with illegals is here.

202

We're doing what we can, but we simply can't hold onto every single petty criminal who can post bail. It's a war and a man-made disaster all at the same time, and we're having to do triage."

It was a surprisingly candid and politically charged rant coming from a serving police officer, but I kept my mouth shut. It *could* all be an interrogator's trap. Or it could be a sign of trust that I wasn't going to rat him out, with the hopes that he could get some of that trust back.

I realized that there was a note of apology in it, as well. Then it clicked.

This guy had been after a man we'd smoked for months. He'd failed. We'd succeeded. Yet we'd gotten *his* quarry at the cost of a firefight in downtown Fort Worth, putting a lot of bystanders and our own client at considerable risk.

He was probably trying to get hold of *any* thread to keep the city from crushing his nuts just because he'd been the man assigned to the case. Since they apparently weren't going to make a public example of us for shooting the men trying to kill or kidnap us, they were probably looking for someone's, *anyone*'s, hide to nail to the wall to save face.

The silence stretched out for an uncomfortable minute. Salazar wasn't looking at me anymore, but instead staring at the photos on the table as if he were a fortune teller and they were particularly recalcitrant tarot cards.

I decided to take a chance. He wasn't getting up, and I *probably* wouldn't hurt our case too much. "Look, Detective, I'd love to help you out. If I knew more, I'd tell you." That came with one hell of a mental qualification, but as far as the actual identities of the *mareros* who'd tried to kill us, I was being one hundred percent honest. I wasn't so gung ho that I wouldn't be happy if the cops took all these bastards out of circulation for us so that all I had to worry about was immediate danger to the client.

I was pretty sure Julie would be happy about that course of action, too. Some of our recent conversations had been uncomfortably short, both because of the demands on my time with this job, and the fact that I simply *couldn't* tell her everything that was going on. She'd start to panic, especially if that dire acronym "MS-13" came up. She wasn't flighty by nature, but everyone has their fears, and she knew enough about *Mara Salvatrucha* to get very, very worried if she found out that I was trading bullets with them.

I'd noticed that the Texans all tended to use the full name for the gang, too. That was an interesting tidbit of information that I filed away for future reference. *Mara Salvatrucha* might have been started in LA, among the refugees of the El Salvadoran civil war, but they were a force to be reckoned with in Texas, such that the locals spoke of them with a certain hostile respect.

"The truth is, though, we don't know who these guys were. Mr. Strand is a high-level finance guy, though he's generally stayed out of the news. It looks to me like somebody's gotten some idea of just how much money he can move around, and they want him either kidnapped for ransom, killed to take him off the board, or…"

I paused. I didn't think that was it, but another possibility had just popped into my head. It didn't match up with all the intel we had, but…

"Or what?" Salazar had caught my hesitation.

I tapped my thumb against my chin. "Or maybe they want to try to suborn him. Force him to work for them." It made some sense, the more I thought about it. I wondered if he'd been approached before. He hadn't said anything, and it was apparent that even if the cartels had tried to get him to work for them, the answer would have been, "No," but it did lend a different cast to events if this was more than just a matter of trying to take Strand out of the game.

Salazar frowned as he thought it over, once again returning his gaze to the photos of the dead men, as if it was easier to look at them as an anchor for his thoughts. "But these guys are *Mara Salvatrucha.* I'm pretty sure even the ones we don't have good IDs for are. The *mareros* work for other organizations as hired muscle a lot—mostly Sinaloa—but they rarely seem to be all that interested in financial wizardry on their own."

I nodded. That much I knew. "I know they started as a bunch of Satanist stoners." When Salazar raised his eyebrows, I shrugged. Maybe I'd given a little too much away, but I didn't think he was an adversary at this point. I thought we'd turned a bit of a corner. "I'm in the security business. Threat intel is kind of a necessity, and MS-13 is in just about every major city in the country. It's worth knowing something about them."

He accepted the explanation with a shrug. "Anyway, like I said, I don't see *Mara Salvatrucha* being that interested in moving money except for moving it out of their victims and into their own pockets."

"Unless they're working for somebody else." I kept my expression as blank as I could. I might have overstepped. So far, it didn't look like the bad guys had local law enforcement as penetrated here as they did in Atlanta, but that didn't mean they *didn't* have anyone in the police department. Even if they didn't, word was probably going to get back to the Feds, and if the Archers were involved, then it would probably get back to them, especially with the old man on the Judiciary Committee.

The number of people we could really trust was extremely small.

If Salazar noticed my sudden hesitancy, though, he didn't react to it. He seemed to be lost in thought, though he clearly didn't like where his thoughts were taking him. "If that's the case, then this becomes a Federal case by default." From his tone, while his face was slack and inoffensive, he *really* wasn't happy about that. "Since I assume Strand does most of his business across state lines, the FBI has jurisdiction."

I was as eager for the Feds to get involved as he was. He would get shoved aside by a bunch of Beltway Bandits, while we'd probably get completely screwed in favor of an unscrupulous private equity firm, Mexican cartels, and possibly worse.

There was a knock at the door before either of us could add to the conversation. When Salazar got up and answered it, a uniformed Fort Worth police officer was standing there with KG behind him. "Are you just about done, Detective Salazar?" The cop didn't look that comfortable. Probably felt like he was between a rock and a hard place. He glanced over his shoulder at our team leader. "Since they're not being charged with anything, their employer wants these guys back."

Salazar looked just as unhappy about that as he'd looked when talking about the FBI. "I don't have much of anything left for now, no." There was ever so little an emphasis on the *for now*. He turned to me. "We might have more questions as the case proceeds. I hope you guys will be available if we need to get in touch again."

In other words, *don't go too far.*

I looked at KG. "I'm sure the office will make sure that we can contribute anything else we can." In other words, *don't hold your breath.*

Salazar got the message, but to his credit, he didn't look all that pissed as I got up and left with KG. He just looked resigned.

Rock and a hard place.

CHAPTER
26

Strand was waiting when we got to our new digs. Well, new stopover, anyway. Strand might have a house outside Dallas, and might make it the center of his operations, but he wasn't tied to it the way an ordinary man might be. Strand was rich as Midas, despite his efforts to gather more support for his financial rescue mission for the Bowmans. He had houses and properties all over the country. It would be next to impossible to pin him down without considerable intel and preparation in advance.

That they'd already come so close told us something, and it wasn't good.

The nearness of the last few close calls was clearly on Strand's mind as we joined him in his suite in the Grand Hyatt DFW. He was sitting on the sectional in front of the TV, which was tuned to the news but on mute. More images of the bloodbath in the intersection outside the Sheraton were plastered across the screen, and Strand's eyes were haunted as he stared at them.

KG went to the coffee table, picked up the remote, and turned the TV off. "You were there, sir. You don't need to keep staring at it."

Strand blinked and shook himself as if he'd just noticed that we were there. "They might have some new information."

KG snorted at almost the same time several of the rest of us did. "Those clowns? Anything they find out is gonna be days out of date, and probably wrong, anyway. All they do is wait for somebody to tell them what to read off a teleprompter." I didn't know how much KG had told Strand about our company's intelligence capabilities, but he must have told him something. After all, it was kind of part of our advertising boilerplate.

In a world of evolving, asymmetric, and increasingly networked threats, you need extraordinary security. Pallas Group Solutions' special-operations-trained professionals have the experience, the skill, and the technology to keep your facilities and personnel safe and secure in the most unstable places on Earth.

Unconventional threats require unconventional solutions. That's why our security professionals are ready and equipped to monitor multi-spectrum threats in whatever country you're doing business in, and act to avoid or neutralize them before they can disrupt your operations.

Don't be vulnerable in a dangerous world. Contact Pallas Group Solutions today.

I'd cringed when I'd first read that, wondering just what kind of awful corporate bullshit I'd gotten myself into in the distant hope that the grass really was greener on the other side. I'd worked with multiple contracting companies over more than a decade, and they were all varying degrees of corrupt, eager to screw their guys over for a little bit of a better percentage. Even the rock star companies, started by veterans and operators, intent on doing it better, eventually got bought out by some soulless corporate hive mind, after which standards tended to drop almost as fast as the pay.

Over time, though, I'd discovered that to some extent, Pallas Group Solutions was dead serious about it. Once I'd found out that Goblin, of all people, was our founder and CEO, that started to make a lot more sense.

I just hoped he didn't see dollar signs and go the way of every other company founder when they started to burn out.

Strand blinked again and straightened, rubbing his hands on his pantlegs. "Right. You're right." He still sounded distracted.

"Mr. Strand..." I might be getting ahead of KG, but I had a growing suspicion gnawing at the back of my mind. "Is there something wrong?"

He took a deep breath. "Not yet. But I can't help but think that it's only a matter of time." He waved at the now-blank TV screen. "This is going to get the FBI involved, and after some of what's happened recently, especially the infiltration of law enforcement in Atlanta, I can't help but think that that's going to go badly."

He had no idea, but right then wasn't the time to say that.

KG already had an answer, though. "In that case, I think it's time to get ahead of that tsunami."

Strand looked up at him with a faint frown. "What do you mean?"

For a moment, KG just studied him, as if considering just how much he should tell our client. "We've come into possession of some documents that, *if* all things are equal, should get the FBI looking into Archer-Lin Investments *very* closely. Documents that indicate they had direct influence on the attacks on you as well as on the Bowmans. Now, the way we obtained these documents may or may not be entirely legal..." I stifled a snort. We hadn't directly been involved in that, but I knew that the B Team had. "That's why they'll be leaked anonymously to the FBI, through several cutouts."

Strand looked back at the darkened TV as he chewed on that one. He had to suspect how we'd gotten our hands on what I assumed were internal emails. Yet in comparison to the use of hired gang hitters to try to kill or kidnap him, the illegality of hacking the opposition's communications rather paled.

Whether or not Strand would see it that way was another question.

Finally, though, he nodded. "Fair is fair, I guess." He squinted doubtfully at us. "I just hope that it's enough." Clearly, he wasn't sure.

I wasn't either. But KG didn't say much of anything, only nodding and heading toward the back of the suite to send a message and get things in motion.

Strand watched him go with the expression of a man wondering if he'd just tied a noose around his own neck.

***

Later, as we were packing up to leave, I stepped aside with KG. "You really think we can trust the FBI to investigate Archer?"

He snorted. "No. Of course not. Especially not if Devon Archer's directly involved." He sighed and ran a hand over his face, then looked at me sidelong with a faint, ironic grin. "We're not expecting anything *good* to come of this, but that's the game we're stuck playing for the moment. I'd call it a chess move, but it's more like high-stakes poker. We don't know exactly all the cards the bad guys are holding, so we throw a big handful of chips in the pot and see what shakes out. My guess is that it's going to somewhat backfire—possibly an investigation into how the leak happened, rather than the content of the emails. But that's intel we can use going forward."

"So, legal recon by fire."

He cocked his head to one side, raising an eyebrow as he nodded. "That's a pretty good way to put it. I might steal that."

"What do we do in the meantime?" I spared a glance at Strand, who was still in a brown study, sitting on the couch, lost in thought, occasionally jotting down notes while his assistants carried stuff out.

"That's a question that I'm still working on. For the moment, our primary remit is to protect Strand. He's decided to move out of the city and head for his ski lodge in Colorado. I suspect that's only going to be temporary, however. There's a lot going on, and he can't just run and hide." KG's eyes moved to our client's back. "He knows it. That's why he's keeping us on. *However*." He folded his arms. "He's really concerned about the ranch. It sounds like he's got enough support to head off any buyout, but there will be a cost, and he's still figuring that out. The people he's dealing with aren't huge philanthropists—nobody in that business is; they do charity because it gets them out of taxes and works as marketing—so they'll want to get something out of the deal aside from just protecting a family ranch from Archer-Lin Investments. It sounds like Strand's still trying to work that out."

"He didn't already? He seems like the kind of guy who doesn't go to the head without a plan."

"Ordinarily, you'd be right. However, this seems to be one time where he just got pissed and acted. He might be regretting that a little bit, but I've got to hand it to him. He hasn't tried to back out, even as the cost has gone up."

I thought about that, studying Strand in turn. Something was bothering me about all this—something beyond the fact that we'd already been in four firefights with MS-13 across three cities.

"I know that look." KG was watching me. "What is it?"

"I just don't see this ending well any way we turn." I spoke slowly, trying to work out the picture in my head as I went. "How is he going to head off a financial powerhouse like Archer-Lin, which not only has connections all over the world, but the de facto backing of the Federal government, without just buying out the Bowmans himself? And if that happens, what's to stop the bad guys from turning up the heat with their cartel buddies until even *he* can't afford to keep the place?"

KG clapped me on the shoulder. "I think that's very much on *his* mind, too. I know it's on Goblin's. Trust me, Chris. Things are moving behind the scenes. Goblin's pretty sure that all Archer-Lin's involvement is as a proxy for somebody else, and he's got our cyber ninjas and a couple other assets digging into it. The lithium's the key. There's no other good reason that this much money and power would be leveled at a little family ranch in the middle of the desert on the border. The cartels might want the infiltration route, but that's minor. There are hundreds of other places they can cross and move north. Hell, Sinaloa and the Gulf Cartel already practically own a huge swathe of the Southwest as it is."

He shook his head. "No, I think it's all about the lithium. Which means that Archer-Lin's Chinese connections are probably *the* big thing we need to worry about, which I doubt Strand's considered more than in passing. That's also why we won't just shrug and walk away if Strand's deal falls apart." He lowered his voice still more, so that I was probably the only one who could hear him. "I know we've still got to get paid, and Goblin knows that even better than I do, but I think we're all here for a little more than a paycheck."

There might be a couple guys whom I'd doubt that about, but he wasn't wrong. And while it was slightly insane—we were talking about our small private security company going up against state-level actors, with all the money and power that implied—I couldn't help but feel a little bit of a warm and fuzzy at the knowledge that we weren't just going to let ourselves get buried by the enormity of the thing for the thousandth time in my career.

Of course, how I was going to explain that to Julie was another matter...

CHAPTER
27

Nick watched the dying light of sunset over the rocky hills to the west as he leaned on the pickup's cab. It was cooling off quickly.

He couldn't say the same for the situation.

Not that they'd gotten in any more firefights, but there had been at least three confrontations with Mexican trespassers along the southern property line over the following two days. None of those trespassers had been openly armed, but they had all been military age males, and all of them had carried that edge that told the professional killers who'd intercepted them what they were dealing with.

The cartel—whichever one it was; they hadn't yet managed to narrow that down, though the running team room speculation had the good money on Sinaloa—was pushing.

He heard the crunch of a footstep on the desert floor behind him and turned quickly, his hand dropping to the Glock at his hip, but it was Jacob Bowman, the oldest son. That explained why Matt, currently down in the cab, hadn't alerted Nick to his approach.

Nick turned back toward the front and his sector. "What's up, Jake?"

The truck rocked a little as the young man climbed into the bed to join him. He wasn't geared up like the PGS contractors were, but he was carrying a rifle and had three mags on his belt. He was relatively loaded for bear, and no wonder, after what had happened already.

He didn't say anything at first, but just set his rifle in the bed and leaned on the roof of the cab, bringing his binoculars to his eyes as Nick shifted over to give him some space.

After a moment, the younger man set his binos down and sighed, glancing at the high-cut helmet with mounted PS-31 NVGs sitting next to Nick. "This is gonna get worse, isn't it?"

Nick glanced over at him. The light had faded to a blue-gray twilight, but he'd been around the family enough over the last few days that he could fill in some of the details that were hard to see in the dimness. Jacob Bowman was a tall, rangy young man, black haired and black eyed, which he seemed to get from his mother. He was probably seventeen, but he carried himself like a much older man. Working a ranch right on the Mexican border probably aged these people faster than most.

He was also pretty good with that rifle. Nick had watched as Casey had put the family through a quick weapons fam, and the big man had been grudgingly impressed with their knowledge and skill. Once again, probably the price of living this close to the nastiest irregular war on the face of the planet.

"Probably." He couldn't bring himself to lie to the kid. What good was that going to do, anyway? Make him feel a little better up until the cartel came back and sawed their heads off? "The rough part about something like this is that you've got to make it cost more for the bad guys than they're willing to pay. These fuckers *worship* death. Losing a few shooters isn't going to be enough."

"What will be enough, then?" It wasn't a pointless question. The kid really wanted to know, really hoped that these hard-bitten older men who'd been through Iraq, Afghanistan, Syria, and a bunch of similar hellholes in Africa would have the solution, the perfect answer to the problem.

214

Truth is, kid, I don't know. Maybe this is one of those situations where there is no way to fix it. No way to win. Nick didn't say that, though. His brutal honesty only went so far.

He ordinarily wasn't the kind of guy who'd even think it. Maybe watching Afghanistan go down in flames had broken something in his brain. He didn't know. Maybe it was just having too much time to think as he stared into the growing darkness, wondering if there were *sicarios* creeping through those volcanic hills toward their position, trying to emulate the Apaches as much as they already emulated the Aztecs.

Jacob didn't prompt him as he thought over what he'd say. The kid just went back to watching the dark, though he may have taken another look at Nick's NVGs.

"We're working on it." It was about as noncommittal and reassuring an answer as he could give the younger man. "Truth is, from what I've seen, there's a lot more to this than just the cartel. They're working with somebody else. If we make it more costly for *them*, and make the cartel lose some drugs and money along the way, then, hopefully, they'll find somewhere else to go, where there's less trouble."

Jacob thought that over for a moment. "I guess that makes sense, but why would anybody else be interested in this place?"

Nick hesitated. *How much should I really tell this kid?* He'd gotten the brief—PGS was nothing if not conscientious about pushing the word down to its operators—but would Jacob really get it if he told him that he and his family were sitting on a treasure trove of strategic minerals that a lot of people would eagerly kill to control?

It turned out that the young man was asking a rhetorical question. Without waiting for an answer, he pointed to Nick's NVGs. "Why aren't you using those?"

Somewhat grateful for the shift in topic, Nick chuckled faintly. "It's not dark enough yet."

Jacob looked up at him. "Will the light burn out the tubes, or something?"

"No, not with these. If it was broad daylight, maybe." He shook his head as he hefted the helmet. "It's just that while it's still this light, there's not enough contrast. Everything gets kind of washed out, and you can't actually see all that well." That had been a problem with NVGs for as long as Nick could remember. The old-timers had griped about it, especially the fact that it hadn't ever really been fixed.

"Oh." Jacob looked out into the deepening twilight again. "I wish I had a pair. Wish I had a lot of the stuff you guys do." He didn't say much more than that, but Nick could hear the subtext, anyway. Like a lot of young men, Jacob hated sitting there on his hands, waiting. He wanted to be out there, in the weeds, taking the fight to the bad guys.

Nick knew the feeling. He was still one of the younger operators in Pallas Group Solutions, though standing in the back of the truck next to a seventeen year old made him feel positively ancient. He'd been getting ready to deploy to Afghanistan for the first time when this kid had been born. Still, he understood the urge, and he knew that he was driven by much the same thing. Why else would he be out here, still making his living with a gun, long after his time in Afghanistan was a distant memory?

Yet he hoped he was older and wiser. Not so old that he lost that warrior spirit, but old enough to recognize that this kid, tough as he might be, didn't have the training that he'd had, and sure as hell didn't have the experience to make up for it. Sure, a lot of kids went to war all over the world with about the same degree of skill, but that didn't make it a good idea to let him try to play Red Dawn in the New Mexico desert.

"Well, it helps to have a company to buy all this stuff for you to use." He was trying to gently deflect the conversation. While he was sure Frank wouldn't want the kid to be out running around in the dark, hunting cartel *sicarios*

216

who would eat his heart if they had a chance, all the same, there wasn't much they could really do to stop him, at least not unless they got instructions from Old Man Bowman. And that hard-bitten old cattleman would probably be proud of the youngster.

Not that Nick could necessarily blame him, but he found that he really didn't want to see the kid go off and get himself slaughtered. Because he was pretty sure that would be what would happen if Jacob tried to take on the cartel.

"How do I join you guys?" There it was. Fortunately, that was an easy enough question to shoot down.

"You have years of experience in special operations or recon, you've done close protection work in war zones, and somebody in the company, or who somebody in the company trusts, vouches for you." He shot Jacob a lopsided grin. "Sorry, kid."

Jacob visibly deflated. He'd been hoping. Probably hoping that, as the world changed, he'd be able to just jump in with a private military/security company and go to work. But it wasn't the '60s or even the '80s anymore. A company like PGS just didn't have the training pipeline to take raw recruits. It would be too expensive, and the alternative was to go the way that many PMSCs had gone in Iraq and Afghanistan, to their eventual downfall. Taking anyone with a pulse just to fill numbers is a recipe for disaster in a war zone.

Nick felt like he should probably say something, but he wasn't sure what. He knew he'd never been the most charismatic guy around, even back when he'd been an NCO. He'd been so blunt that there were still guys, almost a decade later, who hated his guts.

Finally, he reached over and gripped the young man's shoulder, giving him a brotherly shake. "Relax, Jake. The time will come. I have a feeling that there might be plenty of fighting for this place before you know it. You might find you get all you can stomach."

Thinking about the savagery he knew the cartels were known for, he suppressed a shudder, knowing just how prescient those words might end up being.

CHAPTER
28

While Strand did leave Dallas/Fort Worth for his ski cabin in Monarch, Colorado, not all of us went with him.

At the last minute, we got a call from the office. It wasn't Goblin, personally, but one of his office drones. The guy looked pudgy and kind of pasty, but if Goblin had hired him, and trusted him to pass on a message like this, he probably had a past.

"We need a stay-behind element. Not for the *Mara Salvatrucha* assholes, but for the assholes who are hiring them. We've got intel that Devon Archer himself is coming to town, and we need eyes on him. Might be some off-the-books demo work, too."

That had almost triggered a fight. Give this bunch a chance at stretching those destruction muscles instead of close protection babysitting, and things were going to get heated.

Granted, that might have been somewhat relative. Some of us were more mature about it than others, but we were all getting older. Still, even as old-timers in a young man's game, a lot of us hadn't matured all *that* much.

Finally, KG had shouted everyone down and made the assignments himself, without regard for who had volunteered first or last. That put Drew, Phil, Marcos, and me on the remain-behind element. Only four guys was pretty small for a team that might have to fight its way out of a city, but we hoped to avoid conflict. That was what tradecraft was for.

We were back in Dallas, staying at a much lower-grade hotel. It meant we had a longer drive to get to the airport, but it was worth it for the lower profile.

Fortunately, Devon Archer didn't seem to know the meaning of "low profile." The man was an inveterate playboy, and apparently had zero concern about the propriety or lack thereof of flying around in expensive private jets and sweeping through an airport with an entourage like he owned the place, even when he was there to do some more than likely illegal and definitely immoral shit.

At least, we were pretty sure that was why he was there. The man's usual hangouts were all over the country, but the coincidence of his arrival in Dallas this close to the attacks on Strand was a little too much to overlook.

Of course, even with all of those advantages, getting eyes on him wasn't going to be easy. The millionaire son of a senior Senator wasn't going to fly commercial into DFW International Airport. That was beneath him. He flew a company jet into Dallas Love Field.

That might have created more difficulties than ultimately turned out to be the case if our cyber ninjas hadn't been on their game. I didn't have a lot of details, but it sounded like they'd used that keylogger that Nick and Matt had installed on Cooper's computer as a launch point for a phishing attack that had gotten a similar keylogger onto one of Archer's computers.

We hadn't gotten the full brief about how much dirt they'd pulled off it, but KG had had a faint tic in his eyelid as he'd told us about it just before leaving for Colorado with Strand. Our boy was *dirty*.

At any rate, the part of that intel dump that we were concerned with included Archer's itinerary and where he was intending to land and get a car. That led us to Signature Flight

Support, the primary terminal for private and business jets at Dallas Love Field.

Getting in wasn't impossible, but it would be tricky if we were going to put surveillance on Archer. If we were inside, we'd probably get a good positive ID on him and be able to follow, but as soon as he got in a car and rolled out, he'd be ahead of us. We had to figure out an approach that would allow us to pick him up quickly and follow without losing contact.

The end result was a bit of a compromise, which had Drew and I driving racetracks around the neighborhood while Phil and Marcos pretended to be there to pick somebody up. Marcos was waiting in the car in the parking lot, while Phil went inside to wait.

I'd just turned right onto Midway Road for what felt like the umpteenth time when the phone rang. Drew snatched it up and answered, quickly switching to speaker. "Send it."

"He's down." Phil's voice was faintly muffled, but still audible over the background murmur of conversations in a public place. "He just walked in off the tarmac, along with about six other people. They're taking their time, but they are heading for the exit."

"Roger." I sped up, just a little bit. The timing was *almost* impossible to get right, but I could at least get in the ballpark. We needed to be right on Lemmon Avenue, with line of sight on the exit from Love Field, by the time Archer came out.

That was no guarantee that we'd be going the right way, but it was a start.

Phil, for his part, just kept up the running narration of reporting. While his words were one thing, he kept his voice down and he couldn't help but allow some of the act he was putting on for the bystanders leak through. After all, he was supposed to get a call that would tell him that the guy he was waiting for was delayed or diverted, so there was no one to pick up. Otherwise, he and Marcos would have to wait there until someone *did* arrive. The key to camouflage is making it stick, and that counts for social camouflage in a public place as much as infantry camouflage in rural areas, if not more so.

"Coming out. Marcos has eyes on." He hung up, probably making a big to do about it before stomping in frustration toward the parking lot.

Marcos called seconds later. "There's a white stretch limo in the parking lot that got here about fifteen minutes ago. I can't say for sure that it's Archer's ride until he gets into it, but it looks pretty likely."

By that time, I was already turning onto Lemmon, slowing my roll as I headed north again, hoping that Archer didn't go south so that I'd have to pull a U-turn to follow him. Drew was just listening to the phone and keeping an eye out. It was that part of an op where talking was pretty pointless and could actually get in the way. Our game faces were on. We were on the hunt.

"Called it." Marcos wasn't above a little bit of crowing on comms, provided it didn't interfere with the mission. "He's getting in the limo. You won't be able to miss it."

I'd slowed down even more, though I was probably at the limit of how slow I could get before I started attracting attention. The intersection directly across from the entrance to Signature was coming up quick.

"That was fast. They're all in and rolling. Leaving the parking lot now."

Marcos had barely finished speaking when I saw the big, white luxury vehicle pull out into the intersection and turn left, away from us. I let go of a breath I hadn't realized I'd been holding. No U-turn required.

"Eyes on." Drew had picked up the phone to keep it close to his lips rather than lying on the center console. I kept my eyes on the limo and concentrated on staying far enough back that we didn't get spotted.

***

The next couple of hours went by in quiet and increasing boredom, broken only when we called ahead to Phil and Marcos to hand off for a while. Having two vehicles in the follow, we could leapfrog and avoid too much exposure for any great length of time. Some such exposure was unavoidable without at least six vehicles in the box, but we had to deal with the situation and resources at hand. It still made things touchy, since the key to surveillance detection was correlation over time and distance. The more you saw a particular vehicle as time went on and you moved through the city, the more likely it was someone was following you.

Still, Archer's driver must not have really given much of a damn, or simply wasn't trained. He didn't conduct any sort of surveillance detection or countersurveillance that we could figure out, just driving straight toward Corinth and the north shore of Lake Dallas. No radical turns, no sudden changes of speed, nothing to check their back trail. Archer must feel pretty secure.

Of course, Phil hadn't mentioned any security personnel accompanying Archer at the airport, and neither had Marcos. Just his entourage of hangers-on and sycophants. It was possible that there was a security detail in the car, but judging by their behavior on the road, I kind of doubted it.

It stood to reason that even after the firefights we'd already had with his hired goons, Archer was confident enough in his position as a protected scion of a Senatorial family that he didn't think he *needed* security.

Once we got into Corinth, things took a turn for the worse for us, though.

"We gotta back off." Drew was looking at the map on the tablet that we had attached to the dash. Ahead, the limo had just turned left into a wooded, very affluent-looking neighborhood. "We're about to run out of room."

A glance at the screen showed me what he was talking about. Sure enough, that neighborhood was a series of cul de sacs, none of which would offer an easy way in or out. We could still follow Archer in, but we'd be at a much higher risk of detection, potentially with no way to escape.

It wasn't even just Archer and his people we'd need to worry about, either. The kind of people who lived in a place like this—and just judging by the manicured lawns and hedges that lined the street, there was a *lot* of money around here—wouldn't hesitate to call the cops if they saw an unfamiliar vehicle with two unfamiliar men sitting in it, just parked on the side of the street. We'd done okay in our interactions with the local police here in Texas so far, but I wasn't going to stretch that luck very far.

Unfortunately, we had limited options. "Ask Phil if he can get the drone up. Get eyes on that son of a bitch before we lose him altogether."

Drew passed on the word, but Phil just replied, "Stand by." Things went quiet again, as I started to try acting like we were lost. I could maintain this for a few minutes, hopefully just long enough to see where Archer went to ground, but then we'd have to pull off, and that was where the drone would come in.

Of course, we wouldn't be able to keep it on station indefinitely. It had limited battery life, and people would start to notice a buzzing little quad copter hovering around their houses after a while. Unfortunately, these things weren't exactly silent.

There were ways to keep eyes on, though. At the very least, while we wouldn't be able to maintain constant, uninterrupted surveillance, we should at least be able to get enough warning that Archer was leaving to get a follow on him again.

The limo kept going straight, about a quarter mile ahead of us. I was just far enough behind that I could catch the tail end of the vehicle as it went around each minor curve on the way down Post Oak Trail.

The deeper we got, the more I could see that there was no way in hell we'd be able to hang out. Massive, sprawling, brick McMansions lined either side of the road, each with its own roundabout cul de sac driveway and manicured lawns and landscaping. There were hundreds of millions of dollars sunk into property on both sides of Post Oak Trail, and I expected that there were already people calling the cops or the local sheriff about the unfamiliar SUV driving through their neighborhood, just to be on the safe side.

I followed the limo through the next right turn, going around a wooded hill just in time to see the limo take the next left.

"That's gonna be a dead end." Drew was already ahead of me, watching the map while I watched the road. "Keep going straight, toward that fucking castle up there, but slow roll so we can see where he stops."

I did as he suggested. Driver drives. I did hazard a glance at the map, seeing that this road also dead-ended in a roundabout between two more of the huge houses. I figured we'd look around, act like we were lost, then turn around and head out.

Of course, I had the additional duty of watching the limo as it headed down Waterfront Court. I couldn't quite stop, though I slowed down as much as possible to maintain the illusion that I was somebody out of his element and looking for an address, but I still had to keep going before the limo came to a stop. It looked like it was going toward the end of the road, though.

Making the turn, again with that sort of hesitant delay to suggest we weren't sure where we were, I headed back. This time, Drew had line of sight. He looked carefully, then sat back in his seat as we moved on past and back the way we'd come. "He's stopped at the very end house. Looks like they're going inside. Probably going to be there for a while."

I just nodded as I kept going. We had a bit of a dance to go through, but we had our target now. We could set in and wait.

CHAPTER
29

We didn't have long to wait at all. In fact, we really didn't have time to get set in and get a continuous surveillance set in.

"He's moving. Just left in a sports car." Phil was on the drone at the moment, having just gotten it on station.

"That was quick." I had to immediately start looking for a place to turn around. We'd been heading for the nearest hotel, this time a Fairfield Inn and Suites, to set up a temporary operating base. Hotels were good for that sort of thing, allowing a certain degree of anonymity, provided you didn't haul in four hundred pounds of comm gear and weapons for everyone to see. But we didn't have time at the moment.

I had to maintain our current route, ducking under I-35 E and heading back the way we'd come. Phil kept talking us in the whole way, until we finally got eyes on Archer's blue Jaguar F-Type. He was, predictably, driving considerably faster than was legal, and weaving through traffic. I had to fight to keep up without making it obvious.

Fortunately, he didn't go that far. His destination was a bit of a surprise, though.

"Really? Applebees?" Drew's brow furrowed as we pulled into the parking lot. "Why Applebees?"

I shrugged. "Rich people are weird. They get notions. Maybe he likes the menu, or something."

Drew snorted. "Maybe he just has the munchies." I couldn't help but chuckle a little bit. Archer's drug use was an open secret, which made his position as financial mogul that much more obviously corrupt.

Then he sobered. "Or we've got another restaurant meet about to happen."

That was a thought. Restaurants were public places where a lot of people would be talking, and they lent a certain degree of anonymity. Now, how anonymous Devon Archer could really be was another question but, given his aforementioned drug use, he might not think along those lines.

Drew got Phil and Marcos up to speed while I parked the vehicle, then we both made sure our Glocks and other gear were well hidden before we followed Archer inside.

He wasn't hard to spot, even as we found seats in the bar. The man was incapable of keeping a low profile. Gaunt and curly haired, he had a loud, slightly nasally voice that seemed to cut through the low buzz of early evening conversation throughout the restaurant. He wasn't being *quite* loud enough to listen in unaided, but he was definitely making everyone aware of his presence.

I'd positioned myself where I could watch the front door, which also put me in line of sight of Archer. Drew wasn't that far offset, having taken the seat at my right instead of across from me. He'd have to move his head to look toward Archer, while I just had to look up.

We had photos of Archer and his entourage leaving the airport, thanks to Marcos. Neither of the two men in the booth with him right now were in those photos, and he'd gotten out of the Jag alone. I studied his companions, since I already knew who Archer was.

I didn't recognize either at first glance. That didn't mean much. It *might* mean something that one of them was apparently Chinese, and the other appeared Hispanic, though nothing like the MS-13 thugs we'd already crossed swords with. This guy looked like he was in his late forties, early fifties, dressed respectably in slacks and a polo shirt, his graying hair neatly combed, a short, neatly trimmed salt-and-pepper beard on his chin.

Both men looked faintly irritated, and the Hispanic guy kept looking around, especially when Archer's voice rose especially loudly. Our target seemed to be complaining about anything and everything, and it seemed like his two interlocutors were having difficulty getting a word in edgewise.

Drew nonchalantly put a small case on the table just before he got up. "I need to piss." He headed toward the back and the bathrooms.

Coincidentally, that route led him past Archer's table, where he just so happened to trip and drop his phone. He fumbled with it a bit, then shoved it back into his pocket and continued on toward the restrooms.

Except that he hadn't dropped *his* phone. He'd dropped the carefully prepared burner phone that was hooked up to those earpieces he'd left on the table by Bluetooth. I pulled one of them out of the case and slipped it into my ear.

"Mr. Archer." The voice that spoke was faintly accented, but probably speaking better English than mine. It was the Chinese guy. "We did not come here simply to chat. Our information suggests that Merritt Strand is about to offer the Bowmans a deal that would render your attempt at a buyout at the very least prohibitively expensive. What are you doing about it?"

Archer waved a hand impatiently. "Since when did Strand become *my* problem?" He jabbed finger on the tabletop. "I'm supposed to be the front man, not the overall coordinator of shady shit. I provide the money, making this an American thing, while nobody's going to look too deeply into it because of Dad." He stabbed a finger at first one, then the other of the two men. "*You* guys have the capability to take Strand off the board, not me."

"Unacceptable." The Chinese guy wasn't having it. "Your father can bring your FBI against him easily. Why has it not happened yet?"

Archer looked even more impatient. "I don't know why, but he hasn't. Are you going to let that stop this deal?" He turned to the Chinese guy. "What are you going to do when the Bowmans make a deal with Strand to mine that lithium, so American companies don't need your supply anymore?"

"We've handled that before." The Chinese guy was stone-faced and grim.

"Yeah, Molycorp, I know." I frowned slightly, looking down at my phone, which was also linked over the cell signal to the app on the burner currently sitting on the floor under the table behind Archer. We weren't going to have to rely on my memory of listening in for reporting; I had it all recorded, and the burner wouldn't even need to be retrieved. The app we were using wouldn't be easily located even if anyone knew what to look for. It was hidden behind the surface level apps.

I searched for "Molycorp," and it took a minute to find anything. It turned out to be the name of a rare-earth mineral mining company that had run the only such mining operation in the States, until the Chinese had flooded the market in 2002, forcing the company to shut down or go completely bankrupt.

"We can handle him." The Hispanic guy's voice was low and raspy, like he'd smoked a lot.

The Chinese man's reaction was immediate and forceful. "That has already been tried, and it threatens this entire operation."

The man's heavy-lidded expression didn't change, but there was something about his demeanor that seemed to shift, ever so slightly. This guy might look respectable, but I was starting to get some serious cartel vibes off him. He wasn't happy about waiting, nor was he happy about getting called out by the Chinese—whom I was beginning to suspect was PLA or MSS.

This was getting *very* interesting.

They kept arguing, pausing only when the waiter came by, or when someone walked close enough to the table that they could possibly overhear. That included Drew on the way back from the men's room.

"Anything?" He kept his voice down as he slid back into his seat, but I just held up a hand to forestall him as the waiter approached our table, later than I would have expected, but not all that surprisingly. We ordered some appetizers and a couple of beers, and he left.

"If we needed a smoking gun, I think we've got it." I kept my own voice low. "Seems that the Chinese are up to their necks in this, too. If I'm understanding this right, Archer's trying to buy out the Bowmans, after which the Chinese will come in and buy the land from him, either setting up their own mining facility or sitting on the lithium to keep it out of American hands. The cartels are the muscle to make sure that the Bowmans sell." I tapped the phone on the table in front of me. "And we've got it all on audio."

Drew frowned as he pulled his own phone out, just as mine vibrated with a new message. I glanced at it, then stopped, even as Drew put his down on the table. "Well, I guess that tears it, don't it?"

Strand announces that the FBI visited his main offices in Dallas to begin an investigation of his involvement with the Bowmans. Suspicion of financial malfeasance and possible anti-trust law violations.

"That's coming *way* too fast on the heels of our leaks to be coincidence," I agreed. I shook my head. "Suspicions confirmed again."

"So, what the hell are we going to do about it?" Drew glanced over at Archer while he sipped his beer, and the bitterness in his eyes was palpable.

I understood all too well. I'd been in more than one position where one or more of my superiors—or clients—were unscrupulous monsters, but there'd been little to nothing I could do about it, because of their rank or position. Even those higher up who weren't necessarily complicit were willing to cover for them, because of who or what they were, rather than what they'd done.

When that happens, there is no justice. I'm not going to say one way or another whether that means that there's any legitimacy at all left to the guilty parties' authority, but I know what I think about it.

"I don't know, but that's up to Strand and Goblin at the moment." I wondered for a moment just how far I could trust Goblin. Back in the day, I would have trusted him with my life. We'd worked together a lot. But that had been before he'd disappeared into the IC for years. I wondered what that time in that environment had done to him. There weren't many IC people I'd trust so far as I could throw my truck.

Sitting in a restaurant, running surveillance on the son of one of the most powerful men in the country, along with at least two foreign and criminal agents, was not the time to worry too much about that, though. I was committed. Just because the most powerful law enforcement agency in the land was going to side with cartels and Chinese agents didn't mean I could back down and walk away.

Sometimes it's a bit liberating, in fact, to be stuck in a David and Goliath sort of situation. Once you get past the screaming panic gibbering in your lizard brain at the realization of the odds.

Archer seemed to have gotten the same message, because he turned his phone around to show it to the other two. "See? Just took a little time."

The Hispanic dude didn't seem that impressed, but the Chinese agent visibly relaxed. "So, we can proceed as planned, then?"

"Hopefully." Archer put the phone down. "Strand's got good lawyers, though, so it might not go anywhere." He gulped down the last of his beer like it was water. "It will buy us time, though."

The Hispanic guy smiled a little bit, and it was one of the most disturbing expressions I'd seen in a while. He might be playing respectable, but this man was a killer. He'd probably worked his way up the hard way. "We can use it."

Archer put his glass down and pointed at him. "Just don't get too carried away. Things get too nasty down there, and it might draw all sorts of public attention. There's only so much we can sweep under the rug. A few dead people here or there is one thing. Some random violence. An actual massacre?" He shook his head. "Not even my dad can make that go away."

The cartel *teniente* didn't look impressed, but he didn't say anything.

"We should leave separately." The Chinese agent was clearly thinking about security, though it was far too late for that. He started to get out of his seat, but paused, looking Archer in the eye. "My superiors are getting impatient. The overall situation is…delicate." Judging by what I'd been hearing about unrest and economic problems in China, that was probably a hell of an understatement. "This needs to happen soon."

"Don't worry. Everything's coming together." Archer leaned back in his seat and draped an arm over the back. "There's no way that even Strand is going to be able to head this off. We're covered, and it's only a matter of time."

The Chinese guy didn't look all that impressed, but he nodded before he turned and left. I made sure I got a couple of photos before he went out the door. I didn't know if they'd be useful, but it was possible. Not all Chinese spooks were secret squirrels. Some of them were CEOs of otherwise legitimate companies. If we had any ID on this guy, Goblin would be able to get it.

For a moment, Archer and the *teniente*—I figured this guy was probably old enough to be a lieutenant, not a *sicario*—just watched each other across the table. There was no fellowship there, no friendliness. They were two predators—though of different orders—who were momentary allies, nothing more, nothing less.

It was Archer who moved first. Almost spasmodically, he got up, tossed some cash on the table, and walked out quickly, trying not to look scared and failing. His cartel contact watched him go with dead eyes and a faint smile before he got up and followed.

Archer probably had nothing to worry about. The cartel still needed him.

I was momentarily tempted to follow the cartel guy and smoke him. I'd be doing the world a favor.

It was the mission that checked me, but there was something more to it. Not only did I have something to lose—Julie and the boys would suffer the most if it went wrong—but there was a deeper problem to consider.

We had already broken the letter of the law more than once, but that had happened under very specific circumstances where those charged with upholding that law had refused to do so. There are consequences for the abrogation of the responsibility that goes with authority. And while we had taken matters into our own hands, we also had to be ready to face the consequences of doing so.

Yet there were lines we still had to be careful of. If we became as lawless as the powers that be, it wouldn't end well for anyone. We might get away with a lot over time, but a part of me knew that in the long run, it wasn't about what you could get away with.

It was what you could do while still looking yourself in the mirror.

So, I let him go. Not without sending an anonymous tip to the local police department, though. It might not go anywhere. I didn't have an ID for this guy. For all I knew, he could be El Chapo's brother, or he could be some nobody tapped by the cartel to work north of the border and keep his nose clean. So, I just gave a description and said he was acting suspiciously, lurking around kids or something.

Maybe it would slow things down. Maybe it wouldn't do shit. But as we paid our check and left, with a bombshell recording in my pocket, I knew that things were about to get nasty.

CHAPTER
30

Things were moving fast, alright. And not in a good way.

"I expected the investigation, but this is worse than I'd feared." The four of us in the remain-behind element were on a video call with Goblin himself. "Strand is enormously wealthy, but most of that wealth is tied up in various assets. His liquidity isn't nearly high enough to outbid Archer-Lin Investments and their subsidiaries, which can bring *billions* of dollars to bear in a very short time. So, he's been making deals with other financiers, smaller guys who can throw in a few hundred thousand here, a million there. Unfortunately, while the investigation hasn't tied up too much of his assets, it's making some of his partners get cold feet."

Thad just looked tired. He wasn't that much older than me, but he looked like he was in his fifties, not his forties. "If the bad guys can crank up the pressure enough, and Strand can't get the money together to make a deal, it won't matter if his lawyers get the FBI off his back. They'll snatch up the Bowman ranch and the Bowmans might get pennies on the dollar, if they're lucky. And from what you picked up in that recording, Chris, that will mean another strategic mineral deposit in ChiCom hands."

In a way, hearing him use the term "ChiCom" was slightly reassuring, in light of some of the worries and doubts

I'd had since he'd come out of the shadowy world of the intelligence community. Most of those clowns were politically correct to the core and calling the Red Chinese "ChiComs" was *not* politically correct.

"So, what's the play?" Phil was sitting on the bed in my hotel room, his elbows on his knees. His expression was that of a man walking through a graveyard. To have gone through so much, risked so much, only to have it snatched away by such underhanded legal means...

That's what gray zone warfare's all about, I realized, which makes it somehow worse than a stand-up fight.

Goblin wasn't giving up, though. "We do what we can to take the pressure off the Bowmans."

"How?" I thought I knew what he had in mind, but I wanted to hear it from him.

"The most immediate thing we can do is secure the ranch. I can't spare the rest of the A Team, since we're still contracted to protect Strand, but he's currently secure in Colorado. There's a *chance* that they might make another go for him, but he's in a much more defensible position up in Monarch than in downtown Atlanta.

"If you boys are willing, I'm going to send you down to New Mexico and the Bowman place. I'll make sure you still get paid. Might even be sending some additional ammo and tools down there. Nothing Class III, I'm afraid; that's still a lot of lawyer's fees and red tape in the future. But it should hopefully be enough to put the hurt on some *sicarios*."

For a moment, I saw hesitation in Thad Walker's eyes. As if he wasn't sure if he should even be asking us this, even though it was already out there.

We looked around at each other. I'd worked with Drew and Phil in a couple of different countries, and while I hadn't met Marcos before PGS, he was solid as they came. We had some screwballs and somewhat high-strung individuals in the company, but these four were good dudes, and I couldn't ask for a better fireteam.

"Hell." Marcos was sitting in the desk chair while Drew lounged back in the armchair. This place wasn't nearly as big or posh as the suites that Strand had used. "I'd get to fuck up some cartel shitheads and get paid? I'm in."

That seemed to break the ice. I looked back at the screen and the camera from where I was leaning against the wall at the head of the bed. "I think that's your answer, Thad."

Goblin let out a heavy sigh as he nodded. "Thanks, gents. Really. I'll have flights for you within the hour; driving would take too long." He rubbed his chin and grimaced. "Weapons... The TSA is going to throw a shit-fit if you all try to check those." He looked down off camera. "Damn. I'll get a contact moving to pick up the weapons and ammo from you there in Dallas, and we'll have replacements waiting in New Mexico. This is getting complicated."

"How much is this costing the company, boss?" I almost didn't ask, but I wondered. This was a hell of a stretch for a relatively new contracting company.

"A lot." He seemed to steady himself as he looked out through the screen. "Let me worry about that. We'll make it back. Some things are more important than money." He grinned like a skull. "Bet you never thought you'd hear someone in my position, in this business, say that, huh? But in this case, it's true. I took the same oath all y'all did, and this shit pisses me off as much as it does Strand. He might be all but out, but we're not. I'll be damned if I let the cartels, the Chinese, and Devon Fucking Archer run people off their land just so Beijing can maintain its stranglehold on rare earth minerals and Archer can get a few hundred million dollars more to blow on hookers and coke."

He looked down at his watch. "I've got to get moving if you guys are going to be getting on a plane in a few hours. Get in touch with Casper over at the ranch. Cell coverage is a little spotty out there, so keep trying if you don't get through immediately. He'll get you up to speed. They've had a couple of incidents already, so be ready to hit the ground running when you get out there." He reached for the end call button, then paused. "Good luck, gents. I wish I was going with you, but this is the price *I* paid to get this off the ground. Desk work, phone calls, and emails." He shook his head. "I should have roped some eager ladder-climber into the CEO job and been an owner-operator. Oh, well. Good hunting." He ended the call.

There was a brief moment of silence as we all mulled it over. Nobody had said it yet, but the fact of the matter was, we'd just declared war. Not just against Devon Archer and all the corrupted elements of the Federal government he could get to cover for him, but also against the People's Republic of China, and more than likely the Sinaloa cartel.

That was big. Bigger than I think any of us wanted to think about.

And it was about to get darker than any of us were quite ready for.

***

I don't know what kind of hoops Goblin had to jump through to make it happen, but he got us all on the same flight to El Paso. I would have tried to fly into Las Cruces itself, but it turned out that no airliners were going there, despite LRU calling itself an "International Airport."

We got two rental vehicles, even though there were only four of us. Once again, Pallas Group Solutions was footing a hell of a bill but having two mutually supporting elements was better than cramming everyone into one vehicle. Goblin was thinking tactically rather than financially, and I appreciated it.

Both vehicles were Nissans, a Pathfinder and a Frontier. I moved slightly faster than Phil and got the keys to the Frontier. It wasn't going to be nearly as nimble as my Dodge back home, but I preferred pickups to SUVs. Phil grumbled a little, but we loaded up and headed for the rendezvous point outside the airport.

Given the heightened threat on the ranch, we'd debated just driving straight there, but Frank had kiboshed the idea. We'd be traveling along Highway 9, within less than a mile of the border, not to mention the close proximity to Cuidad Juarez, which might not be *quite* the Murder Capitol of the World anymore, but that was a bit hard to be sure about. Frank didn't want us driving that route, especially getting closer to the ranch, unarmed.

So, we pulled into the Bassett Place shopping mall parking lot, staying as far off by ourselves as possible, and linked up with Salt and Hoop.

I didn't know Hoop, but Saul "Salt" Drake and I went way back. The big man was leaning against the back hatch of his SUV with his arms folded as we pulled up and parked alongside, and he cracked a faint, lopsided smile as I got out of our truck. It wasn't much of a smile, but on Saul it was the equivalent of an ear-to-ear grin.

We shook hands, and his grip was as crushing as ever. "Still haven't gotten a haircut, I see." That actually drew a slightly wider grin from him.

"Never." He nodded toward my chin. "Still haven't had a shave, I see." That was one thing that Saul had never been able to stand. He'd grow his hair out to make up for all the years of high-and-tights in the Rangers, but shaving was a daily ritual for him—sometimes twice a day. His jaw was faintly blue from his thick beard, and he couldn't abide the stubble for whatever reason.

I grinned and scratched my own beard, which wasn't quite as thick as Saul's could have been. "Twelve years and counting." I kept it trimmed, because I was still a professional, not Grizzly Adams, but I hadn't actually shaved since my EAS date.

Saul, being Saul, got back to business, jerking his head toward the SUV. "Come on. Let's get you loaded up and get on the road."

The back was stacked with body armor, helmets, NVGs, radios, blowout kits, four rifle cases with Recce 16s and Glock 19s, and four ammo cans packed with preloaded magazines. "All yours. I don't know who Goblin threatened or bribed to get this out here so fast, but we picked it all up a little over an hour ago."

I nodded my thanks as we started to transfer the weapons and gear. We were in the middle of a parking lot, so getting jocked up for a firefight right then and there was inadvisable, but at the very least, as I shoved the weapons cases into the back seat of the cab, I opened them, pulled out the Glocks, and put them up front, along with the holsters and mag carriers. We still had our on-body first aid kits and tourniquets, so we were already carrying those. Go bags would need to be replenished, but that could wait until we got to the ranch.

Hopefully.

We loaded up and Salt and Hoop led out, our two vehicles falling in behind. It was going to be a bit different, falling in on an already established team, but nothing that most of us hadn't done before on contract. Usually, we got shipped in or out of country one or two at a time, switching out with partners ever month or two. I'd done close protection trips where I'd worked with half a dozen different partners over the course of two and a half months.

With our Glocks on our belts and Drew in the back seat to prep the gear and the carbines, we headed out of El Paso, toward New Mexico and the Bowman ranch.

CHAPTER
31

We arrived to find the place in an uproar.

Frank Moretti came out on the porch as we pulled up. "Come on. You got here just as things clacked off."

We hastily dragged our gear and rifles out of the vehicles and followed him inside. There was quite a bit of noise, but none of it seemed to be coming from our guys, or most of the Bowman family men. The three of them were pretty grim, while the little kids were scared, and the mother seemed openly distraught.

"Trevor, this is Chris, Andrew, Phil, and Marcos." Frank introduced us to the patriarch of the family quickly and brusquely. "They're here to back us up, and I might be putting them front and center on this. We still need most of the rest on ranch security."

"What is 'this,' Frank?" I wasn't impatient, exactly, but I'd been up for a while, it had been a long drive from the airport, and it looked like we were about to get thrown into the meat grinder right away.

Nothing like hitting the ground running.

Frank inclined his head toward the back of the house. "Better to brief it back there. The family's already seen it, and they don't need to go through that again." He glanced at where Emilia Bowman was sitting on the couch, holding her two youngest kids close to her, trying not to burst out crying. From

243

the redness in her eyes, perhaps the better expression would be that she was trying not to burst out crying *again*.

We followed Frank into one of the back rooms, what looked like it was a game room during better times. The guys had turned it into a team room, the ping-pong table folded up against the wall and the TV dark, maps put up over the shelves on the walls. He went to the folding table in the middle of the room and picked up a phone. Unlocking it, he brought up a video message and turned it toward us.

A young woman's tear-streaked face filled the screen. She'd been gagged, and a hand was twisted into her hair to wrench her head back to face the camera. I didn't recognize her, but the tears in Mrs. Bowman's eyes told me all I needed to know.

The man holding her by the hair turned the camera to face him. He was wearing a ball cap, sunglasses, and one of those retarded skull bandanas that tryhards use to try to look tough.

"As you can see, we have your daughter. If you ever want to see her alive and whole again, you will wire transfer us two million dollars. I will send the account number soon. Do not call the police or the sheriff. We are monitoring all their communications. If they begin to speak at all about her, she will die. It will take a long time. They will never find us before we have finished her off. I will be sure to send you video, though." He brought the camera even closer to his face. *"Do not fuck with me. Two million dollars, or she dies in agony after my homies and I have had our way with her."* The video ended.

"Ariana Bowman apparently slipped out to visit her boyfriend just after dark." Frank had waited for the video to end before he got down to brass tacks, but not much more than that. "She evidently didn't want one of us chaperoning the meeting, which is understandable for a teenage girl, but under these circumstances was not advisable."

"That's putting it mildly." Phil looked at the phone where Frank had put it back down, an expression somewhere between resignation and disgust on his face. Of course, Phil had a teenage daughter, so he was probably putting the closest thing he had to a brave face on it. He could be a hard case, but I knew he was thinking about his girl. That could either cause some serious problems, or it might just fuel the fire.

Knowing Phil as I did, I figured it was fueling the fire. Those *sicarios* would probably be better off eating their own guns before Phil got to them, *if* we found them.

"Now, she's not dumb, exactly, though she's young enough that her impulse control can obviously use some work." I didn't know if Frank had kids, but if so, he was keeping it together rather well. This was every father's nightmare, and I was sure that every dad on the team was feeling it. "She still should have known better, but the Bowmans have been making supply runs into Las Cruces every week or two for a while. They've had people follow them a couple times, but until now, all the actual violence has been out here at the ranch, not in town." He gusted a sigh. "That's apparently changed."

"I think we know what they meant by 'turning up the pressure.'" I felt a rising anger in my own chest, that had little to do with my sympathy for the Bowmans and nightmares about something like this happening to my own kids. A distant, clinical part of my mind noted that the more we engaged the cartel, the more likely we were going to have to take some serious precautions that this didn't happen to our own families, but for the moment I had that line of thought compartmentalized. No, this rage was the same as I'd felt toward the Al Qaeda in Iraq savages, who'd avoided getting in a fight with us for weeks at a time, only to come back to whichever dirt-poor little farming village we'd patrolled and murder the man whose house we'd used as a patrol base. It was the same rage that I always felt toward the strong who victimized the weak to get at those who might otherwise beat them in a fair fight.

While I might be good at it, a part of me hated this "gray zone warfare" shit. These bastards were willing to torture and murder a teenage girl to get what they wanted. And there were Americans complicit in it.

These fuckers were going to pay. *If* we could find them.

Frank, for his part, was nodding. "There's no way that the Bowmans have two million dollars to cough up. That's why they didn't set a hard deadline. Soon enough, Archer-Lin Investments or one of their shell companies is going to sidle up and make another offer, and with his daughter's life on the line, how is Mr. Bowman going to refuse?"

"Do we have any idea where they might be holding her?" Drew was probably the calmest of everyone in the room, though he was also probably the angriest. Drew's anger was cold and calculating.

"We're working on it. The office's cyber gremlins are already going over the video and all the associated call data with a fine-toothed comb. They made the call from Ariana's phone, and it's turned off, so even if we had a Scorpion, we wouldn't be able to track it down. However, there are apparently ways to get the tracking history, which will tell us where it was when it was last turned off, along with what direction it was moving." He grinned without humor. "For once, Big Tech's ubiquitous tracking and spying can work to our advantage."

"Doesn't somebody have to have account access for that to work?" Marcos was thinking while the rest of us were trying to fight down our bloodlust to get to work.

"They do, which is where we're running into roadblocks," Frank replied. "Ariana didn't share her account password with her parents, so our guys are having to try to brute force their way in."

Marcos was thinking, though, his brow furrowed. "Is this her first phone?"

Frank frowned back. "I don't know."

Marcos nodded toward the living room. "Let's ask. If it's not, and her first one is still around, we might be able to get in and use her account through it." He didn't *quite* smile. It wasn't the time for that. "Teenage girls can be incredibly obsessive about privacy without having the know-how or attention to detail to ensure it. If she didn't unlink her account and we can get into the phone, then we might be in business."

Frank swept a hand toward the door. "Let's go, then. I hope you're right."

Phil looked at me with raised eyebrows, and I shrugged. A lot of guys in this business have knowledge and interests that would surprise a lot of people. Hell, Saul, as big, grim, and taciturn as he was, had a master's degree in mechanical engineering and was close to earning a doctorate.

Marcos had moved quickly, and by the time we got out into the living room, Mrs. Bowman, her eyes still red, was leading him toward Ariana Bowman's bedroom. I hoped this wouldn't take too long.

Frank took me by the arm. "While he's trying to get that figured, you guys need to be ready to move." He led the way back to the team room. "The cyber guys are trying to use as much as they can see of the background in the video to determine a location. There are apparently at least a couple frames where they can see out the window behind the *sicario*, and some of these guys are borderline autistic when it comes to putting some of those details together. Even if Marcos can't put the phone to use, hopefully they'll at least have a neighborhood for you to start your search."

"And if the Bowmans get an offer from Archer first?" It was a concern. We couldn't force Mr. Bowman to hold the line, and with his daughter's life on the line, he had to be thinking through his options. I'd like to think that I'd keep my perspective and trust the highly trained, highly experienced killers who were assuring me that they'd find my kid, but truth be told, wouldn't the offer of the money to get her back be a bit more promising?

Not that I thought the bad guys were going to give her back, anyway. She'd disappear into the web of human trafficking, provided they didn't just kill her for shits and giggles beforehand. But Mr. Bowman didn't know that. Even if he suspected it, he didn't *know* it, and he'd be thinking, weighing his options with the threat to his daughter acting as one huge thumb on the scale. Could he afford to pass up the chance?

"Leave that to me." Frank didn't look like he was enjoying the prospect. "We're expecting that call any minute now, though they might be waiting to let desperation really set in. They're shitty like that. I'll try to buy us time, but it might actually work to our advantage if he agrees. It's not like they'll just roll right up with a contract in the next five minutes. It'll take time to get the money, which is time we can use to find the girl and launch a rescue op."

Of course, a "rescue op" was going to result in a lot of dead people on the ground, but that went with the territory. The trick was making sure the hostage didn't end up among those dead people.

"Let's get as prepped as we can."

CHAPTER
32

As it turned out, both Goblin's cyber guys and Marcos came up with results at almost the same time.

It was still almost too late.

Marcos had just come into the living room when Mr. Bowman's phone rang. The old man, who seemed to have aged a year just since Drew, Phil, Marcos, and I had arrived, just stared at the unfamiliar number on the screen for a moment before he answered it, turning on the speaker so the rest of us in the room could hear. Casey, Manny, Nick, and Matt had joined us, coming off perimeter patrol as it got dark again, and Frank was right at Mr. Bowman's elbow. Mrs. Bowman had ushered the rest of the kids out to the kitchen, and Jacob was somewhere out in the desert with the rest of the team.

"Hello?" Trevor Bowman already had a gravelly voice, but the strain of worry had almost reduced it to a whisper.

"Mr. Bowman?" The voice on the other end of the circuit was young, female, and indecently chipper. "My name is Natalie, and I represent a group of investors who are very interested in your property. There is a considerable opportunity coming up, and we'd like to offer you a really good deal."

They'd just made their latest miscalculation. In trying to act like nothing was the matter, and that it was just coincidence that they happened to be calling that night, their sacrificial lamb of a caller sounded breezy and cheery, in decided contrast to the dread and anguish that gripped the Bowmans. It came across as callous, even if it was unintentional. And I saw Mr. Bowman grit his teeth.

"You fucking vultures." His rasp of a voice rose to a snarl. "You think I don't know what you're doing? You think I don't know why you're calling *now*, of all times?"

"Mr. Bowman…" She sounded legitimately shocked. It was entirely possible that she had no idea what was going on and didn't even grasp why she'd been instructed to call *now*.

"Don't ever call me again." Bowman ended the call with a stabbing finger that he clearly wished was a weapon he could thrust through the woman's throat.

Then he realized what he'd done, and he started to shake.

Frank was at his side, putting an arm around his shoulders. I couldn't hear what he said in the old man's ear, but he eased him down to the couch before his knees buckled and he collapsed. He had to be reassuring him that we weren't going to let anything happen to his daughter.

I just hoped we had the time. The clock had started ticking as soon as he'd rejected the offer.

Frank was clearly thinking the same thing. As hard as he was working to control his facial expression, I could see it in his eyes. He really wished that Mr. Bowman had strung Archer's people along a little bit. Maybe a day. Maybe more. As it was, we were up against it.

Marcos tapped me on the shoulder. "I think I've got something." He kept his voice down, so as not to disturb Mr. Bowman or get his hopes up too high. "The office sent an intel dump, too, and it's matching up pretty good."

If Marcos thought it was good, I figured we needed to move on it, before those animals cut Ariana Bowman up for dog treats. I caught Frank's eye and signaled that we had to go. He nodded and mouthed, "Go."

We were almost at a run on the way out of the room.

Marcos rode with me and Drew, Casey having jumped in with Phil in the trail vehicle. For all we knew, we were far too few for a hostage rescue hit, but odds were pretty good that being sneaky was going to work a lot better than rolling up fast and loud, throwing a cordon around the house and kicking in the door. It wouldn't take much for the bad guys to kill their captive as soon as we rolled up. Besides, we didn't have the gear to look like a SWAT team this time.

"The intel guys in the office think that they've identified North Franklin Mountain in the window behind the kidnapper." Marcos was surprising everyone at how clinical and precise he'd gotten. I don't think any of the team had seen Marcos The Intel Nerd before. We all knew the older, taciturn hardass. "By figuring out the angles, they think that they've narrowed down a line, at least, where the video was taken. It's basically a resection."

"Good thing we're a bunch of old farts in this truck," Drew quipped from the back seat, where most of the weapons and gear were staged. "Otherwise, I might not know what you're talking about. What with GPS and all."

A resection is a technique for determining your location by measuring the azimuths to at least two different points, putting yourself on two lines, intersecting and showing you your grid coordinate on a map. It's a map and compass technique, so a lot of the younger guys, who only used GPS, wouldn't know it.

Marcos was too involved in his brief to even notice the quip. "Anyway, putting that line up against the track left by Ariana's phone tracker history, we come to this." He held up the tablet where I could see it, but I could barely spare a glance from the road. We weren't going all the way to Las Cruces, but rather across the state line into Northwest El Paso, but we still had between thirty and thirty-five miles to go, so I wasn't sparing the horses.

251

"Break it down for me Barney style, Marcos, I've got to drive."

"The track intersects with the line at this address." He tapped the map tablet clipped to the dash, with the route he'd hastily put in as we'd started rolling onto Highway 9. "It looks like they took her to the house, made the video, and then turned the phone off. Unless they moved her again, then that should be our target."

"I doubt they moved her." Drew and I had forced ourselves to watch the video a couple more times, just to pick out any details we could find. "She was shackled to the bed. It was hard to see, but it was there. That place was a stash house. They probably figured that nobody would be looking for the phone until after they sent the call, so that was why they turned it off afterward."

"Don't underestimate these savages." I'd seen it before, seen an unexpected level of professionalism and sophistication coming from two-legged wolves who would torture and murder people just to make a point, or just for the hell of it. "They might be that sloppy. They *probably* figure that we're on our own, and a handful of security guards under investigation by the FBI can't be *that* much of a threat. But maybe they're not. Maybe they did decide to move her, *just in case.*"

"In that case, we need to consider our follow-on actions." Drew was compartmentalizing, as he usually did. I think we all were at that point.

"If she's not there, then she's dead." It was a rough thing to say, but it had to be said. As soon as Old Man Bowman had hung up on Archer's lackey, events had gone into overdrive, even though we hadn't seen them yet. With that leverage removed, all hell was about to break loose. If they couldn't pressure the Bowmans to sell with the life of their daughter hanging in the balance, my guess was that the next step was going to be to kill the entire family and take the ranch by force. The Chinese clearly weren't interested in half

252

measures, and the cartel wouldn't be, either. If nothing else, with Archer's money no longer a factor, it may even become a matter of the cartel doing business directly with the Chinese. It wouldn't stand up under American law, but that close to the border, would they really care?

"We'll have to get back to the ranch fast, then." Drew was thinking along the same lines. "Even then, we might be too late."

"Or we might be just in time to pull a flanking attack." Marcos was just as detached as either of the other two of us. We had to be. Getting emotional at a time like this was a recipe for disaster, even though we were still twenty miles out and I had every nightmare scenario possible going through my head, from a dry hole and Ariana's body showing up in a ditch a week later to getting there and finding that we were just seconds too late. "The rest of the team ain't exactly pushovers."

I hoped he was right, even as I pressed the pedal a little closer to the floor.

***

I'd wanted to approach on foot, spread out in ones and twos, converging on the house at the last moment, allowing no warning until we were right on top of them. It would have meant pistol work instead of carbines, but we had enough 9mm to make that work. Goblin had even sent some of the 33-round mags, for when things really got interesting but we couldn't go to long guns.

If we'd had more time, it might have worked. We didn't have time, though. We stopped in the parking lot of a kitchen supply store for about five minutes to go over what imagery Marcos had pulled off the internet and form a hasty plan, long on speed, surprise, violence of action, and "situation dictates" and painfully short on details. Taking the risk, we'd jocked up right there in the parking lot on the side of Montoya Road, plate carriers, helmets, and all, before piling back into the vehicles and roaring down the road toward our target.

We approached from the south, having done a big J-turn off Highway 20. I was worried about *halcones*, the young lookouts whom the cartels recruited to act as their early warning system, but it was just late enough that the streets in the little neighborhood were pretty empty. We were moving fast for the area, and I got a glimpse of a rather indignant look from a middle-aged woman in a minivan as we screamed past her, going deeper into the residential area, but that was it.

We screeched to a stop in front of the house. I had to push in front of a car parked out front, while Casey brought the Pathfinder in behind it. Then we all piled out as fast as we could, dragging rifles with us. I cleared the street quickly with eyes and muzzle before turning in front of the hood and toward the house.

The window out front was curtained and dark, and the front door was on the other side of a plank fence that completely surrounded the property except for the unkempt, un-cared for landscaping out front. That was an indicator that this wasn't just another neighborhood house, though the vast number of vehicles inside that fence on the imagery was another.

I'd expected all hell to break loose as soon as we braked out front, but everything was quiet, at least except for the pounding music coming from inside. *They probably didn't even hear us. Fucking amateurs.*

Phil and Casey set security on the front, moving quickly to the corner of the street-side wing of the house where they could keep eyes and muzzles on the front gate. Marcos, Drew, and I moved to the big vehicle gate in the fence that led to the back.

It wasn't locked, which was good, but it squealed when I pulled it open. I winced, but Drew had shifted outward with his rifle leveled, covering me through the opening in the gate as

254

I rolled it back. He didn't open fire, didn't make any move that might suggest that we were made and about to get into a firefight.

The music was louder. It sounded like a *narcocorrido*, a northern Mexican ballad about narco traffickers, murderers, and bandits. I couldn't make out the words, but I didn't need to. I'd heard some of them before. Sick shit, a lot of them.

Still, for the moment, I'd take it. It would mask our movement.

That didn't mean we could move as slowly as I would have liked. On a "soft" hit, it paid to move slowly, carefully, and quietly, especially in places where there just might be IEDs or other booby traps set in. The cartels *had* used IEDs, even Stateside.

This couldn't stay a soft hit, though, despite how it had started. We didn't have the time. Ariana didn't have the time.

Leaving the gate open just far enough for one man to get through, I stepped in behind Drew, letting my muzzle drop level past his shoulder as I cleared the gateway and stepped into the yard, moving out to his left as he pushed past the first parked vehicles, their hoods facing away from the house. They provided a bit more concealment as we went, anyway, giving us a bit more of the element of surprise until we were right on top of the bad guys.

The back was a junkyard. There were five vehicles in various states of disrepair along the northern wall, and another eight or so in the back. Drew and I might have crouched down to hide below the hoods, but we were at the point where bullets would do just as well as concealment, so we just glided along as best we could toward the back of the house.

We rounded the corner and came within sight of the patio at the same time, muzzles tracking toward the angle we couldn't see from the side of the house. We were moving quickly but quietly, still unwilling to go loud until we were right on top of the bad guys. Without suppressors, once this went loud, it was going to go *really* loud.

The patio on the back was set in a curve from the corner to the back door. Even as we came around, muzzles sweeping toward that door, a man in black jeans and a dark collared shirt stepped out onto the patio, lighting a cigarette as he came.

For a moment, we were faced with a dilemma. While a part of me knew that we had to kill everyone who wasn't a prisoner in that house, I hesitated at shooting a man without warning, possibly unarmed, on American soil. It was one thing in a warzone, though even there it wouldn't have been an easy thing to justify. "Hostile Act, Hostile Intent." That had always been the ROE, and it was hard-wired into most of us.

The catch was that we'd been able to take detainees as Marines. As private contractors, that got a little thornier.

The next instant, though, the man with the cigarette noticed us, started, dropped the cigarette, and grabbed for the gun in his waistband.

Both of us shot him before his hand closed on the grip. Our rifles thundered as one, and bullets ripped through his chest and throat, spattering blood on the doorway behind him. He staggered and fell on his ass as we closed in, looking up at us with uncomprehending rage, still trying to pull the gun out of his waistband.

I shot him in the forehead from about three feet away as Drew and I pushed on the door, moving fast now that the quiet of the night had been broken by gunfire. He dropped like a sack of shit as his brains painted the patio, and then he was gone as Drew kicked in the door and I rode it to the wall, pivoting to clear the entryway.

We were in an extension, sort of a mud room or storage room. It was a mess, somewhat to be expected, but opened on the kitchen, where another man had looked up, startled, at the gunfire. He was already yelling and darting for the corner of the room.

Drew shot him down on the move, at the same time that the two of us flowed into the kitchen, splitting to dig the corners to left and right as we went. He yelled in agony as his knees collapsed under him and he plowed into the table, just short of the shotgun leaning against it. Chairs went flying and the shotgun clattered to the linoleum. The narco kept dragging himself toward the weapon, so I shot him once more as I swept my muzzle back across the room, then I double tapped him again when he didn't stop moving, my first round punching through his upper back and the second blowing off the top of his skull.

The inside of the house was already pandemonium. The music was even louder in there, and it was now accompanied by high-pitched screams of pain and terror, almost drowning out the angry shouts of the *sicarios*, who were now alerted.

With the kitchen, small dining room, and living room taking up about a third of the house, we had two ways we could go. Drew was already moving toward the short hallway leading to the two bedrooms on the left. I fell in alongside him, Marcos joining us and covering the six o'clock as well as the other bedroom as we moved on the first door.

There was no stack up, no waiting. This had to happen fast. Drew moved up to cover the hallway toward the last bedroom, I kicked in the door, and Marcos and I went through like a battering ram while Drew swung in behind us, quickly clearing the rear as he came.

The bedroom was stripped down to the walls and crammed with about half a dozen people. Four of them were in the corners, huddled in almost the fetal position, their hands zip-tied behind their backs. A fifth was down on the floor in the middle, stripped to his skivvies, battered, bruised, and bloodied.

The man standing over him had turned around, what looked like a blackjack in his hand. He dropped it as we bulled our way into the room, but he immediately reached for something at the small of his back.

Bad call.

The reports of two 5.56 carbines hammering in a twelve by twelve foot room were brutal. The prisoners flinched and cowered as the muzzle blast slapped at them, and the man on the floor was spattered with blood as about ten rounds tore through the *sicario*'s chest and out his back. He fell on the brutalized man on the floor, twitching, and then we swept our muzzles across the rest of the room, quickly evaluating the poor bastards tied up against the wall.

Illegals, more than likely. Kidnap victims, now. Being held by the cartel for ransom, slave labor, or both.

They weren't our concern. We were there for Ariana. Marcos led the way back out and into the hall.

It took a couple seconds to get to the next door. I couldn't hear much on the other side with all the noise, so we just slammed through the door again, making entry with as much fury and violence as possible.

This narco was waiting for us, though.

He had Ariana Bowman held in front of him, her head cranked back by her hair, a knife to her throat. She was in her underwear, almost as bruised and bloodied as the man on the floor in the other room.

Marcos had dug his corner as he'd come through the door, which left me confronting the hostage taker as he glared over her shoulder at me. She was crying quietly, in too much fear with the razor-sharp steel at her throat to make any more noise than that.

I might have tried to negotiate. Tried to get him to put the knife down. Instead, I put my red dot about three inches above his eyeball and squeezed the trigger.

Ariana flinched badly at the concussion and the *snap* of the bullet going right past her ear. The knife cut her, leaving a red line on her neck as my shot blew through the narco's eyeball and cored out his brain, spattering blood, hair, and fragments of bone against the wall behind him. He went limp and collapsed, dragging her down to the floor with him, even as the knife clattered to the floor at her feet.

Marcos had pivoted to cover the door as I moved in, and right then his rifle thundered again as he engaged someone else entering the hallway. There was still that last room.

I wasn't sure I wanted to know what we'd find in there. The whole place stank, and not only with the stench of people tied up for too long in too close quarters without bathing. There was some heavy shit going on in that house.

Drew got to her before I did, his muzzle pointed at the ceiling. "It's okay, we've got you." He glanced up at me for a moment and gave me a quick nod. I returned it. He'd take care of Ariana. We still needed to finish clearing this house. We might not be able to do much about the illegals, but we still *could* kill every murderous cartel gunman in the place.

Marcos and I flowed out into the hallway again, passing the still-twitching body of the man he'd shot from the doorway. Blood was seeping from the dead man's mouth, nose, and a nasty hole in his throat, and his eyes were open, fixed and staring at the ceiling.

I still bent to thump one eyeball with my muzzle as we passed, just to be on the safe side. He didn't even blink.

The two of us came out of the hallway just as a burst of full-auto gunfire tore through the drywall and forced us both to drop to the floor. Shattered plaster and bits of mud and paint flew through the air as bullets carved their way through the walls, tracking higher as the *sicario* in the last bedroom lost control of the recoil.

I started to crawl out into the living room, rolling to my side in an attempt to bring my rifle to bear, when a muffled, thunderous series of gunshots sounded from the front of the house and the burst of gunfire stopped. Casey and Phil had cleaned up through the window.

Marcos and I got back on our feet, fighting our way up with weapons still leveled. That one shooter had apparently been neutralized, but that didn't mean we were out of the woods. I paused just long enough at the doorway to get the nod from Marcos that he was up, visible just out of the corner of my eye, and then we closed on the final bedroom.

It was an abattoir. Bodies were strewn across the carpeted floor, which wasn't just soaked with the blood of the man with no shirt, lying on his face next to the AK he'd sprayed bullets through the wall with. It wasn't just the fresh blood leaking from the other half-dozen corpses lying crumpled against the walls with their hands flex-cuffed behind their backs, either. The carpet was *crusted* with dried blood and other fluids. They'd killed their victims in here before.

Unfortunately, there was nothing we could do for these poor bastards. Some of them looked like they'd been in their teens.

"Clear." There wasn't anything else to say. Whoever had shot the *sicario* on the floor, Casey or Phil, had moved out of the window afterward, so we didn't need to deconflict there, fortunately. That could have been bad.

We moved back to the room with Ariana and Drew, quickly. Drew had her mostly dressed, wrapped in a coat too big for her, and was holding security. I looked down at the other prisoners, none of whom were looking up at me.

"We don't have time, Backwoods." Drew was right. I nodded and keyed my radio.

"Gunner, Backwoods. Four coming out, front door."

"Got you. Come ahead. Make it fast." Typical of Casey, he had to add that last part, as if we were dawdling. We'd been in the house for *maybe* two minutes.

With Drew keeping Ariana's head down, his arm around her shoulders and his muzzle pointed at the ceiling, I led out while Marcos took up rear security. I quickly cleared the front yard, as strewn with trash as it was, then moved to the gate, unlatching it and making sure I made visual contact with Phil before pushing out onto the sidewalk.

We were mounted back up in the vehicles in seconds and driving away. I checked my watch. We'd been on target for a total of four minutes.

Now we just had to get back to the ranch before all hell really broke loose.

CHAPTER
33

Couldn't they have built the house on the hills up there?

Nick was leaning on the cab of one of the ranch trucks, behind one of the M5E1s, the bipods down on the metal. He couldn't load them that well, since even the rubber tips and the pitted, sun-damaged paint didn't make for enough friction, but the elevation was about all the advantage he was going to get.

He also didn't have the night optics he would have liked. The PS-31s were nice, and the company must have dropped a pretty penny on them—he was starting to wonder just where they'd gotten the capital—but they didn't work all that well with magnified optics. In fact, they didn't really work at all. To use night vision with a scope, the NVG had to be mounted *in front* of the optic, and they didn't have any of those mounts.

Something to bring up in the after-action, if we make it through the night.

Judging by the number of headlights gathered down on the side of Highway 9, that was far from guaranteed.

"Sure would be nice to have a belt-fed, wouldn't it?" Matt was outside the truck, which was currently parked in the brush about a hundred yards to the west of the ranch buildings, at an angle to the highway and the road leading up to the ranch house. That way he could still brace himself over the hood while Nick still had some real estate on top of the cab to use.

He had his rifle lying on the hood and his binoculars to his eyes.

"It would be nice," Nick agreed. "But wish in one hand, shit in the other, and see which one fills up first." He almost winced a little at the hypocrisy of the comment, given what he'd just been thinking.

"Story of this job." Matt shifted a little as he scanned the glow on the southern horizon. Nick didn't know what he might be able to see from that position. Even with the little bit of elevation he got from standing in the bed of the truck, he could barely see some of the lights through the brush.

"Kinda overstating the case, don't you think?" Nick tapped the .308 marksman rifle in front of him. "I've been on contracts with way shittier gear. And those were for the US government."

"But at least we had machineguns and thermals then." Matt wasn't giving up. "Don't get me wrong; this is probably the best-equipped gig like this I could have imagined. Just isn't what we had before."

"In other words, we've got to bitch about *something*, even though it takes some looking?"

"Exactly."

Nick forced a chuckle as he got back on glass, though he couldn't help but think that Matt was talking to dispel some jitters. It was a weird time to be making quips, especially for Matt Patric.

None of us are young bucks anymore. We might be addicted to the action, but that's a lot of sons of bitches down there, with a lot of guns. There's too much time to reflect on everything we've got to lose while we wait for what looks like it's gonna be one hell of a firefight. They'd already deployed every asset they had hours before. Now all they could do was wait.

Nick would have preferred to go on the hunt, but with five men gone into town after Ariana, they simply didn't have the bodies or the guns. Not if they were going to keep the Bowmans safe. And that was what this job currently boiled down to.

Keep the Bowmans alive, and they kept the Chinese' and Devon Fucking Archer's hands off the ranch. At least for a while.

That might have been what was eating at Matt, too. Nick was trying not to think about it. *They'll find another way. They've got the money and the time. They'll come back around, come at these folks sideways, and stick a knife in their kidneys.*

Then the radio crackled. *"This is Casper. Drone confirms they're on the move. Single column, coming up the road, ten vehicles, approximately fifty shooters. Stand by."*

Nick settled himself a little more solidly behind the gun, shifting to cover the road. The worst case would have been that the bad guys would have spread out across the desert, advancing on line, spreading out the targets and potentially giving them access to the flanks. Instead, they were coming hey-diddle-diddle, straight up the middle.

They were going to pay for that.

The contractors didn't have any explosives, strictly speaking. Like machineguns, suppressors, and short-barreled rifles, those were NFA items, heavily regulated by the ATF, and they would have not only added to expenses, but they would have put the company solidly in the ATF's gunsights. After all, if they were just a security company, why would they *need* all that hardware? It was a bullshit argument but, given what Nick had already heard about the FBI's choice of who to investigate in this clusterfuck, the last thing PGS needed was extra attention from those goons at ATF.

So, the contractors, with the help of Trevor and Jacob Bowman, had improvised.

The odds that any of the cartel vehicles were using run-flat tires were pretty long, so while they didn't have the same sort of spike strips that law enforcement used, they'd been able to build some workable versions out of rebar and stock steel with the Bowmans' welder. Two of those were currently stretched across the main road that was effectively the Bowmans' driveway.

The lead vehicle hit them at full speed.

All four tires were immediately shredded, and the driver lost control, skidding sideways on the gravel road and flipping over with a catastrophic *crunch*. It wasn't an explosive, but it had done the trick.

The next two vehicles braked hard, swerving to right and left off the road to avoid the spikes. Frank had anticipated that, which was why they'd dug out good sized trenches with the Bowman's skid-steer on either side of the road, angled out a little bit to help disguise them, then filled in with sagebrush and tumbleweeds from the north side of the ranch. The first vehicle went in hard, hitting with an impact that Nick almost felt from five hundred yards away, dust billowing into the air from the hit. The second driver saw the trench, tried to stop and swerve away from it, and only succeeded in skidding sideways into the ditch, the truck tipping over and going in hard.

Nick was watching as the first of the *sicarios* crawled out of the flipped truck, dragging an AR with him. That was a weapon, which meant he was hostile. Technically speaking, that constituted "intent to commit grave harm." Not that Nick was going to hesitate because of legal issues right then, anyway. He put his reticle tick mark for five hundred on the man and squeezed the trigger.

The M5 had an eighteen-inch barrel, so it still spat some fire as it thundered, the buttstock surging back into his shoulder. The roof of the cab being as slick as it was, the gun bucked up and to the right, and he lost sight picture for a moment. When he brought it back down, the man was writhing out his death throes on the ground, partially lit by the one unbroken headlight remaining on the truck.

More gunfire thundered across the desert as the rest of the contractors opened fire. More *sicarios* went down, most of them as they tried to scramble out of the crashed trucks. A few tried to return fire, even as Nick drew a bead on yet another and dumped him with yet another 175 grain match round. Once again, the rifle bucked as he fired, but he was getting better at recovering his sight picture quickly.

Matt was shooting, too, though his 5.56 was somewhat less accurate and less effective at that range. More of the narco shooters dropped, some falling to gunfire, others getting the message and diving for cover.

In the meantime, the rest of the trucks behind the three crashed vehicles started to back up and turn around. Whoever was running the show down there had gotten the idea that just pushing straight up the driveway was not a good idea.

A few more shots chased the retreating vehicles down the driveway, but they weren't in a position to pursue, so pretty soon Frank's voice came over the radio. "Cease fire on the retreating vehicles. Money, Digger, Tonka, and Whack, sweep the roadblock, make sure we don't have any would-be Apaches creeping up on us."

Nick repositioned himself behind the M5, slowly sweeping across the kill zone. He had no targets at the moment, though he was pretty sure there were still at least a few bad guys down there. They'd just gone to ground. These guys might be savages with little training in actual infantry tactics, but they learned quick. They had to in order to survive the constant warfare that was the narco world.

He stayed where he was to cover the four-man maneuver element that was even then piling out of one of the rental SUVs to spread out in a skirmish line, rifles up and NVGs down.

Abaeze Okoro was out on the right flank, closest to Nick and Matt, and his weapon barked first, the flash strangely bright in the dark. Most of the contractors had gotten used to running suppressed, and that was back when they'd been running regular night ops, which for some of them had been quite a few years before.

Nick shifted his hips and his feet to rotate toward where Abaeze was shooting. He couldn't see a target, but that might have just been because he was looking through a scope in the dark. He was going to have to switch to his carbine soon, or the red dot mounted on top of the rear ring.

It wasn't *quite* so dark that he couldn't see another shape moving near the westernmost crashed truck, the one that was tipped over sideways in the trench. There was just enough glow from the headlights to let him see the dark glistening of blood on the man's face and the AK in his hands as he crawled out of the ditch and tried to get a shot at the maneuver element. Once more, Nick's M5 *boom*ed in the night, and when he brought the scope back down, there was no sign of the man with the Kalashnikov.

A crackle of gunfire thundered off to the left, as George and Josh took fire from the vehicle that was nose-down in the ditch and returned it with interest. Nick caught sight of a couple of sparks off the body of the wrecked truck as bullets hit it.

Another .308 *boom*ed from off to the east. That would be Saul with the other M5, ending the conversation. The gunfire went quiet except for the echoes.

Frank's voice came over the radio again. "Fall back to secondary defensive positions and get ready for the next hit. Those guys are going to be out for blood this time."

Nick scrambled down out of the bed as Matt jogged around and got in behind the wheel.

It was going to be a long night.

CHAPTER
34

The next hour felt like a lifetime.

With the enemy having retreated, the B Team fell back to the next line of trenches they'd dug with the skid-steer. Nick handed off the M5. There just wasn't enough light left to use it anymore, not without a forward-mounted night sight. Flipping his NVGs down, he checked that his red dot was dialed down to the NVG setting, too dim to see with the naked eye so that it wouldn't bloom too much in the image intensifier tubes.

He was about to get into his part of the trench, behind the big dirt berm that had been thrown up facing the road, when Frank intercepted him. "Nick, I need you and Matt on scouting duty." He jerked a thumb over his shoulder. "Mr. Bowman's given us the go-ahead to use his four-wheelers. I need eyes up on the hills. The drone's about out of juice and needs to recharge."

Nick nodded. He was already tired, feeling the adrenaline letdown after the action of the initial contact, but getting on the four-wheeler and heading up into the hills would be a good way not to start to drift while sitting in a trench waiting. "I'm on it."

He and Matt started back toward the barn with Frank. "Turns out, Mr. Bowman's actually slightly better equipped than we are." Frank chuckled. "He's got a night scope for his long range rifle, and we don't."

"Shows he knows what he's up against." Nick wasn't going to get upset about it. It was a good thing that at least *somebody* on the defense had the ability to really reach out and touch the enemy.

The four-wheelers were right inside the barn, covered by tarps, and they both started right up. Nick made sure to turn the headlights off. The noise would be enough; there was no reason to give the enemy any more specific indicators of their approach or position. It had been a while since he'd driven blacked out on NVGs, but the PS-31s with their white phosphor tubes were a bit clearer than the PVS-15s he'd used in Afghanistan. It shouldn't be too hard. The hard part would be negotiating the terrain as they got up into the volcanic hills to the west.

With a glance at Matt, getting a nod in return, Nick gunned the engine and headed toward the west.

He quickly angled toward the north as the two of them cleared the ranch buildings. The Bowmans and their hands had already taken some fire from that high ground where they were headed, so the cartel probably had a few preset observation posts up there and, after getting their teeth kicked in on the initial assault, something told him that they might already have some shooters on the move to get overwatch on the ranch. It was over two thousand yards, but the cartels had shown a propensity for using Barrett .50 cals, which could easily reach that far. Maybe not with a great deal of accuracy, not with a half-trained *sicario* behind the gun, but they could still do some damage.

The farther north they went, the less likely that they'd stumble on a group of cartel shooters without seeing them ahead of time.

There was more low ground running northwest in a line that wasn't *quite* an arroyo from just north of the ranch house to the hills off on the edge of the property. That would have been a perfect route, providing good cover, except that it was choked with brush that would slow them down too much. Instead, they followed the line of the seasonal streambed but stayed up on slightly higher ground, weaving through the sagebrush, creosote bushes, and occasional cactus.

They hadn't gotten far before a thunderous *boom* echoed through the night.

Nick braked, straightening up to scan the hills, and Matt skidded to a halt next to him. "That wasn't one of our .308s."

"No, that was a .50." A moment later, he caught the flash from up in the hills as the cartel gunman fired again, the *boom* coming a fraction of a second later. "They're already up there."

"We'd better move fast, then." Matt revved his four-wheeler, which wasn't exactly the best fieldcraft, since it just made more noise, but anyone up near that big anti-materiel rifle wasn't likely to hear it, anyway. "If they've already started in with the big stuff, then they're going to move in sooner than we thought."

Nick nodded. "And they won't be nearly so reckless this time." The element of surprise was gone, and with it went a good part of the contractors' advantage. They had some fortifications, but against close to forty shooters, their ten were still in a bad spot. Especially if they were pinned down by even semi-accurate fifty caliber fire.

He gunned the engine and headed straight for the hills.

It took another few minutes, swerving a few times to avoid thicker stands of brush, to get to the hills. Driving the four-wheelers into the brush in a shallow draw, the two men dismounted, brought their carbines around from where they'd been slung to their backs, and took stock.

There wasn't time for a proper security halt. That .50 was still thundering through the night, and while they hadn't heard more than sporadic small arms fire from the direction of the ranch buildings for the last few minutes, it was only a matter of time before the fight kicked into high gear again.

They took a knee in the sagebrush, about twenty yards from the parked ATVs, scanning the hillside above them and the desert nearby, straining their ears for the sounds of movement or voices that might indicate that they'd been detected, or that the bad guys were closing in on them.

The .50 *boom*ed yet again. Still no sounds of a firefight, though there was a slightly lighter *crack* of a long-range rifle, answered a moment later by the thunder of another .50 caliber shot. Mr. Bowman must have tried to take a shot at the .50 gunner.

"Hope the old man didn't just get his head taken off." Matt was on his feet, and Nick quickly followed.

With their rifles held ready, the two men started up the draw, finding as light a route through the brush as they could without exposing themselves. There was no guarantee that the bad guys didn't have NVGs of their own. The cartels sure had a lot of other top-of-the-line hardware, and the Chinese would have made sure that this bunch especially would be as well-equipped as possible.

Nick fell back until he was about five paces behind Matt. It was easy enough to see his partner in the white phosphor binocular NVGs, and dispersion was something that he hadn't forgotten from his patrolling days in the infantry, even before he'd gone to SFAS.

They worked their way up to the tableland atop the basalt hills. They would be a lot more exposed up there, but they could move faster and they had good sightlines with their night vision. Matt turned sharply southeast, following the line of the hills toward the thunder of the .50 cal.

Nick scanned the hilltops carefully but saw no silhouettes. If the narcos had staged on top of the tableland, they were lying low, which didn't seem like them. More likely, it was just the guy with the Barrett.

He moved out onto Matt's right flank, stepping it out to make sure he didn't fall too far behind. The Barrett thundered once more, and this time he saw the flash, though through some of the brush, making it easier to move in on their target.

Matt froze, throwing up a fist, and Nick spotted what had caused him to halt a moment later. The bad guy with the .50 hadn't come alone.

There was at least one head visible above the brush, made more visible by the fact that the idiot was smoking. The ember glowed like a star against the desert, pointing the *sicario*'s position out as clearly as if it had been spotlighted.

Nick slowed his advance down, rolling his boots carefully against the desert floor and trying his best not to brush against the sage and creosote bushes too much, as he continued to sweep out to Matt's right, searching the brush carefully to see if the cartel sniper had only one or more lookouts covering his six.

There were two. The other one was more alert than the guy smoking, crouching lower in the sagebrush, his rifle held low in front of him, the muzzle high. He was looking straight at Nick, but he didn't appear to have night vision. He didn't react like he'd just seen a man in plate carrier and helmet creeping through the weeds toward him.

He was definitely a hostile, though. There were no friendlies on the ranch that night except for the Bowmans and the PGS contractors.

Nick dropped to a knee next to a creosote bush, making one final scan of the desert in front of him as the .50 *boom*ed yet again, this time followed up by a sudden storm of small arms fire from somewhere below and to the south.

The next assault was already starting.

There was no more time. He rose to his feet to get a better shot and blasted the crouching man, leaning into the rifle and dumping five rounds into the shape of head and shoulders, as fast as he could get the dot to settle again in his NVGs. The guy toppled backward out of sight, but Nick was dead sure he'd gotten at least two good, fatal hits in.

Matt had engaged the smoker at the same moment, almost as if he'd read Nick's mind. Or else, he'd just figured that the renewal of the firefight below meant they *had* to move.

The two of them moved forward, almost side by side, guns up, muzzles sweeping from side to side, red dots now only a couple of inches below the line of sight through their NVGs. Matt fired once as he passed his target. That one must have still been moving, and therefore still a threat.

Nick lowered his gaze and his weapon as he passed the *sicario* he'd shot. He'd been dead on. The picture in his PS-31s was a little blurry that close, but he could still make out the dark, puckered hole punched through the man's cheek, right alongside his nose.

As he did so, he checked the flank one more time, just in case he'd missed somebody. Nothing. Only the desert, rocked once more by the concussion of the Barrett's muzzle blast.

Then they came over the slight rise and the cartel sniper was right in front of them.

Except there wasn't one cartel sniper. There were two.

One was down behind the expected Barrett, his eyes to the scope, but the other had an HK PSG-1. That one must have heard the gunfire behind them, because he had already rolled to his back and was pointing the heavy G3-derived sniper rifle at the two contractors as they crested the rise.

All three men fired at the same time. Nick was only vaguely conscious of the muzzle flash and the *crack* of the bullet as it went past, but the cartel shooter had been ever so slightly *too* fast on the trigger. He didn't have time to make up for his miss, as both Nick and Matt shot him about ten times as they continued to advance. The guy behind the Barrett M82 rolled to his side and grabbed for a pistol. He jerked and spasmed as the contractors' bullets tore into him, but he only stopped trying to bring the handgun around when Matt shot him through the skull, by then only about ten feet away.

They swept the position once more, double checking that there weren't any other bad guys still lurking around, then Nick moved up next to the Barrett and took stock.

Muzzle flashes flickered in two arcs around the southwest corner of the ranch, as the contractors and the Bowmans tried to fight off the renewed assault. More trucks were trundling across the desert from the highway, most blacked out, and far more muzzle flashes were coming from that long, curving line of enemy fighters than were coming from the trenches around the ranch house.

"That's why they took so long." Nick unslung his rifle and set it on the ground as he picked up the Barrett and moved it to where he could get a shot at the advancing cartel shooters. "They were bringing up reinforcements." There were definitely more than seven trucks down there, and more than thirty or forty shooters.

He got down behind the big rifle and got ready to lay some hate.

CHAPTER
35

For a moment, Nick could just take in what was happening. The cartel gunmen had brought up the big guns, not only the Barrett. There were definitely machineguns in the mix down there, MAG-58s from the sound of things. With the disparity in numbers and firepower, this was turning into a *very* bad night.

Time to even things up a little.

Leaning into the rifle, he loaded the bipods, wishing he remembered more of the ballistics for the .50 BMG. It had been a lot of years since he'd been behind a Barrett. He was going to have to shoot, spot, and correct on the fly, which was why he was doing his best to get really good and solidly behind the rifle, even as the urgency of the fight screamed at him to get on the gun and start shooting.

Can't help the boys down there by wasting all the ammo we've got. Granted, the cartel guys had brought a lot of ammo up on the dirt bikes that were lying on the ground not far away. But time was as valuable as ammunition, and you can't miss fast enough to win a gunfight.

With the rifle as rigid as he could get it, he started to search for targets, shifting his hips from side to side. The machineguns needed to be priority. They were the biggest threat, even though there were men on foot with rifles already pushing ahead of the trucks.

He spotted one, overcorrected, and had to shift back. A man in dark clothing was leaning into a MAG-58 in the back of what looked like a Ford Super Duty. It was a full-blown technical, with a post mount for the machinegun bolted into the bed and some sheet steel mounted on the sides.

Unfortunately for the gunner, even if that sheet steel would have stood up to .50 BMG rounds, Nick had a shot down into the back without even bothering with trying to defeat the improvised armor. He put the reticle on the gunner, held over what felt like the right amount, and squeezed off a shot.

The rifle bucked, the big brick of a muzzle brake blowing grit violently out to either side as flame blossomed from the muzzle. The shock was brutal, and he felt like he'd just been punched in the jaw. Still, his position was good enough that he was able to keep the reticle on target, at least mostly, even though he felt pretty sure that he'd blacked out for half a second.

It really had been a long time since he'd fired one of these beasts.

His holdover hadn't quite been on. The round punched into the side of the bed, just above the wheel well, rocking the vehicle with a flash and momentarily forcing the gunner to pause his fire as he looked for what had just happened.

That gave Nick just enough time to correct his hold. He fired again, riding the recoil and handling it a little better this time.

The heavy round was still low, but it took the gunner in the midsection, blowing a massive chunk of his flesh, guts, and pelvis all over the inside of the bed. He dropped, howling, to the bottom of the truck, though his screams were still drowned out by the thunder of gunfire.

The next round was for the cab, shattering the driver's side window and blowing off the driver's head. The truck began to slow, even as it started to swerve, the dead body dragging the wheel over from the momentum of the hit.

He shifted targets, then, knowing that it was only a matter of time before one of the other machinegunners figured out they were under fire and spotted the .50's muzzle flash. Even as he tried to shift and scan through the scope, Matt leaned down close and yelled, "Another technical, two vehicles down and to the right of that one!"

That helped. He picked up the second gunner, and this time his hold was a little better. The narco had swiveled his machinegun away from the ranch and was searching the hillside, but he was a touch too slow and couldn't see well enough. Nick's seven-hundred-grain bullet smashed through his throat, effectively decapitating him and sending his corpse tumbling to the bottom of the truck bed.

Another round immobilized the truck, and then Matt was calling out his next target.

He got a shot on another truck, though his hold was off again, and he missed high. Then another machinegunner spotted his muzzle flash and suddenly he had to go as flat as possible as bullets rained onto the hillside around them. He heard Matt grunt, and then he was just trying to find the machinegun and silence it.

The fire intensified, kicking grit into his face and forcing him as deep into the brush and dirt as he could get. For a moment, he almost froze, just trying to claw his way down through the ground, trying to survive the torrent of high-velocity metal.

To freeze was to die. He might be a small target, but he didn't have much cover at all. He had to take that belt-fed out of commission.

It wasn't that hard to pick out. Wherever the cartels had gotten their hardware, they were using standard 4 ball, 1 tracer, and as anyone with experience can tell you, tracers work both ways.

He followed the dashed line of red glowing sparks back to the stuttering flame of the MAG-58's muzzle blast, lined up what felt about like the hold, and dumped the rest of the magazine.

The recoil was brutal, and he missed with most of his shots, the spread almost as wide as the truck at that distance, but it almost didn't matter. The incoming fire ended immediately. Whether he'd hit the gunner or not, at least the close passage of eight .50 caliber rounds had made the man reconsider staying in place.

Leaving the empty rifle, even as some sporadic fire started to *snap* overhead again, Nick grabbed his carbine and rolled toward Matt, suddenly remembering that grunt and fearing the worst.

His partner was down, but not out. As he dropped his PS-31's tubes back in front of his eyes, he saw Matt cranking down on a tourniquet around his leg. "Took one just above the knee." He was clearly speaking through clenched teeth. "I can still move, but I'm gonna be slower."

Nick got up on a knee. They were above the military crest of the hill, which actually gave them some cover from the closest cartel shooters. The others could still shoot at them, but they were starting to take more accurate fire from the ranch buildings, which precluded much in the way of effective fire on the hilltop.

Grabbing Matt by the plate carrier, keeping his head down as much as he could, Nick started to drag him away from the cartel sniper hide.

Matt was trying to help, but his leg was fucked up. The bullet had probably broken the bone, and he was gritting his teeth, trying not to cry out. More rounds *snap*ped overhead, getting closer as the cartel shooters adjusted. Nick was sure that more dirt bikes with more *sicarios* would be on their way in a matter of minutes.

He got to a fold in the ground and had to stop, just for a moment, to fix his grip on Matt's plate carrier. His partner was heavy, and it had been too long since he'd done a long-distance drag. *Something to add to the training schedule, if we get through the night.*

"Hold up here." The pain in Matt's voice was palpable, even over the cacophony of gunfire below. "You got to go back and get that Barrett, man."

"What?" Nick found himself thrown for a loop. "No. Fuck the Barrett. We gotta get you out of here."

Matt grabbed his sleeve with surprising intensity. "Listen. Croak. If you don't grab that bastard and bring it with us, then they'll just fall back in on it in the next few minutes, and we'll be right back where we started. I've got a tourniquet on, I'll be good. Hell, I can even still shoot." His voice faltered for a moment, probably as another wave of pain passed through him. "But you got to get that damned thing, or we came up here for nothing." He tried to grin, though the expression was a little blurry at that distance through Nick's NVGs. "I'd hate to lose my leg for nothing."

Nick gritted his teeth, but Matt was right. There was no support coming, not unless the hostage rescue team got back in a hurry, and even then, five dudes with a potentially traumatized teenage girl in tow weren't going to be able to do much against the growing cartel dogpile down there. They were it, which meant they had to make every shot count. That included denying the enemy resources that could make the night worse.

"Don't you fucking bleed out while I'm gone." Keeping low, he turned and ran back toward the Barrett.

A gunshot *crack*ed behind him, and he almost froze, wondering if something had just gone terribly wrong. But the shot was echoed a second later by a scream of pain from off to his right. Matt had hitched himself a little higher in that fold in the ground and was covering him.

281

He threw himself flat as a long, staccato burst of fire went over his head, another *sicario* opening up in reaction, the muzzle flash strobing in the dark just up the hill from where the Barrett lay. Rolling to one side, he returned fire, aiming just beneath the flash as he dumped rounds as fast as he could ride the trigger reset, hardly worrying about how the dot jumped and danced in his NVGs.

He hit something, because the incoming fire ceased, and a gurgling scream went up over the desert.

Scrambling to his hands and knees, he practically bear-crawled the rest of the way to the .50, moving as fast as he could. Matt wasn't shooting any longer, and he hoped that meant that there had only been two of the bad guys, and not that Matt was lying unconscious or dead back there. There hadn't been time to check and make sure that the wound in his leg was the only one.

Grabbing the M82 by its carry handle, keeping his head down and his carbine muzzle high, he turned and ran back toward where he'd left Matt. He hadn't heard the dirt bikes as the bad guys had come up on them, not over the gunfire, so he had no way to know if more of them were coming. He just knew that he needed to get off that X, fast.

Matt was still up behind his rifle as Nick threw himself down in the fold. "I can't carry this and drag you." Now that he had the Barrett, the question was what to do with it.

"Pull the bolt. I'll carry it." Matt's voice was hoarse and tight with pain, but he was holding it together. "They can't do much with it without that."

Nick cursed himself for not thinking of that before. *Still, probably better to do it back here, where we've got some cover.* He hastily pulled the retaining pins, pried the upper receiver off, and dragged the heavy bolt out of the rifle. Matt reached out a hand and stuffed it in a cargo pocket, on his unwounded leg. "Let's go. Before they push any more shooters up here."

Nick thought he could hear an engine revving. Matt was right. It was time to get the hell out of Dodge, even if that meant going back down into a besieged defensive position.

Grabbing his partner by the plate carrier again, he started down toward where they'd left the ATVs.

CHAPTER 36

We were flying down the highway, at least as fast as we could manage without standing out enough to get pulled over. Getting stopped by the New Mexico State Police with the hardware we had in the vehicles, not to mention a traumatized girl, would raise too many questions. I was *reasonably* sure we'd be okay, especially since Ariana was crying and babbling her gratitude, but having removed the leverage of their hostage, it was only a matter of time before the narcos hit the ranch.

My phone buzzed, which was less than convenient since I was driving. I'd been the mission commander, so I technically probably should have been in the right seat, but I'd jumped in behind the wheel anyway.

Digging in my pocket, I dragged the phone out, sparing just enough of a glance at it to see that it was Frank. I answered it, putting it to my ear since I had to focus on the road instead of trying to turn on the speaker. "Talk to me."

He almost didn't have to. I could hear the rattle of gunfire in the background. "Don't come straight in. We are engaged, and the highway's going to be a deathtrap. We're under attack by at least fifty shooters, and they already gotten reinforcements once, so we can't be sure that that's all of them. We're holding our own for the moment, but we are badly outnumbered." He was being succinct, simply reporting the situation, despite the absolute hell I could hear going on around him. "I can't tell you not to come in, but you're going to have to come by the back way, and that's going to take time." An even more intense, hammering fusillade of gunfire drowned him out for a moment. "We should still be here. They're not the greatest marksmen. But there are a lot of them, and they might have us completely cut off by sheer volume of fire by the time you can even get close."

He paused then. I could almost hear the wheels turning. "Backwoods, I'm gonna be honest with you. You might be better off going to ground and seeing if Goblin can get us some reinforcements. I don't know what five of you can do. We can hold out for a while, maybe even a couple days. Long enough for a proper response from the State, the Border Patrol, hell, the National Guard."

I hesitated to say it, but I thought he was being more than a little overly optimistic. Still, this wasn't a time to beat around the bush. "By the time anyone can get through the bureaucracy and mobilize, it's going to be too late." I'd come to the conclusion that in most places, no one is coming to save you a few years before. "The Border Patrol's going to be told to stand down, especially if Archer's involved. Can't have them killing a bunch of poor migrants, now. Local sheriff won't have the manpower, and it'll take a week for the Guard to mobilize." I shook my head, even though Frank couldn't see it. "We'll see what we can do."

"Don't get yourselves killed trying to get to us." Frank was sounding a little frazzled. "Especially not if you've got the girl."

That was a factor. We couldn't take Ariana into the middle of a firefight, not in the shape she was in. I glanced in the rear-view mirror, only to meet her eyes. She was trying hard to hold it together, but I thought she might have overheard some of the conversation already. Or if she hadn't heard Frank, she'd heard what I'd said and was putting two and two together.

"We'll handle it, Casper. Just keep the rest of the team alive." I ended the call. There was too much to do.

"What's up?" Drew was watching me. There wasn't a whole lot to see outside the vehicle, as it was dark and we'd all dropped our helmets and NVGs, and I was driving on white light.

"They're getting hit." Under different circumstances, I might moderate what I said to spare Ariana some of the gory details, especially after what she'd already been through that night. We didn't have that luxury, though. "At least fifty shooters. He warned us off going back via the 9."

"That's a long way around." Drew was already pulling up the mapping app on the tablet. "Most of it over unimproved roads, when it's not just straight-up offroading." He snorted. "Rental company's gonna *love* us."

"That's why we got the extra insurance." I was starting to look for a turnoff. If we needed to go around the back way, we'd have to head toward the East Potrillo Mountains soon.

Before I could find that turnoff, my phone buzzed again. I handed it to Drew. "I need to drive."

He grabbed it, frowned at the screen a moment, and answered it. "It's KG." He tapped the button to turn on speakerphone and clipped it into the holder on the dash.

"Little busy here, KG." I was still technically the mission commander, so I should really do most of the talking.

"I'm sure." KG's answer was rather wry. "We suspected as much, since Archer's an idiot, and called the client to gloat."

"You're shitting me." I hadn't been terribly impressed with what I'd seen of Devon Archer's intelligence so far, but then, he was a drug addict as well as a fixer who played fast and loose with the law because of who his daddy was.

"I almost wish I was." KG sounded like he couldn't quite believe it, himself. "He called the client up, told him that he'd won, that there was nothing he or anyone else could do about it, and that it would have been better for everyone if he'd just stayed out of it. The client's *pissed.* He tried calling the Bowmans but couldn't get anyone to pick up. If they're under fire, that would explain that."

"I just got off the phone with Casper," I explained, slowing as I spotted what should be the turnoff. "I'm about halfway between the ranch and El Paso, with Smokestack, Drizzle, Ziggy, and Gunner. The bad guys grabbed the Bowmans' daughter for leverage, so we had to go get her. They've started to hit the ranch in the meantime. Casper says about fifty shooters, but he thinks they can hold out for a while."

"Okay. Stand by a second." KG went quiet, and when I glanced at the phone, I saw we were on hold. I frowned, and Drew mirrored the expression.

"What the hell? We don't have time for this shit." Drew was getting antsy about getting to the ranch, and I saw Ariana shifting uncomfortably in the back seat. Marcos was speaking quietly to her, trying to reassure her that everything was going to be all right, but she could hear every word, and had to know that the situation was looking desperate.

"Okay." KG was back, even as I turned off the highway, trundling onto a dirt county road heading north into the desert. "If you're not in the middle of it, then I've got a new assignment for you. Find us an LZ, within striking distance of the ranch, but not where we'd take fire from the bad guys. We won't be there immediately, but everyone except Scooby and Scrappy are boarding a helo right now. It'll be about three hours, but we're on our way."

I grimaced. Three hours was a long time. A hell of a lot could happen in that amount of time, little of it good. Still, Frank had been fairly optimistic that they could hold out. Maybe the bad guys might even give up.

I doubted it. Not with the kind of money on the line that the ranch represented. They were going to push, and I'd seen enough footage of balls-out firefights all over Mexico that I didn't think these savages were going to back off just because they took a few casualties. In fact, it might just be the opposite.

La Santa Muerte would have her sacrifices, one way or another.

It also stuck in my craw to leave Casper and the rest of the B Team to their own devices while we hid out in the desert. Sure, it was debatable just how much the five of us could do— four, since somebody was probably going to have to look after Ariana—but that didn't make it suck any less.

I had to concentrate on driving. The road was hardly in good shape, it was dark as hell, and the rental vehicle's headlights weren't the best. I was about to stop and put my helmet back on to drive on NVGs. "Good copy, KG. Make sure your radios are working on approach."

Unspoken in that sentence was the instruction to *get moving right the fuck now.*

I'd known manager types in the contracting world who would have reacted like officers in the military, if they even picked up on the subtext. Egos can be fragile things, even— sometimes especially—in this business. Fortunately, though, KG wasn't one of those guys. He got it.

"We will be." His voice faded slightly, as if he was looking over his shoulder. "We've got to get airborne. I'll try to make contact as soon as we're in radio range. Beforehand, if possible. Have those grids for us." He paused for a brief second. He could have ended it there, but he wouldn't. "Hang in there, Backwoods. We're coming." Then he hung up.

"Ever thought you'd be doing an LZ report on a close protection gig?" Marcos asked from the back seat.

"Actually, I have, a couple of times." There'd been a few movements downrange, even on contract, where we'd needed to set up Landing Zones for medevacs, just in case. "Can't say I expected to on *this* job, but this has been a particularly special gig."

We kept driving, into the dark, kicking up dust and going as fast as we could without losing control on the unimproved road.

***

We'd gone about two miles when I first spotted taillights ahead of us.

"That doesn't look right to me." I checked my watch and glanced at the map. "There's not much up this way, and it seems like a weird time for somebody from the Dominquez ranch to be driving home."

"Not impossible, but a weird route, for sure. And I count something like four vehicles." Drew was watching the lights intently, his eyes narrowed. "Might still be locals, though."

A moment later, they turned off to the left, going around the shoulder of the East Potrillo Mountains and heading west. "Guess I was wrong." Drew shifted in his seat, adjusting his carbine so he could grab it more easily. "Looks like they're heading for the Bowman place."

"Either that, or they've got a weird idea of a great camping spot." I slowed down still further. "Call Phil, tell him to go dark and get ready to do some off-roading. We need to get ahead of these fuckers." I suited actions to words and killed the headlights, braking as I did so and reaching back for my helmet.

Ariana handed it to me. I nodded to her in the rear-view mirror, though she probably couldn't see it. Pulling off the side of the road, I stopped altogether and pulled the helmet on, dropping the NVGs in front of my eyes, all the while cursing the fact that the rental pickup didn't have a blackout switch that would keep the brake lights from coming on.

It took seconds, and then I was moving out across the desert.

It was actually easier than it looked. The ground wasn't even by any stretch of the imagination, but it was still *fairly*

290

flat, and so long as I didn't hit a gully that I couldn't see or a rock that I somehow missed, we'd be okay. The pickup handled the brush easily enough, but we could still blow a tire or break an axle if I wasn't somewhat cautious.

We need our own vehicles. That would be cool, but somewhat impractical. We'd have to drive everywhere, and while that might be less expensive for the company than flying, it would take an inordinate amount of time to get anywhere, as well as requiring a whole additional logistical and mechanical support structure.

So, I had to nurse the rental vehicle along, wincing as I hit a depression in the ground particularly hard, almost bouncing Marcos and Ariana off the ceiling. It felt slow as hell, but we *were* starting to outpace our quarry.

The more I watched those four sets of headlights, the more convinced I was that they were moving in to flank the ranch, trying to get behind our guys while the main force hit them from the south. It wouldn't *necessarily* be a game-ender, but it wouldn't be good, either.

If we could cut them off, it might not save the day, but it would keep a bit of the pressure off our guys. And the Bowmans.

"Looks like they're going about the way we were going to." Drew had his NVGs down, as well, the faint glow lighting up his face as he watched the headlights. "Any doubt that these are bad guys is going down the shitter fast."

I agreed, even as I kept my mouth shut and concentrated on driving. This was turning out to be more complicated than I'd hoped. Still, we were gaining, and I had my eye on where I thought we could intercept them.

We still had about five to ten minutes to spare by the time I got to the gully I'd picked out as our ambush point. Well, about a hundred yards downstream from our ambush point. I decided not to risk taking the vehicles down into the gully at that point, so I parked, killed the engine, and piled out with Drew. Stopping before I shut the door, I turned back inside the cab.

"Ariana, I need you to stay here with Marcos. Get down as close to the floor as you can. We'll be back in a minute." I looked up at Marcos. "Sorry, brother. You're the man on the spot."

If it had been Brian, or worse, Jake, he would have put up a fight. Marcos just shrugged. "Don't get shot." I nodded to him and shut the door. For his part, he had his open, just so that he could respond quickly if things went sideways.

Drew was waiting at the front of the vehicle, and Phil and Casey joined us a moment later. "What are we stopping here for?" Casey, it seemed, was going to keep being his usual, belligerent self, convinced he should be the team leader instead of a straphanger. He pointed toward the headlights. "We could head them off right at those hills back there."

"Well, I decided on here." There was a time and a place for explaining rationale, but I wasn't going to waste my breath with Casey, especially not when things were about to go hot. I hadn't worked with him before this gig, but I'd been around him enough in training that I knew what kind of guy he was. He could perform, which was the one reason I figured Goblin had kept him around. I pointed toward the track running through the gully that we'd planned on following. "Let's get set in. Spread out, get low, and don't bed down right *in* the tracks."

I probably didn't need to include that last part, but it was late, we were tired, and we'd already had time to come down off the adrenaline rush of the first of the night's firefights. It doesn't pay to assume things when issuing combat orders, even if they're that abbreviated. I was still glad for the energy drinks that Drew had stashed in the vehicles. I was one and a half in for the night already.

Fortunately, Casey was enough of a professional that he didn't make an issue out of it. He might have grimaced in the dark, but he lifted his rifle's muzzle and turned toward our ambush.

We spread out into a skirmish line as we closed on the gully, decades of infantry training coming back like riding a bike. It took seconds to cover the hundred yards or so to the gully, but in that time the oncoming headlights got brighter and brighter.

Even as I got down in the prone on the desert floor, under a prickly bit of brush and trying not to put my hand right on a thorn—there were far too many out there—I almost hesitated. How did we *know* that these were bad guys? All we'd seen were lights. Sure, there was plenty of circumstantial evidence. But we weren't one hundred percent *sure.*

Yes, we are. No one else is expected. Frank would have called if he knew of anyone on the way. Worst case, we shoot up some tires and engine blocks and maybe have to pay damages down the line.

I couldn't see the rest of the team, but I was the trigger man, anyway. Casey *might* try to jump the gun, but I had the best shot at the oncoming vehicles, anyway.

My doubts were further dispelled as they got closer. I couldn't hear the engines or the crunch of the tires on the gravel and sand of the desert over the thumping Latino music. While I couldn't make out the words, I recognized the tune. I'd heard it in the snatch house. That was narco music.

Setting my red dot just above the driver's side headlight, I shifted my hips to get solidly behind the weapon and opened fire.

The rifle thundered in the quiet of the desert night, and the vehicle lurched to a stop. The headlights were quickly turned off, but that only made it easier to see the narcos—or *mareros*, it was hard to tell which in the dark—as they grabbed their weapons and piled out of the doors, throwing themselves into the rocks and brush on the sides of the gully. They were better trained than I'd thought. I'd half expected them to just try to fight from the car.

I guess years of irregular warfare was weeding out the Active Stupid *sicarios*.

Their unexpected common sense, however, didn't stop them from immediately opening fire with all they had. They couldn't have targets, but they started spraying bullets anyway.

There was something to be said for that as a reaction to ambush. Violence of action goes a long way. It doesn't go as far, however, when the defending shooters can't hit shit, and their muzzle flashes give their opponents something to shoot at.

I quickly shifted targets, aiming for one of the muzzle flashes, and double tapped the man behind it. I didn't hit anything vital enough to drop him immediately, but he went over backward, still spraying rounds into the sky as he toppled. There was too much gunfire to hear any screams, but I'm sure he was not a happy camper. I shot him three more times, even as he brought the weapon back down toward me, and his fire went silent.

Phil, Casey, and Drew were all shooting, raking the front vehicle and the banks of the gully with fire. I shifted to another dim shape trying to hide in the weeds behind the lead vehicle and dumped him with another four rounds.

There was a lull in the fight, then. We'd apparently killed everyone in the lead vehicle, but that didn't mean we were out of the woods. We could sit and wait for the bad guys to make the next move, but that was never a good idea, especially when outnumbered and with limited visibility.

So, despite the fact that a few desultory gunshots were still going overhead with harsh *snap*s, I heaved myself up onto a knee, keeping my rifle in a tight high port, scanning my surroundings for a moment, if only to make sure that I wasn't about to run into a teammate.

It was a good thing I did, too. From my slightly higher position, I could see three or four figures running, crouched over, out of the gully up to the northeast, where we couldn't have seen them from the prone. Drew was getting up, too, so he'd see them in a second, but in the meantime, he was blocking my field of fire. I started to move, staying in a partial crouch myself, to get a shot at them.

A second later, Marcos opened fire from the truck. He had a better angle, and he dropped two of them in the first few shots. I saw one of them go down hard, face planting so brutally that his feet went up behind him.

Then I had a clear shot, and winged another one, following up with a fusillade of five or six shots, leaning into the rifle to keep it under control as I kept moving. I suddenly had to watch multiple directions at once, to make sure I didn't run in front of either Drew's or Marcos's muzzle. Most of us were pretty good at target discrimination, even in the dark, but combat is a bad time to take stupid chances. There are enough risks as it is.

So, I drove forward, standing up possibly more than I should have, my rifle leveled, looking for targets. A head popped up from behind the rearmost vehicle, and I just barely made out the dark shape of a weapon before I shot at it. The head disappeared. No idea if I hit him or not.

Drew was beside me, then. He must have hustled to catch up. Marcos ceased fire as we passed between the truck and the narco convoy, so we had to finish this fast.

Phil and Casey stayed where they were for the moment, dumping more rounds down the length of the convoy, though from the volume of fire they were putting out, and the occasional spark as a bullet smacked off metal, they had also gotten up, probably on a knee. It wasn't an ideal situation, body armor or no, but fighting in the desert, where there's very little actual cover, has its own challenges.

Drew and I swept out to the flank, keeping our muzzles trained on the convoy, looking for more targets even as Phil and Casey hammered at them to keep their heads down.

Another trio tried to break out from behind the rear vehicle, spraying bullets as they scrambled up out of the gully, but they didn't have targets and we did. I shot one up front as Drew knocked the man behind him sprawling. The third dropped to his belly in the dirt, disappearing from view for the moment.

The gunfire from the convoy had died down to almost nothing. I knew for sure that we'd killed at least ten, maybe as many as fifteen. Without knowing how many there were, it was hard to say where that put us, but Drew and I advanced carefully and cautiously on the second vehicle.

Two bodies were sprawled in the brush on the side of the shallow gully. At least one had been hit in the head. His skull was misshapen, and a dark splash of fluid was smeared across the white metal of the side of the vehicle.

Movement caught my eye at the edge of the circle of grayscale night vision, and I shifted my muzzle and my eyes toward it. A man was crouched behind the SUV, muttering to himself in Spanish. I could hear him with my electronic earpro, even over the gunfire.

I came around the back, still checking toward the rear of the convoy every few steps. A rapid, thunderous burst of gunfire sounded in the night, and I heard the bullets go by on the far side of the gully with harsh, supersonic *crack*s, but then everything went quiet, except for the man muttering behind the SUV.

Two things happened at once. I stepped out and cleared the corner at the same time he screwed up his courage—or finished his prayer to *Santa Muerte*—and came up with a lunge, bringing his AK around as he came.

I already had my dot on him as he turned toward me. My first shot caught him just under the collarbone. My second blew his brains across the back hatch of the SUV. His knees crumpled and he went straight down to the dust.

Everything really went quiet, then. Even the music had stopped. Maybe one of us had hit the stereo. There certainly had been enough gunfire flying around. I knelt by the corner of the SUV, watching the still faintly twitching body of the man I'd just killed, and conducted a quick tactical reload. I might have one or two rounds left in that mag.

I scanned up and down the gully. Phil and Casey were indeed up on a knee, covering us, though I was currently cutting off most of their field of fire. Nothing else moved.

Shoving the nearly empty magazine into my back pocket, I stood. "On me."

"With you." Drew was slightly above me now, at an angle where he could quickly engage and cover me as I swept down the length of the convoy.

It didn't take long. I moved from vehicle to vehicle, checking around, under, and inside with the IR-shielded light on my rifle. The narcos had come loaded for bear, but it hadn't saved them. They'd died where they'd bailed out, most of them.

War is hell.

We left them where they lay. There wasn't going to be any flanking attack, at least not for a while. Without another word, we rallied back on the vehicles and mounted up to get moving again.

CHAPTER
37

Nick and Matt made it back to the house just before midnight.

Things had calmed down a little bit. The elimination of the sniper position and the loss of the Barrett had slowed the bad guys, and they were being more cautious now.

Frank had pulled all but two pairs back to the house. Brett and Abaeze were on the west flank, Saul and Manny on the west. The only coverage to the north was from the back of the house itself, but Nick still called ahead on the radio as they got closer. Friendly fire, isn't, and he had no intention of getting smoked because he didn't deconflict.

Every man there aside from the Bowmans was a professional, but it had already been a long night, and dawn was still a long way off. Some had dip, and Mrs. Bowman was keeping the coffee coming, but there was only so much that nicotine and caffeine could do.

"Any Papa Golf station, this is Croak." He didn't know who was on north side security, so he kept things vague.

"Croak, this is Hoop." Mike sounded tired but eager. This might not *quite* have been his baptism of fire, but he was finally getting stuck in after most of a career doing training gigs and never actually getting to fire shots in anger. Of *course* he was eager.

"I'm coming in from the north with Toe Tag. He's going to need some medical attention." Part of why they'd been so slow getting back down off the hill was because Nick had been slowing or stopping regularly to check on Matt. Not just to look to see that he was still upright, but actually stopping and checking that the tourniquet hadn't come loose. "Two four-wheelers, about five hundred yards out."

"Bring it in." Mike paused for a moment, and Nick almost didn't hear his next transmission as he gunned his ATV, trying to get in before either Matt passed out or the bad guys came around and took them in the rear. "Be advised, we've seen a little movement up on the hill, and maybe out in the desert to the east. Come in carefully."

Nick was already moving, checking over his shoulder to make sure Matt was still with him. The other man might have been leaning a little lower over his handlebars, but he was still up, and he gunned his own vehicle's engine to follow as Nick headed toward the ranch house.

He was scanning their surroundings a little more carefully as they got closer, looking away from the lights around the house, not only to keep from whiting out his night vision, but also because of Mike's warning. He'd expected more narco shooters up on the hill. They'd already been coming when he and Matt had fallen back. But that there were more out in the desert was news. A part of him dismissed it as narco incompetence, creating a circular firing squad. But if they were careful, they *could* completely cut the ranch off from the outside.

He gunned the engine again, speeding the last few dozen yards to the house. He saw the flash out in the dark before a bullet went over his head with a *snap*, punching a hole in the wall above the door. Mike, who was in the doorway, barricaded on the doorjamb and watching the northern flank, flinched for a second, then rotated to shoot back.

Unfortunately, in so doing, he cut both men off as he blocked the doorway.

Matt brought his own ATV around in a short arc, skidding to a stop in a cloud of dust, and brought his own rifle up to return fire. He was shaky, the blood loss clearly getting to him, and few of the rounds probably even came close.

Nick was off his own four-wheeler. "Mike, get out here and help." He moved quickly to Matt's side. His partner was starting to sway in the saddle. When he looked down, the other man's trouser leg was soaked in blood. "Shit." He grabbed Matt before he could topple off the ATV, cradling him with one arm and grabbing his carbine with the other before he could accidentally point it at anyone else.

Mike was still sort of hovering. "Get up to the corner and cover us while I get him inside." He looked down as he hauled Matt off the four-wheeler. Sure enough, the tourniquet had loosened, though he didn't think it was so loose that he was spurting. He still needed care, and fast.

"I can walk." Matt wasn't down and out yet.

"You're leaking." Nick already had his partner's arm over his shoulder and was heading for the door. "We've got to get that hole patched."

Whatever Matt said was drowned out as Mike started shooting again, a moment after more fragments of the house wall showered down on Nick's head from another impact. He didn't look, but put on the speed, rushing into the house and dragging Matt through the doorway with him.

Frank was waiting, alongside Mrs. Bowman, who was wearing black nitrile gloves and an apron. There was blood on it. So, somebody else had gotten hit.

"Bring him this way." She didn't blink at the blood soaking Matt's trouser leg and running down to his boot. She was a ranch woman, and a border ranch woman, at that. She'd seen her share of blood, human and otherwise.

Nick helped Matt toward one of the bedrooms. He blinked as they entered and he saw a shape on the floor, covered with a blanket. Josh looked up from where he was repacking a trauma kit, his eyes red and his face drawn.

While he helped Matt onto the bed, currently covered by a blood-splattered plastic sheet, Nick couldn't help but let his eyes stray to the body.

"George took one in the neck." Josh's voice was hoarse. "He didn't make it."

Nick wondered a little at the way his guts twisted at that. George had hardly been the most popular of the team. Saul hadn't been the only one who had disliked the man's constant complaining. But he'd still been a teammate, and it always hurt to lose a teammate.

Time to worry about the living. Mourn the dead later.

Josh was already cutting away Matt's trouser leg. "Looks bad, but not lethal. It might have missed the artery." He squinted in the light of his headlamp. "I'd better throw a pressure dressing on it, anyway. Let the hospital worry about it."

Nick found he had little to do, as Josh started packing the wound with gauze and wrapping the leg with an ace bandage. He didn't want to leave Matt, but there didn't seem to be much more he could do to help.

"Nick." Frank was at the door. "Front and center. They're starting another push." He looked past Nick's shoulder. "You good, Matt?"

"I'm good." Matt spoke through clenched teeth as Josh tightened down the pressure bandage. "Haven't bled to death yet."

"Let's keep it that way." Frank turned to Mrs. Bowman. "I'm sorry to ask, Elaine, but can you take over for Josh? We're gonna need every gun."

Elaine Bowman was already pushing Josh's hands out of the way. "Go. You boys are better shots than me." The

302

distraught mother of a kidnapped daughter had steadied herself as the crisis worsened, compartmentalizing things and simply doing what needed to be done.

Josh handed the end of the ace wrap to her, then hastily cleaned his hands on a couple of alcohol wipes before grabbing for his rifle. He hadn't taken the rest of his gear off. "Let's go."

Nick and Frank were already heading for the front of the house. The sounds of gunfire were intensifying, and there was the unmistakable rattle of at least one machinegun mixed in there. Most of the PGS contractors could shoot pretty fast, but not *that* fast.

The ditches and berms outside hadn't been the only improvements they'd made. There were a lot of sandbags stacked under the windows and by the door. The house was an adobe, fortunately, so the walls actually provided some cover.

Jacob and Trevor Bowman were holding the front of the house by themselves, both armed with their own ARs. Neither of them were currently shooting; the teams out on the front berms hadn't fallen back yet.

Nick moved up to the window, displacing Jacob as he did so. "I've got it, kid."

Jacob might have looked slightly relieved as he stepped back from the window. Or maybe he was disappointed at being supplanted. *He shouldn't be. Kid that age ain't ready for this.*

Not that any of the Bowmans had had much of a choice.

Taking a knee behind the low rampart of sandbags, Nick scanned the front. The Bowmans had left the couple of outside lights on, probably in the hopes of blinding their attackers, but one of them had been shot out, leaving the front of the house in relative darkness.

Nick wondered briefly if it had been the bad guys who'd done that, or if one of the contractors had decided he was sick of being backlit.

He could see muzzle flashes out in the desert, and tracers were zipping through the air toward the ranch house.

No, not so much toward the house. Toward the berms out front. They'd figured out where the bulk of the defenders had set up. That wasn't good.

The window in front of him had already been shattered, so Nick laid his rifle on the sandbags, trying to get a shot at one of those muzzle flashes. It was difficult, though, since he still had to avoid hitting Saul or Manny in the process. He'd have a better shot from the roof, but there was zero cover up there. They really should have put sandbag parapets up there, too, but they'd run out of time.

He shifted right in frustration. He couldn't get a shot. The berm and his teammates were in the way.

Then things got really ugly.

He couldn't hear the buzz of the drone, but he did hear the sudden burst of gunfire and the subsequent explosion as it blew up, about twenty feet above the western berm. A moment later, Abaeze came over the radio. "Need some help out here. I'm hit, and Tonka is fucked up." Abaeze had to be in a lot of pain to let radio discipline slip like that.

"Nick, you're with me." Frank was already at the door. "We're going to have to go get them, then pull everyone back to the house." While he was still maintaining the cool and professional demeanor that had gotten him more than one lead position over the years, Frank was obviously worried. They were losing the last of their maneuvering room.

Nick just got up and moved to join him. "Jacob, Mr. Bowman, we're probably going to need some covering fire soon."

He got a nod from the elder Bowman, and then he and Frank were going over the sandbags and out the door, even as Frank got on the radio. "Salt, Frog, this is Casper. We're moving to Whack and Tonka's position. If you can, join us there, then we'll fall back to the house."

"Roger." Saul was still up, at least. "Moving now."

The gunfire out front redoubled in intensity, as Saul and Manny started to leapfrog across the front toward where Brett and Abaeze were holed up, each man laying down fire while the other ran past him, then either dropped prone or took a knee and picked up the covering fire.

Good to see that even with a few SEALs, we still haven't lost those infantry tactics. Of course, the training that PGS had insisted they all go through probably helped, too.

He and Frank didn't bother with leapfrogging but just ducked their heads and sprinted toward the berm, leaping over the low wall that encircled what would have been a garden in a more temperate environment. Bullets continued to *snap* past their ears as the cartel shooters poured more and more fire into the compound. They must have gotten even more reinforcements, or else they were dead set on melting a couple of barrels.

The two men threw themselves behind the berm, where Abaeze was trying to bandage some of Brett's wounds. Brett, for his part, was still conscious, holding his hand to one eye. Most of his wounds appeared to be from shrapnel, but there was a lot of blood. Abaeze's bleeders were a little harder to see on NVGs, in no small part because of the darkness of his skin, but he'd clearly been hit, too. His right sleeve was dark and wet.

Saul hit the berm next to Brett a second later, not even glancing at the wounded man but throwing himself down on the dirt and laying his rifle over the top of the berm, still panting as he opened fire once again, the muzzle blast kicking grit away from his weapon. In between bursts of fire, he turned his head to speak over his shoulder. "Only the one drone so far, but it's only a matter of time."

"Agreed." Frank had taken a knee on Abaeze's other side, and Nick joined him. The desert out in front of the berms was now a flickering lightning storm of gunfire. It looked like all the remaining cartel shooters had gotten on line and were pouring all the fire they could into the berms.

That meant there was something else coming. Even these savages wouldn't rely solely on volume of fire from the front.

He rolled to his side, searching the dark for a flanking attack, but didn't see it. Maybe the drone was supposed to be the flanking attack, and now the narcos were just trying to keep them pinned down while they figured out what else to do.

"Brett, can you hear me?" Frank paused his own fire as he ducked beneath the berm.

"Yeah." Brett's voice was tight with pain.

"Can you walk?"

There was a brief pause, and Brett gasped as Abaeze cranked down on a tourniquet around his leg. "I think so. I've got at least one chunk in my leg, but I'll crawl if I have to."

"Good man." Frank then keyed his radio. "Money, Casper. Need some covering fire to the south. Watch your fires to the southwest; we'll be coming in fast."

He didn't get an acknowledgement over the radio, but a sudden storm of gunfire roared out from the front of the house, flickering tongues of flame punching through the dark from the windows and door. Frank grabbed one of Brett's arms and Abaeze grabbed the other. "Let's go!"

Nick, for his part, held what he had, crawling back up onto the berm to add his fire to Saul's and Manny's, trying to suppress as much of the enemy fire as possible while Frank and Abaeze got the wounded Brett back to the house.

He dumped the rest of his magazine at the muzzle flashes out in the desert, about five shots at a time, shifting from flash to flash. All too soon, his bolt locked back on an empty mag, fortunately just as the fire from the house redoubled, Frank and Abaeze joining Josh and the Bowmans to cover the men still out on the berm.

None of the three of them needed any prompting. In a fight like that, communication is as much by gunfire as it is by voice. Gunfire is louder, for one thing.

Nick stripped the empty mag out of his rifle and let it fall as he ran for the house, ripping another out of its pouch on his plate carrier and slapping it on the move. He dropped the bolt as he reached the house, some of the fire slackening as Josh ceased fire from the window and Frank pushed out of the doorway to let them through.

A moment later, the gunfire from out in the desert all but ceased. Frank had to yell at Jacob to cease fire and not waste the ammo.

"Now what?" Mr. Bowman scanned the darkness outside. The last of the exterior lights had been shot out in that exchange, and now those without night vision were at a distinct disadvantage. A slight overcast had moved in, so there wasn't much ambient light to work with. Even Nick's NVGs were dark.

"Now we wait for the next shoe to drop."

***

It didn't take long.

"*Hey! You in the house!*" The megaphone the narco was using squealed a little with feedback.

"What do you want?" Mr. Bowman, as soft-spoken as he had been since the team had arrived, could still get some considerable volume in his voice.

"*I want to give you a chance to live.*" The man still sounded cocky as hell, despite the number of his men the contractors and the Bowmans had already killed that night. "*You surprised us to start. I'll give you that. But if* La Migra *or the Army were coming to save you, they'd be here by now. You're alone. All shut up in that little house.*"

"He's got to have another drone up, if he can see that," Josh muttered.

"This place is ours now. It can be that way over your dead bodies, or not. Just put down your guns and come out of the house, one at a time, with your hands on your heads." He might have laughed then. *"You might be tough, and you might be good with guns, but I have more men and more guns than you."*

Mr. Bowman turned away from the window. The look in his eyes was haunted. Almost defeated. "What do we do?"

"We hold what we've got." Frank had to be feeling the same sense of dread. Nick knew that *he* sure was. "They can't storm this place without getting lit up. We've got more cover than they do, and we've still got a good stockpile of ammunition. We do have reinforcements coming, and sooner or later the Border Patrol won't be able to ignore this anymore." He checked his watch. It was getting close to one in the morning. "We can still win this."

"You're already down one man dead and two wounded." Despair was eating at Mr. Bowman, and the look Jacob gave him wasn't successful in hiding the kid's own fear. "If they haven't given up and gone away yet, with the number already on the ground…"

"Look, Mr. Bowman." Frank rubbed the bridge of his nose. "I'm going to be brutally honest with you. That son of a bitch out there is lying through his teeth. They won't let us go. They *can't*. We'll talk to too many people. As soon as we're all out there, unarmed and with our hands on our heads, they're gonna mow us down and toss our bodies in the desert." He glanced toward the back of the house. "At least, that's what they'll do to *us*. I suspect they'll take a little more time with your wife."

Jacob blanched at that and started to stand up, turning toward the window. Saul clapped a heavy hand on his shoulder and dragged him back down.

Mr. Bowman's shoulders seemed to sag. He hadn't asked for this. Hadn't wanted it. Yet here he was, faced with the choice between fighting to the death or being murdered, simply because a bunch of psychopaths from three different countries wanted his land.

After a moment, though, he looked over at Jacob, then back toward the rear of the house, where Mrs. Bowman and the younger kids were holed up. He straightened, took a deep breath, and turned back to the window, his hands flexing around his rifle. "Fine. Let 'em come. We'll put two of them in the dirt for every one of us."

"More than that, Mr. Bowman." Frank had turned back to the doorway, standing next to the doorjamb and barricading on it, bracing his rifle against the frame. "More than that."

CHAPTER
38

The bird came in fast, flaring hard as it approached our makeshift LZ. Without chemlights—which we really probably should have been carrying, anyway—we'd had to improvise, finally settling on setting out personal handheld flashlights and headlamps, with me stationed at the tip of the inverted Y of lights, using my own handheld light to guide the bird in.

Fortunately, we were in the middle of nowhere, so there really weren't any obstacles to call in when KG hit me up over the radio.

The bird settled to the ground in a stinging cloud of dust, and I had to duck my head not to get an eyeful of it. I still got sandblasted, and I was probably going to be spitting out grit for the next couple of days, provided I didn't end up six feet under in the next few hours.

Really should have called Julie one more time.

That wasn't the time for such thoughts, so I shoved them deep in the back of my brain. I couldn't afford to think about my wife and kids right then. That would almost guarantee that I got myself killed and left them a widow and orphans.

I didn't wait for KG and the rest of the team to get off the bird, but jogged up to the side door, compulsively ducking my head even though the still-spinning rotors were a good three feet above my helmet, even if I'd been standing up straight. I'd never gotten over that fear of losing my head to those damned things.

KG was already in the open door, geared up with plate carrier, assault pack, helmet, and with his NVGs down and his Recce 16 hanging from its sling in front of him. I leaned in and yelled to be heard over the roar of the helo's engines. "We've been hearing gunfire from down there off and on for a while. It got really intense about an hour, hour and a half ago, but it's been pretty sporadic since then."

He nodded as he dropped to the ground. "I've had radio contact with Casper. They're still holding on, though Digger's KIA and Toe Tag, Tonka, and Whack have all been hit. They're surrounded and stuck in the house."

"I got the same update from him." It was a good thing we had the radios and weren't relying on cell service. It was next to nonexistent up there. Still, I hadn't told Frank just how close we were, feeling more than a little guilty about hunkering down out in the desert, setting up an LZ, while they were still under fire. We might have headed off a flanking attack on the way, but that wasn't the same thing as going in shooting when they were under fire. "What's the plan?"

"I'd take the vehicles until we got within five hundred yards, but I'm guessing these can't black out all the way." He waved at Ken, Custus, Jake, and Rob to get off the bird and join the rest of the team near the truck and the Pathfinder.

"They can't. Almost got us shot to shit on the way up here." I joined him as he started to jog after Bone.

"We'll have to go on foot, then." He jerked a thumb over his shoulder. "The helo pilot will pull off and go to the Doña Ana County jetport to refuel and stand by. He might have to lift us out in a hurry, depending on what the local authorities' reaction to tonight turns out to be." He looked up as we got close to the trucks and saw the huddled shape in the back seat of the Frontier. Stopping in his tracks, I saw him grimace, more in the glow from his NVGs than anything else.

"Can we convince the girl to get on the bird and wait at the airport?"

I didn't want her tagging along in a firefight, either, but I wasn't sure about talking her into leaving while her family was still under fire. She hadn't broken down yet, despite her ordeal. I worried that telling her she had to wait over twenty miles away, with no way of knowing what was happening to her parents and her siblings, might just trigger that meltdown.

Still, the middle of a firefight in the desert was no place for a teenage girl. She had to go. We didn't dare leave her by herself in the truck, either.

"I'll make sure she understands." I wasn't relishing it. I had boys. I'd never had to deal with a teenage daughter, and I wasn't sure that I wasn't a bit too harsh of temperament for it. But there was no choice.

KG put out a hand to stop me, though. "I'll handle it. I've got a softer touch than you do." He grinned, the expression a flash of white in my NVGs. "That's why I get stuck dealing with all the management bullshit, while you get to run and gun out here. Maybe I should start being an intimidating, scary bastard like you."

I snorted. "Good luck." I veered toward where the rest of the team was rallied up next to the Pathfinder.

Casey was on a knee, covering his sector, facing away from the ranch, but somehow his body language still broadcast his dissatisfaction with being a straphanger with a different team and with no real say in what went down. I gathered that he tended to bully his way into a leadership position most of the time.

The rest were simply set up in a circle, game faces on, weapons held ready. Even Jake was somber. The occasional *pop* of gunfire just over a mile away has a way of focusing the mind. Jake might have been a loudmouth and a pain in the ass most of the time, but Goblin had vetted him, so he brought *something* to the table.

Drew was just finishing up with the final notes on what had happened so far that night. Ken looked up at me as I entered the circle, working the wad of dip in his lip. "You boys have had an eventful night already, Backwoods. Knew I should have pushed harder to come down here instead of going to Colorado."

Right at the moment, I was already too tired to be flippant about it, though I understood what he was getting at. I was exhausted, and a part of me was really dreading what was going to go down in the next hour or so, but all the same, I felt more alive than I had in years. There's something about combat that gets in your blood and never goes away, even as you get older, and should get wiser.

It helps when you know you're fighting in a righteous cause, too. The rage at what was being done to the Bowmans, and why, was still burning, though it was a cold, distant flame now. Professionalism had taken over a while back.

Rage is for before a mission. Not during.

"Can't say you're wrong." I realized that despite everything, I really *would* rather be there in the desert, in combat, than playing babysitter for Strand, even if he was a good client.

When I swung my head back toward the vehicles, Ariana was heading for the helicopter, the crew chief holding out a hand to help her aboard, and KG was heading back toward us. "It took some emotional blackmail, but she's going to the airport for the duration." He stabbed a finger at me. "Chris, you ready to go?"

"Let's roll." The mile ahead was going to suck, not to mention the odds we were probably going to face at the end of it, but better to get it over with.

"Okay. Fast and dirty op order." KG was too much of a pro to just go live without *some* sort of plan. "We all know the situation. Mission is to hit the narcos as hard as possible and force a retreat, at least until we can get local law enforcement and Border Patrol on site. They won't move while there's an active firefight going on. Already talked to some people in the know. BORTAC is still getting stand down orders. Local sheriff is outnumbered, outgunned, and he knows it. He's not going to move, and the law is going to side with him, since the cops really have no obligation to protect people." That was a sore spot with a lot of folks, including a lot of guys in this profession. "So, it's up to us. We're going to proceed on foot, skirmishers left, double time until we're about five hundred yards out, on the narco's flank. At that point we will make radio contact with Casper, and coordinate a base of fire from them, while we hit the bad guys hard and fast." He took a deep breath. "This isn't going to be easy, fellas. We need to kill everyone in our way, and we need to do it before they can figure out what the hell's going on. If some of 'em run, fuck it. Let 'em go, unless it looks like they're going to regroup."

"Get down there, flank 'em, finish 'em. Got it, KG." Jake's attitude wasn't *quite* all the way reformed by the situation.

"Any questions?" KG ignored Jake's comment.

There were none. I might have set Marcos to take point, but decided that with KG taking charge, I wasn't the team leader anymore, so I could focus on shooting and moving. I turned and headed out.

Nobody said anything. The ten of us spread out across the desert and got going, even as the helicopter behind us pulled for the sky, dipped its nose, and roared off into the east.

***

We didn't *quite* run. There were too many unknowns, and Frank had warned us about the drones. There was definitely at least one still up there, and while Frank might not be able to pinpoint it from inside the house, the sound was a dead giveaway where we were, and from there it wasn't that hard to spot it. KG called a halt short of our phase line because he was worried about that thing. So far, we hadn't run into any cartel elements working their way north, but we knew they were there. *Somebody* was still taking potshots at the house from around the perimeter.

"Anybody think they can take that drone out?" KG's voice was a whisper that still traveled up and down the line. "Five hundred bucks to the guy who can drop it."

That's something you'd never get away with in the military, or even most of the contracting world. That KG felt comfortable saying that said something about Pallas Group Solutions.

He'd barely finished speaking when a fusillade of gunfire rippled across the line. It was probably impossible to tell exactly who had just smashed the quad-rotor drone to scrap, but the buzzing suddenly stopped, and the drone fell out of the sky in pieces.

Our approach was now officially blown, presuming they hadn't spotted us with that damned flying lawnmower already.

"Move!" KG was already suiting actions to words, getting up and dashing forward about twenty yards before throwing himself flat again.

Most of us were right there with him. Hanging around after that was just going to get us located, pinned down, and annihilated. Especially if they came at us with trucks, which they appeared to be doing.

Three of the vehicles on the eastern flank were already moving, figures scrambling into the backs. They knew we were out there now, though they'd apparently decided to ignore the noise of a helicopter landing a mile and a half away, and they were coming for us.

KG led the way, angling farther out from the ranch, continuing to bound though he wasn't dropping prone in the brush anymore. It was enough to take a knee. We could just see over some of the sage and creosote bushes that way.

We moved fast. Most of us still fought to maintain a pretty high level of fitness, so we could cover ground with a quickness. Within a minute or two, we were a couple hundred yards east of where we'd engaged the drone, even as the first trucks pulled up, lights flashing around as they looked for us.

They should have known better by then.

Two hundred yards is a long way at night, even on good NVGs, which we had. That just means that volume of fire becomes more important, which was why we were carrying so much ammo.

Flame stabbed through the night as we opened up on the trucks, targeting lights and human shapes where we could. Most of us—myself included—just sort of mag-dumped into the vehicles, bullets tearing through bodies, plastic, fiberglass, and sheet metal. I saw one go down hard, staggering as he was hit three or four times, his light waving wildly before he collapsed.

Only a couple of them managed to get a shot off, and they were quickly suppressed by more gunfire. Then we were up, moving forward in bounds to sweep across the kill zone. A good ambush is over in seconds, but it never pays to assume that everyone's dead until you confirm it.

With KG's hand signal, the team split into two five-man elements, forming a V as we swept down on the bullet riddled vehicles. Another *sicario* stuck his head out from behind the hood of one of the two Super Duties and snatched it back as a dozen of Rob's bullets smashed the remaining headlight and tore through the grill.

I was closer to the front of the vehicles as the V moved across the kill zone, and I paused to prod one of the bodies sprawled halfway out of the passenger seat. The man was obviously dead, but again, it doesn't pay to take chances. I'd come up through the ranks hearing stories from Fallujah about AQ guys playing possum, and the cartels made Al Qaeda in Iraq look like pussycats some days.

The man's head lolled as I poked his eyeball with my muzzle. No reaction. The ragged holes in his shirt and his throat told me the rest of the story.

Rob fired again but held his position. "Got a live one over here!"

I kept moving forward, clearing the other side of the older Dodge I was moving past, sweeping my muzzle across the open ground and checking the pair of bodies that had fallen out of the back. I lifted my muzzle as Ken moved to dead check those two, even as Custus sped up and moved past him. I turned back forward. The driver was obviously dead. Half his brains were painted on the starred and cracked windshield.

The last guy—everyone but Rob had stopped shooting, so I was pretty sure that lone *sicario* crouched behind the Super Duty was the last one—went for broke. Spraying fire wildly in Rob's direction, he sprinted away from the truck and back toward the house.

He was shot at least ten times as he ran. He plowed into the ground on his face and was still.

We finished the sweep in the next minute. We were moving quick, but still only so quick as we could accurately shoot. A few of the bodies were still stirring, and some moans and cries of pain could be heard entirely too clearly with electronic earpro on, but on examination, none of them were in any shape to try to ambush us, and none of them had long for this world.

KG circled his hand above his head and pointed back out into the desert.

We faded, even as a radio started squawking in insistent Spanish and the rest of the narco force started to move to investigate.

CHAPTER
39

We didn't go that far. For one thing, there was no way we were ever going to outrun narcos in trucks while we were on foot. We had to play smarter than that.

What I wouldn't have given for an M203 at that moment. A few well-placed 40mm grenades would do a number on this bunch. It might even be over in a matter of minutes.

That would be too easy, though. Only the military could get those, at least with any useful munitions. And they wouldn't lift a finger to intervene here.

Bounding had been skipped in favor of just getting some distance. We ran straight out into the desert, nobody even looking back until we were a good two hundred yards from the stricken, shot-up vehicles again. By then, I could already hear the engines as the follow up force came looking for us. And they were out for blood. They might not know for sure what had happened, but that a lot of their buddies were dead was pretty obvious.

The dark was our biggest ally then. Without their drone, they appeared to be entirely reliant on white light to see in the night. Even as the first vehicles skidded to a halt in a cloud of dust just short of the first group we'd lit up, intense spotlights and weapon-mounted flashlights were sweeping the brush, looking for us.

Fortunately, KG had led the way farther south, instead of going due west, where we might have been expected to go. We were circling around, getting into their rear area where we could wreak the most havoc. Now the bad guys were shining their lights and looking in the wrong place.

Just ahead of me, KG went down on his belly in the brush, and I followed suit. Sometimes you have to fight upright, but crawling is an infantry skill that, while often overlooked—since it's hardly comfortable—is extremely useful.

In minutes, we were dragging ourselves across the desert floor toward a new attack position. It would take time, and none of us were young enough that it was anything less than miserable anymore, but better to take the time and win than get in a hurry and get slaughtered.

Two more trucks pulled up next to the first, more lights stabbing into the dark. I paused, getting one foot under me enough to lift myself just high enough to see over the brush. These guys had no concept of dispersion and proper intervals. Two of the vehicles were so close that only one could open the doors at a time. Once again, I wanted a grenade launcher so bad I could taste it.

Getting back down, I spotted KG still worming his way through the sage and creosote bushes ahead. We'd had to tighten up our own formation just to make sure we didn't get scattered and lost in the bush. He went a few more yards and then paused, rolling to his side as I caught up to key his radio.

"Casper, KG. Need an update on what you can see."

I crawled up next to him and set security while Casper replied.

"You boys definitely shook things up. They're getting more cautious, but it looks from here like the main body is getting ready for another push while they send flankers after you. Old boy with the megaphone is yelling orders from the back of a truck, immediately to our south."

KG thought that over for a second. We were still close, but not currently engaged, though that was only a matter of time. The narcos who'd responded to our ambush were now starting to spread out from the trucks, forming a rough skirmish line and sweeping the sagebrush with their lights. They still hadn't learned. They would.

Except that KG was thinking ahead, thinking about how to break this attack altogether. He motioned me closer, and I dragged myself to within a yard of him, weaving between a couple of particularly stubborn creosote bushes, hoping that I wasn't creating too much overhead movement that would get us spotted.

"We need to keep going." He kept his voice low, just above a whisper, but still a murmur that wouldn't travel far. He pointed. "Crawl about fifty yards that way, then we get up and move fast. I want to hit that shot caller."

I nodded, twisting my head around to find Drew so I could pass the word along. I didn't really need to, though, since KG passed it over the radio a moment later. He'd just wanted my input, I guess, and when I'd agreed, that had been enough.

It took a little doing to change directions in the brush, but soon we were heading south, the brush crackling around us as we moved as fast as we dared. The lights dimly washed over us from time to time, but we had already moved fast enough to be most of the way outside their search zone. That wouldn't last, since I had no doubt they'd look farther once they didn't find us, but hopefully, we'd stay ahead of their OODA loop and be ready to hit them again by the time they adjusted.

They were getting more cautious, but it wouldn't save them.

An agonizing thirty yards later, KG finally stopped, got up on a knee, and turned to check behind us. I closed in a little bit farther so that I was on line with him instead of still partway in his field of fire, then did the same. Getting up was not fun.

Every joint protested as I hauled myself up onto a knee, keeping my muzzle high until I turned to check our six.

They were moving faster than I might have hoped. The first line of *sicarios* was already getting too close for comfort. A particularly sharp-eyed one would probably spot us once we were up and moving.

For a moment, I thought KG was going to risk it, anyway. Better to break contact and hit them again on our terms. But just then a light swept across our position and one of the bad guys yelled. Even without understanding the Spanish, I knew that one of us had been spotted.

The burst of gunfire the next second confirmed it.

I had started to turn away to get up and move but now I pivoted back, dropping my rifle and looking for targets. The muzzle flashes and flashlights made for pretty easy pickings.

Most of the bad guys were shooting at shadows and dumping on full auto, so they were drilling holes in the sky fairly quickly. We were a little tighter and a little faster.

Once again, 5.56 fire thundered from the brush, and a dozen men went down in seconds. Then we were moving, almost without needing to hear KG yell, "Left side, base of fire, right side fall back!"

It didn't quite work out that way. Instead, we mostly bounded back by pairs. I was shooting at the moment, trying to drill a guy who'd ducked back behind another one of the trucks, so Drew sprinted through the brush about twenty yards before dropping to a knee and sending a trio of shots past my ear. His timing was better than mine; the *sicario* I'd been shooting at popped his head out at just the wrong time and Drew drilled him through the temple.

Then I was up and sprinting past Drew, KG running on my right and Phil on my left.

We went to ground at almost the same time, pivoting and dropping to a knee, opening fire as soon as red dots found targets. The initial shock of our return fire had all but silenced the *sicarios*, though a few were hunkered down behind any semblance of cover they could find and spraying bullets in our general direction. Still dangerous, but less than if they had actually been aiming.

And their muzzle flashes just pointed out where we needed to shoot.

I dumped five more rounds at a flicker of muzzle blast down in the sage as Drew sprinted past me. Then, as that one was silenced, I looked up and scanned our surroundings.

Things had just gone from bad to worse.

Four more trucks were moving toward us, on line, coming from the south side of the ranch. It looked like almost all of the remaining narco force was coming for us. We'd poked the hornet's nest, all right.

I dumped the rest of my mag across the line of the second group, then got up and reloaded on the move as I sprinted toward the highway.

Our volume of fire was up, but if we didn't kill these bastards faster, we were screwed.

Over the crackle and thunder of gunfire, I could hear somebody yelling and cursing in Spanish over a megaphone. Whoever was in charge was *pissed*. This was not going according to plan.

I had gone a little bit farther than I'd intended to and was a good ten yards behind most of the rest of the team. That actually freed up my field of fire to the west, toward those oncoming vehicles.

If we didn't do something, they were going to run us down. So, I dropped to a knee and dumped the fresh mag at the vics, dragging my muzzle across the line of headlights as I rode the reset, my support hand clamped down on the forearm to keep the muzzle steady. I shot out at least one of the headlights, though I was trying to keep my point of aim slightly higher, hoping to shoot through the windshields and kill some drivers if I could.

I definitely hit *somebody*. One of the vehicles suddenly veered off, out of control, and slammed into a second. The voice on the megaphone was abruptly silenced, though a moment later, as the vehicles skidded to a halt, I started taking some return fire.

And by "some return fire," I mean I had to drop prone to keep from getting my head taken off. *Sicarios* were bailing out of the vehicles and spraying bullets as they went. These guys didn't seem to be the greatest marksmen, though the limited visibility was also working against them. They had only occasional flashes to shoot at, while we could see quite a bit more with our PS-31s.

I was moving then, staying low but trying to run and get some more distance on their flank while I reloaded yet again. I was getting down to my last couple of mags.

Fortunately, we weren't actually all alone out there.

Even as we shifted directions and started to bound toward the northeast again, drawing the bulk of the narcos after us, though they were starting to get a little more cautious after the bloodletting we'd already inflicted on them, Frank made his move.

Three vehicles came roaring out from the house, maneuvering around to the west before stopping, only about a hundred yards away from the oncoming vehicles. The doors opened and the shapes of men in plate carriers and helmets bailed out, dropping muzzles level and raking the cartel trucks with fire.

The incoming fire slackened considerably at that first crash of gunfire, as bullets shattered glass, tore through sheet metal and plastic, and ripped into flesh. I saw a dark shape fall from behind the cab of one of the pickups with a limp finality, just as I dropped to a knee again and opened fire once more.

Caught between two jaws of a lethal vise, the cartel shooters kept shooting back. I had to move quickly as a burst of fire *snap*ped past my head close enough that I could feel the bullets go by. I found the muzzle flash and returned fire, hammering five fast shots at it until the incoming fire stopped. Then I was moving again, though with Frank, Nick, Josh, Saul, and Manny out there, we all had to be *very* careful about our fields of fire.

We still needed to be concerned about that element to our right, the second group that had come after us. We'd taken no fire from those vehicles in the last few minutes, but that didn't mean we didn't still have a couple live ones with guns on our flank.

I got about ten yards—my sprints were getting shorter as the night went on and I got more and more tired—and dropped to a knee again, searching for targets.

There weren't any.

It took a second to realize that nobody was shooting back. Gradually, the rest of the team ceased fire, without being told, simply because there was no longer anyone to shoot at.

"This is Casper." Frank sounded exhausted. "You want to do the sweep, KG, or should we?"

I realized I'd never heard KG use his actual name. It's weird, sometimes, the things that pop into your head at times like that.

"This is KG. We'll handle it. We're already out here." He was about five yards from me, between me and the second group. One of those vehicles was starting to smoke. We'd *fucked* it up. "Okay, Backwoods, Smokestack, Chihuahua, and Bone. Check the vehicles. We'll stay on security."

"Bone's down." Jake sounded near panic. He might be an obnoxious prick some of the time, but that didn't mean he didn't care about his teammates. "I'm on him, but he's hit bad."

"Fuck." KG looked around. "Okay, Ziggy, Drizzle, you're with Backwoods and Smokestack. Hybrid, help Chihuahua. Rip, looks like it's you and me on security."

Drew and I were already moving, circling around behind where Jake was trying to stop Rob's bleeding. I wanted to help, but with Custus moving in, already pulling the aid bag off his shoulder, there wasn't much I could do besides make sure the fight was actually over.

The four of us formed a rough line, guns up and NVGs down, and closed in on the bullet-riddled vehicles of the second group. The Toyota Tacoma was smoking, while the Ford was, surprisingly, still running, though all but one window was shattered and there were bullet holes in the fender and the door columns. The driver had gotten out, but I was pretty sure he was the one lying crumpled in front of the bumper. The passenger had gotten it in the side of the head through the window and was slumped against the center console.

The Bronco looked almost unscathed, though there was no movement near it.

Four more bodies lay in attitudes of violent death around the vehicles. We still dead-checked each of them, removing their weapons, just in case.

Something caught my eye in the direction of the ranch house, and I flicked my weapon light once to get Drew's attention. When he turned to me, I pointed with my rifle, even as I started to move past the stricken Ford.

There was a faint trail beaten in the brush, and unless my eyes were playing tricks on me, there was a blood trail there, too.

I didn't have to go far. He sure hadn't.

The man lay on his face in the dust, still clutching his AKM. Despite his position and the brush around him, I could still see plenty of his tattoos. *Mara Salvatrucha*. Not all of these guys were MS-13, judging by the lack of tats we'd seen on some of the other dead bodies, but enough were.

Vicious bastards.

I prodded him in the back of the head with my muzzle, but there was no response. He was completely limp, and, judging by his position, if he'd been alive, he'd be suffocating with his face in the dirt. I kicked the rifle away from his fingers and moved on.

It was a little bit farther to move to reach the final group of vehicles. They were shot to shit; I could see the damage even on NVGs at a distance. Most of the headlights were shot out, and one of the still-running engines was sounding pretty rough. Our 5.56 rounds wouldn't have done any real damage to the engine block, but it they could still do a number on a radiator.

Except for a couple that had fallen half in, half out of the vehicles, we had to be right on the bodies to see them in the dark. Several looked like they'd tried to crawl, while others had clearly died where they'd dropped. More weapons were picked up or simply kicked away from still, grasping fingers.

Not everyone around the final vehicles was stone dead. There were still some moans of pain and agony, and someone was swearing in Spanish in a low, tortured voice that gurgled a little. Lung shot, most likely.

A gunshot *crack*ed on the other side of the Super Duty I was moving up next to. I didn't know for sure who had fired, but knowing some of my colleagues, it might just have been an "insurance round." Homicide in the States, technically speaking, but knowing what I knew about narcos, it might have been entirely necessary, all the same.

I came around the tailgate and found *El Jefe*.

At least, I assumed this was the cartel shooters' commander. He was lying on his back, having fallen out of the bed of the truck behind me, and he had a Beretta 93R clutched in one hand, a megaphone on the ground beside him. Dressed in dark jeans and a black collared shirt, he'd been hit in the collarbone and the guts, but he was still alive.

Shaking, he looked up at me. I must have been little more than a nightmare silhouette against the sky, bulked up by my plate carrier, the twin tubes of my NVGs sticking out from beneath my helmet, my rifle pointed at his face.

It's hard to read expressions on night vision, but I could have sworn he was glaring his hatred at me, even as his life ebbed.

"Don't do it." Not that I knew what the hell to do with a live one. I wasn't a cop, and this wasn't Iraq or Afghanistan, where we could take detainees and turn them over at the FOB. But I saw him start to move, even as my finger closed on the trigger.

He jerked that 93R up, or tried to, and I shot him between the eyes.

The shot echoed off the hills, and then it was over.

CHAPTER 40

That portion of it was over, anyway. The ranch was secure, at least for the moment. How long it would stay that way was another matter.

Matt was stable and doing all right. He'd bled a fair bit from the bullet hole in his leg, but it looked like the round had missed his femoral artery. He'd be fine.

Rob was in a bad way. His plates had saved his life, but he'd taken two rounds in the guts. He'd need surgery, and soon.

That had brought the reality of the situation back with a vengeance. We'd just been in a firefight the likes of which few of us had seen in years. And not only had it happened on American soil, but the powers that be were more likely to side with the narcos than they would with us.

Oh, they'd couch it differently. Throw out a wild story about vigilantes gunning down innocent migrants or something, never mind the guns and explosives on and around the enemy vehicles. To some people, most of them with more money and power than any of us could ever dream of, the truth didn't matter so much as what they could get away with. And even if the truth came out, in six months or five years, the damage would be done.

Trevor Bowman seemed relatively optimistic about Sheriff Hernandez. I wasn't so sure, after some of what we'd seen elsewhere, but we needed medical assistance for Rob, Matt, and Brett, and we needed it soon.

"Better to get the sheriff involved immediately, rather than wait for the EMTs to look at all the bodies and the bullet holes and call him anyway, in which case he'll wonder why we didn't call him." That was KG's take, anyway.

"We *did* call him, KG." Frank sounded even more tired than I felt. He looked worse. "He 'had no one available.'"

"Fuck." KG took a deep breath. "Doesn't matter. He'll come, *now*. The shooting's done." He turned toward the back, pulling out his phone. "I need to call the office. Get some lawyers mobilized thirty seconds ago."

***

The sheriff, the ambulance, the New Mexico State Police, and the Border Patrol all showed up just before sunrise, about half an hour after Mr. Bowman called them again. The place was still in shambles, and we hadn't bothered to try to move any of the blasted, torn up vehicles out in the desert.

We were all dead tired, and I doubt many of us were even that worried about the potential repercussions of what we'd done. Not right then, anyway. We'd done what we'd had to, and I knew I wasn't going to sit still for some second-guessing punk with a badge who'd refused to step up when the time had come.

Frank was thinking ahead, though. Just before we sighted the flashing lights in the distance, he grabbed KG and me. "The A Team needs to get back up to the vehicles and get off the property."

While KG nodded, Casey had overheard and objected. "So, what, we get to be the fall guys?"

Frank turned a glare on Casey that I didn't think I'd ever seen on him. "No, we get to have a little stand down time while the office's lawyers go to bat for us, provided the sheriff doesn't side with us when he sees the carnage out there, which he *should*. This is contingency planning. We might still need a mobile element, in case this does get ugly." He turned back to KG. "No offense, but most of your guys were later to the party, so they should be a little fresher. Sorry, Backwoods."

I just shrugged. "It is what it is." It took far more effort to say that instead of bitching about how dead tired I was than I would like to admit. I wanted nothing more than to pass out for about a week.

We took one of the B Team's rental vehicles and went tearing out to the north with a constellation of flashing blue, red, and white lights in the rear view mirror. We were driving blacked out, and the predawn twilight would help mask us even more.

It felt a little like running away, but Frank had a point. We weren't out of this yet. Only time would tell what form the backlash would take, but if Archer and his cronies got desperate enough, we just might have to go kinetic again.

I just hoped that KG had loaded more ammunition in that helicopter.

***

Nick watched the oncoming lights with a mix of weary resignation, dread, and relief.

At least Matt, Brett, and Rob should get some medical attention. He hadn't really known Rob, but it didn't matter that much. The man was one of them, and the A Team's assault had taken the heat off just when it had been needed.

The sheriff's Durango was in the lead of the small convoy that pulled up to the house. Nick actually started to relax a little bit as he saw just how many had showed up. Three Doña Ana County Sheriff's Department vehicles, two ambulances, two New Mexico State Police cruisers, and one Border Patrol vehicle. If they'd wanted a fight, or an arrest, they probably would have showed up with more than that.

At least, he hoped so.

The sheriff got out first. An older, graying man with a walrus mustache and a pronounced gut, he looked almost as tired as Nick felt. That was saying something. He started to reassess the situation.

What if they had some sort of diversion that kept the sheriff occupied last night? Maybe he didn't hang back out of cowardice, after all.

Sheriff Hernandez kept looking around as he walked toward the front door. "Mr. Bowman? Can you come out and talk for a moment?" His voice was raspy and, if anything, sounded even more tired and haunted than the expression on his face.

Frank nodded to Mr. Bowman. The Pallas Group contractors would back him up, but this was going to have to be his play. The older rancher didn't look thrilled at the prospect, which definitely said something. He didn't trust that *he* wasn't going to be blamed and charged for defending his property, either.

When he got out there, though, he stopped a couple yards from the sheriff and folded his arms. He still had a pistol on his hip, though he'd left his rifle inside. "About damned time you got here, Carlos." He spat in the dust. The weariness and the stress of the night had finally caught up with him, but it had just made him mad, especially when confronted by all the flashing lights that somehow couldn't be bothered while fifty to sixty cartel assassins had been trying to kill him and his family.

"It was a long night for everyone, Trevor." If Sheriff Hernandez was angry about the rancher's condemnation, he didn't show it. "These fuckers made sure of that before they even came after you." He looked over his shoulder, toward the bullet-torn wrecks outside the yard. "Though I'm damned if I can figure out what brought them here."

"There are a few theories about that, Sheriff." Frank stepped out to stand beside Mr. Bowman.

332

"Who are you?" The Border Patrol agent was in full gear, though still lighter equipped than any of the Pallas Group contractors had been the night before.

"I'm the man who was hired to do your job for you." Nick suppressed a wince at the sharp tone of Frank's voice. *Let's just preemptively burn all the bridges, why don't we, Frank?*

Not that he trusted any Feds, after what had happened over the last couple of weeks, but sometimes it pays to be a little more diplomatic.

"He and his guys are the only reason we're still alive." Trevor Bowman was even more blunt. He stabbed a finger out toward the nearest shot-up pickup truck. "Those sons of bitches were here to kill me, my family, and all of my hands, if I hadn't sent them home yesterday. They wanted this ranch, and they were willing to commit a massacre to get it." He glowered at the Border Patrol agent. "If you bastards would do your damned job and secure the border, we might not have had to fight for our lives last night."

"Hey, we do what we can with what we're given." Unlike the sheriff, the Border Patrol agent seemed to want to take offense. "It's not our fault our hands are tied."

Sheriff Hernandez held up a hand to try to forestall the argument. The State Police, to their credit, hadn't said anything yet, but seemed content to back up the sheriff. Nick wondered just how many political battles lay behind *that* bit of jurisdictional prudence.

"Look, gentlemen. Like I said, it was a long night. There were other attacks across both Doña Ana and Luna counties, along with a whole lot of other calls that had every cop and sheriff's deputy tied up from seven o'clock to two in the morning." He sighed. "This does appear to have been coordinated." His eyes strayed to Frank again, as well as the dimly visible shapes of more contractors inside. "I have to follow due diligence, though. This is a crime scene, so I've got to do the whole investigation. Which means everyone here will need to answer questions and be available for follow-on interviews for a while."

Nick understood KG's decision to get the A Team off site even more, then. *Of course* anyone left on the scene was going to be subject to the mountain of red tape and questions that went along with a crime scene investigation. He felt his shoulders slump a little bit. This was going to be a *long* week. Or month. Or year.

Good thing all the weapons and gear belong to the company. He didn't have to worry about his personal rifle and pistol disappearing into a police evidence locker, never to be seen again for a decade.

"Can I have a look around?" The sheriff seemed to want to put the uncomfortable confrontation behind them and get to work.

Mr. Bowman sighed. "Of course. I'd like to come along, though."

Sheriff Hernandez just nodded wearily and turned toward the nearest cluster of bullet-riddled vehicles and the bodies strewn around them. Frank looked back at the house and jerked his head at Nick, who stepped out into the yard and followed. The fight was ostensibly over, but Frank didn't want to take chances.

They got some looks from the cops and the Feds, though the EMTs ignored them as they finally saw the way clear to do their jobs and hustled into the house with stretchers. Nobody said a word, though, since Sheriff Hernandez didn't see fit to comment on their presence.

Nick frowned as they got closer to the vehicles. *What's that noise?* It took a second to realize that it was a phone ringing.

He had to resist the urge to push forward and find it. This was Sheriff Hernandez's show, and if the Pallas Group contractors got too pushy or inquisitive, it might work against them.

Hernandez didn't seem to notice the ringtone at first, but he looked up and around with a frown just before it quit. Then he strode forward, toward where the cartel leader lay. The stench of death was already heavy in the rapidly warming morning air, but it didn't seem to faze the sheriff.

Working law enforcement this close to the border, not to mention Cuidad Juarez, he had to have a pretty strong stomach. As worn down, old, and paunchy as he looked, he would probably have retired long before otherwise.

He found the phone where it had fallen out of the dead man's pocket as he'd dropped, ignoring the bullet hole punched in his forehead. "Huh. Somebody wanted to talk to this guy pretty bad. Twenty missed calls from somebody called, 'Archer.'"

Nick felt his blood go cold, but he kept his expression carefully neutral as he risked a glance at Frank. Frank would have done a poker player proud.

Hernandez gave them both a long look. Before he could ask them anything about it, though, the phone rang again.

For a moment, Hernandez just looked at the screen while it played some raucous *narcocorrido*. Then, to Nick's surprise, he answered it.

He didn't say anything but just held it to his ear. Nick could have sworn that he heard someone on the other end of the connection yelling.

Hernandez just listened, then hung up without a word. He looked up at Bowman, then at Frank. "I'm guessing you gentlemen know more about that one-sided conversation than I do, but it sure sounded to me like some Anglo who wanted confirmation that these narco sons of bitches had killed all of you and had control of the ranch." He tossed the phone back on the dead body's chest and put his hands on his hips. "I'm listening."

335

Bowman turned to Frank. "It's a long story, Sheriff."

"We appear to have plenty of time." His eyes dropped as Frank's phone started ringing. "Or do we?"

"We might not. Can I get that?" When Hernandez nodded, Frank snatched the phone out. "Talk to me." His eyebrows went up. "Roger. Yeah, the sheriff's here, along with some state troopers and a couple of Border Patrol guys. Copy. I'll pass it along." He hung up. "So, that was a friend of ours, over at the county airport. He says that Devon Archer is there with his private jet, and he's been on the phone and seems very agitated."

Nick felt his heart rate spike. The guy behind all of this was right there, twenty miles away, and they couldn't lift a finger to touch him.

Or could they? Was the A Team headed that way right now?

"These friends of yours." The wheels were turning in Hernandez's head, and Nick could almost hear them. "They wouldn't happen to be more security contractors like you, would they?"

"They might." Frank was being a little cagier, even though it looked like the sheriff was at least close to on their side.

"If you can get in touch with them, then tell them to make sure he doesn't leave. I'll deputize them when I get there." His eyes narrowed. "If you trust me that far, I'd like to bring a couple of you along with me." He looked around the wreckage and the bodies. "I've got to leave my deputies here. There's a lot to do."

"We're with you, Sheriff." Frank turned back toward the house as he pulled his phone out. "Just let us grab our gear."

CHAPTER
41

We got the word on the way off the ranch. The helicopter pilot that KG had hired—actually, I suspected that Strand had hired him—called KG, who then had him call us.

"Devon Archer is on the tarmac, barely a hundred yards from here." The fact that the helo pilot knew who Archer was, and what his involvement was, meant that someone, either KG or Strand, had read him in. "He looks pretty agitated. I can only think of one reason he might be here. Hell of a coincidence, otherwise."

"Hell of a coincidence," I agreed. I gritted my teeth as I tried to get the Frontier moving a little faster. "We just hit one of the county roads. It's going to be a little bit." Fortunately, the sun was up, so I could see better, but that wasn't going to overcome the rough state the road was in. "Let me know if it looks like he's going to leave. Last resort, call the law."

"Roger that." He ended the call, and I tossed the phone on the dash. "Archer's at the county airport. If he sticks around, we might get a shot at him."

Drew was quiet for a moment as we bounced over the unimproved road. "Do we really want to?"

I frowned at him, for the brief second I could spare from the road. "What the hell are you talking about? He's been ramrodding this bullshit from the start. If it wasn't for his connections and complete lack of scruples, we wouldn't even be in this mess."

"Yeah, but everybody we've schwacked so far has been demonstrable self-defense." Drew was thinking, putting aside the go-for-the-throat instinct that tended to drive a lot of us. "This would be a straight-up assassination. Bit of a line to cross."

I grimaced as I kept driving. "Maybe we keep him from leaving until we can call the sheriff."

"And what's the sheriff going to do? We've got evidence, but a lot of it we gathered in a rather less-than-legal manner."

I gritted my teeth. He was right. We couldn't just leave it at that, though. Couldn't let this bastard get away with it. His actions had almost gotten the Bowman family murdered the night before.

Almost as if in answer to a prayer, my phone buzzed again. It was a text from Frank. I handed it to Drew. "I've got to drive."

"Holy shit." Drew stared at the message. "Archer tried calling the bad guys and apparently, the sheriff picked up. He's heading to the airport with Frank and Nick. He's given instructions that we're to stop Archer from leaving. Says he'll deputize us when he gets there."

"I'm not sure that's how this works, legally, but I'm down," Marcos said from the back seat.

"So am I." I sped up, clenching my teeth as we hit another rut in the road, flying across the desert toward Santa Theresa.

***

It took entirely too long, even though once we got around the East Potrillo Mountains we were flying down the dirt road through the desert at about forty miles an hour. We still had to cover almost thirty miles to get to the airport.

338

The sheriff was already waiting when we pulled up, with Frank and Nick leaning against his Durango, geared up and carrying their rifles. Apparently, the deputization was already in effect.

"Took you guys long enough," Nick said as we pulled up, stopped, and started to get out.

"We didn't get to use the highway, Nick." He held out a fist and we bumped knuckles. He and I had worked together downrange for a few trips.

Sheriff Hernandez was watching with a stony expression. "Seems to me that you boys weren't already here. Makes one wonder just *where* you were." He glanced at Frank, who shrugged.

"I said we had people at the airport. Never said we had people *only* at the airport."

Hernandez shrugged and let the subject drop. He'd apparently decided who was which side already. "All right, let's go. I'm the actual sheriff, so I'll make the arrest. I just need you to back me up, in case he's got a security detail." He suddenly looked weary clear down to his bones. "If it is *the* Devon Archer, then I'm sure he will."

"Could be worse." Drew was pulling on his helmet. "Imagine if he was the President's son, instead of just a Senator's kid."

"I'd rather not." Crossing swords with the Secret Service was probably the last thing Sheriff Hernandez wanted to do. "Let's go. You're cleared to take vehicles out onto the tarmac. Block that plane and *do not let it leave*."

I nodded. "We're on it." I was fine with letting the sheriff handle this. It might be a temporary solution to a long-term problem, but right at the moment, *any* disruption to this corrupt operation was good. I climbed back behind the wheel, my helmet back on though I'd taken my NVGs off, and waited just long enough for Drew, Phil, and Marcos to get back in before I hit the accelerator, driving toward the runway as fast as I figured I could get away with.

Let Sheriff Hernandez deal with the repercussions. He was the man in charge.

Ken and Custus had piled into the Pathfinder behind us, and they were right on our tail as we roared past the War Eagles Air Museum and down the frontage road toward the hangars at the far end. I was pretty sure I could already see Archer's private jet, a white-and-blue Learjet parked right on the tarmac, facing the runway. Clearly, Archer was poised for a quick getaway.

Why he should bother, I didn't know. Even as I drove, pushing the Frontier just fast enough that I figured I could still make the turn without flipping it, I wondered just what good this was going to do. Archer was untouchable. People had tried to investigate him before and had been stonewalled. His daddy would just make sure it all got swept under the rug.

Still had to try, though.

We came around the bend with a squeal of tires and I floored it again, racing past the plane and bouncing onto the desert median for a moment before I could bring the truck around sharply and screeched to a stop in front of the aircraft's nose. Then we were all bailing out, even as the sheriff's Durango came screaming up with lights flashing and sirens wailing.

It was almost no wonder we'd gotten such detailed reporting from the helicopter pilot. The blue and red AW189 was sitting in front of the far hangar, facing the aircraft. The pilot had just been sitting there in his seat, calling in whatever he saw.

As we spread out, I saw Archer himself, dressed in a t-shirt and khakis, his phone to his ear, standing next to the nearest hangar, staring at the oncoming vehicles with his mouth hanging slightly open. He was clean shaven, and his hair had been combed, like he was fixing to seal a deal or make a presentation or something.

The two men nearby were armed, both wearing dark polo shirts and khakis, both carrying what looked like KH-9s. They were alert, but both of them froze when they saw the lights. Almost as if they didn't know what their boss was up to, and weren't ready to engage a cop.

They got a lot warier when one of them saw us spread out behind the Frontier, in helmets and body armor, with Recce 16 carbines pointed at them.

Archer didn't even seem to notice us. He held the phone up near his head still, but his eyes were fixed on the sheriff's Durango.

Sheriff Hernandez killed the siren but left the lights on. He got out of the vehicle somewhat ponderously, though he was wearing his own vest and had a carbine in his hands. If I hadn't had my electronic earpro on under my helmet, I probably wouldn't have been able to hear what happened next.

"Devon Archer?" Sheriff Hernandez knew damned well who this was, but he was going to play it by the book. "You're under arrest."

"Bullshit. You can't arrest me."

"I can and I will. The charges are multiple counts of aggravated attempted murder and conspiracy to commit murder. Since it happened in my county, I'm arresting you and putting you in the county jail until trial." He held his position, still sizing up the security detail.

Those two weren't sure what to do. One of them was looking from Archer to Hernandez, clearly unsure of what was going on, wondering if he'd chosen the wrong gig. The other one, though... I had my sights close to him. He was ready for action. If that meant smoking a local sheriff, it was no never mind to him.

I'd met a few like that over the years. No vetting process can ever quite weed them all out. The fact that he was probably confident that we were nothing but a show of force, and that Senator Archer would make sure nothing bad happened to him, didn't help.

Archer laughed, though there was a bleakness in his expression and a brittleness in his put-on mirth that put the lie to it. "You don't know what you're dealing with, Sheriff. Do us all a favor and turn around and forget you ever saw me."

Hernandez held his ground. "Not going to happen. I've got a lot of dead bodies on the ground, and you *just so happened* to call the hitter responsible." He smiled without warmth or humor. "Guess who actually picked that phone up."

Archer's face suddenly went slack, and even from fifty yards away, I could see the horror of his true situation go through his eyes. His operation was fucked, the cartel was probably going to come after him for getting so many of their *sicarios* killed, not to mention however many *mareros* we'd dumped out there in the desert. Worse, the Chinese were probably going to find a way to take it out of his hide, too, even if it was a penalty in money and influence rather than blood. And now he was facing a witness his father might not be able to bully into staying quiet.

I never would have thought a soft, drug addled piece of shit like Devon Archer would have been able to move that fast.

He snatched a pistol out of his waistband and shot at Hernandez as he turned and started to run. Hernandez grunted and doubled over, which probably saved his life.

The man I'd been watching most carefully started to bring his KH-9 up to point it at the sheriff and I dumped him, shooting him three times in the chest and once in the head. He wasn't wearing body armor, or at least not rifle plates, because he was already going down by the time my fourth shot punched through his nose and snapped his head halfway around.

Drew was shooting, too. His first shot was fast, and took Archer in the shoulder, spinning him halfway around as he ran, still twisted to the side to point the pistol back at

Hernandez. His second shot took the millionaire son of a senior Senator high in the side, punching through his heart and blowing a chunk of heart and lungs out through his opposite armpit. He collapsed to the tarmac like a puppet with its strings cut.

Hernandez was down, on his knees, clutching his stomach. Blood was seeping through his fingers and his face was pale. He was going to need immediate medical attention. The second bodyguard was on his knees, as well, his KH-9 on the ground and his fingers interlaced on top of his head. He knew the score, even as we closed in, gliding fast across the tarmac with rifles leveled.

"Ken, get on the sheriff's radio and get an ambulance out here." I was already checking the man I'd shot while Custus secured the bodyguard. "Don't worry, Sheriff, we're gonna get you out of here."

Hernandez didn't have much in him at the moment. He just nodded.

I looked at Archer's crumpled body and advanced on it. Blood was soaking the light gray t-shirt, and he wasn't moving. I still kicked the little Glock 43 away from his hand before I did anything else.

His eyes were open, fixed on the horizon, his cheek pressed against the tarmac. The phone had fallen a few inches from his other hand.

The call was still active, at least for a couple more seconds. Long enough for me to see the name "Deng" on the screen, before whoever was on the other end stopped the call.

I picked up the phone, making sure to keep it active. It was going to be a vital bit of evidence, and Sheriff Hernandez was going to need it. If he survived.

I headed back toward his Durango, leaving the body on the pavement. The mission was now to keep Sheriff Hernandez alive.

We were going to need him.

EPILOGUE

Julie picked up on the second ring. "Chris, are you okay?"

"I'm fine, honey." It was true enough. I was still picking a few bits of thorns and cactus spines out of my skin from the fight in the desert, but other than that, I still had all the same number of holes I'd showed up with.

I hesitated. She caught it, but she didn't press.

How was I going to say this? Especially over the phone? We used encryption, sure, but nothing's foolproof. "Look, I can't say much over the phone, but are you carrying on a regular basis?" She'd been off and on about concealed carry, though I hoped that I'd finally gotten her to at least carry while I wasn't around.

"Yes." She was suspicious. "Chris, what's going on?"

"Nothing, hopefully." I didn't *know* that any of us had necessarily been identified. We'd been careful. Still, it pays to be even more careful.

It also pays to be honest with your wife. "We may have crossed swords with some very dangerous people. People with a lot of resources and not many scruples. I don't *think* they'll come after the family, but..."

"But I need to be careful." She almost sounded like she had just relaxed. "Chris, I've been careful ever since you started contracting. It's good to have the reminder, though."

She paused, and when she spoke again, she didn't sound nearly as confident. "Is there anything else I need to know about?"

"Not over the phone." KG was coming over. "I'll explain when I get home. But keep your head on a swivel, and tell the boys to keep an eye out, too. They'll be into it."

"I know they will." There was a certain bittersweet wistfulness in her voice. "They're their father's sons."

"I've got to go, Julie. I love you."

"I love you, too, Chris." Her hesitation was agonizing. Her voice was small and while she was trying to hide it, she sounded scared. "Be careful."

"I will." I hung up and joined KG.

***

KG, Frank, Casey, and I walked into Sheriff Hernandez's hospital room. I traded a fist bump with Deputy Carstairs outside. Carstairs had been the one to accompany the ambulance to the airport, and he'd seen what we'd done to treat his boss. Carstairs was good people.

Hernandez was sitting up in bed, which was better than he'd been doing for the last week. He'd gotten through surgery well enough, but it takes time to recover from being gut-shot, no matter how good the doc is or how tough you are.

He was reading, too, and he looked up at us over the tops of his reading glasses as we came in. "Look who it is." He put the tablet down. "It looks like our nightmare scenario hasn't materialized."

"Really." Frank didn't sound convinced.

Hernandez grimaced. "At least, we're not facing federal charges for killing the son of a sitting Senator. Between your boss's lawyers and my already sworn statement, we appear to have enough evidence that Archer was dirty to head that off."

"So, what's the catch?" I wasn't convinced that we were out of the woods by a long shot.

He got grim. "The catch is that even while Senator Archer is making all sorts of stricken and heartfelt statements distancing himself from his son's illegal activities, I'm sure he's already got people looking into how to come around and slip a knife in our collective ribs. Even if they can't find a legal way to do it..."

"They'll find a way." KG didn't sound mad. He just sounded tired. "Even if it's just another version of what Archer tried to do here. Point some thugs at us and wash their hands of the thing. Meanwhile, they'll hit us with frivolous charges, lawsuits, and any way they can come after us monetarily. It's gonna be a long haul."

"That's not all." Hernandez surprised me. "The Federación is going to be looking for whoever killed damn near fifty of their people. Not only that, but *Mara Salvatrucha*'s going to be out for blood, too." He shook his head. "I hope you boys are ready to fight the war that just started."

"And from the looks of things, the Chinese are probably going to be feeding them intel, too. They're going to be pissed about losing out on that lithium deposit." Frank sighed. "You're right, Sheriff. We are at war. I think we have been for a lot longer than most people think."

"The only thing is," KG said, as he found a chair and sat down, "that now we've got no choice but to fight it." He looked over at Hernandez. "If you need us to leave and have this conversation elsewhere, so you have some plausible deniability, Sheriff, we will."

Hernandez grunted. "Son, I've been fighting this war with one hand tied behind my back for my entire career. You ain't gonna shock me, and I can be almighty selective in my hearing as it is."

So, we settled in to talk lawfare and options going forward. It turned out that Sheriff Hernandez hadn't even mentioned us in his sworn statement, though the paperwork to prove our deputization was filed away somewhere. We might just be able to fade, at least somewhat.

I listened, thinking things over as the conversation went on. Goblin was going to have something to say about all this. In fact, I suspected that the fact he wasn't there spoke volumes in and of itself. He was working things, preparing for the next phase.

I had no doubt there was going to be a next phase. Hernandez was right. There was no going back now.

We were going to have to fight this war, or else get buried as unknown and unsung casualties.

AUTHOR'S NOTE

My previous thriller series, *American Praetorians* and *Maelstrom Rising*, have been largely focused on potential conflicts, set sometime a few years in the future. With the *Pallas Group Solutions* thrillers, of which this is the first of more than one planned series, are a little bit more immediate.

While the war that the Pallas Group Solutions contractors find themselves embroiled in is slightly more kinetic than in real life, its real-world version is no less deadly. Some of the idea for this series came from not only my previous research reading into the convergence between organized crime, terrorism, and state-sponsored espionage and influence operations, but also a passage from *Unrestricted Warfare,* a white paper published in 1999 by two colonels in the People's Liberation Army.

"Aside from what we have discussed above, we can point out a number of other means and methods used to fight a non-military war, some of which already exist and some of which may exist in the future. Such means and methods include psychological warfare (spreading rumors to intimidate the enemy and break down his will); smuggling warfare (throwing markets into confusion and attacking economic order); media warfare (manipulating what people see and hear in order to lead public opinion along); drug warfare (obtaining sudden and huge illicit profits by spreading disaster in other countries); network warfare (venturing out in secret and concealing one's identity in a type of warfare that is virtually impossible to guard against); technological warfare (creating monopolies by setting standards independently); fabrication warfare (presenting a counterfeit appearance of real strength before the eyes of the enemy); resources warfare (grabbing riches by plundering stores of resources); economic aid warfare (bestowing favor in the open and contriving to control matters in secret); cultural warfare (leading cultural trends along in order to assimilate those with different views); and international law warfare (seizing the earliest opportunity to set up regulations), etc., etc."

Several of those methods have been showcased in this story. There will be more to follow.

There is a case to be made that this war is really happening, as I write this. I tend to think that it is. It is the war that the Pallas Group Solutions contractors will be fighting. I hope you will come along for the ride.

To keep up to date, I hope that you'll sign up for my newsletter—you get a free American Praetorians novella, Drawing the Line, when you do.

If you've enjoyed this novel, I hope that you'll go leave a review on Amazon or Goodreads. Reviews matter a lot to independent authors, so I appreciate the effort.

If you'd like to connect, I have a Facebook page at https://www.facebook.com/PeteNealenAuthor. You can also contact me, or just read my musings and occasional samples on the blog, at https://www.americanpraetorians.com. I look forward to hearing from you.

Also By Peter Nealen

Brave New Disorder (Pallas Group Solutions Thrillers)
Gray War
The Dragon and the Skull
Silver or Lead

The Brannigan's Blackhearts Universe
Kill Yuan
The Colonel Has A Plan (Online Short)
Fury in the Gulf
Burmese Crossfire
Enemy Unidentified
Frozen Conflict
High Desert Vengeance
Doctors of Death
Kill or Capture
Enemy of My Enemy
War to the Knife
Blood Debt
Marque and Reprisal
Concrete Jungle

The Maelstrom Rising Series
Escalation
Holding Action
Crimson Star
Strategic Assets
Fortress Doctrine
Thunder Run
Area Denial
Power Vacuum
Option Zulu
SPOTREPS – A Maelstrom Rising Anthology

The Lost Series
Ice and Monsters
Shadows and Crows
Darkness and Stone

Swords Against the Night
The Alchemy of Treason
The Rock of Battle

The Unity Wars Series
The Fall of Valdek
The Defense of Provenia
The Alliance Rises

The American Praetorians Series
Drawing the Line: An American Praetorians Story (Novella)
Task Force Desperate
Hunting in the Shadows
Alone and Unafraid
The Devil You Don't Know
Lex Talionis

The Jed Horn Supernatural Thriller Series
Nightmares
A Silver Cross and a Winchester
The Walker on the Hills
The Canyon of the Lost (Novelette)
Older and Fouler Things